Shadows and Light

Journeys of a Spirit Healer

Joe McMonagle

Contents

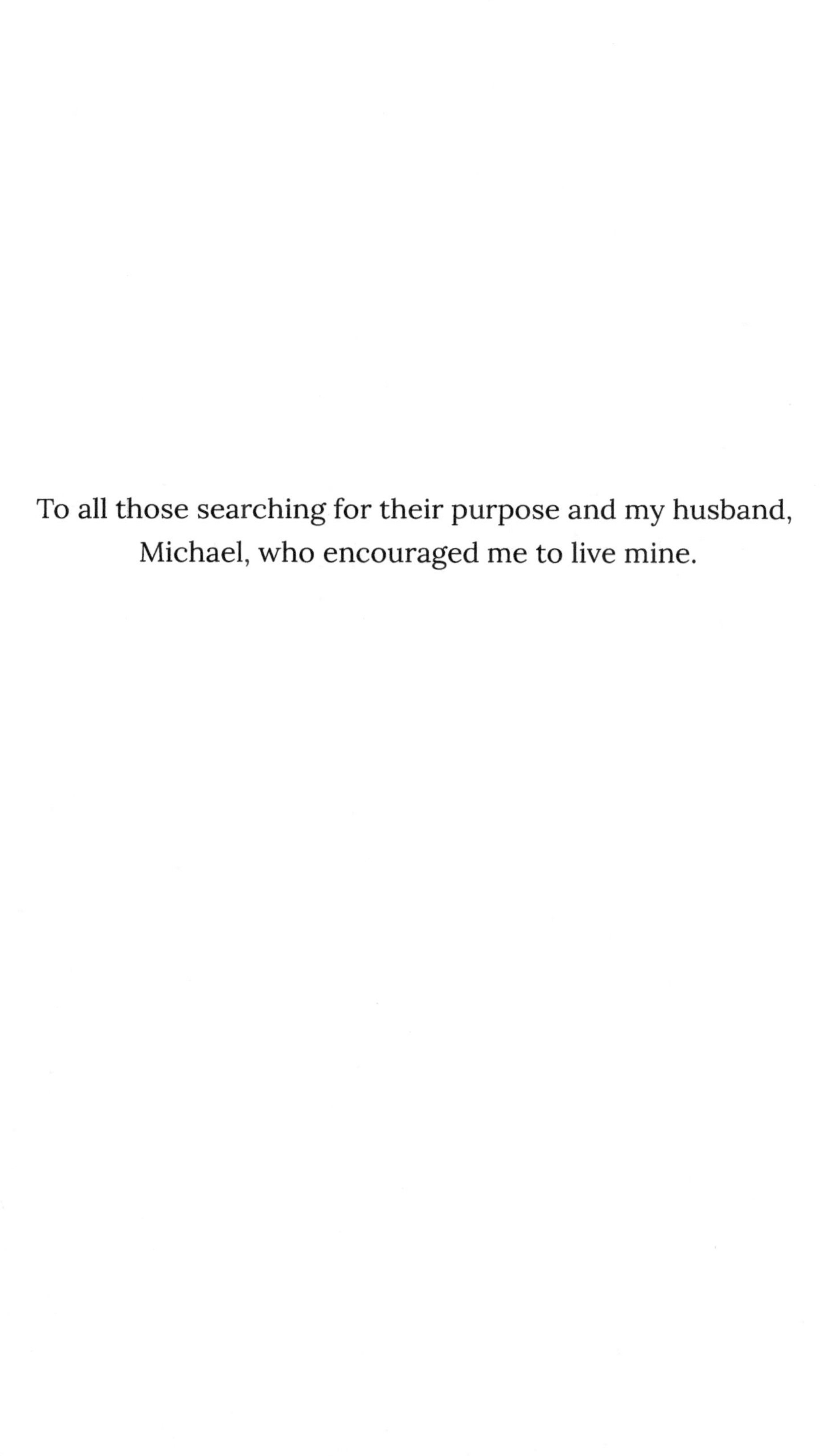

To all those searching for their purpose and my husband, Michael, who encouraged me to live mine.

Chapter 1

"Thom Macirdan, inform your mother I need to speak with her. Now!" a male voice demanded.

Thom had left the storage shed and was walking back to his mother's herb garden, bathed in light from the early morning sun. Strutting up the path was an elder wearing a stern look. "Oh, yes, sir," he replied. He beelined to the front door and called, "Mam, an elder's here. And he doesn't look happy."

"I'll be right there," his mother responded.

"She's coming, sir," Thom informed him.

"At least one of you is respectful," the elder muttered.

Rather than returning to the garden, he stopped at the corner of the house to discreetly watch and listen. Somebody was in big trouble.

As his mother stepped out of the house, he spoke before she even had a chance to greet the elder, "Mrs. Macirdan, you NEED to teach that daughter of yours respect for appointed representatives of Deu."

"Good morning to you, elder," his mother replied slowly, emphasizing each word. "Which daughter? I've got three, you know." Mam's brown hair was tightly bound in a bun, and she wore an apron over her tunic.

Squinting, Thom thought he could see his Mam's eyebrows raised and her mouth quirked slightly. This face differed from the one she often wore when this elder presided at services, constipated. He had learned that word a few weeks earlier while helping his Mam with her patients.

"That Meli," the elder said with displeasure.

"What did she do?" she asked.

"Yesterday in class, she had the gall to ask me why we all had to plead for Deu's mercy."

"OK," his mother said cautiously.

Encouraged, the elder continued, "Well, I already taught the children about our sinful nature," he replied through gritted teeth. "She shouldn't have asked."

His mother remained still.

"After I told her to be silent," he further complained, "she DARED to ask me why... again."

"I see," she responded with a frown.

Before she could say more, he went on, his volume increasing, "But that wasn't all. Last night, I read her answer to the children's assignment. I asked them to explain why everyone was required to attend chapel at least once a week."

"One moment, please," she interrupted him.

"Excuse me," he replied with shock.

"I said, ONE MOMENT, elder," she emphasized. "Meli," she called out, turning back into the home's interior, "Come here, please!"

"Coming," his sister quickly answered.

Thom could barely hear her.

"Oh, elder," Meli said with chagrin when she stepped outside.

"The elder asked about your behavior yesterday," his mother stated. "Did you talk back to him after he asked you to be silent?"

"Yes, Mam," she gulped. Meli's light brown hair looked to be a bit tangled, and her button nose had something on it.

"You know better. Apologize!" his mother demanded.

"Sorry, elder," Meli replied with some remorse.

"But what about her assignment?" the elder demanded, his fists clenched.

"What did you write, Meli?" his mother asked calmly.

"Well," Meli paused, "My exact words were: 'The require-ment to attend chapel every Sunday is antithetical to the belief that Deu is omnipresent.' At the end of my essay, I asserted that we can worship him equally well at home, in nature, and... even in the privy," she added with an impish grin.

"Do you see what I mean?" the elder yelled. "Blasphemy! And I'm tired of her throwing around words she doesn't understand! How does a sixth grader even know them?"

While the elder kept spouting his outrage, Thom remem-bered when Meli began using bigger words. It was the year before, and she had been telling their parents what she had learned in school about leadership. They were shocked when Meli told them she thought the local council had to be more transparent and accountable about how they used the town tariffs. 'Thom's not the only one with a keen mind,' she had informed them. From then on, Meli peppered many of her conversations with grown-up-sounding words.

Returning to the conversation, Thom saw the elder was finally silent, his chest rising and falling rapidly like bellows stoking a fire.

"Did you really mention the privy?" his mother snorted.

"Yes. Isn't Deu everywhere?" Meli asked earnestly. "Why do we have to go to the chapel to worship? He's not confined to the building, is he?"

"I agree. And no, Deu's not," his mother echoed.

Oh, the elder's not gonna like that, Thom thought.

"You didn't agree with her?" the elder yelled. "You MUST worship Deu in the chapel. He demands it," he shouted even louder.

Thom noticed that he yelled like he did in religion class. It always hurt his ears.

"WOMAN," the elder further screamed, "if you're teaching these things to your children, not only will they be damned to hell but so will you."

"Elder," she replied quietly to counter his tone. "I respectfully disagree. It seems to me the good book talks about being able to see Deu in everyone. In other words, Deu could, in fact, be anywhere."

"How dare you preach to me!" the elder yelled.

"Elder, do not shout at me! I'm not one of your students," she stated, drawing herself up to her five-foot height.

"You can't talk back…"

"Furthermore," she continued, now quite loud herself, "you and the other elders seem to have forgotten the good book also talks about Deu's love."

"I beg your pardon," he replied in shock.

"Your overemphasis on Deu as a judge is what prevents us from attending YOUR services every week."

The elder stood mute, his mouth agape.

"Now, I must finish preparing our breakfast before I start seeing patients," she informed him. "I'm sure you have other tasks yourself. Good day!" she stated loudly before turning back inside with Meli and closing the door.

The elder remained motionless for a bit before stomping back down the path.

Oh, that was fun, Thom thought. He'd never heard an elder scolded. But what did antithetical and omnipresent mean? Half the time, he didn't understand what Meli said. He still couldn't believe she had said people could talk to Deu while in the privy, pooping."

Returning to the garden, he knelt by a burdock plant and continued weeding. This herb garden was important to his Mam as a part-time healer. Weeding it was one of his chores. He took it over from Meli last year when she went to work full-time in their Da's pottery.

He wished his younger sister, Reta, could take over weeding. He hated it. It was boring pulling one clump after another, week after week after week. He also hated how long it took to clean out the dirt from under his fingernails. His Mam always inspected them afterward. Crawling to the next plant, he brushed away the red and orange leaves that had fallen from the tree overhead. This plant was especially hateful this time of year because its pretty purple flowers turned into burrs. If he wasn't careful, they stuck to his clothing, which took ages to pick off.

Leaning over the plant, he brushed a lock of his auburn hair from his face, getting dirt in his brown eyes. "Turg," he cursed. He was relieved Mam hadn't heard. His parents did not condone it. Mam had even told him that when she cursed as a child, her Da washed her mouth out with soap. How awful.

Even though Thom didn't like weeding, he did like learning about herbs and healing. His Mam thought he was gifted. That meant that some of his time included studying her healing books. Since most of his day was occupied with school and chores, he had to study after dinner. It always cut into his time to read his novel or write in his precious journal.

"Thom," Meli called from the window of his parents' room, which overlooked the garden.

"What!" Thom replied, annoyed at her interruption.

"Mam wants you to bring in some rosemary. We're having beef tonight."

"Oh wow," Thom replied, starting to salivate. They hadn't had beef since late spring because he knew money was tight.

Returning to the weeding, Thom thought again about his journal, sitting on the left side of his shelf. His family didn't get why he kept one, but for him, there were things he didn't want to tell anyone. Thom started it after his best and only friend, Davi, moved away. He could tell Davi anything. All the kids looked up to him. They even agreed to play Thom's favorite treasure hunt game when Davi suggested it instead of their usual sporty games.

Reaching towards the next weed, he noticed his tunic sleeve. "Turg," he repeated, seeing it covered in burrs. That's what he gets for woolgathering, as his Mam called it. After picking them off, he looked down at his trousers, smeared with mud from the recent rain. He'd have to change before going to school.

"Thom," his mother now called from her window.

"Huh, what?" Thom answered, feeling like he was coming out of a stupor.

"Thom, do you hear me?" she asked.

"Yes, Mam," he replied.

"I've been calling you for a few minutes."

"Sorry."

"Don't forget to bring me a few sprigs of rosemary," she reminded him.

"I won't," he assured her. "Meli told me."

"By the way, I know you were listening when the elder spouted his nonsense. You know that's rude."

"Sorry, Mam," he replied.

"One other thing," she added. "Your tea is still sitting on the table. Be sure to drink it before you leave for school. I added honey this time."

After she stepped away, Thom mumbled, "Blegh." The tea was awful. and that was another reason he didn't like the burdock plant. His Mam brewed it into a tea he had to drink every day. One benefit was improved digestion; his Ma hoped it would help him grow to average height. He didn't think it worked.

Chapter 2

Two days later, Thom was hurrying home to his Da's pottery. He was late. His teacher had asked him to stay after class to talk about his essay. She had asked the students to write about something they had done during the summer. He had written about helping his Mam treat a burn on the arm of a young patient. He smiled and felt himself stand tall, recalling his teacher's comments.

"Great job on your essay, Thom," his teacher had said. "It was well written, and I learned something myself."

"Thanks," he said, blushing.

"You know, when I heard I was getting a student who was not even seven in my fifth-grade class, I was skeptical it'd be a good fit."

"I'll be eight next month," Thom informed her.

"I stand corrected. You do look much younger, given your height," she responded. "Without a doubt, you've proven to me you belong here. Keep it up."

Thom smiled again, thinking about her words. "Hey freak," he heard someone say.

Shaking his head, he looked around and discovered he was passing the field kids always played in. Most of the time, when he walked by this field after class, the kids hadn't arrived yet.

"Hey, I'm talkin' to you, loser."

Thom recognized the voice. It was Kevar. Ever since Davi moved away, Kevar had decided to be the kids' leader. "Leave me alone," Thom replied.

"Look who it is," remarked Shorty, as he was called, who often hung out with Kevar.

"Yeah, the freak," the taller one, nicknamed Beany, chimed in as he trailed after Kevar and Shorty.

"You're not comin' to play, are you? You play like a girl," Shorty whined. By then, most of the kids present in the field had come to watch.

"M...m... my sister, Meli, plays better than all of you," Thom said, shaking inside.

"She's a freak, too," Kevar replied as Thom noticed the cronies moving to either side of him.

"I gotta get home," Thom insisted, attempting to step away.

"You think you're better'n us 'cause you skipped two grades," Kevar stated, pushing him.

Thom knew better than to challenge him.

"Say something," he demanded, "I'm talkin' to you, freak," pushing him harder.

Thom stumbled over something and landed hard on his buttocks. Then, he heard laughter, realizing that Beany had tripped him.

"See, he can't even stand," Shorty jeered, laughing even louder.

"Let's get back to the game," Kevar commanded.

As they walked away, Thom started to stand, grimacing. He knew his butt was bruised. Thom still had to get home. Brushing his trousers off, he stumbled away, hoping his family wouldn't notice when he got home. He didn't want them to know what happened.

After dinner, Thom climbed up to the loft he shared with two of his sisters. Thankfully, they were still downstairs. He had borrowed one of his Mam's salves to apply to his bruises, which were now black and blue. After applying it, he gingerly sat on his bed, kicking off his shoes. At least, he had the evening to himself since his Mam hadn't assigned him any herb reading.

Shifting on his bed, he tried to make himself more comfortable. His butt still hurt. Taking his journal from the shelf, Thom opened it, dated a new entry, Uctiba 9, and wrote, *G, I ran into Kevar today. I wasn't paying attention. He and his bullies pushed me down and called me names again. It hurts. It's not my fault I'm small and not good at sports. If Davi were still here, it wouldn't have happened. I feel like there's a hole in my heart. I really miss him.*

With a heavy sigh, he continued writing, *I found a piece of pottery today. It looks like a lopsided star. It must be special.* Thom picked it up off his shelf and examined it before whispering, "I wish I were special."

Thom placed the shard next to the green stone with a swirly design he found last year. To its right, he saw his greatest treasure, a shiny green triangular-shaped object. He picked it up, running his finger over its predominantly smooth and slightly curved surface. He'd had this forever but couldn't remember where he got it. When his Da let him make pottery, he wanted to make a jar for all his treasures.

Reta popped her head up over the top of the loft ladder. "He's here, Mam," she yelled down. "He's writin' again. Facing him, she announced, "Mam says it's bedtime, Thommy."

"I am in bed," he replied with a smirk.

"But you're full dressed. And you have to kiss Mam and Da goodnight anyways," she replied, sticking out her tongue.

Thom placed the triangular object back on his shelf, closed his journal, and set it on the shelf.

After kissing goodnight to his parents, Thom returned to the loft, undressed, and got into bed. Soon after, he fell asleep.

Ariel didn't usually fly this close to human dwellings, but she needed to take a shortcut back to her mountain in time for her sister to lay her clutch of eggs. She had been delayed returning home when one of her cousins was injured by a sudden collapse of his cave. It was early morning, and she was flying at a height that anyone looking up would assume she was a large bird.

As Ariel was about to pass another dwelling, she detected a bright light on the top of a hill nearby. The dwelling was standard for this area, with mud brick walls and a thatched roof. Is that a juvenile's inner light? she wondered. It's strong enough. She'd have strong words with the parents if it's a juvenile exploring on its own again. We've warned them enough times to stay away from human communities.

Ariel glided in. Landing at the hill's base, below the light, she crept towards it, trying to make as little sound as possible. Ariel was taken aback, realizing the light wasn't a juvenile but a young human child. That level of brightness for a human was quite unusual.

The child turned towards her.

Oh, no, Ariel thought. If the child screams, she'd have to fly off rapidly.

The child waved.

Well, that's contrary to her cousin's experience with human children. This might be foolish, but she wanted to get closer. Something drew her to this child, a male. She noticed cloth wrapped around his waist and something on his feet. What did her cousin call them? Shoons?

Ariel moved closer. She watched as he stumbled his way towards her. Amazing. He had no fear of her.

"Ligh," the child called out.

Interesting, Ariel thought. He can sense her inner light. Curious about the child's glow, she lowered her sensing shield to see greater detail and realized the light was his divine spirit shining through an aura of vivid purple and deep green. This is extraordinary. She'd made it more than halfway up the hill when the boy reached her.

"Brigh' ligh,'" the child repeated, reaching out and placing his hand on her snout.

Ariel felt a strong resonance with him. This boy is unique and must have a powerful purpose.

Using her mind voice, Ariel greeted him, *Hello, little one.*

The child looked startled at first but then smiled.

His brown eyes emitted a holiness. What a wonder! *Hi, little one,* she repeated. *My name is Ariel. I'm a dragon.* Dragons rarely shared their names with humans, but she sensed from her divine guides she should this time.

"Ari? Drager?" the child repeated.

Yes. Ari. Drager.

"Ouchy. Ouchy," he said, frowning.

What did he say?

The child rubbed his small hand across the scale at the corner of her right eye.

Ah, Ariel sighed in relief. That area had been itching, and she'd be shedding soon. As she thought this, a tiny scale came loose and fell to the ground.

The child reached down and picked it up. The triangular scale was about an inch long along each edge.

"Ari better?" the child asked.

Yes, Ariel replied. *Thank you. What's your name?*

"Thommy."

Hi, Thommy. Just then, she heard a female voice call out nearby. *You'd better go back home. Someone is looking for you.*

"Home?"

Yes.

"Bye Bye," Thommy said before waddling back up the hill.

Meanwhile, Ariel turned around, facing downhill. She was close to the dwelling for takeoff but sensed someone coming outside and knew she needed to get away. Using the hill's downward slope to help her take off, she spread her wings and launched into the sky.

Turning back towards Thommy, Ariel saw him getting up. The wind caused by her launch must have bowled him over. Coming around once, she saw Thommy waving. Still using her inner voice, she said, *Goodbye, Thommy. We may see each other again one day.*

The following morning, Thom opened his eyes. What a neat dream, he thought—much better than the nightmares where scary people tried to get him. Lying in bed, Thom wanted to remember what happened. There was a dragon and a little boy, but he couldn't remember their names.

Wouldn't it be great if dragons were real and he could fly on one? He'd fly over Kevar's head and scare him. Then, the kids would see he wasn't a loser.

"Thom," his Mam called out from below. "Would you help Reta get dressed and come down? I need you to pick some herbs from the garden."

"Yes, Mam," he replied. Climbing out of bed, he went to the hook on the wall where he'd hung his trousers the night before. As he pulled them on, he bumped the shelf on which the mysterious triangular object sat, along with his other treasures.

Chapter 3

Thom had been digging clay from a stream bank for the last half hour. This was the first time his Da let him collect the clay without his older brother, Redik. He was proud his Da trusted him and wanted to ensure it was free from any sticks or leaves. Digging his trowel into the bank, he noted he had to use more force than he did a few weeks before. The colder temperatures chilled his hands, not to mention making the ground harder to dig. It didn't help that he was collecting it before most people even had breakfast.

His Da had been teaching him about clay for a month. Last week, he had set up an older pottery wheel for Thom. He wasn't making anything they could sell because he was still learning wheel-throwing techniques. Still, he was finally working with clay. And Thom loved it. Stopping to stretch and stick his hands in his armpits to warm them, he considered the clay. It felt smooth, like a baby's face. Sometimes, he thought he understood it as if it had a soul. When he told Meli, she looked at him like he was crazy. "I'd better keep working," he said out loud. "Da expects me back soon."

Thom had placed his latest pile in the wheelbarrow when his stomach felt like it did after he'd eaten a rotten meat pastie last summer. It can't be from breakfast, he thought. That was almost an hour ago, and Thom only had porridge and one piece of bread with jam. He heard a neigh and the rumble of a vehicle approaching. Without looking, he knew two people were traveling in it. Both men.

How did he know that? Weird. Peaking over the stream bank, Thom saw a carriage with a driver on the outside bench. The other man must be inside. Curious, he imagined the man seated within and felt himself drawn closer, even though he hadn't moved. He started shuddering and soon after threw up.

"Ugh," Thom said with distaste, wiping his mouth on his sleeve. "That was gross."

Peeking again, he saw the carriage driving past and ducked down, even though he was sure he couldn't be seen. The sick feeling was worse, and now he felt afraid, too. Mam said you can ask Deu for help, even though the elders say we're sinful. *Deu, Help!* But he got no reply. Feeling his fear increasing and his stomach threatening to throw up again, he whispered in desperation, "Is anyone up there?" Suddenly, an image flashed of a woman yelling, dressed in a stained apron, and a man running towards her.

That's no help, he thought. Can't you do any better? Please, he pleaded. A picture of a wall appeared before his eyes. Not knowing what else to do, he imagined a thick stone wall between himself and the passenger. As soon as he did, he felt his nausea go away. He decided to remain hidden until he could no longer hear the carriage.

When everything was quiet again, he took a deep breath and felt his fear release, sighing. That was awful. Realizing he had a sour taste in his mouth from the vomit, he scooted over to the stream, cupped water in his hands, and rinsed his mouth, shuddering.

Thinking back to the passenger, how did he know he was bad? Wanting to go home but recognizing he hadn't collected enough clay, he increased his pace. When he collected enough, he made his way back to the pottery. He decided not to say anything about the man. They wouldn't understand. Redik would probably call him a baby anyway.

Arriving at the pottery, his Da commented, "That's a good amount you collected. Thanks for your hard work and for getting up so early."

Thom preened at his Da's praise.

"Tomorrow," his Da continued, "you and Redik need to combine it with our two other clays to create our special mixture. When you're finished, is the clay ready to use?"

"No," Thom answered confidently. "We have to wait at least a month before creating pieces."

"Correct. Good job," his father praised him. "Don't you have school today with Madame Rosearn?" his father asked.

"Yes. We're learning fractions today."

"Ugh," Redik grunted, who was working near the kiln. "I hated fractions." Redik wore a thick smock over his tunic as he helped his Da load and unload pottery from the kiln. He had a wiry shape and shoulder-length dark brown hair.

"I loved them," his sister Meli interrupted, sitting on one side of the pottery. "They were stimulating."

"You would. And stimulating? You sound like a dictionary," Redik retorted.

"None of that, Redik," his father admonished. "What design are you adding to the platter, Meli?"

"Interlaced geometric shapes," she answered, "They have their basis in fractions, by the way," smirking at Redik.

"Basis in fractions," Redik sputtered. "Come on, Da. No one talks like that."

"Redik," his Da said, frowning with displeasure. Looking at Meli's design, he said, "It's very nice. Why don't you add it to the rest of the dish set before I fire them."

"Sure, Da," she replied with a wide grin.

Turning to Thom, his Da said, "Go clean yourself up and head to school. I know you're helping your mother with patients this afternoon. I'll expect you early tomorrow."

"Yes, Da," he replied.

As Thom cleaned up at the pump outside, the cold water made him shiver, bringing back the memory of the carriage passenger. "Oooh. I hope I never feel that again," he whispered. "The wall helped me feel better. Looking up to the sky, he wondered, *Was the idea from you, Deu? If so, thanks.*

"But how did I make the wall? It's a little freaky. I think I'll write about it tonight."

Chapter 4

"Oh, by God's foot!" Rel yelled. "No! I wasn't supposed to die. I was masked and washed my hands before touching any of the patients. No, No, NO," their voice grew louder. Rel had been heading to a meeting with their guardian angel in the divine realm. Passing through a Sanctuary, a redwood forest that one of their previous incarnations had imagined while living on earth, Rel had stopped to appreciate its beauty. They were about to continue when the part of their most recently incarnated self returned with a whoosh.

"Rel!" a voice called.

Rel continued ranting but didn't respond.

"Rel!" the voice repeated.

Rel looked towards the voice and saw their friend, Jeshua, zooming towards them.

"Finally," Jeshua muttered with relief. Noticing Rel was in human form and that of the most recent incarnation, Celes, Jeshua transformed into a human as well, specifically the male he often took. Running up to her, he tried to hug her, but she was too agitated.

"Calm down," Jeshua admonished. "Rel, calm down, please," he pleaded, reaching out and touching her shoulder.

Hearing Jeshua's plea, Rel took a deep breath and asked, "How did you know?"

"Come on. You know how connected we are," Jeshua reminded her. "I was with Archangel Metatron when I sensed Celes' soul returning to you. I honed into your energy and found you yelling like a banshee, not to mention cursing in a way even your incarnate wouldn't have used."

"Oh, Jesh," she said, her voice breaking. "It... it... it...all went wrong. This wasn't suppo'... supposed to happen," she said, gasping for air.

"Breathe, Rel," Jeshua encouraged, taking her hands.

Pausing to wipe the tears from her face, she whispered, "But... I was particularly careful. How could I have gotten sick and died so quickly?"

"I don't know," Jeshua replied with sympathy.

"Now my life's purpose is unfulfilled," Rel added dispiritedly.

"Rel," Jeshua interrupted. "First, are you aware you look like Celes?"

Rel looked down and saw she was wearing her healer apron. "Oh," she muttered quietly before transforming into an energy sphere. "I must have unknowingly changed into her when she returned to the divine realm."

"Talk to me," Jeshua encouraged, returning to their natural state.

"You know I sent signs and messages to Celes to encourage her to be a healer. Even though she didn't know they were from me, she paid close attention to them," Rel explained.

"Yes," Jeshua agreed. "You were quite pleased when she followed her neighbor's suggestion to study healing despite her father's warning that many wouldn't approve of a woman."

"Exactly," Rel said. "She risked her reputation to challenge her village's mores. I was excited about the steps Celes took toward living her purpose. I did wish she realized there were divine forces like me, her higher self, supporting her. I was especially looking forward to chatting with her in her meditations or prayers. But she wasn't there yet in her faith journey."

"Rel," Jeshua interrupted, getting back to the main issue. "Since Celes was a healer, didn't you consider the possibility she might catch something from her patients? Wasn't that discussed at your last pre-incarnation meeting?"

"Yes," Rel answered. "But I thought it was almost impossible given her natural immunity. You were with me when we watched her first start treating the sick villagers. She was very careful."

"True," Jeshua admitted. "Even if getting sick was a slight possibility, it was still there."

"I guess," Rel replied, still discomfited. "When you were incarnated as Jesus, did you think you would be crucified?"

"No," Jeshua admitted. "I knew the authorities had made threats about what I was teaching, and I expected some repercussions. But I didn't expect that. I did have to accept it. Back to you, though, how are you doing?"

"I still feel like my head is spinning. That is if I had a head," Rel said with a smirk.

"Good, your humor's returning," Jeshua said with a grin. "Do you think you're settled enough to talk with Metatron? As your teacher, I don't think they'd appreciate hearing you cursing. Although, as a being who incarnated on earth, I'd imagine Metatron might've cursed once or twice."

"They probably did," Rel replied. And yes, I'm a little better."

Jeshua and Rel's spheres folded into themselves and disappeared.

They reformed in Archangel Metatron's office, as humans would call it. Metatron's cube was spinning in the center of the room, its interlocking circles, stars, triangles, and other geometric shapes glowing with the violet energy flowing through it.

"Aren't there more sparks now than there were before?" Jeshua asked Metatron.

"Yes, but it's settling down again, at least to how it was before," they replied, nodding towards Rel. "I wish it would spark even less. The negative energies caused by the polarization between people on Earth continue disrupting the flow between there and here. And that's despite more people turning to us for help."

Rel remained silent, his sphere a little dimmed.

Turning away from the cube and towards Rel, Metatron asked, "Dare I say, welcome back?"

"Yeah. Thanks," Rel mumbled.

"I sensed how disturbed you were when Celes died. But I know from personal experience that the unexpected and undesired can happen on Earth."

"I suppose," Rel said with a sigh.

"Metatron," Jeshua interrupted, "do you want me to stay, or did you want a private chat?"

"Hmm...private, please, Jesh," Metatron answered. "Thanks for seeking Rel out."

"You're welcome," Jesh replied. "Rel, come look for me when you have time. Then, we can have our customary greeting." Jeshua's energy sphere folded into itself and vanished.

"Tell me how you feel about Celes' life," Metatron encouraged.

"It was a failure. Her life was a waste," Rel replied, disconsolate.

"A waste? Don't you think that's a bit of an exaggeration?"

"No," Rel replied. "At my pre-incarnation meeting, everyone agreed to Celes' life purpose as a healer. When the male healer asked her to assist him, it seemed like a perfect opportunity."

"I agree."

"The situation also gave me a chance to start resolving fears of incompetency which lingered from my last incarnation," Rel continued.

"I saw that, too. You must have been very pleased when Celes suggested to the male healer that they keep surfaces clean and bleach soiled bedsheets and clothes."

"Yes, I was," Rel agreed. "But she got sick anyway. I still don't know how."

"I'm sorry that happened," Metatron said. "I was hoping her natural immunity would pull her through. But like I said..."

"I know the unexpected can happen," Rel replied, letting go of the weight of Celes' death.

"I'm not surprised you were upset. Lightworkers are sensitive beings," Metatron added. "Tragedies, like you experienced, are more difficult to handle, much less understand. If it's important you know how Celes got sick, we could check with the higher self of the male healer, who also died," Metatron suggested. "What do you think?"

Rel considered this before responding. "No. If Celes got sick due to something the male healer did, knowing wouldn't help advance my path as a lightworker."

"I was hoping you'd say that," Metatron replied. "It shows you are indeed moving toward full lightworker status.

For a time, they remained quiet.

Breaking the silence, Metatron spoke, "Why don't you take some time to yourself? Afterward, talk with Sereh and the rest of your divine team. We can talk more at another time."

"OK, Thanks," Rel replied before folding into themself and disappearing.

Four months passed, according to the human calendar. Rel stood outside the Gaia chamber, where his pre-incarnation meeting would be held. For this meeting, he decided to appear as a human male. Looking through luminescent energy walls that rippled slightly, Rel saw the chamber was full of beings in human form. He knew from experience that it offered a wider range of communication options.

"Lightworker-Reliant, you can go in," Spirit Guide-Jak announced.

"Thanks," Rel replied. Stepping into the chamber, he saw Jeshua first and made his way over. They greeted each other with their usual routine: slapping their hands, tapping each foot with the opposite hand, twisting at the waist, bumping their rumps, and ending with a hug. "Your timing's off a bit, Jesh. Not to mention, you started to bow instead of twist. We changed that two incarnations ago," chuckling.

"I forgot," Jeshua admitted. "But you were too fast," he countered, laughing.

Looking to his right, Rel saw his guardian angel, Sereh. Walking to her, he gave her a hug.

"Are you ready for this?" she asked, reaching out and grasping his hands.

"Yes, he replied, "Thanks again for staying with me when Celes first died. It helped. But I know I'm ready for what comes next."

"You're welcome," Sereh said. "And I think you're ready, too," placing her forehead against Rel's. "Remember, I'm always with you," she whispered, "even with the part of you that incarnates."

"I know," he said as warmth grew in his heart. Standing straight a minute later, Rel saw God beyond Sereh's wings. "Do you know why God's here?"

Sereh gave him an enigmatic smile.

"Not telling, huh."

Out of the corner of his eyes, he saw someone rush in. It was Lightworker-Sens, who was also in training.

"Sorry I'm late," Sens apologized. "I was delayed at Spirit-Jen's life review."

Metatron nodded. "We understand. Life here isn't all about floating on clouds, as some on Earth presume."

"Why is Sens here?" Rel asked Sereh.

"I don't know," she answered.

"Hi, Rel," Metatron said, interrupting them. "I overheard you wondering about God and Sens' presence. That will come clearer soon."

"Could I have everyone's attention?" Spirit Guide-Jak called out. "Would you all take your seats? We're about to start."

Rel went to the front circle of chairs and sat down. Sereh sat next to him.

When everyone was settled, Jak continued, "Welcome to Lightworker-Reliant's pre-incarnation meeting. Since Archangel Metatron oversees all lightworkers, he'll run this meeting."

"Thanks, Jak and everyone," Metatron added, looking at the large crowd present. "As you all know, Rel is a lightworker trainee. As always, with these meetings, we'll start with Rel summarizing his last incarnation. Rel…"

"Sure," Rel replied. "… and then she died."

"Consequently, you could not make much progress on Celes' life purpose, correct?"

"Yes," Rel replied.

"What about your spiritual development?" Metatron asked.

"I didn't make progress there either," Rel replied. "Once I got more accepted as a healer, I had hoped to use my role as an opportunity to raise questions with the local elders about some of their teachings."

"Sereh, do you have anything to add?" Metatron asked.

"Only to say Celes' death didn't allow her time to discover her other healing ability."

"Oh, I forgot to mention that." Rel agreed. "Sorry."

"Now, Rel, would you share what we've identified as your purpose in your next life?"

Once Rel had told them, Metatron asked the assembled, "Any questions?"

"I have one," God said. "Why is Rel incarnating so soon? I know the reason, but I want everyone else to understand, too."

"Why don't you answer, Rel?" Metatron suggested.

"Sure," Rel answered. "After talking with my divine team, including Metatron, they thought, given my stage of development, my next incarnation needed to occur about six months after my previous life ended. My understanding is that I'm close to reaching full lightworker status." He noted a few of those gathered nodding.

"You should also mention the other unusual aspect," Metatron advised.

"OK," Rel responded, "I wasn't sure. I'll be incarnating into the same world Celes lived in, but not in the same land."

"Why?" someone in the back row asked, who Rel couldn't identify.

For a good while, discussion ensued.

"Well, that was lively," Metatron said. "We appreciate everyone's comments. Now, Rel, have you considered your gender and the family into which you might be born?"

"Somewhat," Rel replied. "As to gender, male. That's why I took a male form. I have some thoughts I'd like to discuss with you about the family. But I need a little more time to think about it."

"Sounds good," Metatron replied. "Come seek me out when you're ready. Before we conclude, I want to give God and Sens an opportunity to speak."

"I'll be brief," God said.

Hearing some murmurings, God added, "Yes, I know. I do have a tendency to run long."

"You can say that again," Jeshua said, winking towards Rel.

"Anyway," God replied. "Given your next life's purpose, which Metatron previously shared with me, and your willingness to risk, we've identified a special opportunity for you, which includes Sens. Rather than discuss this with the entire group, let's chat after everyone else leaves."

"OK," Rel replied, curious and giving Sens a pointed look.

"Was that brief enough, Jesh?" God asked with a wink.

"I stand corrected," Jesh responded, whereupon he stood up, his mouth twisted in a wry grin.

Rel heard some groans and laughter.

"OK, OK," Metatron interrupted. "Let's end the meeting. But before I do, I want to acknowledge how much I appreciate your playfulness, Jesh and Rel, including your greeting routine. Some in this realm have forgotten the lighter side of life here. It's important we model that here and with our incarnates."

"Thanks, Metatron," Jeshua and Rel replied.

"You're welcome. And thanks, everyone, for coming," Metatron said.

Some while later, Rel sought out Metatron. "I've chosen the Macirdan family," Rel informed him. "They live in Docha-leigh, the largest land on the Sandrim continent."

"Why them?"

"The mother, Winni, is a part-time healer. Her mother was also a healer. It's almost certain my incarnate will inherit some abilities."

"Is the father also a healer?" Metatron asked.

"No, he's a potter," Rel answered. "He looks to be quite good. It could be fun to develop that skill."

"OK," Metatron confirmed. "What about their spirituality?"

"They practice the Iosan faith," Rel explained.

"And how do you think that will work?

"I don't know," Rel confessed. "The Macirdans seem like good people, but, like you said, sometimes the unexpected happens."

"Good," Metatron replied approvingly. "When do you expect the incarnation process to begin?"

"In about 10 weeks," Rel replied.

"OK. Let me know if you have any questions during the process."

"Will do," Rel confirmed. "Are you coming to the welcome back gathering for Spirit Guide-Dev's incarnated self?"

"Of course," Metatron answered. "I'll see you there."

Chapter 5

A month ago, Rin had set up his practice in Potai-cruth. Gazing out the window, through the icicles hanging from the eaves, he reflected on his journey here. It had taken a lot of wandering in this part of Docha-leigh in his guise as a traveling healer to locate the energy of the boy the seers had foretold. He now knew the boy's name, Thom Macirdan.

The mystery of Thom's energy, its nature, and its role in the prophecy intrigued Rin. He had begun the search months before as part of his duties as a member of the covert group COM, established by the queen of his land, Niamh, and her spouse, Pethuric.

From inquires he made to the local chandler, now his landlord, he learned Thom was the son of Uric and Winni, who lived on the outskirts of town. And like the foreseers described, Uric was a potter, and Winni was a part-time healer. He had also learned Winni was overloaded with patients since the town healer had died. Rin couldn't help but feel for Winni and her burden. He hoped she would welcome his assistance. He hadn't sought them out because his guides had told him it was important they come to him. He didn't understand, but he trusted them.

Rin was short for Rinbalden. Why his parents gave him that name, he'd never known. Rin was of medium height, 5 ½ feet tall, with dark brown hair graying at his temples. He had pale skin, so he always wore a big floppy hat outdoors to avoid sunburn. Most people thought he looked silly. For him, the hat was functional. Since he traveled quite often, he was also slender. But he knew he'd gain a belly if he stayed in one place too long. One of his weaknesses was sweets, like cakes and sweet muffins.

Rin didn't know how long he'd live in Potai, as the locals called it. He also still didn't know Thom's current age. The first foreseer's vision put his age at around seven. When the vision occurred, he'd been on an assignment in Dunal to investigate a marked increase in thefts in the area, which was likely the work of a ring of thieves. His mind went back to that time.

Rin had placed another bag of herbs on the shelf. He'd been here for three months, working with the local healer and surreptitiously investigating the situation. He was pleased with his progress but hadn't yet identified the ringleaders. Returning to the side counter to fill another bag, he heard the door chime. He saw a tall man enter. It was Crevan, another member of COM. What's he doing here? He'd sent an update to Niamh and Peth a week ago.

"Can I help you, sir?" he asked.

"Yes," Crevan answered. "My lord requested I buy salves to treat minor cuts and burns. Do you have any recommendations?"

"Of course," Rin replied. "Follow me to the shelf across the way."

When they had privacy, Rin whispered, "Crevan, is there some crisis?"

"Not that I'm aware of," he assured him. "But the message is urgent, and they want you to return immediately."

"Understood," Rin replied. "Let me tell the healer there's a family emergency, and I must return home. I'll meet you outside as soon as I can."

"Sounds good," Crevan replied, leaving soon after purchasing a few jars of salve.

Once outside, Rin read the message. It didn't mention the nature of the emergency, which prevented him from estimating the length of time he'd be away from Dunal. When he explained this to Crevan, Crevan offered to take over the investigation. Readily agreeing, Rin shared what he had discovered. Returning to his room at the inn, he gathered his things and got on the road to the capital, Freas-a-chos, or Freasa.

Rin rode through the night, arriving before sunrise the next day. This afforded him a few hours of sleep in his room in the Keep before he awakened to a sound.

Rap—rap—rap.

Climbing out of bed, he shuffled to the door, a bit bleary-eyed, and opened it a crack.

"Sir Rinbalden, sir," a young page squeaked, shifting from foot to foot. "Um, the Queen asked me to give you a note," she said shakily, extending her hand towards him.

"It's OK, lass. I won't bite you. Thank you for bringing me the message. Do they expect a response?"

"They didn't tell me."

"OK. Thank you again. Job well done."

The page blushed and dashed off.

Am I truly scary? Rin asked himself. Closing the door, he read the note. It explained the monarchs were in a meeting for another hour. Good, he thought. I have time to beg for some food in the kitchen.

The cooks obliged him with some bread, jam, and a bowl of porridge. When he was in town, he always spent time with them, sharing stories about the characters he met on his travels. Unabashedly, he also knew it would result in a gift of some sweet baked goods. This time, the chief cook, Mari, offered him a cinnamon apple muffin. After he finished, he headed to the monarchs' private sitting room in Cleirigh Hall.

Knocking on the door, Rin heard a female voice call out, "Come in, Rin." The door he opened was a hidden entrance to the sitting room. It was needed to prevent the general Hall population from being aware when covert messengers came on private business. Rin found Peth seated on a couch and Niamh at the desk.

"Thanks for coming as quickly as you did," Peth greeted him. "Have some coffee and your favorite muffin. We know you're obsessed with them."

"I wouldn't say obsessed," Rin countered.

"What would you call it?" Peth asked. Peth was about thirty, lean but muscular since he continued to train with the weapons master. He had dark brown hair, a skin tone the color of wheat, and almond-shaped brown eyes, which often twinkled with mischief. At the moment, they looked pensive.

"I'd say I... favored them... strongly," he replied with a grin.

Peth smiled before saying, "I'd imagine you didn't get much sleep."

"No, I didn't," Rin replied. "But your message said it was urgent. Since you still had your usual budget meeting, I presumed it wasn't time-sensitive."

"Interesting way to put it," Peth replied, tilting his head. "It is, and it isn't."

"Let me finish up this letter, Rin," Niamh interjected.

"No hurry," he replied, settling on a chair across from Peth and taking a bite of a still-warm muffin.

Minutes passed before Niamh joined Peth on the couch. Niamh was a year younger than her husband. She had reddish-brown hair and a darker complexion. Despite being shorter than her husband, she bore the same strength. Like Peth, she still trained with the weapons master.

"Good to see you, Rin," Niamh said. "As Peth implied, your comment was ironic. Three of our foreseers came to us two days ago. Each had very similar visions."

"I sense something unusual about them," Rin commented. "Otherwise, you'd simply share the transcriptions."

"Astute as ever," Niamh noted. "All of them are about a child."

"The same child?" Rin asked.

"Yes," Peth added, "But we wanted your assessment."

"I know visions of children are rare, but I still don't understand the urgency," Rin said, his brow furrowed.

"The child, a boy," Niamh added, "will exhibit powerful gifts at a younger age than usual. The urgency stems from wanting your impression of the visions while they're fresh in the seers' minds. Past experience has told us that when you hear them directly, you often learn additional details that may be important."

"True," Rin confirmed. "What else aren't you telling me, Niamh? I know you sometimes withhold information, even when we were in school."

"I did," she admitted. "Back then, I liked surprising you all. This time, I don't want to influence what you hear."

"Good enough," Rin replied.

"We'd like to invite them back now," Peth added. "Are you OK with that?"

"Certainly."

Using the bell pull, Niamh rang an assistant. When he arrived, she asked him to request the seers' presence in their smaller audience chamber next door.

Pethuric, Niamh, and Rin were seated when there was a knock.

"Come in," Pethuric called out.

Three people entered: two women and one man. "Good morning, your majesties and Healer Rinbalden," the foreseers chorused, bowing to each of them as they approached.

"Good morning," they replied, standing to greet them.

"Thank you for coming," Pethuric continued. "Healer Rin, I believe you've met Seer Trethlyn and Seer Arion."

"Yes, I have," Rin responded. Trethlyn was in her late 60s, with gray hair tied in a bun. When he'd interacted with her before, she always asked about his health. She knew from her sister, who was also a healer that sometimes they forget to take care of themselves. Arion was in his mid-50s, with thick red hair, a long goatee, and a bit disheveled. Arion was quite conscientious of details, sometimes to a fault. Behind them, he noted that the second woman, not long out of her teenage years, approached more tentatively, her eyes downcast.

"I'd like to introduce you to Apprentice Seer Lalia," Pethuric said. "She's new to our foreseers. Her gift made itself known a few months ago."

"Congratulations, Seer Lalia," Rin said. "I'm pleased to meet you."

"Thanks, sir," she mumbled, looking up briefly.

"Would you all like to sit?" Peth asked.

"Thank you," they replied.

"We'd like you to share your visions with Healer Rinbalden," Niamh said. "Seer Trethlyn, would you start?"

"Yes, your majesty," she responded.

"Before you share your vision," Rin added, "would you also tell me where you were and the time of day you had it." He wanted to make sure they were indeed separate visions rather than one vision that was compromised by overhearing the others.

"Yes, of course," Seer Trethlyn replied. "I had my vision three nights ago. I was awakened from sleep by a blindingly radiant light. Reliving the vision, she explained, "The light energy passes through me, and I feel a healing warmth."

Rin nodded, sensing the light and warmth she described. He wished he could see what she saw, but his abilities didn't extend that far.

She continued, "After a few seconds, the light diminishes a little. It's still quite dazzling. I realize that it's a child, a boy child, to be specific. His luminescent aura has swirling streaks of vivid green and purple. And I have to say his energy exudes a sensitivity and purity that I haven't felt often. Even through this vision, I feel uplifted."

"What was the boy doing?"

"He's in a garden, standing among rows of plants. He's speaking to them because I see energy flowing from him to the plants."

"He may have some earth sense, then," Rin said. "Can I presume you can't hear what he's saying? I know that ability hadn't exhibited itself in you or other foreseers here last I heard."

"Lalia heard some sound in her vision," she answered. "We're hopeful that ability persists."

"Very impressive, Seer Lalia," Rin said, looking towards her, whose face had turned red. Trethy, can you determine the boy's age?"

"Maybe around seven, given his height, but I have the feeling he's a bit older. I've only known a few children his age."

"Please continue," Rin encouraged.

"I see the boy look up. Now my vision shifts to the front of the home, where a woman is carrying a young child toward a door with a healer sign. It's back to the boy, and I'm sensing he's tuning into the child, and get the impression he knows what's wrong with her. Now, some distance behind the boy, I see a dark cloud approaching that's not associated with the weather. It's most disturbing."

"Can you say more about the dark cloud?" Rin asked.

"It was oily, and my sense was that it was going to cover his entire being in an attempt to control him."

"OK. I'm sensing your feelings now. Other than his height, can you describe the boy?"

"Unfortunately, his light was too bright for me to make out his features, even his hair color."

"Understood. Would you tap into where he lives?" Rin asked.

"I'll try. Lalia, I'm going back into my vision and changing my viewpoint to a higher perspective," Seer Trethlyn explained. "OK. I see farms and a few homesteads. The boy's home is on the outskirts of a town. On one side, past a garden, I see a hill that slopes down into a valley. I don't see any signposts with the town's name."

"That's OK," Rin replied. "Do you get the sense of its general location?"

"South. Maybe southeast. I can't say exactly, but I think it's about a week's ride away."

"Good information," Rin stated. "Oh, what about the time of year? I should've asked earlier."

"Maybe the beginning of spring. There are a couple of small piles of snow here and there. I can also see the trees and flowers budding."

"Anything else? Rin asked.

"Just that this will occur sometime in the future, maybe a few years," she added.

"Thank you, Seer Trethlyn."

"Yes, thank you, Trethy," Niamh said. "Seer Arion, would you share your vision?"

"Yes, your majesty," he replied. "Mine happened the next morning. I was behind in transcribing a previous vision, and I'd gotten up early to finish. I had completed the task when I felt a searing headache. Gratefully, it was brief. But it was followed by the same radiant light Trethy described."

"Interesting," Rin noted.

"The vision is coming into focus. I see that the light is coming from the boy. Unlike Trethy's, there's a black shadow tinging his light, and it feels oily, too."

"I'm also sensing that," Rin commented. "Where's the boy in your vision?"

"He's working at a wheel in a pottery," Arion told them. "It looks like he's creating a bud vase, but it has an unusual shape. He's about to place a small blue stone in the stem. Interesting."

"OK, Arion," Rin said, "I don't need any more details about the vase. Can you determine the boy's age?"

"I can't tell his height because he's sitting down. I'll look around to see if I can find a clue."

Rin remained silent.

"There's part of a book showing next to the stool the boy's sitting on. Let me see if I can get closer, Arion said. "Oh, it's a math book for sixth graders. Would that put him at 11 or 12 years old?"

"Likely," Niamh offered.

"I know that you're indoors," Rin continued. "But can you determine what time of year it is?"

"The doors to the pottery are open. It looks to be a nice day. The trees still have leaves. They're mostly green, but some are beginning to change color."

Mmm, Rin thought to himself. "Arion, did the math book look new?"

"Oh, I'm sorry. I should have mentioned that. Yes, it was."

"Then, it's Siptema or thereabouts when school starts," Rin concluded. "Excellent. Can you provide me any further details about the boy?"

"No, he glows too brightly for me, too," Arion admitted. "And I can't perceive auras like Trethy can. I do sense a connection between the boy and the clay of the vase. That also suggests an earth sense."

"Can you tell me any more about the black shadow?" Rin asked.

"Some. Its source is from another person in the pottery."

"Would you focus on that person then?" Rin asked.

"Certainly," Arion replied, pausing. "I can't tell if it's a man or woman because the shadow's obscuring the person."

"Tell me more about the shadow," Rin requested.

"It exhibits an undulating quality, with darker and lighter shading. It's also in constant motion, which is a bit disorienting."

"I suspect that's from imperfect shielding," Rin suggested. "Can you sense or see anything through the lighter areas?"

"I'll try," Arion said. "I get a glimpse of high-quality clothing, and the person's overweight, but I still can't tell if it's a man or woman."

"That's unfortunate," Rin said. "Stick with it a bit longer if you can."

"The person's tall, but that's about it," Arion offered. "I need to stop soon; my headache's returning, and I can tell it's going to be severe."

"That's enough about the shadowed figure. Are there others there?"

"The figure's talking with a man, who I'm certain is the boy's father. He's muscular with reddish-brown hair and probably in his late thirties. I see some of the same shadow over him, by the way. There's also a third person, a male teenager. But no shadow."

"Good," Rin said. "Is there anything else that stands out about the setting?"

"The pottery pieces are exquisite. I'd love to get my hands on a few."

"Thanks," Rin added. Since your vision is in a pottery, you wouldn't see any signposts. But do you have an impression of where it's located?"

"Southeast of here. But I can't tell you how far away."

"Thanks, Seer Arion," Rin said. "Now..."

"Sorry to interrupt, Healer," Arion apologized. "I do want to mention that it's important that this boy not fall into the merchant's hands."

"No need to apologize," Rin assured him. "Thanks for telling us."

Before Rin could speak up again, Niamh spoke, "Seer Lalia, this might seem a bit overwhelming since you are new to your gifts. We also know this is the first time you've come to us. Please take your time."

"Yes, your majesty," Seer Lalia replied shakily.

"Tell us what you saw as best you can," Niamh encouraged.

"OK. I was eating in the kitchen the same morning when Arion had his vision. I had slept in and missed breakfast. One of the kitchen helpers was a friend, and he brought me some porridge, a roll, and jam. I was sitting at a side counter when I saw a light so bright it almost hurt."

This third vision also starts with a bright light, Rin mused. It could be the same boy. "Go on."

"The light is getting smaller but doesn't go away. I can now see a little boy standing at the top of a hill. Just like Seer Trethlyn and Seer Arion, the light makes him too glarey. So, I can't describe him. From his size, he might be my youngest cousin's age, who's a toddler."

"About three years then," Rin suggested.

"Yes, sir," she replied.

"Please go on, Seer Lalia," Rin said.

"The toddler gives off great power and seems to be talking to someone. I can't see who but my sense is that she's a female and is very wise." Shaking her head, she says, "That's all I got." When I came out of it, my friend was standing near me. He was holding my spoon. I guess I dropped it. My vision didn't last very long. I'm very, very sorry," she said, lowering her head.

"Lalia," Seer Trethlyn spoke, "None of us control the length of our visions. Arion and I sometimes wish ours were longer or at least clearer."

"Did you sense when this will happen?" Rin asked.

"In the next day or two," she replied without looking up.

"One more question. Lalia, if you don't mind me calling you that."

She shook her head.

"Since you were outside, can you go back into your vision and change your perspective to see the location?" Rin asked.

"Lalia," Seer Trethlyn interjected. "Remember what I taught you. Imagine yourself floating above the scene but still very much present. And remember to ground yourself before you move."

She nodded and took a few breaths. "The hill is on the right side of a house. There's a garden there too. I'm hearing sounds from the inside, like metal clanging. It's morning. I think they're preparing breakfast."

"I love that you're getting sound," Rin interjected. "Can you hear any voices?"

"I hear a woman's voice yelling," she answered. "But I can't tell what she's saying."

"No worries," Rin said. "Can you move your perspective even higher?"

"I'll try," she responded.

"You're doing great, Lalia," Trethlyn encouraged.

"I'm seeing the entire house. There's smoke coming from a chimney. And it looks like they're building an extension. Oh, and there's a pottery next door because I see some ceramic pieces through the window. I hear sounds from there, too, but no voices."

"Good," Rin replied. "Can you move out further to see more of the area?"

"Oh," Lalia uttered with disappointment. "I'm really sorry. I lost it," looking down again.

"You did great, Lalia," Trethlyn assured her. "We know this is new for you."

"One last question, Lalia," Rin spoke. "Did you sense any blackness nearby?"

"No."

Looking at each of them, Rin asked, "I'm getting the impression you believe your visions are about the same boy?"

"Yes," Seer Trethlyn replied.

"Thank you for bearing with me," Rin said. "Your visions confirm that none of you inadvertently listened in on the others. And I also have a sense your visions are about one boy."

"I agree," Niamh added. "Thank you for your time and for using your gifts in service to our land. You are invaluable. And your visions are one example."

"Thank you, your majesties," the three replied, bowing again before departing.

"Let's go back to our sitting room and discuss this a bit more," Peth suggested.

After each of them had gotten a cup of coffee and Rin another muffin, they all sat down again.

"What do you think Rin?" Niamh asked.

"Like I said, the visions are of one boy. The light they experienced was the boy's spirit."

"I don't recall our foreseers ever having similar visions," Peth commented. "Niamh, were you aware of any from your mother or grandmother's foreseers?"

"No," she replied, "Those which I heard were always distinct."

"I might've heard rumors in my travels," Rin said. "What's important is this boy has a very powerful spirit, and a special purpose. It could be he has a very strong healing ability, but I can't say without meeting him."

"A special purpose. Interesting," Peth commented.

"His gifts will start showing quite early. Gifts usually don't surface until around twelve. I've worked with two who had gifts emerging at ten but no younger. One, a girl, ended in tragedy."

"That must have been awful for her parents," Niamh said.

"It was," Rin admitted. "About the boy, I'm more disturbed by the progression of darkness two of them described."

"I must say, Arion's description of the cloud overshadowing him and his father gave me the willies," Peth added.

"I understand. That person is bad news. My sense is that he wants to corrupt the boy's untrained gifts."

"We agree," Niamh said.

"We both thought it important for the boy to be found before then and trained by a suitable person," Peth explained.

"By suitable person, do you mean me?" Rin asked.

"Yes," Niamh replied.

"Makes sense," Rin agreed. "As to identifying the person, I wish Arion could've determined whether the person was male or female. We do have some useful clues, including the characteristics of the cloud. But it would have been helpful if Arion was able to identify the person's trade."

"I agree," Peth said, shaking his head.

"The good news," Rin continued, "is that he's safe for now. But that will change in a few years as his gifts start emerging."

"Good point," Niamh replied. "Do you have any thoughts about how to handle this? I have some, but we'd like to hear what you think."

While Peth and Niamh sipped their coffee, Rin considered the situation. Finally, he spoke up. "Given the boy's gifts won't emerge in the near future, I think I should continue as I have been for a couple more years. I do travel through the southeast on occasion. When I'm in that area, I'll keep my senses open to see if I can detect either the boy or the merchant. They both have very telling energy signatures. I'll also listen for any mention of quality potters."

"Good idea," Niamh said.

"In about three and a half years," Rin continued. "I'll resume my traveling healer guise and search for the boy. My hope is I'll have found him and can witness the vision Trethy described. What do you think?"

"That matches the plan we came up with," Niamh stated. "In the meantime, Peth and I will ask others in COM to stay alert for any new merchants that our traders have dealt with. I'll keep my senses open, too. You remember I have a bit of prescience myself."

"I do," Rin replied.

"How were things progressing in Dunal?" Peth asked. "Were you able to determine if a group of thieves was operating?"

"Yes, there was, but I haven't been able to identify its leaders," Rin replied.

"Did you want to head back there?" Peth asked.

"Actually," Rin replied, "I think Crevan is better suited for this one since he used to work for the constabulary. I'm grateful he offered to take over."

"Good," Niamh replied. "Again, thank you for coming. I don't believe you are handling any other tasks for the next couple of weeks."

"For the most part," Rin replied. "I did want to wander about the Acadium a bit. I want to talk with some of the teachers and older students to see if any might be potential candidates for COM."

"You have a talent for that, Rin," Peth remarked. "I know I don't. We'll let you go. Can I presume you're going back to your room to sleep?" he asked with a wry grin.

He smiled back. "See you later."

Emerging from his memory, Rin still felt disturbed by the merchant's dark shadow and his potential impact on Thom. He hoped his mother, Winni, might visit his shop soon. Getting up from the table where he was crushing some herbs, he tripped and spilled half of them. "Oh, Turg!" he cursed. "I need to find a bletter way to secure those floorboards."

"Bletter," Rin uttered, shaking his head. "Yep, I'm upset. That's when I add Ls to my words. Maybe the BETTER solution," he said with emphasis, "is to talk with my landlord about fixing them. I have many skills, but fixing stubborn floorboards isn't one of them."

Returning from talking with his landlord, Rin was putting up some jars of salve when he sensed Thom Macirdan was nearby. As the foreseers had said, his spirit was almost blinding. Shortly afterward, the shop door opened.

"Before you step in," a woman commanded, "be sure to stomp off the snow from your boots. We don't want to be tracking snow into the healer shop."

Through the open door, Rin could see a little girl and the woman stomping their feet on the ground. He saw Thom thumping his boots against the shopfront wall.

Once they entered, Rin greeted them, "Good morning, madam. Good morning, children. That was some snow we had last night."

"Yes, it was, sir," she answered.

"Thank you for cleaning the snow off before coming in. Not everyone is as conscientious," pointing to a puddle on the floor."

"You're welcome," the woman replied. "My husband and I require it of our children before they come into our house. How could we not require it when we visit other establishments?"

"Well, I do, thank you," he said. She's very considerate, which bodes well for her as a healer. "How can I help you?"

"My name is Winni Macirdan. I'm sort of a part-time healer in the area."

"Sort of?" Rin asked.

"Yes, sir. You see, our town's healer died four months ago. Before he died, I helped him out on occasion. Since then, people have relied on me in this area. But I'm not fully trained."

"Were you apprenticing to him?" Rin asked.

"No, sir," she answered. "Years ago, soon after my husband and I married, I did have an apprenticeship. But before I completed it, the healer moved away, and we couldn't follow because Uric had set up his pottery business, and we had our first child."

"And you couldn't finish your apprenticeship with the town healer before he died?"

"Unfortunately, no," she responded. "He was elderly and lacked the energy to take on anyone."

"I see," Rin replied. "And who do you have with you?"

"These are Thom and Reta," she answered, "two of my seven children."

"You have a large family," Rin commented.

"Yes. My husband, Uric, and I wanted a large one. Me, because I grew up in a large family, and Uric because for most of his life, it was just him and his Da."

Looking down, Rin noticed that Thom had extended his hand to him in greeting. "Oh, sorry, lad. I should've paid more attention. Nice to meet you, Thom. I'm Healer Rinbalden," he said, shaking his hand.

"Nice to meet you, sir," Thom responded.

Holding Thom's hand, Rin perceived his aura clearly. It showed translucent green, a healing color, the purple Seer Trethlyn had mentioned, and a little blue. He also detected that Thom's gifts were beginning to emerge. Remarkable, given his age. It won't take much for them to activate fully.

"And how old are you?" Rin asked Thom.

"I'm eight years and three months," Thom replied.

Huh, Rin thought. He's small for his size. It's understandable why Trethy wasn't sure about his age. Let me confirm one aspect of Arion's vision. "Given your age, are you in third grade?"

"No, Thom replied. "I'm in fifth, Healer Rin...bal..den," he enunciated carefully.

"Well done," Rin complimented him. "You can call me Healer Rin, by the way."

"Thom's advanced for his age," Winni said. "Some call him precocious, but not in a good way."

"How small-minded," Rin commented.

"I agree," Winni said. "We teach our children to speak their minds. Sometimes, it gets them into trouble. Of course, Thom here is more precocious than most of my other children."

"The other kids call me a freak."

"I'm sorry to hear that, Thom," Rin replied tenderly.

"Thanks," Thom mumbled, his eyes lowered a bit.

Turning to the little girl, Rin asked, "And you're Reta?" She nodded.

Rin detected a nascent earth sense in her, which would emerge soon. The auric colors overlaying her spirit showed shades of brown and green. It's going to be quite strong, he thought. She may even have healing gifts. "And how old are you?"

"Almost five," Reta replied. "I want to help in the garden. I like dirt."

"Soon, dear," her mother replied. "Maybe in a couple months."

"Dirt is good," Rin said to Reta. Looking closely at Winni, he saw vivid green and blue auric colors overlaying her spirit. He wondered if any of her other children had gifts. "What brought you here today, Mrs. Macirdan?"

"Please call me Winni," she said. "You see...are you planning to remain here long?" she asked.

"Six months to a year," he replied. "Why?"

"Now that my older children can help care for my younger ones, I have more time. I wondered...um... if I might apprentice with you?" she asked, her words bursting out of her like a startled deer.

"I would be happy to," Rin replied. He now understood why his spirit guides told him not to seek her and Thom out. She had to come to him to ask for training despite her fear. "On one condition."

"Anything, sir," Winni replied, sighing with relief.

"No more of this sir business. Please call me Rin. Or Healer Rin if you like."

"Healer Rin, yes," Winni replied. "Oh. I was hoping you'd teach me. But I wasn't sure you would have the time or even be willing. Too many have come to me for treatment that I had to turn away because I didn't know what to do."

"OK. How about if I come out to your place twice a week initially? Then I can see your healing set up and be with you as patients come for treatment."

"Could you? That would be wonderful, Healer Rin. Sometimes, Thom helps me. Would it be OK if he was there too?" she asked. "We'd understand if you said no."

Glancing at Thom, he saw his eyes widen and nod. "Certainly," Rin agreed, smiling. "Would it fit your schedule if I come this Widna-dae and Moone-dae in the afternoon?"

"Um," Winni said hesitantly. "Moone-dae won't work because we have a family gathering. Could you come on Setr-dae? I don't mean to make trouble."

Rin couldn't tell Winni he would adjust his schedule to fit hers. "Let's see," he said, pretending to consider. "Yes, Setr-dae works, too."

"Oh, thank you, thank you," Winni replied with a grateful smile.

"Now, how are your healing supplies, like herbs and salves?"

"I'm fine on herbs, but I could use some salves, including those for burns. I haven't quite come up with one strong enough."

From the shelf behind him, Rin picked up a few jars. "These are good for burns," he said, handing her two jars with a blue ribbon tied around each. "This one, with the green ribbon, helps with cuts and abrasions. I'm also throwing in a few herb bags you can use to brew tea to treat digestion issues. It's a combination I developed some time ago."

Oh, no, Thom thought. Will Mam make him drink that tea, too? He hoped it didn't taste disgusting.

"Thank you, Healer Rin," Winni replied, placing the bags and jars in her basket.

"I have a question for you, Winni," Rin said.

"Yes," she replied.

"You mentioned your husband has a pottery business."

"Indeed, and a good one," she said with pride.

"Do you know if he makes jars like these? They have lids that clamp shut securely to help the salves retain their potency," he explained.

"Unfortunately, no," she replied. "But I'm sure Uric could."

"When I come out in two days, perhaps I can chat with him?"

"I'm sure he'd happily speak to you, Healer Rin. I'll let him know when we get home."

"Thank you," Rin replied.

"Can I help make them?" Thom asked, looking up at his mother.

"You'll have to check with your father," she replied. "But I'm sure he'll say yes. Your smaller hands will be a plus to shaping the jars."

"Thanks, Mam," Thom replied. Turning to Rin, he said. "I'll make you good jars, Healer Rin."

"Thank you, Thom. I'm sure you will."

"We should head on our way," Winni added. "Thank you again."

"I'll see you Widna-dae," Rin replied.

After they left, Rin smiled. "That was easy. Thanks for the heads up, guides," he said out loud. Thinking back to the seers' visions, he thought to himself. Given Thom's age, I hope I didn't miss witnessing Trethlyn's vision.

Chapter 6

"Rinbalden," Dermot Lodan muttered to himself. "You'll get yours. As a result of you, grandda had to turn his horse business over to Da and my stupid brother. It's all lies," he yelled. No one listened to him when he insisted the documents were planted and his grandda's signature forged. He was waiting in a private room in a run-down tavern on the outskirts of Freas-a-chos, the capital of Docha-leigh. He'd reserved it under the name Mitch Justan to keep the meeting secret, particularly from his family.

"Do you need something, sir?" a server asked, stepping into the room. "I heard you yell."

"Bring me another pint!" he demanded. After she returned and was about to leave, he yelled, "And close the door."

"Yes, sir."

"Where are those fools?" he grumbled. "They better not have skipped town. I hope I didn't hire the wrong thieves." Sipping his ale, the image of his grandda came to mind, sitting in his office with his head in his hands and refusing to attend family meals.

"I'll ruin you, Rinbalden," he yelled, slamming his mug on the table and splattering his drink. "I don't care that you're friends with the monarchs. They won't be able to protect you."

Dermot had finished his third mug of ale when the two arrived. "You're late. Where were you?" he demanded. "I'm paying you good money, and I expect you to be here on time."

"Sorry, Mitch, we was held up, ya might say," a short husky man said, snickering as he removed his thick patched coat and hung it on a wall hook.

"Held up. Thet's a good un, Vern," the taller one replied, hanging his ragged coat on another hook. "And thet was clever helpin' da lady what slipped on da ice. She din't even know'd thet she was robbed."

"I was smooth," Vern admitted, grinning. "Again, sorry we was late."

"Enough," Dermot stated. "Make sure your main job is dealing with my problem."

"Ya means Heal…," the taller one started to say.

"My Problem, Finn!" Dermot emphasized. "I'm sure no one is listening. But I don't want to take any chances. Have you learned where he is?"

"My frien' in the kitchen overheard one of dem seer people talk the other day," Vern stated. "He's not in the capital, but she didn' know where he went."

"Find out!" Dermot yelled. Pausing, he considered the situation before saying, "Perhaps it's a good thing he's away from the fool monarchs."

"Ya still haven't told us, Mitch, what ya want us to do when we fin' im," Vern said.

"I don't know," Dermot replied. "Create a scandal. Maybe have him accused of having an affair with someone's wife or, better yet, someone's husband. Or have a patient die under suspicious circumstances. You figure it out."

"But ifn' he's not in da city, how does we fin' him?" Finn complained.

"I heard that he sometimes functions as a traveling healer," Dermot informed them. "Ride to other towns and ask."

"We'll be needin' more money, Vern said.

"Fine," Dermot agreed. "Send me updates regularly, care of this tavern, telling me where you are and if you found him. If I learn where he is, I'll get a message to you," extending a small bag of coins to Vern. "This'll get you through the next few months. I'm sure you'll find a way to supplement it."

"No doubt," Vern replied.

"I need to get back," Dermot said. "Wait a bit before leaving. Maybe have an ale. I don't want anyone seeing us together."

Chapter 7

I t was early spring. Rin had been coming to the Macirdan home for two months. Last week, Thom overheard Rin telling his Mam she was a natural healer and was happy with her progress in such a short time. He was proud of her. Later that same day, Rin complimented his emerging healing skills. Much to his chagrin, he blushed.

After spending the morning at school, he'd worked in the pottery. His Da had finally let him help make Rin's jars after demonstrating that he knew the correct ratio of clay, sand, and water for their Macirdan mixture, as Redik called it. His first two jars didn't make it. The first cracked because he had not let it dry completely before firing. The second broke when his younger brother, Kavan, ran into him as he carried the finished jar to the shelf. But since then, Thom had made two more. He was very proud of them. His Da let him create a larger jar for himself as a reward. It was purple and would hold his treasures.

He was now working in the garden as Rin wasn't coming today. It was chilly, but the sun on his back warmed him up. The sky was the color of the blue jays nested in a nearby tree. The female was now brooding. The air smelled of chamomile, peppermint, sage, and a little basil, the plant he was now tending.

Reta had started working in the garden the week before. She always had a big smile on her face. She was a natural. Mam even gave her permission to plant a flower garden nearby. Being partial to purple, Reta planted sweet alyssum and lobelia among the other flowering plants. For reasons Thom couldn't explain, he felt drawn to purple, like his treasure jar. Even his nemesis, the burdock plant, which was now flowering, was the same color.

"You seem to be doing better," Thom told the plant before him. In the last month, he felt more connected to nature and even enjoyed gardening a little. He could feel the life of the plants, trees, and even animals. He still didn't like weeding, though.

As he continued working, he detected two energies coming closer to their home. He thought they were both girls. Then, he heard a child's cries and a woman's unsuccessful attempts to comfort her. Something was wrong with the little girl's stomach.

After finishing in the garden, Thom walked to the far side of the house and entered the door to his Mam's healing room. "How is the little girl's stomach?" he asked.

"Mirabel's a little better," his mother replied. "I gave her the special ginger tea mixture that Healer Rin made and a sweet biscuit baked with psyllium. I also sent her mother home with a bag of psyllium to sprinkle on Mirabel's food."

His mother paused, "Wait. How did you know what was wrong with Mirabel? Did you talk with her mother?"

"No," Thom replied. "I just felt what was wrong. I don't know how. Do you?"

"Not exactly," his mother responded. "Your grandmam could. But I can't. I would've been able to treat Mirabel more quickly had I known. She's only now beginning to talk. Let's ask Healer Rin."

"OK," Thom agreed, looking out the window and considering her words.

"Also, I'd like it if you helped a little more, especially for my young patients," she said, startling Thom to focus on her again.

"I'd like that," he said. "Do you think Healer Rin would agree?"

"I don't see why he wouldn't," she answered. "You can ask him the next time he comes."

When Rin returned, Thom explained what happened.

Turg! Rin cursed inwardly. He had hoped he'd be here when that happened. Turning to Thom, he asked, "Can you take me back to when you sensed the mother and daughter approaching? Were you able to see them?"

"No," Thom responded. "I was in the herb garden around the side of the house."

"Weeding again?" Rin said, smiling, knowing Thom didn't like doing it.

"No," he answered, "I was... um... sort of talking to the plants."

"I didn't know you did that," Mam commented. "That was one of the first things your grandmam encouraged me to do."

"Oh. It seemed natural, I guess. And I think the plants become sturdier when I do."

"Correct," Rin confirmed. "It's natural because humans are made of the same stuff as plants. By nature of their gifts, healers have an affinity for living things. What you've been doing is part of your earth sense gift. We can talk about that at another time. Back to the mother and child, though."

"While I was working," Thom continued, "I sort of felt two energies approaching, one stronger than the other. And they both felt girly. I guess females is a better word."

"Feminine," his mother corrected him.

"They both felt feminine," Thom repeated. "Then, I heard Mirabel crying and her mother trying to quiet her. I felt bad for them. When I wondered what was wrong, I kind of knew Mirabel's energy was all twisted in her stomach."

"Anything else?" Rin asked.

"Nope."

"OK," Rin replied. "The ability you described is sometimes part of the healing gift. About half the healers I know have it. For some, it surfaces when their gift first emerges. Winni, I suspect you'll be able to sense it soon."

"Oh, that would be helpful," she replied. "I thought I didn't inherit it from my Mam."

"Since your mother had it, it's almost certain you will," Rin explained. "Thom, I'd like you to spend more time helping your mother with patients."

"Mam suggested that too," Thom explained.

"Winnie, you do have good instincts," Rin told her.

"Thanks," Winni said, blushing a little.

"Thom," Rin continued. "I know you're helping your father. Can I presume you also go to school?"

"Yes," Thom replied. "Three mornings a week."

"I'd also like Thom to attend more of your training sessions, Winni," Rin explained.

"I'd like that," Thom said.

"Winni, let's sit down with Uric and devise a schedule that covers Thom's various responsibilities."

"Good idea."

Turning back to Thom, Rin said, "I know with pottery, healing, gardening, and school, you'll be fairly busy, but we also want you to have time to play with your friends."

"Um," Thom replied, "That's OK. I want to learn as much as possible."

Hmm, Rin thought. There's something behind that. But I won't pry.

"Why don't you stay for dinner, Healer Rin?" Winni interjected. "You, Uric, and I can talk afterward."

"I'll take you up on your offer. Thanks," Rin replied.

Over the next couple of months, Thom lent a hand with his Mam's patients in the afternoons. Occasionally, he accompanied her to visit patients who were too frail or unwell to venture out. Irrespective of the patient's age, Thom unfailingly discerned their ailments. As his mother had suspected, his gift proved particularly beneficial for children under two.

Working more with his mother, he also noticed that he picked up the same energy in animals as humans, like with their horses. It came and went, though. When he mentioned this to Rin and his Mam, Rin explained that it was the being's life energy or spirit.

As new aspects of his gift emerged, Thom documented it in his journal. For one entry, he wrote, G, *it's a little scary being able to do this. I like helping people. But even Rin's surprised at how much my ability is growing. I keep hearing Kevar calling me a freak. I don't like being called names. My stomach gets all messed up.*

Chapter 8

"**R**emember to use those crutches!" Rin yelled at the middle-aged man hobbling away from his shop. He thought he heard a grunt. Some people don't realize that healing takes longer if they don't properly care for a broken bone.

It was a beautiful day in the mid-70s, with puffy, white clouds drifting over an expanse of blue. It was a perfect opportunity to enjoy noon supper on the patio of the town inn. Waiting for his meal to arrive, he took a deep breath, enjoying the fresh air, knowing it would grow warmer and more humid in a few weeks.

Winni's training is going very well, Rin thought to himself. She knows more than she thinks. In another few months, she'll complete her apprenticeship. Thom's gifts were fast developing, too. In time, he'll make a very good healer.

For these last months, Rin kept his ears and eyes open for the figure Seer Arion had described. From his time in this area, he suspected the person was likely a male merchant because he hadn't seen any female merchants come through. He had pursued a few possibilities that he soon after discarded. It amazed him how many overweight merchants there were. They were like a breed. If it wasn't crucial that he find the person, it would be comical.

After finishing his meal, he walked through the market toward the stall of the leatherworker, Kari. She was creating him herb pouches. The sample she showed him the week before was perfect. It was deep enough to hold a considerable amount but also could be rolled up to a compact size for traveling. He wanted her to create a half dozen more.

While Kari explained possible changes to the pouch, Rin noticed two merchants strolling by. Both matched Arion's description. They stopped at the jewelry dealer's stall behind Kari's. He tried to listen in but wasn't successful.

"Rin, what do you think of my suggested improvements?" she asked.

"Sounds good," he responded. He hadn't heard everything Kari said, but he knew her work and trusted her. "Go ahead and make the other pouches. Here's the amount we agreed on," he said, handing her some coins. Moving away from her stall, she stepped closer to the merchants.

"That's much too much for this... trinket," one of the merchants insisted belittlingly.

The second one echoed, "Too expensive, indeed. I saw something similar in the capital for half the price."

"But, sirs. That ring is 14-carat gold," the dealer insisted. "I doubt you'd find any reputable dealer who would part with a ring like this at that price."

"What are you implying?" the first merchant shouted, waving his hands and drawing the attention of people walking by. "I know quality workmanship and...THIS IS NOT IT!"

Listening to the exchange, Rin opened his senses and felt a wrongness about the man yelling. Lowering one of his shields to view him with his inner sight, he detected auric colors of red and yellow, indicating passion and dishonesty. Sadly, he knew those were not uncommon for merchants either. What disturbed him was that his aura was almost opaque, obscuring his true spirit. That could be the dark cloud that Arion and Trethy sensed. Looking at the other merchant briefly, he noted a similar aura. Rin decided to make inquiries about both.

That was a wasted day, Rin groaned, dropping down on his bed. He had started trailing one of the merchants mid-morning when he saw him in the market. Part of the day was spent at the tailors, watching the man get measured for a new coat. Then, he followed him to the inn, where the merchant spent a leisurely lunch with a well-dressed woman he couldn't identify. Finally, the merchant led him to a manor a few miles outside town. He had to dash to get his horse to follow. He almost lost him a few times. Peering through a window, he saw the merchant greet another well-dressed woman, likely his wife, with a peck on the cheek. Was the first woman his mistress? He wondered. He stayed there until they sat down to dinner. Rin noticed the beautiful dishware and concluded that it was made by Thom's father.

Quickly undressing and slipping under the bedcovers, he thought about the merchant again. He had doubts that he would buy more dishware. Although, it wasn't impossible. He'd trail the other merchant after checking on a few patients tomorrow.

Chapter 9

Today had been a long day for Thom. The morning had started with a quick breakfast of porridge before sunrise. That was followed by helping his mother prepare herb packets. She brought them with her when she traveled to neighboring villages to treat their sick. Thom went with her. The work had taken the entire day. Halfway through, he realized he could sense a person's illness more easily. By the time they returned home, despite feeling tired from the work and sweaty from the summer day's heat, he was happy he could help.

Climbing up to the loft after dinner, Thom would turn in early. But first, he went to his treasure jar. Tonight, Thom would add a little fluffy white feather. He'd found it on the path outside the pottery. It struck him as strange because it wasn't there when he entered the pottery seconds before.

Taking the lid off the jar, Thom placed the feather inside and pulled out his green triangular object. Rubbing his fingers over its smooth surface, he felt an unknown connection. Sometimes, Thom carried it in his pocket. He still didn't know what it was. But he no longer asked Deena to repeat the story of when she found him with it. The last time he did, she got all red in the face and even growled.

Thom sat down on his bed. Reta was already in hers. Meli was still downstairs with his mother, helping her finish some needlework on a wedding shirt for Bedum. He was getting married at the end of Uctiba and would move into his new home soon to get it ready. Then, Meli would move into Bedum's old room and Thom would get the coveted window alcove. He could hardly wait.

Looking towards it now, Thom thought he would string a cloth across the opening. He wasn't sure why Meli hadn't, but she didn't spend the same amount of time here as he did. He often climbed up to the loft when no one was around to read his book or write in his journal.

OK, Thom thought. He needed to get to sleep. If his Da caught him yawning in the pottery, his Da wouldn't let him make Rin's jars. He undressed, slipped under the covers, and was dead to the world.

Thom.

Is someone calling me? Thom wondered. He opened his eyes but discovered that he wasn't lying in bed. Instead, he was sitting on a soft surface in a room with light walls that seemed to move. *Where am I?* He noticed an amorphous shape drawing closer to him. Oddly enough, he wasn't afraid.

Thom, the voice repeated.

Thom focused on the shape drawing nearer from which the voice seemed to come.

Oh good, you can hear me.

Where am I? And who are you?

To answer your second question, I'm Sereh, your guardian angel.

My what?

Your guardian angel, she replied. *I believe your faith includes angels, doesn't it?*

Yeah, Thom said. *But I don't think I've ever heard about guardian angels. Sometimes, I do fall asleep in my religion class. The elder is really dull.*

I know. You look sweet with your head on the desk, even with the drool.

What! You saw me, he said, looking down embarrassed. Looking up again, he said, *You know, I can't really see you. You're all foggy.*

That always happens with first visits, Sereh replied. *And as to seeing you, that's my job. I watch over you. I know you've felt lonely since Davi moved away. I also know you keep your feelings hidden by staying busy. By the way, I'm impressed with how much you've learned from Healer Rinbalden.*

Thanks, he replied. *Learning's getting easier. I like learning from Rin, but he's old. He can't be my friend like Davi was. I miss having someone to play with.*

I understand, she replied.

Why do the kids have to play sporty games all the time? With Kevar as the leader, that's all they play. I did try to play with them once, but they made fun of me when I couldn't run fast enough.

I'm sorry. The night after that happened, Sereh commented, *I saw you crying. I wanted to hold you.*

Yeah. It was hard, Thom said, his eyes welling up with tears.

Again, I'm sorry, she said with a soft voice. *You may not feel it now, but you're not alone. And I'm not the only one with you. Other angels, Deu, and spirit guides are with you, too. That's why I had the owlet drop her feather on the path.*

The feather was from you? Thom replied, his mouth dropping open.

Yes. Feathers are a way of letting someone know a divine being, like me, is sending you a message. This time, it was to get your attention, as if I were knocking on your door.

Thom looked at her in amazement, straining to make out more details.

As to your first question your body's still in bed, Sereh answered. *When you're asleep, your mind and spirit can travel. I know you've had dreams in which you felt like you were somewhere else.*

Yes, Thom replied.

Other times, you can travel to the divine realm, where we are now.

I'm not sure... I can't... Thom replied, confused.

That's OK. You'll learn more…

Do you mean when I'm older? I hate it when grown-ups say that.

When some say that, it's to avoid answering because they don't know how to teach children, she explained. *What I meant was that someone will teach you more about it soon.*

OK, Thom replied, sighing.

I need to go soon, Thom, Sereh said. *Please remember I'm with you every moment of every day and love you very much. And be assured you'll make friends with kids who value you. I have to leave now, but I want to encourage you to learn all you can while at home. It's important.*

What…? Thom started to ask. As Sereh's shape dissipated, he felt like he was falling into himself.

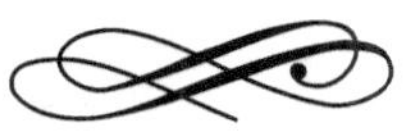

"Sereh, Sereh!" he called out.

"Shh," Meli whispered. "You'll wake Reta."

"Huh," Thom mumbled, feeling a bit dazed.

"You were calling someone named Sarah," Meli answered as she walked by Thom's bed on the way to her alcove. "Who is she?"

"Um," Thom replied. "I don't remember."

"The only person I know named Sarah is Mrs. Hinsman, who lives in town. But you wouldn't call her by her first name."

"No," Thom agreed. "I thought I met someone named Sereh. Maybe I was dreaming."

"Either way, you don't want to wake Reta," she whispered. "You know how cranky she gets when she's woken up."

"Yeah."

"You were like that when you were her age," Meli commented. "And just as whiny."

"Hey," Thom objected.

"Go back to sleep," Meli hissed.

"You're not the boss of me, Meli."

"I am older. And anyway, everyone else has gone to sleep. Perhaps you'll dream of Sarah again," she said with a smirk.

Thom grunted in acknowledgment. Was Sereh someone from a dream? Closing his eyes, Thom fell asleep with a smile on his face.

Chapter 10

Thom was working steadily at his latest piece, a water pitcher. It was still pleasantly cool in the pottery for a summery day. He knew that would change once his Da fired up the kiln and the air outside grew warmer. School would resume in two weeks, and he wanted to spend as much time as possible helping his Da until then. Starting early in the morning gave him time to help his Mam with her patients in the late morning and attend Healer Rin's afternoon training, which now occurred three times a week. For some reason, he knew it was important to work extra hard.

Looking down at the pitcher, Thom was pleased. This was the first time he'd created anything besides Rin's salve jars and larger pots. He hoped to fire it this afternoon before dinner if his Da approved it. He was proud of what he created. His Da had been impressed, even with the treasure jar he'd made some months back.

When Redik joined him and his Da in the work area, Thom was intently shaping the pitcher handle. Suddenly, a wave of nausea hit him. "Ugh," he groaned. His mind immediately flashed back to his encounter with the man in the carriage a year ago, shocked the experience had stayed with him. Hearing a horse and carriage arrive outside, he wondered if this was the same man. Soon after, someone rapped on the front door of the pottery.

"Redik, would you answer that?" his Da called out. "I'm about to put some pieces into the kiln, and Thom's at a critical place with his pitcher. Tell the customer I'm coming."

Thom returned his attention to the pitcher handle, but his stomach roiled as the awful feeling intensified. He hoped he didn't throw up. Taking his hands away from the handle, Thom sat unmoving. He could hear his Da talking to the man through the workroom door.

"Yes, we can combine clays to create your set, like we did with the Baron's," his Da said. "After we mix it, we'll have to let it rest for about a month before we can create a sample dish for you to evaluate. I can show you our clays if you come into our work area."

"Redik and Thom, this is Lord Samiltun," his Da announced. "He's commissioning a set of dishware."

Reluctantly, Thom stood and turned, watching Redik shake the lord's hand. Lord Samiltun was a tall, stout man with dark brown hair that was balding. Despite his stoutness, he had a narrow, stern face with high cheekbones. His clothing revealed he was wealthy. A long brown overcoat with a maroon silk lining was trimmed in gold with matching buttons.

Thom forced himself to walk to Lord Samiltun when his Da gave him a look. As he reached out to shake hands, his gaze fell upon a sizable gold ring on the lord's right hand. Thom tried to keep his hand steady when their hands clasped, but he knew it was shaking and was sure the lord noticed.

"Nice to meet you, young man," the lord commented. "I see you work for your father, too, for someone so young. You must be gifted."

"All my children are gifted," his Da asserted.

Still holding Thom's hand, Lord Samiltun nodded inwardly. This was indeed the same boy he saw last month in the marketplace. He sensed that the boy had a unique energy, but a part of him also felt repulsed by him. Intriguing... He needed to determine more about this boy's energy.

Thom knew the second he shook Lord Samiltun's hand that he was the same man from before. The lord's hand almost felt slimy. Preparing to withdraw his own, he felt something being jabbed into his stomach and twisting. Looking down, he saw nothing, but it reminded him of a dasher his Mam used to churn butter.

"Lord Samiltun," his Da said, "Let me show you our clay and more of our pieces."

When Lord Samiltun finally released his hand, Thom scooted back to his wheel and took deep breaths as his stomach threatened to revolt. He pretended to focus on the pitcher, all too aware of the continued twisting sensation and a coldness that started spreading. Recalling how he had mentally put up a wall, Thom repeated it. This time, he also decided to push back.

Hmm, Lord Samiltun thought. The boy pushed his energy probe away. Some resistance. This could be from his gift, but it could also be a natural body reaction. He needed to probe him at another time and more intensely to determine the cause.

"If you come back in five weeks, Lord Samiltun," his Da said, "that will give us four weeks to allow the clay mix to set and a week to create and fire a sample piece of your dishware for you to assess."

"I can't wait that long," Lord Samiltun countered, knowing he wanted to return to test the boy again. "Surely you can have something to show me in two weeks."

"Sir, I don't know if you're aware," his Da replied. "But clay mix needs about a month before it's workable."

"I've heard some potters wait no more than a week. I'm being generous by giving you two," Lord Samiltun replied, annoyed that this commoner was challenging him. "May I remind you," he continued, "you'll be making a tidy sum with this commission and free publicity when people learn who made the set?"

"True," his Da agreed. "But our clay is distinctive, as you saw from my samples. We could allow the mix to age for a little under three weeks. It might not be as high quality or as durable."

"Very well," Lord Samiltun replied. "I'll be back in three weeks." The gall, he thought to himself. Even though he wanted to return for the boy, he couldn't let it seem like this potter won. "If it's not ready, I'll go to a potter nearer my home who I'm certain will provide me with what I need."

Thom noticed that his Da didn't respond.

After the lord had left, Redik commented, "Da, that guy didn't seem to care about what you said."

"Redik, you will be respectful and call him Lord Samiltun. But you're correct. He wasn't listening. I pride myself in what we produce, like the dishware he saw at Baron Hetherford's estate. I wouldn't have accepted this job if it weren't for the large commission. We can use the extra income for your brother's wedding."

Thom was cleaning up when everything grew quiet and still. His father and brother were stationary. Even the dripping water from the pump appeared to freeze. Something's going to happen, he suddenly knew. Thinking of Lord Samiltun, he became unnerved.

Seconds passed. Then Thom heard the water hitting the metal basin below the pump: plink, plink, plink. Shaking himself, he dried his hands and tried to put it out of his mind. He had to get to Mam's healing room to help with her patients.

Lord Samiltun. Rin was convinced Lord Samiltun was the merchant who would try to influence Thom. He was one of the merchants he'd encountered in the market more than a month ago. Last week, Winni and Thom had stopped by to say hello when they'd come into town. When they left, he had noticed Lord Samiltun watching them. Thom, in particular. At the time, Rin read Samiltun's intentions but couldn't detect anything untoward.

The red flag that decided him occurred at the inn where he ate noon supper. At an adjacent table, a woman casually mentioned that Samiltun had commissioned pottery from Uric. Rin wanted to take Thom away immediately, but his spirit guides warned him that events needed to progress as foretold.

As unhappy as Rin was about waiting, he trusted his guides. He had to be prepared to leave at any time, which meant keeping a close eye on Samiltun. Accordingly, he reduced his hours at the shop.

That evening after dinner, Thom went up to his alcove, now that Meli had moved. There was enough room for his bed, bookshelf, and a few hooks to hang his clothes. Trying to get comfortable on his bed, he realized he was still upset by Lord Samiltun's visit and the incident at the pump, as he was calling it. He had a little privacy with the curtain hanging over the entry.

Gazing out the window above the treetops, Thom noticed that the stars began appearing. He wished there was someone out there who he could really talk to. Thom would've told Davi if he still lived nearby. He felt his eyes drawn to one star, yearning for some comfort.

Thom's gut roiled again. "Is anyone out there for me?" he whispered desperately. Pulling out his journal, he wrote, *G, I wish I could talk to my family. I do love them. But I've always felt different. I'm quiet and think a lot. That's why I like being by myself. Mam and Da don't understand. They keep telling me to go out and play.*

Pausing from his writing, he looked outside again. "Is anyone listening? Da's new customer really bothered me. When he shook my hand, I knew something was off. He wants something from me. But I don't know what or why. What do I do?"

Returning to his journal, he wrote, *Lord Samiltun feels dangerous. Redik called him rude, but I don't think he or Da think he's dangerous. Maybe I'm imagining it. Meli says I have a wild imagination. But, G, I can't put my family in danger. Maybe I should run away? I'd miss them and would be lonely. But I feel that already.*

Thom closed his journal and set it back on the shelf. As he laid his head on his pillow, his thoughts kept swirling. Finally, feeling emotionally exhausted, he fell asleep.

Thom, can you hear me? a voice asked.

Thom grunted.

Thom! the voice repeated with greater insistence.

Huh, Thom mumbled groggily. *It can't be morning yet, can it?* Instead of his usual view of the window and bookshelf, he was surrounded by walls that glowed and rippled. He was definitely not in his alcove, but it felt familiar. Before him, a figure formed. *Wait,* he spoke toward the figure. *Are you.... Sereh... my guardian angel?*

Yes, she replied. *And as you suspected, you've been here before.*

You're real? I thought I made you up.

No. I'm real.

You're clearer this time, he remarked, seeing a young woman with blue eyes and shoulder-length brown hair. He also noted a warm feeling around his heart.

I'm glad, she replied.

Aren't you supposed to have wings? I read that in my religion workbook.

They're folded behind me.

Oh, Thom replied.

Someone to Thom's left cleared their throat. He saw two more figures who hadn't been there before. *What's going on, Sereh?*

Others wanted to visit with you. This is Archangel Metatron, pointing to his left. *Jeshua is next to him. Your faith calls him Iosa. I hoped my presence would make this easier. I didn't want you to be overwhelmed.*

Iosa! Deu's only-begotten son! Thom yelled, using the phrase his elders taught him. *Too late!* he smirked.

Now that's the kind of humor we like to hear, Metatron replied. *We're glad you're better able to see Sereh. It means you feel more connected to her and this realm.*

Realm?

The divine realm, Metatron informed him. *It's where divine beings dwell, including humans who have died. We wanted to talk with you because of your encounter today with Samiltun.*

How do you know about him? Thom asked.

You did mention him in your prayer earlier. But we also know because we watch over and support you.

I think Sereh told me that, Thom said.

I'm sure she did, Metatron agreed.

Thom saw Sereh nod.

Metatron continued, *Feeling connected will be vital when you discover your gifts and learn your purpose.*

My gifts and purpose? Do you mean with pottery and herbs?

No, and yes, Metatron replied. *Thom, you're a lightworker-in-training. And before you ask, a lightworker is dedicated to bringing light and hope to people struggling and searching for meaning.*

OK, I guess, he said, a little uncertain. *And I'm in training?*

Yes, he answered. *You'll develop lightworker skills through your experiences.*

A lightworker, Thom replied. *I don't know...*

Give it time, Iosa encouraged. *You'll understand it more later.*

I've heard that before, huh, Sereh? Thom said, winking at her.

More humor. I'm glad, Metatron said. *And you're not scared, are you?*

No. But you don't feel scary, Thom admitted.

Jeshua whispered privately to Metatron. *I hope he stays that way, given who's about to appear.*

Metatron nodded. *Did you want to ask us anything, Thom?*

You said something about my purpose. What do you mean?

Your purpose is the area you want to dedicate your life to.

Like Da's being a potter and Mam's a healer?

That could be, but it could also be something a person does outside of their daily work or coming out of a dream or a passion.

What's my purpose?

You'll have to discover that yourself. That's part of the human experience. The reason for our visit is to inform you that Samiltun has detected one of your gifts. In its untrained state, he might try to corrupt you if you came under his influence.

How? Thom asked, his eyes growing wide.

By using his gift to influence you and your parents and even try to change you, Iosa said. *It might be difficult for one as young as you. How old are you, by the way?*

I'll be nine in Nuvima.

Yes, that is young, Metatron agreed. *We have a plan under-way to keep you safe, and it involves someone quite gifted.*

You don't mean Rin, do you? Thom asked, hoping.

Yes, Iosa replied.

That's a relief, he said, feeling a little better.

We'll also be here to help, Iosa added.

Thom looked at Sereh, who smiled and took his hand in hers.

I had a feeling something was going to happen.

Makes sense, Metatron added. *You have a bit of prescience. That's the ability to sense what's coming in the future.*

Thom shook his head in disbelief but remained silent.

Thom, Metatron added, *there's someone else we want you to meet.*

Just then, another being appeared.

There's no way to make this easy, the being said. *Your Iosan faith calls me Deu.*

What! Thom scooted away on his knees, bowed his head, and launched into a rapid-fire confession. *I'm sorry. I'm trying to be good. I know the elders yell at me for not paying attention. I'm sorry for fighting with Meli and Reta. Reta's really annoying, but I know it's wrong.*

Thom, Deu said, attempting to interrupt.

I'm sorry I disobeyed Da when he told me to help Bedum with the horses. I promise I'll never disobey again. Please don't send me to hell, Thom pleaded. *I'll be good.*

Thom, Deu said with tenderness. *Take a breath. I won't send you to hell, even if it did exist. I have to say that I'm displeased that your elders describe me as someone you fear rather than someone who cares and loves you. Please come closer and sit. Please.*

Thom reluctantly returned.

Thank you, Deu said. I do love you, even if you're unsure. By the way, I'm impressed with your pottery skills. The pitcher you created was beautiful.

Thanks, he replied, relaxing a little.

I want to talk to you about your journal writing, Deu explained.

How did you know...?

Besides the fact that I watch over you, I'm G.

Really? I don't understand.

G's the first initial of a name some call me, God, Deu explained.

I never knew why I started my entries with G, Thom admitted. Why did I...?

Let's call it intuition, Deu said. How do you feel after writing?

Mostly a little better, he answered. And maybe less lonely.

Like you're unburdening yourself to a friend, Deu remarked. We know it's been hard since Davi moved away. You'll make new friends even if you don't think you will. Please understand that I hear you each time you call out or put your quill to paper.

Thom considered what Deu said. This makes sense, and his body was all tingly.

You're feeling something, aren't you? Iosa asked. Tingling?

Yeah, Thom replied.

Whenever you feel that, Iosa explained, know we're with you and you're connecting to our divine energy.

It's almost time for us to go, Deu said. Continue learning as much as you can about pottery and healing.

I promise, Thom said. It does seem like I'm learning faster.

Ah. Unbeknownst to Rin, Deu said, he might have inadvertently used his gifts to help you.

Should I thank him?

No, Deu replied. You already do that enough.

He nodded, then frowned.

What's wrong? Jeshua asked.

Kevar and the other kids make fun of me because I talk more like a grown-up. Should I pretend I can't?

Never, Deu answered. Your divine spirit is coming through more. That's something to rejoice about, not hide.

OK, Thom said.

We're sorry you went through that, Metatron said. Those kinds of challenges make you more sensitive to other people's pain, which will be of great value to you as a healer.

And please try to believe I do love you, Deu added. You won't remember much from this visit, but you should at least remember that.

I'll try, Thom replied.

Sereh squeezed his hand as he saw the four of them fade.

A rooster crowed.

Thom awoke feeling rested and at peace. He looked out his window and saw that dawn was about to break. Getting up and dressing, he once again felt an urgent need to learn as much as he could. When he parted his alcove curtain, he saw Reta and Kavan still sleeping. Stepping lightly so as not to wake them, he made his way to the ladder. After climbing down, he went into the kitchen, finding his mother. "Good morning, Mam."

"Oh, Thom. You're an early riser today. Even your Da's still in bed. Since you're up, would you feed the chickens? I know Reta took it over from you, but I'm sure she'd appreciate it."

"Sure, Mam," he replied. "Will you be treating anyone today?"

"Yes, I'm going to Widow Senter's to make sure her leg wound hasn't become infected. Why do you ask?"

"Can I go with you? I'd like to learn what to look for."

His Mam smiled. "Sure, but I thought you wanted to spend your time in the pottery."

"Not all of it. I still want to learn from you and Rin. I got up early to make sure I'd have enough time."

"That's fine. Let your Da know. I'm leaving for the Widow's around late morning."

"OK. Thanks," Thom replied.

Chapter 11

Thom was working on a vase when he felt Lord Samiltun's loathsome energy. It wasn't long before he heard the carriage. "Da," he called out. "I think we've got a customer." He didn't want to tell him it was Lord Samiltun because he didn't think his father would understand how he knew.

Shortly after, footsteps crunched on the gravel path leading to the pottery. And, before anyone could stand, Lord Samiltun walked into the work area.

"Oh, Lord Samiltun," his Da said. "I was about to take your sample bowl out of the kiln. Redik, would you help me?"

Lord Samiltun grunted.

Thom felt his presence behind him.

"And what are you working on, lad?" Lord Samiltun asked.

"Um," Thom gulped. "A bud vase." This time, the probing felt stronger and touched various parts of his body, like his Mam would do when she examined a patient.

"That's an unusual shape," Lord Samiltun remarked, placing his hand on Thom's shoulder.

Like before, Thom pushed back, but he didn't think it was as successful. "Yes," he replied. "The customer wanted the mouth of the vase curved to make the flower more visible."

"What are those blue stones for?" he asked, pointing to the left of Thom's wheel.

By now, Thom was gritting his teeth and shivering. He didn't like the lord touching him, and his stomach started yelling at him. "One of Da's specialties is adding decorative stones to the clay before firing it."

"And what about the pink in the dish there?" he asked, pointing.

Why can't he leave me alone, Thom thought, feeling his breath quicken. "Sometimes, we add a splash of color for accents," he told him, shrugging his shoulders, hoping that the lord would remove his hand. But to no avail.

"Interesting," Lord Samiltun commented, shifting his hand slightly to see if he could read the boy better.

In desperation, Thom pretended he needed a tool on a bench nearby and stood up, forcing the lord to remove his hand. "Is there anything I can help you with?"

"No," Lord Samiltun responded. "It looks like it will be a nice piece." He still couldn't determine the nature of the boy's gift or strength from his examination. If his gift was substantial, which he thought it was, he'd be a great asset. As young as he was, he was undoubtedly untrained. That would make controlling him easier. Now, he needed to make him and his father more amenable.

"Lord Samiltun," Da called out. "Your sample piece is ready to evaluate."

Lord Samiltun stepped away from Thom and went to the other side of the work area to a table where his Da had placed a blue bowl.

Thom resumed his work on the vase, feeling his breath ease. Focusing on smoothing the curve at its mouth, he realized he felt warmer. That's weird. The pottery wasn't any hotter than usual. While he sipped a cup of water nearby, he relished Lord Samiltun's praise for his craftsmanship. Maybe he could earn money by making a few pieces for him.

Leaning back and stretching, Thom overheard his Da say, "You're asking me to add more of our clay mixture 4 to your clay? Easily done. The new mix should be ready in ten days. Is that agreeable?"

"Yes," Lord Samiltun replied. "I must say, I'm very impressed with young Thom's work. Would you consider apprenticing him to me a few days a week? I could set up a little pottery behind my home. I could even teach him merchanting. Having a combination of merchant and potter skills would enable him to set up his own shop one day."

Thom looked back when his Da didn't respond.

I think he needs a bit more encouragement, Lord Samiltun thought.

Thom noticed the lord's hand twitch a little.

His Da finally replied, "Maybe. Learning about merchanting would be good. I'll need to speak to my wife."

"Of course," Lord Samiltun responded, sneering inwardly.

After the lord left, Redik said, "Da, didn't you say you didn't like the man the last time he was here? Are you really considering apprenticing Thom to him?"

"I might have misjudged him," his Da replied. "He was very nice this time."

When Lord Samiltun returned to the pottery to see the new sample, his primary goal was the boy. Stepping into the work area, he sent more energy toward Thom and his father to make them more receptive to the apprenticeship.

Thom tried to listen while his Da showed the bowl to the lord. Wouldn't it be exciting if he had his own pottery? He didn't even consider how odd it would be for a boy his age.

"This is perfect," Lord Samiltun exclaimed. "You're very talented, Mr. Macirdan. Please proceed with making my dishware. Since you're an honest man, here's half the agreed cost."

"That's very generous, sir," his Da responded. "The standard down payment is 25%."

"Yes, I know. However, I'm impressed with your work and believe it merits it."

Looking around the work area, Lord Samiltun spied the vase Thom had completed on a shelf nearby. "Oh, I see Thom finished his vase."

Thom had turned around to face Lord Samiltun and his father.

"The blue complements the vase's brown glazing. And the pink splash makes it something special," Lord Samiltun said to Thom. "You are quite talented."

"Thank you, sir," Thom replied, turning red.

This boy's pottery skills could be beneficial to him as bribes, Samiltun determined. Deciding to probe him once more, he discovered there wasn't any resistance.

Sitting at his pottery wheel, Thom felt something pop inside himself.

"Mr. Macirdan," Lord Samiltun said, "Have you considered my proposal?"

"Yes," his Da replied. "We're seriously considering it. Thom does assist my wife, Winni, with treating her patients. Let me talk with her again to see if our younger daughter can take his place."

"I understand. Will you be able to show me some completed dishware in two weeks? Of course, I don't expect all of it to be done by then."

"Yes, we'll have pieces to show you," Da replied.

Outside the pottery, Rin had been eavesdropping on the conversation. He sensed Samiltun's energy influence Thom and his father, and the energetic probe. Rin knew the time was approaching for him to take Thom away.

After Lord Samiltun left, Rin returned to his shop to consider the situation. Samiltun's last probe significantly affected Thom, about which Samiltun was unaware. First, it fully activated Thom's healing gift. Second, it triggered a much stronger gift. One that Rin couldn't identify. He now knew why his spirit guides told him to wait before taking Thom away. It was now time for him to implement his plan.

Rin had to hide the strength of Thom's gifts for when Samiltun returned. But before that, he needed to set the stage for their departure. He'd return in two days to suggest to Thom's parents that he get special training. He'd already given his landlord notice about closing his shop. In ten days, he'd start camping near the pottery to ensure he was nearby when Samiltun came by again.

Rin was putting away his breakfast pot when he heard a carriage on the road and sensed Samiltun's presence. He mounted his horse and took his shortcut to the pottery, arriving before Samiltun. Sensing Thom inside with his father, he first removed any lingering traces of Samiltun's energy manipulation from both. Afterward, he placed a fake shield on Thom and tuned his senses to the goings on within, especially his hearing.

"As you can see, Lord Samiltun," Rin heard Uric say, "we've created 12 of the 20 place settings. Let me show you the pieces."

Lord Samiltun saw Thom working away. Once again, he probed him and finally broke through the boy's natural shield. He knew his repeated energy probes would win out, he thought smugly. Nothing could defeat his skills. Now, he could determine the strength of the boy's gift, extending his senses. Blinking his eyes several times, he was shocked. What? It's negligible. How did he misread that? Worthless child! "He won't be of any use to me," he mumbled audibly.

"Lord Samiltun?" Uric called out, "Did you say something?"

With some irritation, he focused his attention on Uric and grumbled, "Yes, yes. These are good. I'll need the rest in six days."

"Excuse me. Six days?" Uric replied, bewildered. "You previously agreed to eleven more days. We have other commissions we're handling."

"I don't care," Lord Samiltun replied, irritated that this commoner challenged him again. "Mine should have your full attention. If you can't deliver, I expect full reimbursement and will tell everyone you're unreliable."

"But, sir!" Uric protested.

"No buts. Those are the conditions. Now, I have other more important business to attend to."

Rin watched from the side of the pottery as Lord Samiltun stomped out and climbed into his carriage. OK, he thought, if they set out on the road tomorrow, they could put a considerable distance between them and the pottery when Samiltun returned, just in case he decided to retest Thom. Rin's next task was a quick trip into town to pick up the last of his supplies and collect the horse he purchased a few days ago. Then, he'd have another chat with the Macirdans.

Chapter 12

Late morning, Rin rode to the Macirdan's place and tapped on their door.

"Oh, Healer Rin," Winni exclaimed. "Were we supposed to meet today? I thought we wouldn't see you until tomorrow."

"Ah. Winni," Rin replied. "Plans have changed. I need to talk with you and Uric. It's urgent."

Winni turned to Reta, standing nearby, "Go and tell your father that Healer Rin is here and needs to talk with us."

"If Thom is also in the pottery, would you have him come too?" Rin asked.

"Of course," Winni replied. "Reta, go get them both. Please come in, Rin, and have a seat at the table. Do you want some hot cider? Now that it's Fall, the temperature's gotten colder."

"Yes. Thank you," Rin replied. "How are you feeling?"

"I'm good now that my morning sickness has ended," she replied.

"Excellent," Rin said.

As Winni poured Rin a mug of cider, she asked, "Is everything OK? Did Thom do something?"

"No," Rin answered. "But I don't want to say more until Uric and Thom are here."

When they arrived, Uric apologized, "Sorry we couldn't get here sooner. Thom was putting one of Samiltun's pieces into the kiln, and we had to be extremely careful. Rin, did Winni tell you about Lord Samiltun's sudden change of attitude?"

"Yes."

Settling on a bench across from him, Uric asked, "What's going on?"

Pausing to consider how to explain this, he finally said, "Do you remember when I mentioned Thom had a notable healing gift and would benefit from private training?"

"Yes," Winni replied. "Wasn't that the afternoon you said you'd be away a few days?"

"Correct," Rin replied.

"Uric and I talked about it a few nights ago," Winni continued. "We're hoping you'd train him."

"I will. And thanks for taking my suggestion seriously," Rin replied. "There's a catch."

"Is this why you said it's urgent?" Winni asked.

"Yes," Rin replied. Where should he start? he wondered. "Thom has a strong gift in physical healing, as you know. But two weeks ago, I discovered one that's significantly more powerful."

"Another gift that's more powerful?" Thom said, his jaw dropping open.

"Yes," Rin replied. "It's likely related to physical healing. I don't know what it is, but I'm certain I'll identify it during your apprenticeship."

"Great," Winni replied. "We aren't sure how to pay, but we'll figure something out. Will that mean he has to live at your shop?"

"Don't worry about the payment. It's covered," Rin assured them. "As far as Thom living at my shop, no. And this is where the urgency comes in. I need to take Thom away."

"What? Why?" Winni asked.

"Uric, you mentioned your customer, Lord Samiltun," Rin remarked.

"What does he have to do with this?"

"The thing is," Rin answered. "Samiltun... how do I put this? He has a gift himself, but not in healing. Using it, he detected Thom's. When he visited the pottery, I was nearby and sensed when he probed Thom. You were aware of it, weren't you, Thom?"

"Yes," he replied.

"And you also pushed against it?"

"Yes, how did you know?" he asked.

"Wait," Uric interrupted. "I'm confused. You said you were nearby. How did you even know Lord Samiltun visited us? I didn't think you were training Winni and Thom on those days."

Hmm, Rin thought. He wanted to keep this as simple as possible. "No, I wasn't. I first encountered Samiltun a couple of months ago, and he came across as someone to be wary of. When I heard he commissioned pottery from you, I decided to watch him—but without him knowing."

"I see," Uric replied. "And what do you mean by probe?"

"Oh, sorry," Rin apologized, "I'm used to talking with other healers who do it regularly. It's similar to what Thom did when he detected what was wrong with Mirabel. Can I presume that Winni told you about that, Uric?"

"She did," Uric said. "It still amazes me. I'm happy that Winni has that ability now, too."

"Yes, I was relieved when it finally came on," she said sincerely.

"As you know, Winni," Rin continued. "I have a strong healing gift. That includes an ability to detect when others are using theirs. When Samiltun probed Thom the first time, I had no reason to say anything because he could simply have been curious. What Samiltun did was impolite, but I've known others who have done it. I was concerned, though."

"You didn't trust him," Uric added.

"No. I didn't," Rin agreed. "A month ago, I felt him influence you, Thom, and Uric to make you more favorable to him. That's when I knew Samiltun was dangerous, especially to you, Thom, because you're still in the early stages of training. If you had apprenticed to him, he could've used his gift to manipulate you to do anything he wanted, including criminal activities."

Thom's eyes widened, and his mouth went slack.

"I thought something was wrong with that guy," Uric growled. "But we needed the commission. I didn't think he was dangerous."

"I didn't like him. I should've said something," Thom admitted. "But I knew we needed the money, too. I also thought you might think I was crazy."

"I'm sorry we made you feel that way, Thom," Winni replied, reaching out and touching his hand.

"I want to throttle him," Uric growled again, his eyebrows narrowing.

"I understand," Rin replied. "I'm sure you know that's not a good idea because it would land you in jail. I'm certain he has connections in high places. Not to mention that any such action would likely end your business."

"Listen to him, Uric," Winni warned.

Uric grumbled.

Rin continued, "Before Samiltun visited you this morning, I placed a shield over Thom. When Samiltun probed him, he detected a gift of minimal strength and concluded he had misread Thom's potential abilities."

"A shield?" Uric asked.

"It's an energetic layer...how do I say this? You might think of it as something similar to the glazing you add to your pieces, strengthening the clay. In this case, the layer protected Thom."

"I guess that makes sense," Uric replied, a bit calmer.

"If Samiltun can't detect Thom's gifts," Winni said, "why do you have to take him away?"

"Keeping this shield on Thom does take some effort. I'll teach him to create his own as part of his training. But there will be times when I'll need to remove it. I don't want to risk the possibility that Samiltun might be nearby."

"I see," Uric said.

"Where do you want to take him?" Winni asked. "Will we be able to visit, or can he visit us?"

"Honestly, no. And I don't want to tell you where I'm taking him in case Samiltun tries to force you to tell him. I don't think he will, but I don't want to take the chance."

"How long will Thom be gone?" Winni asked, holding Thom's hand even more tightly.

"It's hard to say. Perhaps years."

"Years? Uric!" Winni gasped, her eyes wide with disbelief. "No, no, no. This can't be true. Can't you do something to stop Samiltun?"

"I'm sorry, Winni, but no," Rin replied. "And in truth, even if that was possible, others could stumble upon Thom and try to influence him."

"Uric, it'll be torture not knowing and not being able to..." she broke off, looking shattered, tears streaming down her cheeks.

Thom sat there trying to absorb this. "Can you get rid of my gifts?"

"No," Rin replied. "Thom, I understand that leaving will be hard. But once you're trained, your gifts will benefit many. And you'll be safe from Samiltun and others like him."

"Winni, I don't think we have any choice, hon," Uric advised. "We already trust Rin and know he'll keep Thom safe."

Winni nodded and whispered, "When do you need to take him?"

"Tomorrow morning," Rin replied. "I know this doesn't give you much time to prepare, but we need to get as far away from here as possible."

"Ugh," Winni emitted a heartbroken groan.

Looking at his wife, Uric said, "How about if we have the whole family over for dinner tonight, and we'll make it something special. Redik can ride to Deena and Rian's to invite them and her little one."

"The twelve of us will be together again," Winni said, plaintively. "I like that. It's been a while. Even if I don't like the reason for it this time."

"We won't tell anyone else about Samiltun," Uric commented. "We'll explain that Rin's going to apprentice Thom and that they have to leave immediately."

"OK," Winni mumbled, her head bowed.

"Winni, why don't you help Thom pack," Uric continued. "I'm sure we'll have a wonderful farewell dinner," he said, his voice breaking a little.

Turning to Thom, Rin asked, "Do you have any questions?"

"How will we get to where we're going?"

"Ah. I purchased another horse. You do know how to ride, don't you?"

"Yes. I haven't ridden much, but I do know how."

"Good," Rin replied. "I'll leave you all now. Winni and Uric, thank you for trusting me with your son. I know this is difficult. I promise to take good care of him and keep him safe. I'll see you tomorrow."

Winni nodded, still looking stunned.

Chapter 13

Early the next day, Turi-dae, Thom was putting his breakfast dishes in the sink when he heard the sound of horses approaching. He'd finished packing the night before, and his saddlebags were by the front door. Stepping outside, Thom noticed the sky was overcast and the air chilly. He was glad he was wearing a jumper.

"Hi, Healer Rin."

"Good morning, Thom. Are you ready to go?" Rin asked as he dismounted and untied the second horse trailing behind the one he had ridden.

"Yes, I'm ready," he replied. By then, Thom's family had also joined them outside.

"Good morning, Healer Rin," his Da said. "I'm sorry that you had to purchase a second horse. We couldn't afford to buy another, and we can't spare any that we have."

"No worries," Rin replied. "That's one of my responsibilities as his teacher. Let's secure your bags to your horse, Thom."

"Bedum, would you help him load his bags?" his Mam asked her oldest son.

Bedum and Thom were securing his second bag when Thom felt inside his pocket and realized it was missing. "Um, Healer Rin," he said. "I forgot one thing."

"Go and get it," he replied.

Thom dashed back towards the front door.

"What's going on?" his Mam uttered.

"You forgot something, didn't you?" Meli smirked.

"Yes." Climbing up to the loft, Thom walked to the shelf by his bed, took the lid off his treasure jar, and pulled out the triangular green object. How could he have forgotten this, rubbing the object like a talisman? Whatever it was, Thom believed it essential to take with him. At the last second, he took the entire jar, figuring he could squish it into his saddlebags somewhere.

"You forgot your jar," his mother commented as Thom returned. "Will it fit in your bags? I thought they were full."

"I'll make it fit."

"Good," Rin said. "You were quick. If you want to say your final goodbyes in private, go ahead. I'll wait here."

When Thom came outside, his eyes were red from crying.

Not wanting to embarrass him, Rin nodded and mounted his horse. "OK. Let's be on our way."

For a time, Rin remained quiet, knowing that Thom probably needed time to collect himself. Riding along, he noticed the leaves blown from the trees by the light wind. He was grateful it wasn't winter when they'd have to deal with snow. Today, the roads were clear. Once it arrived, they wouldn't be camping outside, that's for sure.

After traveling a bit longer, Rin slowed his horse to ride alongside Thom. "How are you holding up?" he asked.

"I'm OK," Thom mumbled.

"Thom, even though I've known you for over half a year, we've never had a heart-to-heart talk. But I've noticed you're usually quiet."

"I suppose," he replied softly.

"OK. Let me take a guess at something."

Thom shrugged.

"You feel like you're different from everyone, the neighbor kids, and even your family. You don't have friends because they don't understand you. When you're not working or in school, you spend time alone wondering why you don't fit in and if there's something wrong with you."

Thom turned his head towards Rin and frowned suspiciously. "How do you know this? Can you read my mind?"

"No, Thom, I can't. I can read your aura, though," Rin offered.

"What's that?"

"Oh, how stupid of me," Rin replied. "That wouldn't have been something your Iosan elders taught you."

Thom shook his head.

"Did you know that our bodies give off energy?" Rin asked.

"No," Thom said uncertainly. "We did learn about the brain in school."

"What did you learn?"

"It sends signals and messages and controls our actions," he answered.

"That's correct," Rin replied. "Those signals are energy, as is the heat your body gives off when you're playing. The aura is also a form of energy."

"OK," Thom said. "I guess that makes sense. How does my aura tell you what I feel?"

"Essentially, it reflects a person's personality," Rin explained.

"How?"

"Have you ever noticed that some people make you nervous and others calm you down?"

"Maybe," Thom replied.

"Think about some of the people you know," Rin suggested.

"Well, I guess one elder makes me nervous sometimes."

"OK," Rin said. "What about people who make you smile when you see them?"

"My friend, Davi, was like that."

"What you're feeling is the energy from their personality."

"Huh," Thom said, tilting his head, considering.

"Each aura," Rin continued, "exhibits colors, and each color has a specific meaning. For you, I see some gray, which means sadness. I also see blue, which means honesty, and green, which is associated with healing. The last color I see is purple. That represents a spiritual connection."

"I give off colors," Thom said, astonished. "I kind of like that."

"As part of your training, I'll teach you more about your aura and spirit."

Thom nodded, looking over at Rin, showing some curiosity.

"It makes sense that you're sad," Rin commented. "Anyone in your situation would be. I'm hoping I can help you through it. I won't try to talk you out of your sadness because it's important that you honor your emotions. I need you to share with me what you're feeling, thinking, and even sensing."

"Sensing?"

"Yes," Rin replied. "Some months back, remember you told me about the little girl, Mirabel?"

"Yeah."

"You said that you felt something was wrong with her. That's what healers call sensing. With that same healing gift, you can also sense and connect with animals."

"I think I knew that," Thom said. "Then, sensing is feeling in another way?"

"That's a good way to put it," Rin replied. "You do have a sharp mind, Thom."

"Thanks," he said, a little embarrassed.

"One thing I want to mention about your gifts and that I didn't tell your parents," Rin continued, "is that normally they don't show up until a child is around twelve years old. That yours made itself known a few months ago indicates that it will be strong."

"Didn't you say that my newest gift is really strong?" Thom asked.

"I did," Rin replied. "The thing is that when a gift first emerges, it's usually at its weakest strength. But for yours, it's already quite strong. And, it's likely to grow even stronger."

"Is that a good thing?"

"It depends on the child," Rin said. "How do I say this? For pre-adolescents, it's sometimes difficult for their bodies to adjust to channeling their gift, much less having the mental capacity for it."

"What about me?" he asked anxiously.

"Mentally, you'll be fine, given how quickly you learn," Rin assured him. "Also, the fact that you had the wherewithal to push against Samiltun indicates you already have a little control."

"I think I had a little help from Deu," Thom admitted.

"Say more," Rin asked.

"The first time I sensed Lord Samiltun was about a year ago when digging for clay. I was so scared that I called out to Deu. Then, a picture of a wall appeared in my mind. I imagined one in front of me. In the pottery, I did it again when Samiltun probed me. I pushed against it."

Huh. Self-protection somehow gave Thom access to his gift, Rin reflected. Speaking out loud, he said, "I'm glad to hear that. Being connected to the divine will be helpful. I'll explain why at another time. Like I said, I'm not concerned about your mental state. I wonder whether you can physically handle it due to your body size."

"Yeah, I'm a runt," Thom said, looking down.

"Thom, look at me," Rin said. "First, don't call yourself names. And about your size, I'll ensure you get physical conditioning and training. I'll also proceed slowly with your gift training to enable your body to accommodate it."

"Do you think I can get bigger and taller?" he asked, his voice hopeful.

"Yes, I do," Rin assured him. "I want to mention something else about your newest gift. My sense is that it's connected to your fiercely glowing spirit. It shines through your aura most vividly now, a change that I believe Samiltun triggered."

"I don't know what to say," Thom said, shaking his head.

"I'm sorry. I'm going into more detail than I intended," Rin apologized. "My point is that because I don't know what it is, you may experience sensations I'm unfamiliar with. I need to know about them so I can help you. That's why I brought up my observation about you being quiet. For that reason alone, you need to tell me."

"I'll try."

"Thanks. Any questions?" Rin asked.

"Um," Thom paused uncertainly, "Can you tell me where we're going?"

"Ah. Yes. I didn't want to tell your parents for the reason I told them. We're heading to a land called Eiren, across the ocean, off the northwest coast of Docha-leigh. One of the reigning monarchs is a friend. I also know healers there who can help me identify your stronger gift."

"Across the ocean," Thom exclaimed. "I've never seen the ocean."

"That means you've never been on a ship either," Rin added. "I hope you'll do OK with ocean travel. It takes some people a little time to get used to it."

"Um," Thom replied. "I don't know. But it sounds exciting."

"It should be," Rin agreed. "Now to the practical details. You may have noticed that you have a bedroll and a third bag attached to your horse. That includes camping supplies. Most days, we'll camp outside, at least until the first snow. Your brother, Bedum, mentioned that your mother packed an extra blanket and warm clothes. I have another blanket for you, too. But don't worry, we'll stay at inns or traveler shelters when it snows. I'm fine with camping when it's nice. But I am too old to do that in snow."

Thom nodded.

"Our travel days will be long," Rin continued. "Some days, we'll stop early to give me time to teach you. Today, we'll ride until early evening. It may be difficult for you. We'll take a few short breaks. But the bottom line is that you'll be sore from riding until you've adjusted."

"Mam thought that would happen. She packed some salve in one of my bags."

"Good. I have some, too," Rin replied.

"During our ride today, I'd like you to think about situations where you might've used your gifts. These would be times when you felt something or did something that seemed odd or unusual."

Thom looked puzzled.

"Not quite getting it, are you?" Rin remarked. "OK. We talked about you feeling different from other people. Think of any experiences when you were most aware of that. What did you do? What did you feel? If there were people involved, how did they respond?"

"OK."

"Oh, one more thing. Do you know how to cook?"

"A little," Thom replied. "I can make porridge, but my parents and older siblings did more cooking than me. I can chop vegetables, though."

"That's a start. You'll be learning how to cook, too," Rin replied. "Enough talk. Let's settle into riding. You'll notice that you'll get into a rhythm. Since I'm setting the direction, you can settle back and have time to reflect. And since the sky has cleared, it looks like a fine day for riding."

Some hours passed, and it was mid-afternoon when Thom knew he had a problem. His legs and groin ached, and his back was screaming at him in pain. He didn't want to say anything, not wanting Rin to think he couldn't handle this.

"Gnghnaaaaaaa," Thom groaned a while later, unable to keep his pain to himself.

"Are you OK, Thom?" Rin asked.

Oh no, he heard me, Thom thought. "Um..."

"Getting some pain from the riding?"

"Yeah," he replied. "Bedum warned me about balancing and sitting correctly. But I guess I didn't do it right. Sorry."

"That's OK," Rin said. "Let's stop briefly. Did he show you any stretching exercises?"

"Yes."

"Go ahead and dismount and go through them," Rin said. "Unfortunately, we have a couple more hours of riding ahead of us."

Thom swung his leg over the horse, moaning, and slid to the ground. As he stretched, he felt soreness in parts of his body that he'd never been aware of.

Rin remained in the saddle looking on, thinking. He really is small. He hoped this wasn't too much for him. Unfortunately, he had no choice. When they were on their way again, he asked, "Better?"

"Some."

"When we stop for the evening, you can put on some salve to help with the pain."

True to his word, as sunset drew near, Rin led them a short distance off the road to an open area surrounded by trees.

"I've camped here before. It's private enough that no one will see our fire or hear us."

"Umph," Thom uttered, dropping to the ground.

"Still feeling some pain?" Rin asked sympathetically.

"Yes."

"Let's start with you walking around a little to loosen your muscles," Rin suggested. "While you're doing that, I'll tie up our horses."

After the horses were groomed and happily munching on the grass nearby, Thom offered, "Would you like me to collect wood for the fire?"

"Yes," Rin said. "I was going to ask you that very thing. I'll start preparing our meal."

By the time Thom had a stack of wood ready to go, Rin had pulled out a pot and had placed some cut-up vegetables and meat in it. "Can I presume you know how to build a fire?" he asked.

"Yep," Thom replied.

"Before you do that, let's deal with your pain. Go ahead and dig out the salve from your bag and apply it," Rin said.

Applying the salve helped.

"How's that?" Rin asked.

"Much better."

"I know it won't take the pain away, but it will make it more tolerable until your body adjusts. Why don't you get the fire started? I'll go get some water from the stream nearby."

By the time Rin returned, Thom had a good fire going.

"Nicely done," Rin complimented. "Why don't you set up the bed rolls, and I'll cook our meal?" Crouching down to pour water into the pot, he tripped, and his waterskin went flying. "Turg!" he cursed.

"Are you OK?" Thom asked.

"Yes," he replied. "Only my pride is bruised. I do need to make another trip to the stream, though. I'm making stlew by the way."

"Stlew?" Thom repeated, his lips quirked.

"Oh, turg!" Rin cursed again. "When I'm upset, sometimes I add an L to a word that doesn't belong there. I occasionally get odd looks, like the one you gave me. I meant stew."

Thom smiled, thinking it was nice that his teacher sometimes made mistakes.

When Rin returned with the water, he carefully poured some into the pot. Thom watched as Rin added crushed herbs from a cloth bag.

"We'll have meat in the stew tonight because I picked up some before we left. But we won't get it often unless we stop at an inn," Rin explained.

"I'm used to that," Thom replied. "We don't have meat often at home anyway."

As the stew cooked, Rin asked Thom, "How are you feeling?"

"Tired."

"Understandable, it's been a long day. Dinner should be ready soon."

While Rin tended to the cooking, the aroma of sizzling meat drifting his way, Thom used that as an opportunity to pull out his journal and write. *G, it's been a long day. It was hard leaving this morning. Mam was sobbing when I hugged her goodbye. Da was crying, too. It would've been better if Healer Rin could've taken away my gifts. Why do I have them, G? Can Deu take them away? And Healer Rin doesn't even know the name of my newest gift. I must be a freak. And how do I tell Healer Rin? I don't know if I can.*

He sat there quietly for a time. Then, sighing, he closed his journal and stashed it among his bedding. Looking up, he saw Rin watching him.

"Might I ask, do you keep a journal?"

"You know about journals?" Thom asked.

"Yes, I do," Rin admitted. "I've been keeping one since I was ten."

"Really," Thom said. "My family doesn't understand."

"Mine didn't either," Rin told him. "Does it feel good to write down your thoughts and experiences?"

"Yeah," Thom answered. "I feel lighter."

"Good. I'm glad," Rin said. "If you didn't have an outlet, I'd be very concerned that your feelings, like fear and hurt, would get stuck inside you. If they're not released, they can fester and impact your gifts."

"That's why you want me to talk to you," Thom said.

"Not just that," Rin explained. "I also don't want you to be unhappy. And before you ask, I consider your journal private and would never read it without your permission."

"Thanks," Thom said, a bit relieved.

"But, until you talk more to me about what you're experiencing, I'll likely pepper you with questions."

"OK," Thom replied.

"I think the stew's ready," Rin said. "Let's eat."

Chapter 14

After they ate, Thom and Rin cleaned their bowls and the pot and settled by the fire afterward. Thom felt better after eating. Although the temperature had dropped since it was almost dark, the warmth of the fire kept him toasty.

Rin cleared his throat. "Before you tell me about your experiences, I want to tell you more about the fake shield I put on you yesterday and shielding in general."

"The fake shield prevented Lord Samiltun from really sensing my gifts," Thom said.

"That's correct," Rin continued.

"It sounds kind of weird knowing I have a shield."

"In truth, it's your second shield. Your first shield showed itself with the wall you envisioned. It's called your natural shield, and you were extending it when you pushed against Samiltun's probe."

"I did? I mean... I was? I didn't know that. I knew I wanted him out." Thom replied.

"I understand," Rin said. "That came from your instinct, which was very good because you responded to something that felt wrong. I'll teach you how to strengthen your natural shield and create others layered over it. First, each shield can serve a specific purpose, like the one I placed on you. I'll want you to take over that one eventually."

"OK," Thom replied. "What purposes might there be for the other shields?"

"That will depend, in part, on what we discover about your gifts. To continue, you mustn't drain yourself around people as a healer. There are times when a healer will unknowingly offer healing without intending to. That can be dangerous if the person uses all their energy. Healers must maintain control when they heal."

"Yeah, I did notice being tired after spending an afternoon helping Mam with her patients," Thom admitted.

"Well, that certainly could've been from using your healing energy. In your case, your tiredness more than likely was a natural result of it being the end of a busy day."

"Like I feel now, you mean," Thom concluded.

"Yes," Rin said. "Also, the healer doesn't want to use all their healing energy for minor problems that can be treated in other ways. If they do, and a major healing becomes necessary, the healer wouldn't be able to help. Does that make sense?"

"Yeah," Thom replied.

"Healers set up shields to prevent them from unknowingly being drained of energy and control how much of their gift they use. That's enough about that for now. Are you ready to share your experiences with me?"

"Yeah," Thom replied.

"Take your time," Rin encouraged.

"OK," Thom said. "You already know I feel different from my family and the neighbor kids."

"Yes. Would you tell me more about how you felt different from other children?"

"Sure," Thom said. "Well, I'm smaller than them. But even if I wasn't, I always knew my life would not be like theirs. My friend, Davi, said that he always felt good around me. I felt really connected to him. When he moved away, I felt alone."

"It's notable that you knew your life would be unique," Rin said. "That shows a level of spiritual awareness uncommon for someone your age. The fact that Davi felt good around you implies that your healing nature was evident even to him. That's good to know."

"Then, there was Kevar," Thom continued. "He's a bully. He made fun of me and called me a freak. Mam said to avoid him, but that was hard to do. He always gave me a nasty look, like I was doing something to him. Do you think he was picking up something from me like Davi?"

"Possibly," Rin replied. "Do you know what Kevar's family was like?"

"They're not very nice," he answered. "One day, Kevar's mother brought him to Mam for treatment. He'd been hurt. I heard them when they first arrived. She was very demanding and expected Kevar to be treated right away, as if they were the most important people in the world. Mam had called me to bring more hot water into her healing room.

When I did, Mrs. Sauntus got all still and insisted I leave. I didn't understand why she acted that way until Mam told me that some wealthy people behaved oddly."

"Hmm. It could be that your goodness felt threatening to Mrs. Sauntus."

"A threat?" Thom frowned. "But I didn't do anything to her. That was even the first time I saw her. Sometimes, I did want to punch Kevar."

"I don't mean you physically threatened her, but that ...how do I say this? As I mentioned, you have a very bright spirit. Its brightness comes from your innate goodness. Most can't see it, but some can feel it without realizing it."

"OK," Thom said.

"And for those who are unkind, your goodness drives them away, as if you were pushing against them."

"I didn't like being around her either."

"That's her aura," Rin explained. "Because your auras clashed, Mrs. Sauntus didn't want you there. For Kevar, I'd imagine that he was bullied at home and didn't have the power to stop it. In response, it sounds like he took out his frustrations on you. How did the other kids treat him?"

"They were scared of him. They did what he told them, even throwing rocks at squirrels and birds."

"Were you scared of him too?" Rin asked.

"Yes," Thom replied. "But he couldn't make me hurt animals."

"Good. And that meant Kevar couldn't control you," Rin said. "Deep down, I suspect that he was afraid of you."

"What?" Thom asked. "He didn't act like it."

"If you were around him now, since your gifts are emerging," Rin explained, "I think you would sense his fear. Anything else?"

"Yes," Thom said. "I once heard a neighbor talking to my Mam about me. I remember her exact words 'cause they sounded strange."

"What did she say?"

She said, "*Whenever your Thommy looks at me, I feel like he's looking into my soul. It gives me the shivers.* I didn't hear Mam's response. I still don't understand what she said. I didn't make googly eyes at her or anything."

"Do you remember if she said anything else?" Rin asked.

"No," Thom replied.

"Did you have any other such encounters?"

"Maybe," Thom said. "One day, I ran into a neighbor, Hugo, when I was returning home from delivering medicine for Mam. Hugo is my oldest sister's age. He was about to hit me for running into him when I looked at him and felt that he was nervous and excited. Hugo suddenly stopped and made a weird face. Then, he took off. Da said he ran away with his girlfriend soon after."

"Interesting," Rin commented. "Your sensitivity as a burgeoning healer enabled you to feel his emotions."

"Burgeoning?" Thom said. "I think Meli used that once. That means growing, doesn't it?"

"Yes," Rin answered. "How old were you when the last two happened?"

"About seven, I think," Thom replied.

"Did that happen before or after your first encounter with Lord Samiltun?" Rin asked.

"I think after," Thom answered.

Even without Samiltun's influence, his gifts were making themselves known, Rin mused. That's unusual. Turning to his spirit guides, he thought, *do you agree?* The message he immediately heard back was that Thom's path in this life would be unusual. Speaking out loud, he asked, "Did anything change after your neighbor chatted with your mother?"

"Oh, I didn't think about that before, but yes," he answered, "Other adults started looking at me oddly."

"I suspect that's both because you were looking more intently at them unknowingly and that Mrs. Endelrun is a bit of a gossip."

"You're right about that," Thom agreed, grinning.

"Very good. Anything else?"

"There was Mirabel. But I already told you about her.'

"Yes, you did. Is that it?" Rin asked.

"There's another thing that happened, but...um..." Thom hemmed and hawed. "It wasn't really an experience either because it happened while I was asleep. It could've been a dream, but it didn't feel like one. But maybe... I don't know."

"It's OK, Thom. Please tell me."

"It was after you started training Mam and me. In the middle of the night, I heard someone calling my name. At the time, all I remembered was that I felt peaceful. Meli told me I was calling out the name Sereh. But since Samiltun's visit, I've recalled that Sereh was my guardian angel and was watching over me. You think I'm crazy, don't you?"

"I'm glad you told me," Rin replied. "And no, I don't think you're crazy. I'm sure it happened. I'd call it a visitation. I know that the Iosan elders only talk in a general way about angels. When they do, it's about their appearances long ago. But they're real, as are guardian angels. I'm sure Sereh is yours."

"And she's really watching over me?" Thom asked.

"Not just her, but also Deu, Iosa, and spirit guides, who all dwell in heaven," Rin explained. "And before you ask, spirit guides were spiritual teachers when they lived on earth."

"That's a lot of people watching," Thom said. "It sounds a little creepy."

"It's not meant to. It's coming from their love for you," Rin assured him. "They also offer advice and send signs and messages. They never tell you what to do, but they want to help. And they always encourage you to use your intuition or gut feeling to make good decisions."

"My gut feeling," Thom said. "Is that when I know some-one isn't nice even before talking to them or if doing some-thing feels right or wrong inside?"

"Indeed," Rin said.

"That reminds me of something else," Thom said. Scram-bling over to one of his saddlebags, he withdrew his purple jar. "Um. This is my treasure jar. It's probably childish, but sometimes it brings me comfort. I have this green triangle thing I've had since I was young. I still don't know what it is or how I got it."

Rin smiled encouragingly.

"But this is what I wanted to show you," Thom explained, pulling out a white feather. "Sereh told me that she had an owlet drop this feather in my path the night she visited me. She said it was to get my attention, but I think she said it normally means that divine beings support me. Why am I remembering that now? It's kind of weird."

"For divine visitations, it's common that people don't remember details. They often come out when it fits the situation," Rin explained.

"I still think it's weird," Thom said.

"I'm glad you received the feather and have those treasures," Rin said. "And thanks for sharing your experiences. They help me plan your training."

"Are Sereh, Deu, and everyone are all aware of what's happening?" Thom asked as a yawn erupted. "Oh, sorry."

"No worries," Rin said. "Yes, they are. Let's stop there. It's been a long day, and we have another one tomorrow. Let's get some sleep. I'll throw a few more branches on the fire to keep it going until morning."

Settling into his bedroll, Rin heard Thom's deep breathing. The poor boy fell asleep not long after climbing into his bedroll.

The following morning, Rin and Thom finished the previous night's stew for breakfast. Filling up their waterskins, they saddled their horses and continued their journey.

Chapter 15

After months of searching, Vern and Finn had located their prey in the town of Potai-cruth. They'd also discovered the healer was teaching a married woman, Winni Macirdan. After exchanging a few messages with Mitch, they developed a plan to use that information.

Sitting down for noon supper one Turi-dae, Vern looked back at the serving girl who had taken their order and asked Finn, "What did the wench say?"

"She tol' us our food was comin' soon. Din't ya hear her?" Finn replied, scratching his head.

"I'm talkin' about the affair rumor," Vern whispered through clenched teeth.

"Oh, ya mean yestirdiy, when I went out wit' her," Finn replied.

"A course," Vern replied, his voice grumbling. "Ya said she trusts ya now since youse been seeing her a few weeks."

"Yea, she's real nice," Finn said, grinning.

"What about the rumor?" Vern repeated, his face growing red.

"Saurry Vern," Finn replied. "Her frien' in da bakery said she'd gossiped with a few people at da market and at ta tradin' shop."

"Good," Vern said. "I also heerd the stablehands talkin' about it the other day. We can go ahead with the last part of the plan."

Finishing the last forkful of an extra-large piece of pumpkin pie da serving girl had brought them, Finn belched, saying, "Thet was good."

"Yeah, it was," Vern agreed. "Now, ya remembers what to do?"

"I knows, Vern. You minded me yesterdiy," Finn whispered. "I'm nots stupid. But how's do we know da woman'll be wit da healer?"

"I've been watchin' the shop for a month," Vern explained, trying to keep his voice down. "She gets trainin' from the healer every Turi-dae afternoon. Let's go."

Standing in the alley, Vern watched Finn cut his arm. "Make it bigger," he demanded. "Anyone'd be able to treat that." Grabbing the knife, he made a three-inch gash in Finn's arm.

"Ow!" Finn yelled, seeing the blood pour out of his wound. "What da turg ya doin'? Ya tryin' ta kill me?"

"Shut it and go!" Vern replied. "I'll come afta ya start yelling and make a bigger ruckus."

When he didn't hear Finn yelling, Vern ran to the healer shop to find Finn pounding on the door.

"Where's da healer?" Finn yelled. "I need da healer!"

Hearing the shouting, the tailor next door came out. "Oh, Finn, that's a bad cut," she said.

"Where's da healer?" he repeated.

"Healer Rinbalden closed his shop about a week ago," she answered. "I thought everyone knew."

"Na, we didn'," Vern replied.

"I'm bleedin' ta death," Finn whined, even louder.

"Go to the Macirdans," the tailor suggested. "Winni can take care of you."

Chapter 16

Thom was still sore from the riding, but his legs and butt ached less. He must be getting more accustomed to horse riding. He had also noticed he felt more connected to his horse, Brule. Maybe it helped him find his rider's seat, as his brother described.

"Thom," Rin called out. "We'll make camp for the night in about an hour."

"It's not even mid-afternoon," he said, his eyes lighting up when he heard they'd get a break.

"I know. But we've been riding hard," Rin replied, "and we've come a good way. It's time to officially start your training."

Setting up camp took longer because the location hadn't been used before. Thom and Rin cleared the brush and created a safe fire pit and a space for their bedrolls.

"OK, Thom," Rin said. "Come and sit in front of me."

Thom brushed a few pebbles from the ground before sitting down cross-legged.

"First, I want to teach you about grounding and its relationship to shields. Grounding is key for building good shields and living in general," Rin explained. "It keeps you stabilized when facing challenges."

"What do you mean by grounding?" Thom asked.

"Of course, you wouldn't know about that. It's the experience of being connected to the earth and sharing its strength. But I think the best way to explain is by showing you. Sense into me, like you did with Mirabel. Then tell me what you notice about my relationship with the ground."

After a moment, Thom spoke. "I sort of feel like you're attached to the ground. Not really attached…, but somehow connected. It's almost as if you are part of the earth. But that doesn't make sense."

"In truth, it does," Rin interrupted. "We are part of Mother Earth. All of nature, including humans and animals, are made of the same stuff. In a way, when you talked to the plants in your mother's garden, you talked to part of yourself. What you're detecting comes from your earth sense. All people can ground, but those possessing the earth sense can do it more quickly."

Thom nodded.

"Stay focused on me. Am I stiff or relaxed?" Rin asked.

"Relaxed."

"When you ground, you don't have to be stiff, which can happen if you rely on your mind. In this case, your body is the connector. Relaxing connects you to the earth more strongly. I want you to relax your body and clear your mind. If your mind intrudes, take a few deep breaths and have your mind focus on breathing."

Attempting to do as Rin said, Tom's mind kept trying to help by repeating the word 'relax,' which resulted in the opposite. Shaking his head in frustration, he attended to his breathing again, inhaling and exhaling slowly a few more times.

"Good," Rin replied. "I can see your body relaxing and your mind quieting. Do you notice any areas of tension?"

"My legs."

"I'm not surprised," Rin agreed. "You're still getting used to long riding days. Concentrate on your leg muscles and tighten them. I know it sounds counter-intuitive."

"What does counter-intuitive mean?" Thom asked.

"Oh, it means that it sounds the opposite of what you would think to do."

"OK."

"Good. Notice your legs' tightness… and tighten them even more," Rin encouraged. "Careful, don't bite your tongue."

Thom released his jaw as he squeezed his muscles tighter.

"Keep holding it," Rin encouraged. "Now, relax those muscles. Then relax them even more. Notice the difference between how they felt when they were tight versus now."

"Huh," Thom grunted. "My legs are really relaxed."

"Great," Rin continued. "Next, bring your attention to your buttocks and legs touching the ground. Even rub your hands against the dirt, feeling its grittiness."

Doing as Rin instructed, Thom also noted the ground's coolness.

"Good," Rin said. "Feel the strength of the ground and that it's holding you up in a way."

"Yes, I'm getting it," Thom admitted.

"Imagine a thick rope, starting at your heart, that runs down your spine and deep into the earth's center. Feel it pulling you downward, but not in a restrictive way."

Rin remained silent to give Thom time. "What do you feel?" he asked.

"Powerful."

"Good," Rin affirmed. "That's grounding. Every morning, take time to practice. Eventually, you'll find you don't have to be seated on the ground to be grounded. For instance, you can even do it while riding Brule."

"I don't know," Thom said, smirking, "It almost sounds... counter-intuitive."

"Humor. I like it." Rin continued. "Let's move on to shielding. Before we began, I removed my fake shield from you so you'll only see what's innate to you. Close your eyes, tune into your inner self, and ask your body to reveal your natural shield. When you do, tell me what your mind's eye sees."

"Hmm," Thom answered, considering. "I see what looks like heat waves, similar to what I see over a road when it's hot."

"How thick is it?" Rin asked.

"It's thicker near the ground but not as much higher up," Thom told him.

"That's because you grounded first. Next, imagine the ground is feeding you strength, and your shield is thickening."

"Yes, it's happening," Thom said, smiling.

"Keep going," Rin said. "Anything else?"

Still with his eyes closed, Thom raised his head towards Rin's voice and froze.

"What's going on?" Rin asked. "You look startled."

"I'm seeing ribbons of color around you. A lot of green, but some purple, blue, and brown, too. It's all flowing around you. Am I doing this right? I don't think I'm doing this right."

"Breathe, Thom," Rin said.

"Wait. What's going on?" Thom spoke, opening his eyes. "I'm not seeing anything now. I'm sorry. I messed up."

"It's OK," he assured him. "It's all normal and good. I suspect you lost your grounding due to your anxiety. Close your eyes and reground. Then, sense into yourself again."

"Huh," Thom replied. "I see colors around me, and my natural shield is closer to my body."

"What else do you see? Rin asked. "Describe it in as much detail as possible."

"I see blue, green, and a little purple. The colors are flowing around me like they're dancing. Sometimes, they form lines and shapes. Other times, they are waves and swirly things."

"Good," Rin encouraged. "Anything more?"

"Yes, I see sparkles of light shining through. They're very bright."

Rin thought to himself. Thom's a natural. He's seeing details I've never seen, and he's a beginner. Speaking out loud, he said. "Open your eyes, look at me, but stay grounded and relaxed."

"Oh. I see your colors again, even with my eyes open."

"Good. I was hoping that would happen," Rin said. "What you're seeing is an aura. I mentioned it some days ago."

"I remember."

Rin continued, "As energy, your aura is part of your energetic body, which is the same energy that makes up Deu. This energy is your spirit or soul and attaches to your physical body when you incarnate."

"We're the same as Deu?" Thom asked.

"In a way. We're part of Deu," Rin corrected. "Earlier, I said it was good you were connected to the divine. Because you share the same energy as Deu, you are automatically connected. Seeking help from the divine strengthens that bond and can be a resource for you as you grow into your gifts."

"I don't really get it."

"Leave that for now," Rin suggested before continuing. "When a spirit incarnates, an aura appears around it. A baby's aura is translucent yet displays a shifting array of colors akin to a kaleidoscope. The predominant hue is white, representing the essence of the spirit shining through. As an individual matures, distinct colors become more pronounced, much like what you observed in both you and me."

"OK," Thom said.

"Ideally, those colors reflect the person's purpose in life if the person is aligned with that purpose. Are you following me?"

"Kinda," Thom said. "The elders told me about souls, but I never heard the rest before."

"They wouldn't," Rin stated. "The colors represent distinct characteristics. Green can mean nature, but it can also mean health, often seen in healers. And envy. Blue implies honesty and loyalty. Purple signifies spiritual awareness and enlightenment. I'll go over the other colors in a future lesson. Do you understand?"

"I get it in my mind," Thom replied. "But... and, this might sound weird, not in my heart. It's hard to explain."

"You're doing well, and it doesn't sound weird," Rin said. "You're saying you understand the words, but their truth hasn't settled into you in a knowing way."

"I guess," Thom said. "Once, I said something like this to an elder, and he told me to stop thinking. He said they're the ones who know everything, and I should listen and do what they say."

"How unfortunate," Rin commented. "Many elders want you to memorize beliefs and rules. They don't want you questioning or trying to figure things out. Believe it or not, their reaction comes from fear of getting it wrong and losing power."

"Uh-huh," Thom responded. "That makes sense."

"Do you feel comfortable going on?" Rin asked.

"Yeah," Thom answered. "Can I tell you something?"

"Always," Rin said.

"You said purple was spiritual."

"Yes," Rin confirmed.

"Well, about a year ago, Reta planted purple flowers in her garden. She loves purple, like me. Do you think purple's in my aura because of my connection to Deu?"

"I do. We are often drawn to colors that resonate with us and reflect our personalities."

"Oh," Thom said. "I didn't think about that."

"Shall we focus on you creating another shield?" Rin asked.

"Sure," Thom replied.

"For this part, I want you to imagine a new shield in front of your natural shield. Ask your body-mind to create it," Rin instructed.

"My body-mind?" Thom replied, scrunching up his face in confusion.

"Sorry," Rin responded. "Put simply, you have two minds. Most folks are familiar with the brain-mind, for lack of a better term. Your body also has a mind. They work together in service to your spirit and, in this case, to create your shield. Your body-mind guides your brain-mind to create the shield. Relax into it and trust that your body-mind will handle this."

Thom took a deep breath and gradually exhaled before trying.

Rin sensed a shield forming outside of Thom's natural shield. "Good," he encouraged. "Imagine your new shield is also connected to the earth and strengthened by it and your spirit."

"I see it," Thom exclaimed. "It's working."

"Very, very good. Now, I want this shield to hide your gifts. Direct that intention toward it."

"Do you mean I should have my brain-mind, um... ask it of the shield?" Thom asked, unsure.

"No," Rin said. "How about trying this? Think of your intention as a ball of white light. Then have it move into your heart and settle there."

"OK," Thom said. "It's there."

"Imagine it expanding to encompass the whole of you." Rin waited, then tuned into Thom. "Yes, I can tell your second shield accepts the intention."

"Rin," Thom interjected. "You talked about seeing my aura and my spirit. Do you also see my gifts? Do they show up as a shape or something?"

"Excellent question," Rin replied. "Like your aura and spirit, your gifts are energies. But your spirit makes them evident through your aura."

"Will the shield make the colors disappear?" Thom asked.

"Ah," Rin responded. "Another good question. Not unless the purpose of the shield is to conceal something like the fake shield does. Any other questions?"

"No. I gotta think about it for a bit... using both of my minds," Thom said with a twinkle in his eye.

"Yes," Rin replied. "And well said. I want you to continue strengthening your shields. I'm going to place my fake shield back on you. When yours is strong enough, I'll remove it."

"Got it," Thom said.

"You did great. One last thing," Rin said. "Like you've heard, a key part of this work was to use your imagination."

"Yeah," Thom said. "Does that mean I was making it all up, and it wasn't real like Meli says?"

"No," Rin replied. "Just the opposite. Using your imagination, you create reality from potentialities."

"Huh?" Thom asked, frowning.

"What I mean," Rin said, "is you invite something like shields to come into existence by believing it's possible. In fact, letting your imagination run free enables the unexpected and deemed illogical or impossible to come into being. And your intention that it be for the highest good drives that creative force."

"Hmm. I gotta think about that, too," Thom admitted.

"Understood. How do you feel?" Rin asked.

"Tired."

"Why don't you take a nap?"

Thom nodded, slipping into his bedroll. He was instantly asleep.

Rin remained seated. He was amazed at how effortlessly Thom saw auric colors. Even more astonishing was his ability to perceive patterns, movement, and bursts of light---a likely result of Thom's more powerful yet unknown gift. Recognizing his own fatigue, Rin decided he'd also nap before starting dinner.

The next morning, Thom awoke before the sun rose, but it was light enough to see. Noting Rin was still asleep, he decided to revisit the exercises from yesterday. Sitting on his bedding, Thom wrapped his blanket snugly around him. First, he grounded, feeling his connection to the earth. It felt almost warm to him, which was helpful, given the chill in the air. Now, Thom would check his shields. Closing his eyes, he opened his senses but couldn't see anything. What was he doing wrong?

Thom was about to check on his grounding again when he realized that his nose was runny. "Turg!" he cursed. Wiping his runny nose on his sleeve, his frustration mounted. He refocused on his grounding, confirming it was in place. But when he checked his shields again, there was still nothing. What was he doing wrong? He couldn't help but feel a pang of disappointment. He had managed it just fine yesterday. Rin's words about the body-mind and brain-mind echoed in his head. Maybe, his brain-mind was trying too hard.

"OK, body-mind, go for it," Thom whispered. He waited and waited and waited. Suddenly, he felt a cramp in his left foot. Was his body-mind trying to tell him something? Or was he imagining there was a message where there was none? He remembered what Rin had taught him about tightening and relaxing his muscles.

Once more relaxed, Thom took a break, adding a few branches to the glowing coals to reignite the fire. Looking east through the trees, he saw the sun peeking over the horizon. It's gonna be a nice morning. *Good morning, Deu, Sereh, and Mother Earth,* he mind spoke.

Sitting down again and returning his attention to his shields, Thom asked his body-mind to help. He instantly saw that his natural shield was strong and connected to the earth, and Rin's shield was also strong. The shield he had created, however, seemed thinner.

OK, he thought. He'd ask his body-mind to work with Mother Earth to strengthen it. Feeling a powerful energy surge rising from the ground, he lost his balance and became dizzy. When he settled, he noticed all his shields were brighter and thicker.

After about an hour spent strengthening his shields and testing his grounding cord, Thom needed another break. Since Rin remained asleep, he decided to write in his journal. *Gosh, G, I can't believe all this stuff's happening to me. I still feel different. But I also feel more like me, I guess.*

This sounds weird, he thought. *Body-mind, can you help me figure this out?* Thom felt silly talking to himself, not that he hadn't done it before. What if he asked Sereh? Rin mentioned that she, Deu, and the guides wanted to help. But what prayer should he use? He tried hard to remember a formal prayer that matched his desire but couldn't think of any. Seeing Rin stirring, he closed his journal and began preparing their morning meal.

They'd been traveling for a good while when Rin spoke up. "Remember when I talked with you a few days ago about your guardian angel and Deu giving you advice or sending messages?"

"Yes," Thom replied, his jaw dropping open.

"I wanted to talk to you about it. You probably didn't learn much about that in your religious education."

"No," Thom answered. This is spooky, he thought, knowing he'd asked for help from Sereh earlier.

"I know in the Iosan religion, you had to memorize formal prayers," Rin said.

"Yeah," Thom replied. "The elders always made a big deal about us praying in a specific way. They even told us how to sit, kneel, and hold our hands."

"What would happen if you didn't?" Rin asked.

"The elder would yell at us and tell us Deu was angry. Sometimes, she even warned our soul was in jeopardy."

"Sounds a bit scary," Rin remarked.

Thom nodded. "Aren't you Iosan, Rin?"

"Not for many years. But I remember going through something similar. It upsets me that things haven't changed. I know the Iosan faith teaches about Deu being loving. But too often, the elders depict him as a judge and someone to be afraid of."

"It reminds me of those folks who stand in the town square yelling that we're all going to hell," Thom added. "They also say we must have a personal relationship with Iosa."

"Why would anyone want to have a personal relationship with a being who is out to get them?" Rin said.

"I wouldn't," Thom said.

"But I digress," Rin continued. "My point is that divine beings care deeply about you and are eager to help. All you need to do is ask; formal prayers aren't necessary."

"They aren't?" Thom responded. "What do I say?"

"You talk to them like you do with me. You mentioned you write to G in your journal. What about?" Rin asked.

"About what I did that day, how I feel, and the stuff I learned. You said I should also write questions."

"Yes," Rin responded. "Have you tried?"

"A little," Thom said.

"Good," Rin replied. "I also suggest you verbalize it, either out loud or within your thoughts."

"OK," Thom responded, with a hint of skepticism.

"And," he added, "you can direct the chat to one being, like Sereh or Deu, or even to a group."

"I feel like I've heard this before," Thom replied. "But it wasn't from an elder. You know, I've felt closer to Deu for a while. Sometimes, I even get a tingling feeling."

"I don't know about the tingling," Rin replied. "But I'm glad you're feeling a stronger bond."

"This morning, I asked Sereh to help me figure this out," Thom confessed. "I didn't get an answer, but you answered my question."

"Often, the divine communicates messages or answers through other people," Rin explained. "And messages can even come to you through unexpected means, a song you hear, a word on a sign, or even a feather, much like the one your guardian angel sent you."

"Hmm," Thom thought. "I wanna think some more about that."

Chapter 17

A week later, it was early afternoon when Thom and Rin were riding through a hilly area. They hadn't seen any farms or people for a while. Since it was late Uctiba, the trees had lost most of their leaves. Thom found himself squinting ahead along the road.

Looking at Thom, Rin asked, "The sun's bright, isn't it? Aren't you wishing you had a hat like mine?"

"Yes," Thom said. "But maybe one that doesn't look so funny."

"We'll be stopping at the inn in next town, Lifford, in an hour or two. Maybe we can find a hat for you there," Rin suggested.

"OK. Thanks," Thom replied. He was looking forward to the inn. He wanted a warm bath, a comfy bed, and good food. It wasn't so much that the stew they had wasn't good. But it was boring to have it all the time. He had to admit that he was proud his cooking skills had improved enough for him to prepare their meals.

"We're making good progress," Rin said. "I think you'll like the inn. The food is tasty and plentiful. And we can get something other than stew. We'll both have a chance to take a bath too."

Is Rin reading his mind? Thom wondered again. No, he said he couldn't do that and wouldn't if he could. He had noticed that he and Rin awoke at the same time and both liked quiet time in the saddle. The word "aligned" popped into his head. Da says that when talking about how he and Mam take care of our home. It kind of makes sense.

Earlier today, Rin warned him that this area sometimes had bandits. As they approached a bend, Thom decided to lower his newest shield, his fourth. He created it following an incident at the last inn. Rin and Thom had been enjoying a quiet meal when an argument erupted between two male customers. The argument led to a brawl involving half the patrons. He remembered cowering in the corner, paralyzed by the intensity of the emotions, until Rin came to his aid. His new shield enabled him to control the influx of emotions. He wondered whether he could use his empathic gift to detect people.

Lowering that shield now, Thom projected his senses and immediately felt someone ahead. "Rin," he whispered. "There's a man on a horse around the bend."

"Thanks, Thom," Rin replied. "Let's stop and see what happens."

Thom noticed Rin loosening the staff which he had strapped to his horse. Seeing Rin nod to him, Thom removed his slingshot and a few stones from a saddlebag and placed it in front of him.

Soon after, a man wearing a uniform rode towards them. "Oy," he called out, "What's going on here?" The man was tall and muscular and wore a stern look.

Rin didn't say anything as he reached for his waterskin.

"Oy. I'm talking to you, old man," he repeated. "What are you doin'? I heard you coming up the road and then stopped."

"Yes, we did," Rin replied. "I needed some water."

Stay silent, Thom repeated to himself, heart beating rapidly from fear. Rin had previously instructed him to play someone deaf and mute should something like this happen. He was determined to play his part. Breathe; that's what he needed to do to calm himself.

"If you expect to go any further on this road, you'll have to pay the toll," the man stated, riding closer.

"This road never had a toll before," Rin replied. "Is this something the Lifford council recently imposed?" he asked, counterfeiting confusion.

"Yes, and I'm a deputy of Lifford. Too many folks have tried to get by without paying. Enough chatter. Get off your horses and pay me!"

Now calmer, Thom noted the poor condition of the deputy's uniform. He saw Rin nod to him, his signal to spook the deputy's horse. With the man focused on Rin, he loaded a stone in his slingshot and let it loose. It hit the ground in front of the man's horse, causing it to rear up. At the same time, Rin grabbed his staff and charged the man.

While Rin was battling the man, Thom sensed two individuals approaching from behind. Glancing back, he saw a man and woman riding towards them on a single horse. As Rin had instructed, Thom swiftly spurred his horse into action, racing up the road toward the town. Reluctant as he was to leave, he knew he couldn't help Rin and had to fetch aid. Hearing the man and woman galloping after him, he urgently whispered, "Faster, Brule, faster."

Despite Brule's attempt to run as fast as he could, they closed in on Thom, corralling him amidst the trees. He had no choice but to stop. Both were yelling, but he continued feigning deafness and muteness. Shaking his head, he gestured to his ears and grunted. Meanwhile, the woman had dismounted.

"It looks like the kid cain't hear or speak, Berta," the man said. "Why don' youse git on his horse and ride back with im."

"What do ya think I was doin', Gridiot!" the woman yelled.

"Dervig tol' ya ta stop calling me that," the man yelled.

"Then, stop actin' like an idiot, Gurr...iid," Berta sarcastically replied.

Berta was short and muscular, with shoulder-length black hair. She wore trousers and a tunic that looked old but cared for. Grid, on the other hand, was heavy, with grimy brown hair. Like the first bandit they encountered on the road, he wore a ragged uniform.

Thom's heart raced from the ride, and he tried to calm himself again. Berta climbed behind him on the horse, and he gagged from her smell and decided to take as few breaths as possible.

When Grid and Berta brought Thom back, Dervig had secured Rin on his horse.

"Took you long enough," Dervig complained.

"He took off fast!" Grid whined.

Noticing Rin's hands were tied, Berta asked, "Why'd ya tie the old man up? Ya usually knocks em out and leaves em by the roadside."

"The old man's a healer," Dervig explained. "He can fix up Grid's leg. I see you didn't knock the kid out."

"Uh, no. I was goin' to," Grid replied, "But he cain't talk or hear. An' won' be able to tell nobody nothin'."

"How do you know he's deaf and mute?" Dervig asked suspiciously.

"He grunted and pointed ta his ears," Grid replied.

"Did you make sure it wasn't an act?" Dervig asked.

"Um, no," Berta answered.

Uh oh, Thom thought, feeling his heart start to race again. Rin had prepared him for this, too. Connecting strongly to the earth, he thickened his natural shield. It wouldn't block out sound, but it would briefly reduce it.

Dervig grabbed his sword and a long knife from his belt. He ran the knife along the sword's edge, making a screeching sound. Grid and Berta clapped their hands over their ears. Rin and Dervig winced. In contrast, Thom did not react.

"OK. It's a good thing you weren't wrong," Dervig said. "Let's get back to camp. Then the old man can look at your leg, Grid."

Thom sighed with relief as Dervig led them off the road. Once they passed a hill, Thom saw the ruins of the cottage, behind which were bedrolls and the remains of a fire.

"Get the kid off the horse and tie him up, Berta," Dervig commanded as he pulled Rin off his horse. "Then tie up the horses. Grid, hop over by the fire. I'll never know why you had to play with your knife while we were waiting."

"Bored," Grid whined.

"Oh, shut it," Dervig replied. "You're lucky the old man's a healer. Hopefully, he won't have to chop off your leg."

"Chop it off!" Grid cried out in alarm.

"Old man," Dervig called out. "I'm gonna cut your bonds loose. If you try anything, Berta there will slit the kid's throat."

Looking up at her, Thom gulped. He was terrified. His body started shaking, and he thought he might throw up.

Noticing Thom's reaction, she laughed.

Deu and Sereh, Help! Thom mind-spoke.

Also alerted to Thom's fear, Rin sent a pulse of supportive energy through the shield he still had on Thom. "I'll need to get some of my healing supplies," he told Dervig.

"Fine," Dervig replied.

Feeling the strength of Rin's support, Thom's fear eased a little. He watched as Rin went to his saddlebags and pulled out some supplies. It also looked like he palmed a little bottle.

"What's your name, old man," Dervig asked.

"Pollard," Rin replied.

"OK. Pollard, get to work. See if you can save the leg," he said, chuckling.

Thom heard Grid groan.

"Sir," Rin said, turning toward Grid. "Would you move away from the tree and to the other side of the fire? I'd like to take advantage of the sunlight."

"Careful not to tip over the stew pot, Grid," Dervig said. "If you do, I'll take it out of your portion of today's gains."

After Grid relocated, Rin knelt beside him and rolled up his pant leg. Grid's cut was two inches long.

"Will I lose my leg, healer?" Grid asked.

"No," Rin assured him. "But I must clean and sterilize your wound before I stitch it closed." Looking at Dervig, he said, "I'm going to need some hot water. And some whiskey."

"Yeah," Grid cried out. "I could use me some whiskey."

"It's not fer ya, Gridiot," Berta called out, still standing next to Thom.

Thom had forgotten she was next to him. Glancing at her, his eyes widened when he saw the knife in her hand. It looked very sharp and had a jagged edge. His heart started beating rapidly again. *Deu and Sereh, are you there?*

"Berta," Dervig warned. "Call him by his correct name. She's right, though. It's to clean your wound, idiot. What do you need water for, Pollard?"

"I want to apply bandages infused with thyme, an antibacterial. After I stitch the wound closed, I'll wrap them around it."

Dervig pulled out a pot from his saddlebags and poured some water from his waterskin into it. Setting the pot next to the simmering stew pot, he handed the waterskin to Rin.

"Thank you," Rin replied. After cleaning the wound, he reached into the herb pouch he had taken from his saddlebag and added a pinch of thyme to the water pot.

Grabbing the whiskey Dervig had placed near him, Rin turned to Grid and said, "This is going to sting."

"Ya sure I cain't have some whiskey, Dervig?" Grid pleaded.

"No. Deal with the pain."

Grid let out a yell as Rin poured whiskey on the wound. Handing the bottle back to Dervig, he thanked him. "Grid, I'd suggest you find a stick or something to bite down on while I stitch this." It took roughly ten stitches.

Then Rin took the pot containing the antibacterial water off the fire. He dipped a bandage into it, wrung it out, and wrapped it around the wound. Looking up at Dervig, he said, "I'd like to apply another bandage in about an hour. He should stay off the leg for the night."

Dervig nodded. "Go over to the deaf kid, Pollard. Berta, tie him up, and when you're done, get Grid's bowl and spoon."

When Berta walked away, Thom gave Rin a fearful look. Once again, he felt another pulse of assurance and saw him mouth the words, *Breathe. It'll be OK.*

Trying to believe him, Thom took long, deep breaths and felt his heart slow.

"We'll be keeping a close eye on you while we're eating," Dervig informed them.

"And I'm keepin' my knife handy," Berta added. "I'm good at throwin' too."

The three bandits sat by the fire to eat. All was quiet except for the clanking of their metal spoons on bowls.

"Let's finish the stew tonight," Dervig said. "I want to get away from here. I don't want anyone from our old squad to stumble on us. We need to find a town with more traders traveling through."

Grid and Berta grunted before reaching for the pot to get more. Dervig also took more of the stew.

Dervig patted his stomach and let out a satisfied burp. "That was good camp food," he remarked. Seeing the empty pot, he instructed, "Berta, go rinse them out," gesturing toward the pot and their tins.

"Ya know, jus' cause I'm a woman doesn' mean I'm supposed ta do the dishes," she complained.

"Shut it and do what you're told," Dervig reiterated. "Grid will do it when we get to our next camp."

Thom and Rin remained quiet, listening to the threesome talk about their day's work. An hour later, Thom saw the three were asleep where they sat.

Turning to Thom, Rin said, "Let's make our escape."

"Won't they wake up?" Thom asked.

"Not a chance. I gave them enough of the valerian root tincture to render them unconscious for hours."

"I was wondering what was in the bottle you palmed," Thom commented.

"You saw that. I must be slipping," Rin grimaced. He got up and untied Thom.

"How did you get loose?"

"When Berta tied me up, I held my hands tight against the rope to fool her that she had tied me up securely. Her knots were amateurish. Anyway, go and saddle our horses. I want to finish treating Grid."

"What? Why?" Thom asked.

"Because I'm a healer, Thom, like you will be. Even though Grid and the others are bandits, I'm committed to healing. But don't worry. When we get to town, we'll inform the constable."

Rin quickly applied a new bandage to Grid's leg. After tying the bandits' horses to the back of theirs, he whispered, "Let's get a move on. If we hurry, we should be able to get to Lifford before the sun sets."

When they reached the end of town, Rin said, "We'll head to the constable's building first. I treated an injured deputy here some years back."

After trotting up to a brick building, Rin said, "Stay here with the horses. I'll talk to the constable."

When Rin returned, Thom saw him with a tall man wearing a clean uniform and a metal badge pinned to his left chest.

"Thom, this is the constable," Rin said. "Constable, this is my apprentice, Thom."

"How do you do, sir," Thom said.

"I do well," he replied. "You'll be a great healer if you're as skilled as Healer Rin."

"Thank you, sir," Thom replied. "What's happening?"

"As I explained inside to Rin," the constable said, "Dervig was a lieutenant deputy here, and Grid was his assistant. I fired them when I discovered they were bullying townsfolk, particularly young women. I don't know how Berta got mixed up with them. I sent out three deputies with a cart to their location. Given how much valerian root you gave them, Rin, they're unlikely to wake up until they're secure in cells."

"Very likely," Rin agreed.

"I'll take their horses. I know of a few poor families who could use them," the constable continued.

"Glad to hear it," Rin said. "Thank you."

Turning to Thom, Rin said, "Let's head to the inn. It's a bit late, but I'm sure they'll still have some of their excellent dinner. We might have to wait until tomorrow for baths."

"That's OK," Thom replied, relieved to be alive.

As they rode away, Rin said, "You know, given what we've been through, let's stay here two nights. We can replenish some supplies and enjoy real beds for a change."

Thom awoke, noting frost on their room's window.

"It's a beautiful morning, isn't it?" Rin remarked, already dressed. "Not a cloud in the sky. It's a good day for riding, even if it's chilly."

"I guess," Thom mumbled. It may be beautiful, but he couldn't appreciate it. The bandit attack still gave him collywobbles, even though Rin wanted him to learn self-defense. Dervig looked like he could handle his sword. And Berta seemed very comfortable with her knife. What could his puny sling do against them? Before they had ridden out, Thom had grabbed a few more stones for his sling.

"Thom," Rin said, breaking into his thoughts. "Still thinking about the attack?"

"Yes," he replied. "We both could have died. I know you said you're going to start training me in self-defense. But what good is that? I'm small."

"I understand," Rin said. "But don't underestimate the skills of someone small. Opponents often dismiss people who are small, thin, or even older. I once saw a woman take down a man three times her size."

"How?" Thom asked.

"Leverage," Rin explained. "When the man was about to hit her, she grabbed his arm and used his momentum to flip him. While he was stunned, she hit him in his tender spots. It incapacitated him."

"Will you teach me that?" Thom asked.

"No," Rin replied. "I'll leave that to your weapons trainer in Eiren. I am going to teach you how to use a staff. It's a standard weapon for most healers."

"Will I have to learn knife or sword fighting?" Thom asked.

"Most certainly," Rin answered. "But, like all healers, you're probably a bit disturbed by the idea of hurting people."

"That's what I thought," Thom said. "It feels off, like it's not me."

"I understand."

"Yesterday, while writing in my journal," Thom went on, "I was thinking about what I would do if someone tried to hurt my family. Even if I learned how to use knives or a sword, would I be able to use them in defense?"

"I see," Rin said. "First, anything at hand can be a weapon. If you're outside, that might be a rock or a branch. If you're inside, a chair, pot, or even a dish can be effective."

"OK," Thom replied, a bit uncertainly.

"I'd suggest you keep writing about it," Rin suggested. "You might even chat with Sereh or Deu. By the way, how's that going?"

"Oh, I don't know. I talk to them or try to, but I haven't heard direct answers."

"Give it time," Rin said.

They'd been riding a few hours when Thom looked toward the sky and saw clouds gathering. Before they left this morning, the innkeeper said it was supposed to get colder and might even snow. He wondered if it would snow on his birthday in a few weeks. This would be his first birthday away from home. Mam would have made him her special gingerbread buns filled with lemon curd. And his family would sing him the birthday song.

Thom didn't think Rin knew about his birthday. He needed to forget about it. "Great," he muttered. "Now I'm sad, on top of being scared from the attack."

Chapter 18

The day after they left Lifford, Rin started Thom on defense training. He first taught him about balance, which, not surprisingly, began with grounding. That was followed by teaching him how to move smoothly as he twisted his body, lifted his arms and legs, and made fast 360-degree turns that left Thom dizzy.

One evening, while their dinner was heating on the fire, Thom spoke up after completing the exercise sequence for the fourth time. "I think I'm finally getting the hang of them. But I thought you were going to teach me self-defense. I almost feel like I'm dancing."

"Perfect analogy," Rin complimented him. "They are very similar to dance. A key to self-defense is both balance and movement. An attacker can come at you from any direction. You must be prepared and respond rather than react. Have you noticed that you no longer get dizzy when you spin now?"

"I didn't."

"And the movements train your muscles to handle changing positions often," Rin added. "They also help you learn to deepen your breath and stay relaxed while remaining centered. Did you realize your body-mind is the main player here rather than your brain-mind?"

"I didn't think about it," Thom replied.

"Exactly," Rin said. "You didn't think about it. When you began these exercises, your brain-mind tried to control the moves, causing you to trip up. After your brain-mind let go, your body-mind took charge, and you became balanced. When you defend yourself, your response must be automatic, without requiring thinking. Thinking takes too long, which could lead to injury or even death."

"Got it," Thom said. "It's almost like how you want me to automatically raise or lower shields based on what's happening."

"Correct, Thom," Rin replied. "You know, you are quite intelligent and quick-witted. I keep thinking you might not understand, given your age. I've worked with students five years older who didn't understand even after I explained a concept multiple times."

Thom blushed but remained silent.

"Tomorrow, we'll pass through a village where I know a woodwright who will make you a staff. All you've learned about movement will flow nicely into incorporating it into your self-defense training."

The next day, mid-afternoon, Rin and Thom tethered their horses to a hitching post outside the woodwright's business.

Walking inside, Rin called out, "Good day, Woodwright Alder!"

"I'm coming," Thom heard a male voice respond.

A middle-aged man, slender but muscular, with short red hair, walked through the doorway behind the counter. "Rin," the man called out. "I thought I recognized your voice. It's been a few years since I last saw you."

"I know, Haz," Rin replied. "It comes with the territory of being a healer. You can call me a roamin' healer."

"That sounds like the start of a song a bard might sing," Haz bantered. "Are you thinking of changing careers?"

"Not a chance," Rin replied, laughing. "Not with my voice."

"What brings you by?" Haz asked. "You didn't lose your staff, did you?"

"No. Over a week ago, my apprentice, Thom, and I were attacked by bandits," Rin explained. "We were able to get away, but I realized Thom needed to learn some self-defense now."

"Nice to meet you, Thom," Haz said. "Call me Haz. Sometimes your mentor forgets about introductions."

"Nice to meet you, Haz," Thom replied.

"Sorry," Rin uttered. "I can get quite single-minded at times."

"Where did the attack happen?" Haz asked.

"Outside of Lifford," Rin replied, providing the details.

"Can I presume you want me to create a staff for Thom?" Haz asked.

"Yes," Rin replied. "I've been training Thom in movement exercises for the last week. He's ready to start working with a staff."

"Hickory wood?" Haz asked Rin.

"Of course."

"As luck would have it, I have some lengths of that wood that would be perfect," he volunteered. "Thom, would you come closer? I want to size you up."

It felt weird to Thom to have someone scrutinizing him from head to toe.

"How old are you?" Haz asked.

"Almost nine," Thom replied. He hoped Rin would get the hint and ask him about his birthday.

"OK," Haz said. "I can have the staff ready first thing tomorrow morning."

"Perfect," Rin replied. "The usual cost?"

"Yes," Haz answered.

As they left Haz's shop, Rin told Thom, "We'll stay overnight at the inn down the road."

"OK," Thom replied, disappointed that Rin hadn't picked up on his hint.

After a quick breakfast, Rin and Thom rode back to the shop early the following day. Stepping inside, Thom saw a long wooden staff with metal bands around each end leaning against the counter.

"I knew you'd come early," Haz said, stepping through the back doorway. "Go ahead and pick it up, Thom," he instructed.

When Thom grasped the staff, he noticed it was almost two feet over his head. "Um... isn't this too long?"

"It is, and it isn't," Haz answered. "If you weren't a growing lad, you'd be right. When I examined you yesterday, and yes, I know it might have felt a bit creepy, I noticed your trousers were short. I suspect Rin's training and the food you're consuming is the cause of your growth."

"You always had a good eye, Haz," Rin commented. "Until you're taller, you'll have to stand on a rock when working with your staff."

"How does the staff feel, Thom?" Haz asked him.

"Good," he replied.

"Sense into it, Thom, with your earth sense," Rin suggested.

Thom did as Rin instructed. He felt the staff possessed an inner strength and was oddly majestic. Sensing into it a bit longer, with his mind's-eye, he saw a very tall tree. There were nuts on the ground beneath it. In the near distance, he saw dark clouds and flashes of lightning.

"What are you getting?" Rin asked.

Connecting more strongly with the staff, he said, "The wood is strong, and it's from a deeply rooted tree. I bet digging up the roots after lightning hit it was hard."

"In fact, it was," Haz uttered in amazement. "How did you know?"

"Um," Thom replied. "I sort of saw it."

Rin smiled. "Another aspect of your earth-sensing gift is coming through, Thom."

"Earth sensing," Haz repeated. "I've heard about that but didn't know that included seeing a tree's history. He's young."

"Thom is a unique lad," Rin admitted. "We'd best get going."

"Let me first attach a staff holder to your saddle, Thom," Haz said.

While Haz did so, Thom tried to figure out how he had seen the tree.

Soon after, Thom and Rin rode out of the village and continued west.

"Sometime tomorrow," Rin went on, "we'll take a road that goes more north. It will end at the port city of Bethemel, where we'll catch a ship to Eiren."

"Oh. I think my aunt, my father's sister, lives there. I've never met her, though," Thom commented.

"Unfortunately, you won't this time either, Thom," Rin informed him. "No one in your family can know where you're headed."

Chapter 19

Vern and Finn were riding hard to the town of Lifford. A few days before, Mitch had sent them a message that the healer was on his way to Eiren. Lifford was on the main road west and a logical stopping place.

"When we get to town, I'll do the talkin'," Vern said. "You don' talk good. I want folks to believe I knows the healer."

"Who ya foolin'," Finn replied. "Ya don' talk like upper folks."

"Yeah, but I can fake it," Vern stated. "We're comin' to a crik. Let's wash and put on our good tunics."

Riding into town, they stopped at the local trading post.

"Stand straight," Vern demanded before entering the post. "And look honest."

"How ya look honest?" Finn asked.

"Don' touch nuthin or say nuthin."

Pushing open the door, a chime rang.

"Can I help you, gentlemen?" the owner asked.

Vern looked at Finn and nodded. "Yes, sir. We're trying to reach Healer Rinbalden. There's a family emergency. Sorry, we aren't very presentable. We've been riding fast on the road."

"An emergency. That's not good. Unfortunately, the healer and his apprentice lad left here over a week ago."

Turg! Vern cursed to himself. *How did we miss im again? Mitch is gonna be angry. And he said nuthin about a kid.* Speaking to the owner, he said. "It's important we get the news to him."

"I believe they're heading to Bethemel," the owner offered. "There's a cattle trail you can take that would help you catch up with them. But it's rough riding, and no traveler shelters or inns along the way."

"Where's this trail?" Vern asked.

"About a mile west of town," the owner explained.

"Thanks," Vern asked. "Do you have message people coming through youse... your store?" Vern asked.

"Yes, the courier is coming through tomorrow," he answered.

"Thanks," Vern replied. "Do you have a quill, ink, and paper?"

"Certainly," he replied. "It will cost you a few coins for that and the courier."

Vern and Finn stepped over to a nearby table with the supplies.

"Wutcha' thinkin' Vern?" Finn asked. "And whas' with da kid? Mitch said nuthin about a kid."

"I knows," Vern replied. "I have an idear. We ride fast to Bethemel and beat em there. Then, we kidnap the kid and demand money from the healer. It won' look no good if he cain't protect his apprentice. I'll write Mitch and let im know. I'll also tell im we need more money since we're dealin' with two."

"Oh, thets good, Vern," Finn agreed.

"Git some travel food while I writes the note," Vern said. "We'll be eatin' on the road."

"It's gettin' colder," Finn commented. "Look, I kin see my breath."

"Yeah, well, we're headin' inta winter," Vern replied. "Let's go. We still gots a few hours of light."

Chapter 20

As they continued their journey to Eiren, Thom's training now included staff work. Rin divided his time equally between his gifts and the staff. For Thom's gifts, Rin created challenges to help him refine his grounding technique, fortify his shields, and heighten his sensitivity in reading auras. With the addition of the staff, Rin first had him practicing the movement exercises. After several days, he taught him defensive strategies.

Thom's previous aches from horse riding were replaced by those gained from his imperfect defenses. Added to them were bruises. Rin had explained that they'd become his teachers, reminding him of where and when he needed to better defend himself. After each lesson, Thom tried to believe that as he applied the salve to his body, grimacing each time he hit a tender spot.

The weather had gotten much colder recently. Thom was now wearing his coat on top of his jumper. He added a layer of leaves beneath his bedroll and an extra blanket. For the last few days, he'd been trying to use his earth sense to determine whether it would snow. Maybe his gift wasn't strong enough. To be on the safe side, when he bedded down for the night, he pulled the blanket over his head.

A full week had passed, when, in the middle of the night, the snow finally descended. Despite Rin's careful choice of a camp nestled amidst trees, they awoke to discover a thin layer of snow covering them. "Oh, turg! I shlould have known," Rin grumbled. "Shloud? There I go, adding Ls again. I hope Thom didn't hear. I don't like sounding foolish."

Thom busied himself with putting his bedroll away. It was still kind of a relief when Rin did that.

"Thom," Rin said, interrupting his thoughts. "From now on, we'll stay at inns or traveler shelters. The shelters are one-room lodgings free to use when it rains or snows."

"Thank goodness," Thom replied happily.

"I didn't tell you before," Rin said, "but I have a slight gift for weather sensing. Unfortunately, it's not always consistent and timely."

"That's neat," Thom replied. "Not the part about your gift not being timely, though."

"The good news is this storm passed and was a minor one. But I sense there's a larger one close on its heels, arriving late this afternoon," Rin explained. "That means we'll have to ride fast."

Shortly before dinner, they reached the Inn at Dunigal, feeling exhausted and damp. Handing their horses to the stablehands, they rushed inside, seeking refuge. Checking with the innkeeper, they learned only one large room was available, and it had three beds. Faced with limited options, they reluctantly accepted it, albeit at a higher cost than they usually paid. After dropping their bags in their room, they returned downstairs to get a bite to eat.

"Why don't you get a table by the fire and warm up," Rin told him. "I'll order some food."

Thom was rubbing his hands together near the fire when a gust of wind blew against the shutters. Then came a loud noise, as if a giant from one of his stories was hammering her fists against the door. Startling him, he cried out, "What was that?" Glancing around, he saw the inn door slam open as the stable boy entered. Not having much success closing it, Rin and the innkeeper went to his aid.

"There be huge hailstones, bigger'n my fist," the boy exclaimed. "One missed my head by inches!" indicating with his fingers.

"How are the horses and animals?" the innkeeper asked.

"All safe an' warm with plenty of feed," he answered.

"Good. Go to the kitchen and get yourself warmed up."

Thom stayed sitting by the fire, waiting for Rin to join him. After what seemed like a long time, he did.

"OK," Rin said. "Our dinner should come shortly. We'll likely be here for a few days until the storm passes and the roads are clear."

Ah, Thom thought to himself. That's why it took Rin a while. He was asking about the storm.

"Would you mind changing seats?" Rin asked.

"Oh, no, sorry," Thom replied, moving to another chair. "Your hands are red. Was that from helping the stable boy?"

"It was," Rin replied, sighing as he rubbed his hands before the fire.

Shortly after, a server placed two steaming bowls of soup on the table, brimming with vegetables and meat. Following closely behind, the stable boy arrived with a fragrant, just-out-of-the-oven loaf of bread.

As they ate, Thom noticed fewer hailstones hitting the outside wall. But the wind had increased. He could tell that snow was falling more heavily and was very glad they were not on the road.

They had finished their soup and bread when the server returned with hot cider for Thom and mulled wine for Rin. She also brought two pasties with an apple and raisin filling.

While Thom ate his pastie, Rin remarked, "While we're here, we'll work more on your shields. It's a perfect opportunity to teach you how to make them more malleable and give them texture. I'll tell you more tomorrow."

"Umph k," Thom said before swallowing the last bit of pastie.

"Since we rode hard today, why don't we both turn in," Rin said. "I'm sure you're exhausted. I know I am."

As tired as he was, Thom expected to fall asleep quickly but couldn't. This is crazy. Why was he still awake? Trying to calm himself, Thom recalled Rin had said meditating could relax you. Eventually, it worked, and he drifted off to sleep.

When Thom awoke the next morning, he could still hear the wind blowing outside. It didn't sound as intense. Maybe the worst was over. Looking over at the next bed, Rin was still asleep, with his mouth agape as it often was when he was sleeping. Luxuriating in the warmth of the bed, he stretched. He was grateful they weren't camping, especially since it was Nuvima. Then he remembered what day it was. It's Nuvima 15. He was nine years old today, and no one knew. "Happy birthday to me," he whispered dispiritedly. "Yeah, me. I should've said something to Rin."

Looking back toward Rin, he realized there was no reason to get up. He supposed he could greet Deu and Sereh and tell them it was his birthday. Maybe he'd hear from them this time. He patiently waited but heard nothing. The next thing he knew, someone was shaking him.

"Thom, it's time to get up if you want breakfast," Rin said, shaking him again.

"Huh," Thom replied groggily.

"Breakfast. Eat," Rin emphasized.

"Oh," Thom said. "I was awake earlier. I guess I fell back to sleep."

"We both must have been exhausted," Rin said. "We'd better get a move on."

Thom grabbed his trousers from the hook on the wall and pulled them on. Slipping on his shoes, he followed Rin down to the tavern.

The server saw them when they came in and waved them down. "The innkeeper suspected you might sleep late after he heard how long you were on the road yesterday," she said. "He had the cook set aside some porridge, bread, and butter for you. Have a seat, and I'll bring it out."

"Thank you, lass," Rin replied.

They were able to settle again by the fire because the room had few patrons. Thom wondered whether the others were in their rooms or had left.

Soon after, the server brought their breakfast. "Did you want hot cider, tea, or coffee?" she asked.

"Tea," they both said.

After finishing his meal, Thom sipped his tea, thinking. If he was going to say anything about his birthday, he'd better do it now. "Hey Rin," he said nervously, "Guess what? Today's my birthday."

"Today?" Rin replied. "Well, Happy Birthday! You're what, nine?"

"Yeah," Thom said.

"We need to celebrate, but our options are a bit limited. I'll come up with something we can do. I hope that's today. What would your family do for your birthday?"

"When my friend Davi lived nearby, he'd come over, and we'd play games. Mam would prepare a big meal and serve her special birthday buns for dessert. And my whole family would sing me the birthday song."

"You're missing them, I'd imagine," Rin said.

"Uh, huh," Thom said, his eyes downcast.

"I'm sorry," Rin said sympathetically. "Maybe we can figure out something to lift your spirits. Why don't you head up to our room? I want you to work more on your shields.

Also, would you push the furniture around to create space on the floor? I'll be up in shortly. I want to check with the innkeeper about the weather first."

Thom nodded, trudging up the stairs.

Poor lad, Rin said to himself as he headed to the kitchen. He wanted to check with the cook about the special meal he arranged the night before. He hoped she could make the gingerbread buns with lemon curd. When he finally climbed the stairs, he was happy everything was set. Last night, the cook wasn't sure whether she had preserved lemons to make the curd. Thankfully, she did. When he reached their room, he saw an open space in its center. Thom had also placed two pillows on the floor, on which they could sit since they didn't have chairs.

"Will this work?" Thom asked.

"Perfect," Rin answered.

For the next 2 ½ hours, they worked. Rin first checked the strength of Thom's shields. He was amazed when he discovered Thom's fifth shield, which he learned Thom had inadvertently created while playing with his aura.

"Your new shield is quite strong," Rin said. "I'm impressed."

"Thanks," Thom replied, blushing.

"Have you defined its purpose yet?" Rin asked.

"No," Thom said. "Maybe something about auras, but I'm not sure."

"No rush," Rin said. "You can take your time to decide. I've heard some healers have a shield with a changing purpose," Rin said. "Maybe you can set that as your intention."

Thom was fascinated when Rin showed him how to apply degrees of roughness, slipperiness, and even stickiness to his shields. He explained that adding texture could come in handy when a person with another gift, like Samiltun, tried to manipulate him.

"It's about time for noon supper," Rin said. "How do you feel? Are you tired?"

"No," he replied with amazement.

"That's because you're staying grounded, and the earth is feeding you energy," Rin explained. "Again, good job! Let's head down to supper."

Rin gestured for Thom to lead the way down the stairs. As Thom stepped into the tavern, he saw a large crowd and nearly jumped when they all yelled, "Surprise," followed by "Happy Birthday, Thom!" His jaw dropped, and his eyes filled with tears. Turning to Rin, he said, "You knew."

"Of course, you silly boy."

Breaking down into sobs, Thom tried to speak. "I didn't think... I don't..." unable to complete his sentence.

Rin enfolded Thom in his arms, letting him cry. He's still a boy, he reminded himself, despite being advanced for his age.

When Thom had stepped back from the embrace and wiped his eyes, Rin gestured to the server, who directed them to what had, by default, become their table. Someone had strung letters on the wall above it that spelled out Happy Birthday, Thom!

Thom started crying again, turning red out of embarrassment.

"It's OK, Thom," Rin replied.

Soon after, the server brought their meal: cooked chicken smothered in a cream sauce, herbed rice, and roasted parsnips.

Thom was all smiles as he enjoyed the meal. Unlike his brothers and sisters, he liked parsnips. After indulging in a second helping, Thom leaned back from his empty plate. It was almost as good as Mam's.

After the servers cleared their plates and those at the other tables, one returned with a metal tray bearing desserts.

As she approached, Thom's eyes widened. "Are those gingerbread buns?" he exclaimed, glancing at Rin for confirmation.

"Yes, they are," the server answered, "with lemon curd filling."

"But those are my special birthday buns Mam always makes," he said, tearing up again.

"I know, Thom," Rin replied. "Your mother made me promise you'd have them on your birthday."

"She did?" Thom said. "It's almost like my family is here too."

Rin nodded and began the birthday song, to which everyone joined in enthusiastically.

When the server set down the tray before him, Thom counted nine buns, one for each of his years.

Looking up, he saw the cook, who he learned was the innkeeper's wife. She'd come out of the kitchen and stood nearby with her husband. "Rin explained you had to leave home because a dangerous man was after you. We all agreed we'd try to make your birthday special." Speaking more loudly, she said. "There wasn't enough lemon to make buns for everyone. The rest of you will have apple crumble for dessert."

"I can share," Thom offered.

"If you want," Rin said.

While they were eating, Thom asked Rin, "Did you tell them everything about why we left?"

"Oh, no," Rin assured him. "Only enough that they'd be willing to help with this little party."

In the end, Thom ate two of the buns, gave one to the stable boy, who, it turns out, was the son of the innkeeper and cook, and cut up the remaining to allow everyone to have a taste. When he'd finished his second bun, Rin pulled out two packages from underneath the table.

"Are these...?" Thom asked.

"Gifts," Rin said. "Yes."

The first Thom opened was a pair of new trousers.

"These should fit you for a little while at least," Rin grinned. "At least I hope they will."

"Thank you, Rin," Thom said. Opening the second package, he discovered a book called *The Adventures of Tam*

Silluwin. On the cover, he saw a teenage boy standing at the bow of a ship next to another man who looked to be the captain. "Oh, I love adventures. Thank you, Rin! How did you know?"

"It's not from me, Thom," Rin answered. "It's from your parents. They asked me to give it to you on your birthday."

When the floodgates opened again, Rin handed Thom his handkerchief.

As they were getting ready to go upstairs, Thom thanked everyone and hugged the cook, the innkeeper, and the stable boy.

Once they reached their room, Rin said to Thom, "No more training today. Why don't you spend the afternoon enjoying your book?"

"Thanks, Rin. I don't need to be told twice," Thom replied, giving him a long hug. "I can't ever thank you enough."

"You just did, Thom," Rin answered. "You just did."

The following morning dawned clear. Rin and Thom headed downstairs to breakfast, learning the roads were still unpassable. The innkeeper explained that work crews were clearing the major thoroughfares. He also mentioned that the sun might melt the snow on the lesser roads if the day remained bright.

As they finished eating, Rin turned to Thom and asked, "What if we offer to help?"

Thom readily agreed. Rin was added to the snow removal crew. Thom first helped the stable boy with the horses. He then helped the kitchen crew make sandwiches and took them, along with muffins, biscuits, and hot coffee, to those shoveling snow.

By noon supper, the worst of the snow was removed. Since Thom had his afternoon free again, he decided to write about his birthday celebration in his journal. Afterward, he returned to reading his new book about Tam and his travels with his father, the captain.

The afternoon and evening went by quickly. Before blowing out the candle by the bed, Rin told Thom, "If it's warmer tomorrow and the skies are clear, we'll get on the road after breakfast."

Chapter 21

Rin and Thom had been traveling for about two weeks since they left Dunigal. Most nights, they stayed in traveler shelters. Tonight's boasted a fireplace, a cupboard with basic food supplies, and two trough-like boxes for their bedrolls. There was also a place in the back for the horses.

They had finished breakfast, and Thom had packed away the pot from the morning porridge when he asked, "Should I bring more wood inside for the next visitors? There was a large pile of it."

"Good idea," Rin replied. "The nearest town is responsible for the shelter's upkeep, but bringing in more wood would be a kind gesture."

After completing the task, Thom attached his saddlebags to Brule.

"Are you ready to leave?" Rin asked.

"Yep."

Now that the roads were clear again, they moved at a brisk pace. Three hours into their ride, Rin suggested they stop. "The temperature is a bit warmer today," he said. "I want you to run through the staff routines first, followed by a little sparring with me."

After forty-five minutes, Rin said, "Let's stop. You're certainly improving. But I'm concerned you're holding back. Are you afraid you might hurt me?"

"Yeah," Thom admitted.

"I know I'm older, but I'm in relatively good shape. When we get to Eiren, I'll find someone to work with you who can give you a good workout."

"I'm not excited about that," Thom groaned. "I know I need it, but I'm sure that will come with more aches and bruises."

"Indeed," Rin replied. "Let's get a quick bite while you cool down. Then we'll be on our way. We still have a few pasties left over from our stay at the inn two nights ago."

Rin and Thom had ridden for two hours when Thom heard what sounded like an animal whimpering. He looked over to see if Rin had heard it, too, but he didn't seem to.

They rode for a while longer. By then, the whimpering had become much louder, pulling Thom toward it.

"Rin, I feel like something's calling out to me. You don't hear it, do you?

"No."

"I have to find it. It's hurting a lot and has me twisted up inside."

"Is your fourth shield raised, Thom?" Rin asked.

"Yes."

That's strange, Rin thought. That's his empathy shield. He shouldn't be absorbing another's emotions. Aloud, he said, "We'll explore why your shield doesn't block the pain after we've determined what's causing this. Let's hold here. I want to see if I can sense something untoward."

Thom waited, but it ached not to keep moving.

"OK," Rin announced, "I don't detect any wrongness, but we'll go cautiously. I don't want to ride into another bad situation."

Thom was already partway down the road before Rin finished speaking. A few miles further along, he saw a trail. He pointed to it and said, "It's somewhere down there."

"OK," Rin replied, "Be careful. There might be tree roots or rocks that could lame Brule."

Making his way up the trail, Thom detected the sound of livestock. Emerging from the woods, he came upon the back of a stone cottage with a thatched roof and green shutters. A large red barn was next to it. By this time, the whimpering was almost excruciating for him.

Rin trotted next to Thom and said, "Didn't you hear me tell you to slow down?"

"It's tormented. I need to help," Thom spoke through gritted teeth. "And my pain's worse."

"OK. Let's ride around to the front door." Once there, they dismounted, and Rin called out, "Hello, the cottage."

There was no response.

"Hello, the cottage!" he repeated.

The door opened, and a man with short dark brown hair and a muscular build stood in the doorway. He was in his mid-20s.

"We can't help you if you've come for food or money," he stated.

"We're not here for either," Rin replied. "I'm a healer. My name's Rin. And this is my apprentice, Thom. Is everyone OK?"

The man looked at them suspiciously. "Your apprentice seems to be in some pain," he said, pointing to Thom, bent over and holding his stomach.

"Please!" Thom pleaded, "I need to help. Who's sick?"

The man's face relaxed. "Aye, there is someone sick. My son. I don't know what you can do. The other healers couldn't help."

While the man was talking, Thom pushed past him. Crossing the threshold into the main room, he heard moans coming from the door on the right. Following the source of the moans, Thom entered the room to find a young woman hunched over a bed, her brow furrowed with worry as she tended to a tow-headed toddler. The woman, her light brown hair hastily braided down her back, loose strands framing her worried face, struggled to comfort her child. With a cloth in hand, she gently dabbed at the child's forehead, her expression mirroring his pain. As the toddler continued to writhe in the grip of excruciating agony, tossing and turning on the bed, Thom's heart dropped. Here was the source of his own agony. Somehow, he'd been sharing in the child's suffering.

"I'm sorry, baby," the woman whispered. "I know it hurts. I'll dampen this cloth with cold water."

Standing, the woman turned and saw Thom. "Who?" she said, confused. The man who answered the door entered the room, followed by Rin.

"They're healers," he said.

"Would you let Thom touch your son?" Rin asked.

Looking confused that a child would be tending her toddler, she nodded.

Thom knelt next to the bed. He placed one hand on the crown of the toddler's head and his other over his heart. Almost immediately, the toddler settled. Thom heard his mother gasp.

"That's the first time our boy has quieted down all day," the father told Rin.

Turning to the toddler's mother, Thom asked, "Would you go to the bottom of the bed and put your hands on his feet?"

She complied.

Sensing into the boy, Thom felt something wasn't right. The boy's connection to his body was fragile. He lowered all his shields and saw twisting and jagged energy strands. What the turg is that?

Focusing on the strands, he realized he was looking at two spirits fighting for control: one was the boy's, and the other belonged to a girl. Instinctively, Thom knew the girl was the boy's twin who hadn't survived birth. Somehow, she attached herself to her brother.

Without knowing what else to do, Thom forced his abilities open further to help him connect with both spirits, especially that of the girl. When he did, Thom was shocked to see pulses of green and purple burst from his hands to enfold her. How did he do that? Watching as the pulses smoothed out the strands, he mind-spoke to the girl, *It's OK, little one. I'm here. You're angry and scared and don't understand what's going on. Your time has passed. Return to the divine realm and be comforted.*

Thom froze a moment. How did he know what to say?

Providing more energy to supplement the pulses, Thom noticed the spirit strands begin unwinding. He realized very quickly that he was exhausting himself. But Thom couldn't and wouldn't stop. From nowhere that he could determine, he felt an energy surge that enabled him to continue. He kept encouraging the girl to let go until her spirit eventually unwound from her brother's and faded.

Knowing Mother Earth could strengthen a person's grounding, Thom channeled her energy toward the boy's spirit and body, uniting them further. Gradually, the boy's breathing became more regular and relaxed. Opening his eyes, Thom saw the boy had fallen into an exhausted sleep. He was pretty depleted himself. "Depleted?" What made him think of that word? He was plain tired.

Rin looked on, smiled, and nodded. He couldn't tell what Thom had done, but he'd ask him when they had time to themselves. Seeing Thom slump against the bed, he turned to the parents, "Your toddler's fine now." Looking at the man, he said, "Would you help me put Thom in the bed next to your boy? Thom's worn himself out. I'd like to keep them together."

Good job, Thom!

Huh, Thom mumbled.

Thom opened his eyes and saw a magenta light. *Where am I?* He seemed to be in a larger version of his alcove at home. *But I can't be home.*

No, *you're not home, Thom,* a voice from the light assured him. The light coalesced into the shape of a human male. *Since you've been traveling, I wanted to appear somewhere familiar,* the being responded. *My name is Archangel Metatron, by the way.*

You're an archangel? Thom said with surprise. *Wait, have we met before?*

We *have before you left your home,* Metatron replied.

I don't think I've ever heard the elders speak of you, Thom continued. *They told us stories about Archangel Michael and Archangel Gabriel, but not you.*

I'm mentioned in a few places, but not in your holy book, Metatron answered. *But that's not important. How are you?*

Am I dead? he asked nervously.

No, no. You are very much alive. In fact, you're sleeping next to the toddler you healed. You did a great job. Your spirit is visiting me in the divine realm like you did when a few of us last visited you.

Sereh was there, wasn't she? And two others? Thom asked.

Yes, he replied. *We also know you've been talking to Sereh and Deu lately.*

They're really listening? Thom asked. *Why don't they answer?*

They have, but not always in ways you expect. By the way, a few of us here, myself included, helped ensure the bandits didn't see Rin pour the valerian extract into their food.

You did? Thom replied. *Thank you. That was scary.*

I know, Metatron answered. *We're pleased Rin is teaching you self-defense. Back to the healing. You did an amazing and dangerous thing, given that you are mostly untrained. You saved a life but almost lost yours.*

What?

Yes. You weren't conscious of what you were doing. Archangel Raphael and I reinforced your spirit a few times and sent healing pulses to the girl.

Th... Thank you, Thom replied, a bit stunned. *I didn't realize.*

We know. That's why training is essential.

What happened to the girl twin? Thom asked.

She's here in the divine realm and is being looked after by her grandparents.

Good, he said, relieved. *And the toddler is OK, too?*

Yes, he'll recover, Metatron replied. *You have a powerful gift—of a type and strength that hasn't been seen in your time.*

Is this the gift Rin can't identify?

Yes, Metatron replied. *Samiltun's probe triggered its emergence, and your healing of the toddler fully activated it.*

So, it was a good thing Rin took me away.

Yes, it was, Metatron agreed. *The thing is that while Healer Rinbalden can teach you about your physical healing gift, he won't be able to teach you about this extraordinary gift.*

Who will teach me? Thom asked.

A variety of people. Be assured you'll meet them at the appropriate time.

Will I ever see my family again?

Yes, but you'll be away for a time, Metatron replied. *Use your time well. Try not to figure it all out. Your brain-mind is wonderful, but you also need to trust your spirit-mind and your body-mind. They each have their own wisdom.*

I've heard about my body-mind and my brain-mind, Thom said. What's the spirit-mind?

More or less your intuition, Metatron answered. *It comes from your divine spirit. By the way, your healing also created a channel connecting you to this realm and, more directly, to the wisdom of its dwellers.*

More wisdom, Thom said, a little uncertainly.

I want to tell you a few more things, Metatron stated. *Be careful not to push yourself. You may get frustrated by being unable to put things together and even feel hopeless.*

All things will come in time. Above all, listen to your inner knowing and be wary of anything that doesn't resonate.

Thom sat there quietly, trying to absorb it all.

I know this is a good amount of information, Metatron said.

Thom nodded.

Final word: trust. Trust we're always here with you, even if you don't feel it or don't seem to get a response. As usual, you won't consciously remember what I've said. But some of it will surface when you need it.

OK, Thom replied.

Good. You'll soon be waking. Be aware that you'll need time to recover. Rin's guides will tell him to travel slower. Remember, you are unconditionally loved.

Thank you, he replied.

Rel walked back and forth in his dwelling, waiting to hear from Metatron about Thom. He had transformed into a male form earlier because it allowed him to pace, hoping it would relax him. He knew his incarnated self, Thom had almost died, and Metatron was visiting with him. Although he had wanted to be present for the meeting, it was too soon in Thom's spiritual development to learn about his higher self. He finally became calmer and sat down when he felt a pulse from Metatron and, soon after, materialized.

"How is he?" Rel asked, jumping up before Metatron had a chance to say anything.

"He's fine," Metatron assured him. "Thanks for keeping your distance while I met with him."

"It was difficult, given what happened to Celes," Rel admitted. "I had to keep singing "he's OK. Thom's OK. Metatron knows what he's doing," repeatedly to the tune, *I saw Three Stars on Solstice Day*. It mostly worked."

"Good," Metatron approved. "Like I said, Thom's OK now. But your concerns were valid."

"Thanks," Rel replied.

"He'll need time to regain his strength and heal the gift channels he opened," Metatron explained. "They're raw." Metatron went on to tell Rel everything else that happened.

"His open channels also give Thom greater access to our wisdom here," Rel commented. "That includes me, I presume."

"Of course," Metatron confirmed. "Go ahead and tune back into him."

"Wow," Rel commented. "He now has a stronger connection to me than Celes had before she died."

"That's interesting," Metatron said. "I look forward to seeing if these new channels impact how quickly he learns, including the development of his major gift."

"I agree," Rel concurred.

"I'd better get back to the other light-worker trainees," Metatron explained. "Will I see you at charades?"

"I don't know," Rel replied. "They're not really my thing."

"Oh, come on," Metatron encouraged, "God joined us in our last game, and you would have fallen down laughing at how awful God is at it."

"That would be fun to watch."

"Good. And it will take your mind off Thom for a bit."

After Metatron departed, Rel sat back down, taking a deep breath. "To use your curse word, Thom, you scared the turg out of me."

Chapter 22

Thom felt a puff of air blowing on his left cheek. As he turned in that direction, he saw the brown eyes of the toddler staring at him. He directed his senses toward him and noted the boy's aura looked good.

"Who you?" the boy asked.

"I'm Thom. What's your name?"

"Rindo. Where, Mama?"

Thom heard distant voices. "I think she's in the other room. Do you feel OK?"

"Hungry," Rindo replied.

That's a good sign, Thom thought. "OK. I'll take you to your Mama." Sitting up, he noticed that he wasn't wearing shoes. Seeing them on the floor, he slipped them on and stood. Turning back to the boy, Rindo had raised his arms toward him. He scooped him up, set him on his hip, and headed towards the door.

Stepping into the other room, Thom saw Rin and Rindo's father and mother sitting by the hearth at the room's far end. The woman looked over.

"Mama, hungry," Rindo demanded.

The woman stood up and rushed over to them, taking Rindo in her arms and kissing him all over.

"Mama, hungry!" Rindo insisted, squirming in her arms.

"Yes, yes. I'll get you some bread. How is he?"

"Good. Rindo's hungry, like he said," Thom answered, seeing great relief wash over her face.

"Winslaw hasn't wanted to eat for a few days." She went to a basket on the table, picked up a slice of bread, and handed it to him.

"Oh. His name's Winslaw," Thom replied. "He told me it was Rindo."

"Yes, that's how he pronounces it," the mother replied. "I'm sure it will become his nickname. You're Thom?"

"Yes."

"I'm Lida Barrelson, and this is my husband, Storen," she said. "The infant in the basket is Winslaw's brother, Benno. We've been talking to your teacher, Rin."

"How long was I asleep?" he asked.

"About three hours. Are you hungry?" Rin asked.

Thom nodded.

"Let me get you something to eat," Lida offered.

"How are you feeling, Thom?" Rin asked.

"OK, I think. I feel like I've run a long way. And I sort of ache all over, even inside. It's like I've stretched muscles I've never used before."

"Let me look at your aura," Rin said, focusing on him. "Physically, you're tired, and your colors are dimmed. Your blue and violet are fluctuating."

"Oh," Thom replied. "I didn't realize."

Lida handed Thom a large bowl of stew and a chunk of bread.

"It's mostly vegetables, but it should be filling," she explained.

"Thank you," he replied.

"Go ahead and eat," Rin said. "That will help replenish your energy. I ate earlier with Lida and Storen."

As Thom ate, he realized he was ravenous, quickly finishing the food.

"Do you want more?" Lida asked.

"Maybe a little."

"Of course," Lida said, refilling his bowl and setting it before him. "I always make a big pot as the boys eat a lot."

This time, Thom took his time, savoring each mouthful.

"More?" she asked.

"No, thank you. That was good."

"Here's some cider," Storen said, extending a mug to him.

"Thanks."

"Can you tell us what you did?" Lida asked. "We were frantic. Winslaw had these spells before, and herbs seemed to settle him. But nothing the healers did prevented them. This morning, the herbs didn't help at all. We thought he'd die."

Thom looked at Winslaw, who had fallen asleep against Lida's chest. How should he explain this? he wondered. Pausing, his intuition told him to be direct. "Did Winslaw have a twin?"

Lida and Storen looked at Thom in shock.

"Yes," Storen replied. "When Lida was pregnant, she was expecting two. But there was a problem while she was giving birth, and our little girl died."

Thom looked at Lida, whose head was bowed. "I'm sorry," he said.

Storen noticed and turned to her. "It wasn't your fault, luv," he said. "You were very careful and always followed the midwife's advice. There was nothing we could do."

Lida remained silent.

"How did you know Winslaw had a twin?" Storen asked.

"You see.... I felt your daughter's spirit along with your son's. Somehow, her spirit didn't return to Deu when she died. As Winslaw was being born, her spirit sort of twisted around Winslaw's."

Lida and Storen looked at him dumbfounded.

"What I felt from your daughter was confusion," Thom continued. "She didn't understand she had died. She battled Winslaw to survive. I told her she had passed, to let go, and be at peace."

"I never heard of anything like that before," Storen stated.

"Are they both OK?" Lida asked.

"Yes," Thom answered. "Your daughter is at peace. And your son has room to really live."

"How did you know to do this?" Storen asked.

"I didn't," Thom replied, still amazed at what happened. "I followed my intuition and responded to what I felt and sensed."

"Lida, Storen," Rin interjected, "Thom is new to his gifts. He still has much to learn about them."

"You are god-touched," Lida stated.

Thom furrowed his brow as a brief memory of meeting a divine being flitted across his thoughts. Shaking his head, he replied, "I don't know."

"We can't thank you enough for what you've done," Lida said.

"I agree," Storen added. "It's late. We should all get to bed. You're welcome to stay the night."

"Thank you," Rin replied. "We're going to get on the road very early."

"We understand. Can we give you some food for your journey?" Lida asked. "I have a few vegetable pasties and can also give you cinnamon-apple pasties."

"That would be much appreciated," Rin replied.

"I'll get them together while you set up your bedrolls," Lida said.

"You sleep closer to the hearth, Thom," Rin suggested. "The warmth will do you good."

As Lida placed a cloth bag on the table, she said, "Thanks again. Please let us know if there's anything we can do for you."

"You're welcome," Thom replied, finishing unrolling his bedding.

"Good night," Lida said, carrying Winslaw into the other room.

Storen followed with the infant. "Goodnight," he said before closing the curtains between the rooms.

Thom slipped into his bedroll, turned his back to the fire, and closed his eyes.

What seemed like a short time later, Thom felt a poke in his back.

"Thom, we need to get on the road," Rin insisted, shaking Thom's shoulder.

"OK. I'm awake," he mumbled. "What time is it?"

"It's before dawn."

Thom nodded and scooted out of his bedroll. After living on the road for over a month, he swiftly packed his belongings. He grabbed the bag of pasties and followed Rin out to their horses.

Once on the road, Rin spoke up. "Go ahead and get out those pasties, Thom. Let's eat them while they're fresh. I know you're hungry already."

Thom smiled. He opened the bag, handed one of the vegetable pasties to Rin, and took one himself. Biting into it, he smiled. It was full of carrots, potatoes, and root vegetables. It also had a slight spiciness. His mother didn't make hers with the same spices, but he enjoyed it immensely. He consumed his second vegetable pastie and was about to grab the sweet pastie when Rin spoke.

"Um… Thom." Rin interrupted. "Would you hand me my second vegetable pastie?"

"Sorry, Rin. Let me take out my cinnamon-apple pastie and I'll hand you the bag." When Thom took a bite out of the pastie, he was in heaven. The apples weren't mushy, and the sweet filling was thick and included raisins.

They both finished their pasties in silence and continued down the road. It was still dark, but the moon gave them a little light, augmented by the snow that reflected it on either side of the road.

"When it gets lighter," Rin spoke, "I'd like to increase our pace."

Thom grunted in agreement. *Rin's worried about something,* he thought.

"We'll wait until noon supper to discuss the healing," Rin explained. "While we ride, reflect on what you sensed, felt, and thought, starting when you first became aware of Rindo's situation."

"OK," Thom replied.

After riding hard for hours, Rin called out, "We're approaching an area ahead where we can stop. Let's build a fire. I want us to be comfortable while we talk."

After they'd eaten their supper, Rin handed Thom an apple. "Lida also gave us two of these."

Thom gratefully accepted it. Their travel food was filling, but it was a far cry from this morning's pasties. After eating, he still felt tired. He wasn't looking forward to their afternoon ride. But he'd make the best of it.

"Would you take me through what you experienced yesterday?" Rin asked. "Visualize yourself on the road when you first detected Rindo's predicament."

"I hear whimpering, like an animal's hurt," Thom told him.

"When you say you hear, was it truly a sound?" Rin asked.

"Maybe it was vibrations that were sound-like," Thom said. "I'm not making any sense, am I?"

"It's OK," Rin said. "Where in your body do you notice the vibrations? Let your body-mind help you."

Thom shook his head in frustration. "My brain-mind wants to help figure it out."

"I understand," Rin remarked. "Our brain-mind is used to being in control. Close your eyes, take a deep breath, and hold it for four counts."

Thom did as he was instructed.

"Now, release it."

"Good," Rin said, hearing Thom's outrush of air. "I'm going to give your brain-mind a simple task. Do you hear the creek nearby?"

"Yes."

"Turn your mind to that sound. Let any thoughts flow like the water moving over the rocks and pebbles in the creek bed."

"OK," he replied a little skeptically.

"I know this sounds strange," Rin assured him. "But lightly attend to that."

"Alright," Thom replied, tuning to the sound. "My brain-mind is quieter now."

"Good," Rin complimented. "Next, ask your body-mind where the vibrations are centered."

Thom did as Rin asked, but it was difficult. *Bring in your spirit-mind,* a voice said into his head. Where had he heard spirit-mind before? "It's still difficult," he said to Rin, "But I'll ask my spirit-mind to help."

"Your what?" Rin asked.

"It's also called intuition, someone told me," Thom explained. "About the vibrations, I'm feeling them below my stomach."

"OK," Rin said. "That's your root chakra, which makes sense as it's associated with survival. I'll tell you about chakras at another time. Let's skip to when you identify the two spirits in Rindo."

"I saw them battling over control of his body. I'm afraid both would die if I didn't do something."

"Keep going," Rin said.

"I sort of forced myself open more to connect with them and offered comfort. Suddenly, purple and green pulses shot from my hands to the girl. I didn't know how or why? It kind of scared me," Thom admitted.

What the heck were those? Rin thought. He'd never heard any healer mention them. He needed to find someone to help him figure out this gift.

"Rin, did you hear me?" Thom asked. "Should I continue?"

"Oh, yes, shooting pulses," Rin replied. "That would be frightening," he concurred, trying to keep his voice calm. "What happened next?"

"I sent healing energy to both," Thom explained. "Eventually, the girl relaxed and released Rindo."

"How did you feel during this?" Rin asked.

"I felt weak," Thom said. "But, I got energy boosts occasionally, especially near the end. Did you help me?"

"I didn't," Rin replied. "You were doing something I couldn't detect."

"Oh," Thom said, astonished.

Rin sat quietly, and then said, "It's urgent that I get you to Eiren. Unfortunately, that means longer days in the saddle. I want to get to Bethemel in no more than two weeks. Let's get going."

Chapter 23

Ten days had passed since they'd left the Barrelsons. Thom was relieved no more snow had fallen. He shivered despite being bundled in a jumper and a thick coat, realizing he still felt tired from healing Rindo. Thom didn't want to say anything because Rin kept pushing them to ride longer and faster. Every time he took a little longer to put his bedroll away or clean the traveler's shelter, Rin got angry.

While on the road that morning, Thom overheard Rin talking to himself. He was calculating how much further they had before getting to Bethemel. He learned the queen's cousin, Gabi, lived across the sea in Eiren. She was Rin's good friend from their Acadium years, and she married the Eiren prince before he became king.

We're making good time, Rin thought, relieved. He knew he'd been pushing Thom, but it appeared Thom was handling it well. He was still gobsmacked by what Thom had done and couldn't help but wonder what his divine guides thought.

They were passing an inn when Thom interrupted Rin's thoughts. "Do you think we can stop and have a meal here instead of eating travel food?" he said hopefully.

"Sure, but let's make it quick," Rin replied. While he spoke, a white feather wafted down and settled on his saddle. "Hmm," he grunted. "A message from my guides?"

"Are you OK, Rin?" Thom asked.

"Yes. Let me ask you, how's your energy?"

"I'm still pretty tired. But I didn't tell you because I know how important it is to get to Eiren quickly."

Rin suddenly felt a jolt of energy. He knew it was from his guides. OK, *you've got my attention*, he mind-spoke to them. *Did you really have to send that, though? I'll check in with you after we eat.* Speaking to Thom, he said, "On second thought, how about if we stay at the inn for a few days to give you time to rest?"

Thom looked at him with a huge grin.

"Go find the ostler to stable our horses," Rin told him. "I'll get us a room."

"Sure," Thom replied, dismounting and approaching the stable. His gaze was drawn to the dripping icicles hanging from its eaves.

Rin secured a room for two nights, with an option for a third. It also included the use of bathing facilities. After dropping off their bags in their room, they returned to the tavern for dinner. Both were silent while they ate.

Eating his soup, Rin thought again about Thom's healing. He was certain there was more to it than physical healing.

While Thom bathed, he'd ask his guides. Glancing at him, he saw Thom was half asleep, holding a piece of bread halfway between his plate and his mouth. "Thom," Rin said.

"Huh," Thom replied, coming out of his stupor.

"You're exhausted and filthy. Why don't you get a bath? I'll bathe after you. But take your time."

Thom nodded, stuffed the bread into his mouth, and headed upstairs to their room.

Soon after, Rin finished his dinner. When he got to their room, he saw Thom had already left. It was time for him to chat with his guides. Forty-five minutes passed when Thom returned, his skin red and shriveled. "How was your bath?"

"Good," Thom replied.

"I'll get mine now. Why don't you climb into bed and get some rest," Rin advised.

As Rin bathed, he reflected on his chat. Regret gnawed at him for not seeking the advice of his guides sooner. While they didn't berate him, and never would, they weren't pleased. They reminded him that his higher self was present at Thom's pre-incarnation meeting. "Thom's gift is somehow tied to his spirit and auras," he mused. "I've never heard of such a gift. Eiren isn't the place for him. We need to go to the Glakkadeth Archipelago."

At breakfast, Rin asked, "Do you feel rested? Thoroughly check in with yourself. I don't want you telling me what you think I want to hear."

Thom sat quietly, attuning to his aura. He noted its colors were brighter but less vibrant than they had been. He did discover more purple, however muted, which he shared with Rin.

Interesting, Rin thought. The increase in purple must be from his unknown gift. To Thom, he said, "I sense you need more rest. We'll stay here two more days."

"Thanks," Thom replied. "I didn't realize how much Rindo's healing drained me."

"Neither did I," Rin admitted. "And I should have. Sorry. But it does make sense because you were using brute force. I need to tell you that our destination has changed from Eiren to the Glakkadeth Archipelago."

"Why?" Thom asked.

"When I chatted with my guides, I learned that your healing gift is somehow related to your spirit. Glakkadeth is a better place to go. There's a monastery there, and I'm hoping one of the monks will know about your gift."

"Oh," Thom said. "Do you know what my gift is called?"

"Unfortunately, no," Rin said.

"You said it was an archipelago," Thom said. "Isn't that a group of islands?"

"Yes," Rin replied.

"Are we still going to Bethemel?"

"No," Rin replied. "Glakkadeth is a good distance south of Docha-leigh. We'll catch a ship in Dridley. A river runs by the edge of town. We'll take a riverboat downstream to the port. Why don't you rest and read your novel today," he advised. "You haven't finished it yet, have you?"

"No. I've been too tired to read lately."

"Again, apologies," Rin said. "Today, I'll purchase riverboat tickets. I'll also sell our horses since we can't take them on board. We'll keep the saddles because we'll need at least one horse when we reach Glakkadeth."

Thom rested the next day and the day after, napping between meals, reading, and meditating. He had mixed feelings about selling the horses. While he was glad that he was no longer riding, he would miss Brule. Brule had seen him through a long trip, including the bandits' incident.

Chapter 24

The morning arrived without a cloud in the sky. Snow had fallen during the night, but the storm had been weak compared to the one two days before. Looking out their room's window, Thom noticed the new snow hid the slushy tracks created by people, horses, and carriages trudging back and forth across the inn's courtyard. Rin and Thom were taking the riverboat south that morning. Since he'd never been on a boat, much less downriver, he was excited about seeing new towns and people.

Standing behind him by the wash basin shaving, Rin asked, "How do you feel?"

"Better," Thom replied. "I have more energy and feel more grounded."

"Enough to travel today?"

"Yes."

"Good," Rin replied. "I've arranged for a cart to take us to the boat. Since it should take six days to get downstream, you'll have more time to rest. The cart will pick us up in the courtyard in an hour. You'd best finish packing before we get some breakfast."

Thom discovered that traveling downriver turned out to be boring. Even though the boat stopped twice daily to offload and take on goods and passengers, the wharves in each town were identical. As the riverboat approached a quay in Dridley, Thom was amazed by the spring-like weather. He was happy to change out of his winter clothes. He and Rin were on deck.

"To situate you, these quays are on the city's west side," Rin explained. "I see they're building a new warehouse. That means trade is good."

"Where are the ships anchored?" Thom asked.

"At the port, southeast of here," Rin replied.

As Thom watched the activity around the wharf, he was overwhelmed.

Noticing Thom's reaction, Rin said, "A few people out and about, huh?"

"A lot."

"Wait until we get near the port," Rin advised. "The streets will be more crowded, and then, you'll see a great deal of hustle and bustle."

"Oh, dear," Thom said, frowning. He'd never been to a city before. The largest group of people Thom had seen was at the Solstice Day gathering in their town a year ago. There were fewer than a hundred people, and he didn't enjoy it.

"Rin... um," he said hesitantly. "I'm not good in crowds. I get tired quickly."

"That makes sense," Rin replied. "Remember what I told you about empaths absorbing other people's energy. Now that one of your shields can block that out, you should be OK." Rin noticed the gangway had been set up between the boat and the quay, "I see they're ready for us to disembark."

"Oh. I'd better go get my stuff." Thom said.

"No need. The sailors will unload our belongings," Rin replied. "We'll be taking a carriage to the port. I know of a few places near there where we might stay."

After disembarking, they found a carriage. Once their baggage was loaded, they were on their way. Thom looked around as they traveled through the streets. Since it was two days before Solstice Day, Disime 21, he saw lights, garlands, and other decorations strung about. He felt sad, knowing he'd miss his family's usual holiday activities.

Reaching an intersection, a pedestrian dashed in front of them, barely missing being run over, startling Thom out of his reverie. "That was close!" he exclaimed.

"You'll get used to it," Rin said. "Sometimes, I imagine the pedestrians are performers engaged in a dance when navigating around wagons, vendor carts, and carriages. I understand messengers undergo special training to dash through the city. While we're here, we'll have noon supper at an outside café. We'll be in the perfect place to watch. It's quite amazing."

"How long will we be staying in Dridley?" Thom asked.

"I'm hoping under two weeks," Rin replied. "I need to find a ship that takes passengers."

They rode the rest of the way in silence.

Rin and Thom stopped at two inns before they found one that could take them for two weeks. They secured two rooms with shared a door. One, the larger of the two, contained a bed, wardrobe, desk, and a table with two chairs. The smaller one only had a bed and a wardrobe. Thom assumed he would get the smaller room until Rin told him to take the one with a desk. Schoolwork?

Since the inn had an outside patio, they decided to have supper there. As they waited for their food, Thom confirmed what Rin had said about pedestrians. He even saw two messengers hop on and off carts to get around, much to the chagrin of their drivers.

After swallowing a mouthful of fish, Rin said, "Since our new destination is Glakkadeth, you'll need to learn Glakkadian. You wouldn't have had to learn another language had we gone to Eiren."

"That's why you gave me the room with the desk," Thom commented. "I had a feeling."

Rin smiled and said, "I knew you'd pick that up. While onboard the ship, I hope to find a sailor willing to continue your self-defense lessons. It takes about eight weeks to get to Glakkadeth. You'll have time to learn the language in addition to training."

"You've been there before?" Thom asked.

"Yes," Rin replied. "For a time. Are you about finished?"

"Yep," Thom replied, popping the last bit of apple into his mouth.

"OK. Let's go. Our first stop is a bookstore."

Rin led them to Tradith Square. Along the intersecting streets, merchants sold their wares.

At the center of the square, Thom saw a fountain surrounded by benches. Along the edge of the square, vendors selling food, jewelry, and household goods were nestled in between the trees. Rin took them down one of the more prominent streets. They passed a stationer's shop and a printer's house before finally stopping at a bookshop.

Stepping inside, Thom's jaw dropped when he saw the number of books it contained. Shelves teeming with books stretched from floor to ceiling, while tables showcased an array of literary treasures and assorted items.

"A book fan, I see," a portly gentleman said from behind the counter.

"Yes, sir," Thom agreed. "You have so many books."

"I can't seem to stop myself from ordering more, much to the chagrin of my daughter, who runs the shop with me," the man answered. "I'm Mr. Leabhar."

"I'm Thom. This is my teacher, Healer Rinbalden."

"Nice to meet you, Thom and Healer Rinbalden," Mr. Leabhar said. "How can I help you?"

"Do you have a Glakkadian grammar, dictionary, and workbook?" Rin asked.

"I do," he replied. "I have new copies of all three and used copies of the grammar and the dictionary." He led them to a shelf dedicated to languages.

Rin pulled a used dictionary from the shelf. "Used for this is fine," he said to Thom, handing it to him.

Flipping through the book, Thom noticed that the front section provided the meaning of each Glakkadian word and the corresponding Dochalan word, while the back section had the opposite.

"For the grammar," Rin remarked, "a used copy could be acceptable, but it depends on its condition." He looked at a few before selecting one. "This has a minimum of worn pages. It also has notes in the margins with good suggestions about pronunciation and a few corrections. We'd best get a new workbook, with exercises paired with the grammar lessons."

Thom looked down at the three books he held. He realized he was essentially going back to school. Thom had appreciated having the last two months off. He did like learning, but most of the teachers at home were boring. *Maybe learning a new language will be fun.*

"Sir, I wonder if I might propose another book," Mr. Leabhar asked Rin.

"Of course," Rin answered.

"Since this is for the lad, might I suggest you buy a novel for him in Glakkadian? It might help him learn the language."

"Yes, please, Rin," Thom begged.

"That's a good idea," Rin agreed. "Where might we find those?"

Mr. Leabhar led them to another set of shelves. "We have all kinds of novels, including thrillers, romance, and fantasy," he explained.

"I love fantasy," Thom interjected.

"OK," the seller said. "We have a variety of even those: adventurers traveling the land and fighting battles, sailors riding the seas, and even those with magical creatures, like dragons or tree sprites."

"Dragons," Thom responded excitedly.

"Oh, dragons appeal to you," Mr. Leabhar said, smiling. Pulling a book off the shelf, he said, "Here's one you might like. It follows the experiences of a young man trying to raise a dragon. It's the first one of a series. I have the first three."

Thom looked towards Rin.

"Let's get the first book," Rin said.

"OK," Thom agreed, with a big grin.

"We have that in new and used as well," the seller mentioned.

"Used," Rin replied.

"Are there any books you'd like, sir?" Mr. Leabhar asked Rin.

"No, but thanks for asking."

Rin purchased the four books, and the seller put them in an old cloth bag for Thom to carry.

Leaving the shop, Rin said, "Let's go to the stationer's shop. I need some paper and ink. Do you need any?"

"I could use some ink and perhaps another quill," he replied.

When they exited the shop, Rin asked, "Do you think you can return to the inn by yourself, Thom?"

"Yes, sir," Thom replied.

"Good. I'm going to the harbor to inquire about ships to Glakkadeth. Keep an eye out for pickpockets. I didn't tell you to bring your staff with us this time because I knew your hands would be full and I'd be with you. But, in the future, take your staff."

"I will."

"I'm hoping I can find a ship quickly, but I might not be back until dinner," Rin explained.

"OK," Thom said. As he walked back toward the inn, he realized he wanted to buy Rin a Solstice Day gift. He had a little money from helping his Mam out and from selling a few pottery pieces. What would Rin want? He stopped in front of a millinery. Rin does wear that weird-looking floppy hat. But he didn't have enough money for one of them.

Continuing through the square, Thom noticed three bedraggled children loitering near the fountain and eyeing him. Were they checking him out to rob? Thom held the bag of books and the stationery package against his chest. Looking around, he saw two people in uniform passing through the square. He followed them since they were heading in the general direction of his inn.

A block from the inn, Thom had yet to find a gift. He spotted a trading post that sold a collection of goods and went in. Behind the counter stood a man of medium height with curly black hair and skin that was almost black. He also noticed a shorter woman with a similar complexion arranging shirts on a nearby table. She had a green cloth wrapped around her head. Rin had told him Glakkadians had darker complexions and that some lived in Dridley.

"Can I help you, lad?" the man said with a notable accent.

"Yes, sir," Thom replied. "I want to buy my teacher a gift for Solstice Day, but I don't have much money."

"I can help him, Admah," the woman said, but without an accent. "You're looking for a gift for your teacher, lad."

"Yes, ma'am."

"Is your teacher a male or a female?"

"Male."

"And what does he teach?"

"He's a healer, and I'm his apprentice."

"Ah, a noble profession," she said. "That must mean you have healing gifts. You certainly have the demeanor of a caring and sensitive healer."

"Um... thanks," Thom said, reddening.

"I have an idea," she said. "Healers must always wash their hands before and after treating patients. I have a little gift basket that has antibacterial soap and lotions. I'd imagine his hands dry out often."

Thom nodded.

She picked up a basket and said, "This one also has a shaving brush and soap. Does your teacher have a beard, or is he clean-shaven?"

"Mostly clean-shaven," Thom answered. "Sometimes, he says he can't be bothered."

"Will this work?"

"Yeah," Thom said. "But how much is it?"

"May I ask how much money you have to spend?"

"Not a lot," he replied, taking all of it from his pocket.

"Ah," she murmured. "Let me think." Lifting the basket, it slipped from her grasp. She retrieved it from the floor and lamented, "Oh, dear. How clumsy of me. The soap now bears a slight dent. I couldn't in good conscience charge you the full price. How about three crowns, five shillings, and two pennies? It'll leave you with more than half your money."

"But that's less than half the price?" Thom said.

"True, but it's damaged," she responded, giving her hus-band a wink without Thom seeing.

"Are you sure?" he asked.

"Absolutely," the woman said.

"Thank you, ma'am," he replied.

"If you take it to the counter," she continued, "you can pay my husband. He'll wrap it for you."

Soon after, Thom left the shop and returned to the inn. Once in his room, he placed the books on the desk and hid Rin's gift in one of his saddlebags. Sitting at the desk, Thom picked up the novel and began flipping through it. A page opened—a drawing of a dragon in flight, with a young man straddling it. "This is cool," he said out loud, fascinated by the dragon's scaled body, squared-off head, and golden wings. Shaking his head, he realized he should start learning Glakkadian. Setting aside the novel, he opened the grammar and workbook.

Thom worked steadily for ninety minutes, stopping to stretch his neck and back. "Ungh," he groaned. Satisfied with his progress—having mastered greetings, food orders, and transactions, Thom decided it was time for a break. His stomach growled in agreement. He had an idea. He'd return to Tradith Square, buy something to eat, and continue studying by the fountain. Before leaving, he grabbed his staff.

Arriving at the square, Thom walked around to see what food was being sold. Behind one cart, he noticed a young woman wearing an orange tunic with geometric designs. The tunic's intertwining shapes mesmerized him.

"Hey!" the woman called out to Thom. "You, boy!" she said again when he didn't respond.

"Oh, yes, ma'am," Thom replied. "I'm sorry for staring. That was rude." he said, looking down.

"Yes, it was," she replied. "And, don't call me ma'am. I'm not that old! Call me Khali. I'm only fourteen. I take it you haven't seen someone with my skin tone before."

"Actually, ma'am... sorry, Khali," Thom said, still embarrassed, "I have. I was looking at your tunic. It's beautiful. I've never seen anything like that. Again, my apologies. My name is Thom. You speak Dochalan well and don't have an accent."

"Thank you for the compliment about my tunic," Khali replied. "And, yes, I don't have an accent because I was born here, in Dridely. My father was born in Glakkadeth."

"Oh," Thom replied. "May I ask another question?"

"Go ahead," she answered.

"Do you speak Glakkadian, too?" he asked.

"Of course! Growing up, my parents spoke both languages in our household. We also lived in Glakkadeth for a while because my grandparents and cousins live there." Looking pointedly at Thom's staff, she said, "Do you know how to use that thing, and are you going to try to rob me?"

"Oh, no," Thom answered with alarm. "I'm still learning to use it, but my teacher suggested I take it when walking alone."

"Your teacher's smart. The pickpockets prowl around the square. Constables do walk the neighborhood, but some pickpockets are clever. And some are kids, who people don't always notice."

"I saw a few earlier today," Thom explained. "They were watching..." he started to say when his stomach growled.

Khali heard it and smiled. "Might I interest you in a little sweet to fill your vocal stomach?" she asked.

Thom stepped closer to her cart. He saw long pieces of twisted fried dough with sugar sprinkles and cinnamon.

"They're Sweet Spice Twisters," Khali explained. "Chili powder gives them a kick."

Thom's mouth began to water. Should he ask for some in Glakkadian? he wondered. He decided to give it a try. "May I bought two?"

Khali smiled and responded in Glakkadian, "Yes, you may." Responding in Dochalan, she added, "You got the verb tense wrong, though."

"I did?" Thinking again about what he'd learned, Thom repeated his request, "May I buy two, please?" He added "please" to be courteous, given his earlier rudeness.

"Well done," Khali replied. "You're learning Glakkadian?"

"Yes, my teacher and I are going to Glakkadeth." Thom pulled out the grammar and showed it to her.

"Oh, this is funny," Khali said, chuckling. "Your grammar used to be mine! You can see my comments in the margins. Some were tricks my Pa taught me when I was learning. Others are notes about changes made to the language in the last five years, including slang. Did you buy the workbook too?"

"Yes, and a dictionary and a novel," he replied.

"What novel?" Khali asked.

Thom pulled it out and handed it to her.

"*Demba's Chronicles: The Discovery!*" Khali shouted with glee. The vendors nearby gave her a disapproving look.

"*Demba's Chronicles: The Discovery*, is that the title?" he asked.

"Yes. It's the first book of my favorite series. Demba's the main character. But early in this book, he meets a girl named Abi," she explained. "And they both raise... I shouldn't say anything more because I don't want to spoil it."

"Do you mean they both raise dragons?" Thom asked.

"Yes," Khali said.

"The bookseller told me," Thom replied. "I also flipped through a few pages and saw a drawing of a teenager on a dragon. That's one of the reasons I got the book. He said it was a series but didn't say how many. I don't have much room in my bags anyway."

"You'll be able to get the rest of them when you get to Glakkadeth," Khali informed him. "It's still a popular series there."

"Great."

"How long will you be in Dridley?" Khali asked.

"I don't know. Maybe two weeks. My teacher's looking for a ship."

"Oh," Khali replied, her eyebrows raised. "If your teacher..."

"Healer Rin," Thom offered.

"If Healer Rin doesn't find one, my father might be able to help. His brother, my uncle, makes regular trips between Docha-leigh and Glakkadeth."

"Really? I'll tell him."

"And," Kahli continued, "while you're here, I'm willing to help you learn Glakkadian."

"You will? Thanks," Thom replied. "Let me check with Rin about paying you for it."

"Hmm," Khali paused, thinking. "I have a proposal. I sometimes have errands to run. If you can tend my cart for an hour every morning and afternoon when we're both here, we can go over what you've learned and practice it."

"That would be great, Khali," Thom replied. "I should probably still check with Rin, but I think he'd be OK with it."

"That's fine. Were you going somewhere now?" Khali asked. "Do you have to get back?"

"No," he answered. "Rin's not due back at the inn until dinner. I planned to study more and then try to read the novel."

"I've got an idea," she said. "Why don't you sit next to me? If you get stuck while studying, I can help you figure it out. And maybe I can read a little of the novel to introduce you to Demba and Abi's adventures? Sometime while you're here, I'll show you how to tend my cart."

"I'd like that," Thom replied.

She picked two twisters from her tray and handed them to Thom. "These are on the house."

Thom settled on the low wall behind the cart to munch on the twisters. They tasted terrific, and he liked their spiciness. Khali had a jar of water that she kindly offered him to drink. After wiping the sugar and cinnamon from his hands, Khali taught him how to cover the cart. Then, he went back to studying the grammar.

Khali's guidance really made a difference. As he learned, he discovered that speaking the language was easier than writing it. However, ending every sentence with the same raised pitch he used when asking a question in Dochalan felt strange.

It was late afternoon. Khali had been reading from Demba's Chronicles. They didn't get far because whenever she came upon a word Thom didn't know, which happened quite often, she'd define it and ask him to use it in a sentence. He struggled a little, but he knew the more he learned, the easier it would become.

"It's getting close to dinner," Thom said. "I'd better head back to the inn to see if Rin returned."

"OK," Khali replied. "I'll be going home soon myself. You're really picking up Glakkadian fast, and your accent is improving. Will I see you tomorrow?"

"Yes, if Rin lets me tend your cart," he replied.

Returning to the inn, Thom noticed Rin hadn't come back yet. He set his books down, sprawled out on his bed, and dozed. Time slipped away, and Rin burst into the room before he knew it.

"Turg! Turg! Turg!" Rin muttered. "What inclompetents! Turg! I'm doing it again. This is ridiculous."

"Rin," Thom tried to interrupt.

Rin began pacing the room. "First, the clerk couldn't find the list of ships that travel to Glakkadeth. Then, after he found it, he broke his quill, and it took him forever to find a replacement."

"Rin," Thom spoke up again.

"If that wasn't bad enough," he grumbled, "he didn't include the dock numbers. How was I to know they added nine new docks? After wasting a lot of time searching, I had to return to the clerk and stand in a long line before I could get him to add the numbers."

Thom remained silent as Rin continued pacing.

"But the fool had the numbers wrong," Rin hollered, his temper going full steam. "Where do they get these idiots? From a school of the clueless. When I finally returned to the docks and found the two ships going to Glakkadeth, the first captain wouldn't return there for over a month. The other told me they had no room. Grrr."

Confident that Rin's tirade had sputtered out, Thom spoke again, "Rin, I might know of a ship we can take."

"What, what?" Rin said with surprise. "Oh, sorry. I thought I was in my room. It was a very unproductive afternoon. What did you say?"

"I said I think I might know of a ship we can take."

"How do you know that?" Rin asked, a little irritated. "You didn't go to the harbor, did you?"

"No. I met a food vendor, Khali, in the square. Her uncle's a captain."

"Tell me how you met her again?" Rin responded, sitting on the side of Thom's bed.

Thom explained how he met Khali and that she would help him learn Glakkadian. He also shared with him all that he had learned.

"That's great," Rin responded. "I'm impressed. I'm certainly fine with you helping Khali with her food cart. I'm also relieved you have a lead on a ship. Perhaps you can introduce me to Khali tomorrow?"

"Of course," Thom said.

"Let's head down to dinner," Rin added. "I think they started serving a half hour ago."

Chapter 25

After breakfast the next day, Thom and Rin went back to the square. On their way, they passed by the same children Thom had seen loitering the previous day. He gave them a look, holding his staff securely to show them he could defend himself. Of course, he wasn't sure he could because he was still learning. But they didn't know that.

Approaching Khali and her cart, Rin greeted her in Glakkadian, "How do you do, Khali? I'm Healer Rin. Thom told me how you met and that you would help him learn Glakkadian. Thank you. I'm fine with him covering your stand for an hour or two each day in exchange."

"That's great, Healer Rin," Khali responded in Glakkadian. "I'm happy to do it. It gets a bit boring standing here for hours at a time. By the way, you speak our language well."

"I lived in Glakkadeth some years back," he replied.

"How much of this are you getting, Thom?" Khali asked.

"A little," he admitted.

"Thom mentioned your uncle is the captain of a ship that travels to Glakkadeth," Rin said in Dochalan for Thom's benefit.

"Yes, that's right," Khali replied, also in Dochalan.

"Is your uncle and his ship in port?" Rin asked.

"No," she replied. "He's due in a week or two, but my father would know exactly."

"Do you think I could talk with him?" Rin asked.

"Probably," Khali replied. "My parents run a trading post close to the harbor. I can take you if Thom can tend the cart?"

"Sure," Thom replied.

"Perfect," Rin said. "Before we head there, might I buy one of your sweets, Khali?"

"Oh, please. On the house. They're Sweet Spice Twisters."

"They smell wonderful," Rin replied.

Rin grabbed a twister, and Khali led him away.

Thom spent the time learning Glakkadian and selling Twisters. Since it was morning, he had a good number of customers. Two of the children from yesterday stopped nearby and were watching him. The girl looked a little older than him, and the boy seemed about his sister Reta's age. Thom picked up his staff and did a few exercises.

Glancing at them while he was doing that, he noticed they looked hungry. He wondered if they'd had a sweet recently. Setting his staff against the wall behind the cart, he checked his pocket and found a few coins. Looking in their direction, he gestured for them to come nearer. When they hesitated, he gestured once more, urging them to approach.

Thom watched as they drew closer. "Would you like a twister?" he asked. "I'll pay for them."

"What's in it for you?" the girl asked, narrowing her eyes.

"Nothing," Thom said. "I figured you might not have had a sweet in a while."

The girl smiled a little.

Thom selected two twisters from the tray and gave one to each.

"Thank you," the girl said, casting a pointed glance at the boy.

"Fank oo," he mumbled with his mouth full.

Thom was just handing another customer a Twister when Rin and Khali returned.

"Any problems?" Khali asked him.

"Nope. You do a good business in the morning."

"I know," she agreed. "There's always a bunch of people running late who haven't had time for breakfast. I was thinking of selling coffee, too."

"Great idea," Thom replied.

"Good news, Thom," Rin said. "Through Khali's father, I secured space on her uncle's ship, the Bittaye Biashara."

"When are we leaving?" Thom asked.

"Not for another three weeks," Rin answered. "While it means we'll be staying in Dridley longer than I hoped, we'll get a good-sized cabin. It includes a fold-down desk for your studies."

"That will give me more time to learn Glakkadian," Thom said. "What's the other good news?"

"Khali's parents, Admah and Fatou Bittaye have invited us to their Solstice Day celebration tomorrow."

"Wow, that's nice of them," Thom said.

"It will also give you a chance to practice Glakkadian with my parents and younger brother," Khali added.

Thom smiled. Why did the name Admah seem familiar?

"Since I took care of my errands while Rin was talking to my parents," Khali interjected, "I can handle the cart for the rest of the day."

"OK," Thom agreed. "Then I can study in my room this afternoon. See you tomorrow, Khali."

As they walked away, Thom turned to Rin and said, "Since we'll be with Khali's family tomorrow, shouldn't we buy them a gift?"

"Good point," Rin replied, considering. "For the parents, I can get a bottle of wine. Do you know what Khali might like?"

"A headscarf, I think. But I don't know what to get Khali's brother, Annan. Khali said that he's 11 years old. I wouldn't know what to get him even if he was my age. I don't think I'm a typical boy."

"I'm sure we'll find something," Rin assured him. "Let's head back to the inn for noon supper. We can shop afterward."

Rin's statement about being able to find gifts almost seemed like a foretelling. Two blocks away, they found a business that sold spirits. Next door was a clothing shop. Thom bought a magenta headscarf with a swirl design.

Walking one block further, Rin and Thom found a shop selling children's toys. Stepping inside, they saw a few teenage boys standing by a table displaying a miniature wooden ship. The boys were oohing and aahing. Nearby were boxes that had images of the ship sketched on them.

"That's cool," Thom remarked. "It looks like the ship is a model you assemble."

"Can I help you, gentlemen?" the owner asked, who was standing behind a counter beyond where the teenagers were standing.

"Yes, thank you, ma'am," Thom answered. "We're going to a friend's home tomorrow, and we want to buy a Solstice Day gift for her brother, an 11-year-old whom we've never met. We don't know what to get him."

"He's a local, then," she said. "Do you know his name?"

"Yes, Annan Bittaye," Thom answered.

"I know the lad," she answered. "He's destined to follow his uncle to the sea and is obsessed with ships. Do you see the model?"

They looked back.

"Boys," she called to the teens, "Off with you. If your parents were going to get that for you, they'd already have it hidden away. If not, you can encourage them to buy it for your next birthday."

Turning back to Rin and Thom, she said, "Sorry about that. The boys have come by every day to stare at it. I think the model would be perfect for Annan."

"Thank you very much," Thom said.

Rin purchased the model, and they left the shop.

"Why don't you head back to the inn to study," Rin directed. "Take the gifts with you. I have some other errands to run, including picking up a few things for our trip. I'll try to make it back for noon supper. But if I don't, go ahead and eat. I can get something while I'm out.

Rin had told Thom they were expected at the Bittaye's home at 1:30 p.m. It struck Thom as odd that they didn't depart much before the time they were due.

When they left the inn, Rin steered them towards the square. A block away, he stopped in front of a door to the left of the trading post where Thom had bought Rin's gift.

Oh, my, Thom thought. What a strange coincidence.

Khali opened the door after Rin's knock. "Good Solstice, Healer Rin and Thom!" she exclaimed.

"Good Solstice to you too, Khali," they replied in unison.

Khali led them up the stairs to the second floor. Thom had decided to stand behind Rin to signal Khali's parents to say nothing when they saw him.

When they entered the living area, Khali's parents greeted them, "Good to see you again, Healer Rin. This is our son, Annan."

"Good to see you, Admah and Fatou. Nice to meet you, Annan," Rin greeted. "This is my apprentice, Thom."

"Good to meet you..." Admah stopped, catching sight of Thom, who shook his head.

"Nice to meet you," Thom said.

"Please come in, and Good Solstice to you both," Fatou said.

After a delicious meal and wonderful celebration, Rin and Thom thanked the Bittayes and walked toward their inn.

"Khali loved the headscarf, Thom," Rin commented.

"Yes, I'm glad. And I was shocked when she and her family gave me two more books in the Demba's Chronicles series. I'll need to find some room for them in my bags. Now, I'll have plenty to read on the ship."

Rin cleared his throat.

"Of course, I'll still be learning to use my gifts from you and studying Glakkadian," he assured Rin.

"And hopefully getting some more self-defense training," Rin added.

"Oh, yeah," Thom said, not looking forward to the return of the aches that would come with it. "It was fun to see Annan's eyes bug out when we gave him his gift. He told me he was going to the shop tomorrow to thank the lady who helped us."

"And thank you, young man, for your toiletries gift," Rin said. "I'm sure you don't think I smell," he said with a smile.

"What a coincidence that you bought my gift from Admah and Fatou."

"Yes, and you seemed to like the hat they bought you. It's not as... floppy as the hat you have," Thom said, grinning.

"Yes, I liked it," Rin replied. "Now I have two hats to use."

"And thank you for the beautiful journal, Rin," Thom said, sincerely.

"You're welcome," Rin replied. "I know how important it is to you. When I saw you were nearing the end of your current one, I thought it appropriate."

"Yes, definitely," Thom replied. "And this one doesn't have stains on the cover, where Reta spilled her cider a few months back."

Arriving back at their rooms, Rin and Thom spent the rest of the evening relaxing, talking, and writing in their journals.

Lying in bed that night, Thom closed his eyes, smiled, and whispered, "It was a wonderful day, Sereh and Deu. Thanks. Family, I hope you had a good celebration, too."

Chapter 26

The next three weeks were packed for Thom, but he swiftly fell into a routine. Each morning, upon waking, he greeted Sereh and Deu, hoping they might respond directly. They never seemed to, which made him wonder if he was thinking about this wrong. After dressing, he'd meet Rin downstairs for breakfast. Since Dridley was a port town with visitors from other countries, the inn offered a variety of foods, including fare native to those cultures. One morning, Thom ate grilled tomato slices with his eggs. Another morning, he ate a fried ball made of beans, which was too spicy for him.

Following breakfast, Rin and Thom alternated between training with the staff and continuing to work on his shielding. The shield training was anything but easy. Rin had him changing their textures and raising and lowering them automatically. One of the most annoying aspects was when Rin tried to scare him or make him angry. The first time he did this, Rin had yelled at him for not following instructions. He felt terrible until Rin assured him it wasn't true, explaining it was a deliberate attempt to provoke him as part of the training.

Late mornings, Thom would head to Khali's cart. They decided he'd have one longer shift rather than two shorter ones. When Khali returned from her errands, she'd test him. Then, they'd read more of Demba's Chronicles.

Thom spent much of the afternoon on his own. He dedicated an hour to working with his staff. Since Rin was usually occupied with errands, he was saved from sparring matches. Then, up until dinner, he'd nap, read, or explore the city.

In the evenings, he and Rin spent time together in his room, relaxing and talking. He felt like he was getting to know his teacher better. He'd also review the new vocabulary he learned. As a reward, he'd reread the pages of the novel that Khali and he had read earlier in the day. With each turn of the page, he'd imagine himself traveling alongside Demba and Abi as they soared in flight on their dragons or confronted dangers.

Rin and Thom would write in their journals for the remainder of the night. Thom had even started writing in Glakkadian. And, silly as it sounded, he kept his entries brief because he didn't want to start writing in his new journal until he boarded the ship. Their departure symbolized the beginning of a new phase of his life, and he wanted his journal to reflect that.

It was two days before they were scheduled to depart. Khali's uncle, Captain Musa Bittaye, had returned five days earlier and confirmed their space on his ship. Thom was returning to the inn after helping Khali with her cart. She had shut down early because she had to help her parents review their shop inventory.

Thom was satisfied. He'd made good progress on learning Glakkadian. Thom had completed two-thirds of the workbook and was halfway through the novel. He loved reading about Demba, Abi, and their dragons. Khali had been a big help. He realized he wanted to give her a gift for teaching him and being his friend. It was really nice to have a friend again.

Thom recalled passing a gift shop a few blocks back. When he stepped inside, a bell rang, announcing his presence. The shop was packed with all kinds of goods. As he wandered around, he noticed an open area towards the front.

"Who is it? Who's there?" a male voice demanded gruffly.

Thom replied, "Um. I'm Thom, and I wanted to buy a gift, sir." He went to the back of the shop, where the voice had originated, and approached a middle-aged man with short gray hair, attempting to move the sales counter.

"Oh, it's one of you thieves," the man growled. "Well, you won't be able to steal another thing because I'm moving the counter closer to the door. That way, I can keep a better eye on my goods. If all you kids didn't look alike, you'd be in jail."

"Sir, I'm not a thief, sir. I want to buy something." Pulling out some of his money, Thom showed it to the owner.

"Yeah. Sure. I know that trick," the man grumbled.

Maybe he should go, Thom thought. But what if he could convince him he wasn't a thief? He lowered his third shield, intent on sending positive energy into the man's pulsing red aura.

Suddenly, there was a loud crash behind him. Turning around, Thom saw a carved wooden angel lying on the floor. It must have fallen from the table. One of its wings was broken.

The man looked at the broken angel before glaring at Thom. "You'll pay for that."

"But sir, I wasn't near it," Thom argued.

"There's no one else in the shop. It had to be you," the man insisted.

Thom was quiet. Maybe this was a message from Sereh or Deu warning him. Feeling ashamed, he checked his aura and discovered the blue had dimmed. Uh, oh. *Sorry, Sereh and Deu,* he mind-spoke to them.

"I'm very sorry, sir," Thom apologized. "I'll pay for the angel." He carefully picked up the broken angel and its wing, placing them on the counter. While counting his coins, he saw a beautiful bracelet with multi-colored beads hanging on the wall. He knew that would be Khali's gift.

"Sir, may I also buy that bracelet?" Thom asked, pointing.

"Well, perhaps you aren't one of the thieves," the man admitted.

When the man handed him a bag with his purchases, Thom said, "Sir, would you like me to help you move the counter?"

The man's eyes softened even further. "Oh, I'm sorry lad. I know all kids aren't thieves. I've had a few bad days. And yes, I would love some help with the counter."

Leaving the shop with the angel, its broken wing, and the bracelet, Thom felt a pang of sadness, knowing he'd spent all his money. "That was a tough lesson," he mused. Yet, he found solace knowing he helped the man.

Over dinner, Thom told Rin what he'd done.

"I agree that the angel was a clear sign," Rin told him. "Trying to influence anyone, even in response to someone misjudging you, is wrong like you thought. Lord Samiltun's first step along his path could have begun that way. You must always use your gifts to serve the highest good. As you noticed, your honesty color dimmed. I'm glad you checked that."

"Oh, digi!" Thom cursed. "I don't want to become like Samiltun. I didn't realize. I'm sorry, Rin."

"Did you learn digi from Khali?" Rin said.

"Sort of," he answered. "Khali accidentally dumped half of her twisters on the ground last week. The birds had a field day eating them. Is it real bad?"

"Just a mild curse," Rin assured him.

"Good," Thom said. "I wouldn't want to say something bad. But..."

"I get it; you were upset," Rin replied. "Perhaps you should tell Sereh and Deu about it this evening."

"I will," Thom assured him. "I'll also thank them for the message."

"Good idea," Rin said. "After we finish eating, I think I have some adhesive to glue the angel's wing back on. Your angel can further remind you to always use your gifts for good."

"True, thanks, Rin," Thom replied.

Thom returned to Khali's cart the next day and presented her with the bracelet.

"What's this?" she asked.

"You've helped me a lot with learning Glakkadian, and I also wanted to give you something for being my friend, even though it wasn't for a long time," Thom answered.

"You don't buy someone a gift because they became your friend," Khali countered.

"I know. But I haven't had any friends for a while," he admitted. "It was nice to have someone closer to my age to hang out with and enjoy Demba's Chronicles. The gift is mostly to say thanks for teaching me Glakkadian, especially the correct pronunciation."

"OK," Khali replied, "You're welcome. I know the pronunciation can be tricky. And I accept your gift. It's beautiful," she said, slipping it over her wrist. "You leave tomorrow?"

"Yeah," Thom replied.

"Let's see how much more of the novel we can get through? We're getting to one of the good parts," Khali said.

"Hey, don't tell me!" Thom protested.

"Of course not," Khali defended herself.

Before he left, Khali handed him some money.

"What's this?" he asked.

"Your earnings," she answered. "You were a great seller of the twisters. I've been getting more customers since you started tending my cart. And your suggestion to sell milk, along with the coffee, was a good idea for parents who buy twisters for their kids."

"Thank you, Khali." Looking down at the coins, Thom discovered he had almost the same amount of money he had yesterday before he bought the angel and the bracelet.

Chapter 27

Vern and Finn had been in Bethemel for a few weeks. Vern had found a place in town where they could stash the kid without anyone noticing. Meanwhile, Finn kept watch on the road, waiting for the healer and the kid to arrive.

It was late evening, and both were in their room.

Vern was pacing. "They shoulda' already got here. Even with em goin' slow and stoppin', they shoulda' been here over a week ago. Are ya sure you didn' miss em?"

"I wutched da road, Vern," Finn insisted. "Maybe ya missed em when youse was wutchin'."

Suddenly Vern stopped pacing and said, "Tomorra, I'll go by the port. I'll ask if they seen someone what looked like the healer and the kid tryin' to purchase tickets to Eiren. Why didn' you think of that?"

"I don' know," Finn mumbled.

"Aight," Vern said. "I'll go there in the mornin'. Ya keeps an eye on the road, jus' in case."

Late morning the next day, Vern sought Finn in their usual spot, a low wall across the main road at the edge of town.

"Vern. Youse here, fin'ly," Finn said, rubbing his hands together from the cold. "Ready ta take over? My hands is freezin.'"

"Did ya see em?" he asked, ignoring Finn's complaint.

"Nope," Finn replied. "I talked wit' a man and woman what came through Liffor'. They didn' pass no man and kid comin' here."

"That's good thinkin', Finn," Vern said.

"See, I knows stuff too," Finn reminded him. "What about youse?"

"The clerk didn' see no man or kid in the last two weeks. She even tol' me no ships from Eiren come in or went out durin' thet time neither."

"What should we do?" Finn asked. "We runnin' outta money."

"Give me a second to think," Vern said, sitting on the wall. "They shoulda' been here by now. Maybe they went sumplace else. But Mitch shoulda' sent us a message. Somethin's wrong. Mitch's gonna pay either way."

"Dern right," Finn agreed.

"We'll keep a lookout for another week, in case Mitch sends a message," Vern told Finn. "If we still don' git one, we'll send im a message tellin' im we're staying here for the rest of the winter. But, when we git home, we're out. We wasted too much time. While we're here, we can do a little robbin' to make this worth our while."

"I likes thet," Finn replied.

Chapter 28

On their day of departure, Rin rented a cart to take them to the dock where the Bittaye Biashara was moored. They arrived early in the morning and found sailors loading what turned out to be the last of the cargo. The ship looked huge to Thom. It had three tall masts. Khali had informed him they were the foremast, the mainmast, and the mizzen mast, each with six sails. Khali had even taught him the Glakkadian words for them, as well as those for port, starboard, and stern. He spied her on the top deck, talking with a tall man with rich, dark, weathered skin.

"That must be Khali's uncle," Thom said.

On seeing Rin and Thom, Khali waved and pointed them out. Together, they made their way down the gangway.

"Healer Rin, nice to meet you this fine morning. I'm Captain Musa Bittaye," the captain said, extending his hand in greeting.

"Good morning to you, Captain Musa," Rin replied, shaking the captain's hand.

"And this must be Thom," the captain said.

"Yes, sir. Good to meet you," Thom answered, also shaking his hand.

"Khali's been telling me a lot about you, including that you're learning Glakkadian," the captain continued, now speaking in that language.

Translating the words into Dochalan in his mind, Thom replied, "Yes, sir. She's a great teacher."

"I'm impressed with your accent. Have you really only been learning for three weeks?" the captain asked.

Again, Thom was silent briefly before responding, "Yes, sir. I enjoy learning it."

"You seem to be a natural," the captain replied, switching to Dochalan.

"Thanks," Thom replied. "In my head, I still have to change Glakkadian into Dochalan and then convert my answer into Glakkadian. It makes talking pretty slow."

"That's OK," he assured him. "You'll have plenty of opportunity to practice onboard. We're all loaded, except for your things," gesturing to the belongings the cart driver had unloaded on the dock.

"I'll go get mine," Thom replied.

"No need," The captain assured him. He signaled three sailors nearby, who gathered their belongings and carried them up the gangway.

"Khali," the captain said, "Why don't you show them their cabin."

"Yes, uncle," Khali replied. "Follow me."

Stepping onboard, Thom commented, "I didn't expect the ship to be this big."

"Yeah," Khali replied. "Uncle Musa does trade a lot. He needs room for sailors, the cargo, and sometimes passengers like you. Occasionally, he even transports animals. But none this time."

Khali gave them a quick tour before leading them down a ladder to a lower deck. Gesturing towards a doorway, she said, "This is your cabin."

Thom followed Rin and Khali in.

"I know you paid for a good-sized cabin, at least for a ship, Healer Rin," Khali said. "But I thought it might be helpful if you had a large enough room for a stand-alone desk and two chairs. That way, Thom will have a place to study, and you'll have room to work, too. I convinced Uncle Musa to upgrade you. You still have bunkbeds, like most cabins."

"Thanks, Khali," Thom replied.

"Thank you," Rin echoed. "I see our things have already been delivered, except for the saddles and the horse blankets."

"Oh," Khali answered. "Uncle's storing them in the room where he usually houses the animals."

"That's very considerate of you and your uncle," Rin said.

"No problem," she stated.

TOOOT-TOOOT-TOOOT-TOOOT

"Four blasts," Khali announced. "The ship's about to depart."

Thom and Rin followed her to the main deck.

Before disembarking, Khali turned to Thom and gave him a hug. "It's been great getting to know you," she spoke in Glakkadian.

"It's been a pleasure knowing you, too, Khali," he replied more formally in Glakkadian. "And thank you for being my teacher."

"Well done! By the way, on the ship, you'll learn more informal Glakkadian, along with another curse word or two besides the one I let slip," Khali smirked. "I'll miss you."

"I'll miss you too, Khali," Thom said.

Turning to Rin, Khali offered her hand. "Good to meet you, Healer Rin."

"And you too," Rin replied. "But none of that. After spending Solstice Day with you and your family, a hug is in order."

Khali gave her uncle a quick peck on the cheek and said to them, "May you have fair winds and following seas on your journey." Turning, she ran down the gangway to the dock.

"What?" Thom replied, confused.

"That's the nautical phrase for a good voyage," Captain Musa explained. Speaking to the sailors near him, he said, "Let's get underway."

Immediately, the sailors jumped into action while the dock crew removed the gangway.

"Let's stand over there," Rin said to Thom, pointing to an area away from the activity.

As the ship pulled away, Thom could see Khali waving goodbye. He waved back until she and the dock were no longer in sight.

"Let's go back to our cabin and unpack," Rin told him.

Lying on his top bunk, Thom awoke and stretched. He was still a little stiff from his self-defense training yesterday. Eight weeks ago, soon after they set sail, two sailors had offered to assist in his self-defense training. He was proud he was getting better. But two weeks ago, the sailors had teamed up and begun playing the roles of pirates, and they were now more aggressive.

Hearing deep breathing in the lower bunk, Thom recognized that Rin was still asleep. The sea seemed to be quieting down after last night's storm. He'd become "attuned to the mood of the water and the ship's response," as Captain Musa referred to it. By now, he'd gotten used to the rising and falling of the bow and stern and the rolling motion. But his first ten days were awful. He spent a lot of time near the railing, throwing up the little food he could eat, mostly bread.

Like his time in Dridley, the voyage had been busy. In addition to studying Glakkadian, Rin had taught him about the people and land of Glakkadeth, including its democratic leadership. He was shocked when he learned that the head of the land, the Prezdan, was married to another man.

The ship's cook told Thom about the land's primary faith, Aaliswan, one morning when he stumbled upon him meditating in the galley. He explained they called their supreme being the One. Thom recalled that Rin hoped to find him a teacher from the local monastery when they got to Birkemi. Maybe he'd learn more about Aaliswan from one of the people there.

Of course, Rin continued working with Thom on his physical healing skills. Since he couldn't help much with Thom's spirit-related gift, Rin suggested he take note of any new abilities. None had surfaced since he healed Rindo.

Despite all that was going on, there were times when Thom felt sad being away from home. His family didn't know where he was, and he couldn't contact them. He imagined seeing his father working in the pottery and his mother treating patients. Bedum was getting married in two weeks, and he felt bad he was going to miss that. He understood why, but it still hurt.

Very quietly, Thom climbed down from his bunk and pulled on his trousers, letting his tunic drape over them. On his way out of the cabin, he grabbed his Glakkadian grammar, the dictionary, and the novel. Thom had completed the workbook a few weeks before. He had also started the third book in the Demba's Chronicles series. When he stopped reading yesterday, Demba and Abi were imprisoned by a demonic overlord, and he had drugged their dragons.

Thom first headed to the galley. "Good morning, Cooke," he said, greeting the man working at the stove. Cooke was tall and surprisingly slender, contrary to what most would think given his profession.

"Good morning, Thom," he replied.

"Did you hear the rain last night? It was coming down hard," Thom commented.

"Aye, it was," Cooke agreed. "But that's usual for this time of year, now that we're approaching Glakkadeth."

"Back home, we get rain in the spring, but it's not this heavy," Thom said.

"That's because this is the start of our main rainy season, which goes through Mei. We also have a minor one near the end of the year."

"Don't you have a winter?" Thom asked.

"No," Cooke replied. "The other seasons we have are dry ones."

"Oh. Rin didn't mention that," Thom replied. "I can't say I'll miss winter."

"I'm not fond of it either," Cooke said. "Some of our voyages were far north of Dridley, and I could never get warm. By the way, your accent's improved since you first boarded. You're speaking Glakkadian more naturally."

"Thanks. I still think in Dochalan and have to translate," Thom confessed.

"That should change if you stay in Glakkadeth long enough. Do you know how long that will be?"

"No. Rin hasn't said." Thom answered. "Will you need help today?"

"Yes. Thanks for asking. Please come by an hour before noon supper to chop vegetables."

"Of course."

"Help yourself to some porridge and biscuits. I still had some currants left. I added them to the biscuit batch."

"Yum, that sounds good," Thom replied.

"Here's a little jam for the biscuits. But don't say anything to anyone."

"I won't. Thanks, Cooke," Thom said.

"Uh, huh," he grunted.

While eating, Thom asked, "Did you ever have another name besides Cooke? It's funny that's your name, even though you have an 'e' at the end."

"Not that I know of," Cooke replied. "My Mam called me Junior when I was a child. She was the cook at the local inn and I helped her. When I signed on to my first ship, I was a junior cook. But rather than calling me Junior or Junior Cook, they called me JC. Now that I'm the only cook, I go by Cooke. I added the "e" because officials in some countries didn't believe Cook was a real name."

"Huh," Thom grunted, his mouth full of porridge. After consuming two bowls of porridge and three biscuits, he took his bowl to the sink, rinsed it off, and placed it on a rack.

"Thanks for the jam. The biscuits were good with the currants."

Cooke nodded. "I'll see you later."

Thom made his way topside and found a place midship where he could study. After almost two hours, he felt good about what he'd completed. Now Thom could get back to the novel. He was reading that Demba and Abi's dragons were preparing to escape when he heard a yell from the crow's nest. Making his way towards the sailor to find out what happened, he saw Cooke heading towards the bow and followed him.

"Ah, lad," he said when Thom stopped beside him. "Do you see the dark smudge way out there?"

Thom squinted, "Yeah. Is that Glakkadeth?"

"Yes. It's the northernmost island called Umojai," he informed him. "You're seeing its mountains."

"Are we going to land there?"

"Not immediately. We're sailing directly to the isle of Rohan, where we'll drop you, Rin and some cargo off. We head back to Umojai after that."

Rin came up to them and nodded in greeting. "Do you recall, Thom, that Glakkadeth is an archipelago of 12 islands?" he asked.

"Yes," he answered. "And the capital of Glakkadeth is on Umojai."

"Correct," Cooke replied.

Thom also remembered Rin's explanation that the islands formed a spiral, with Umojai being the largest on the outer arc. Rohan was the innermost island.

"When do you think we'll get there?" Thom asked.

"It'll be two more hours before we get to the archipelago and another hour before we get to Rohan," Cooke replied. "We'll get to your stop around mid-afternoon."

"Thom," Rin interrupted. "Cooke mentioned you agreed to help him prepare noon supper."

"Yes," Thom replied.

"I'd like you to have your final workout with Budergi before you do that. She told me you've made good progress. Wasn't your last workout with Momodou?"

"Yes," Thom answered. "And I'm glad Budergi thinks I've gotten better. My body doesn't always feel that way from all the bruises and bumps I've gotten from her."

"I'd best be off to confer with the captain about the supplies we need," Cooke remarked. "I'll see you after your workout, Thom," Cooke smiled. "Be sure to clean yourself up before joining me."

"Yes, Cooke," Thom replied. "I'll change into my older trousers before looking for Budergi," he said to Rin.

"Good," he replied. "I'll see you at supper."

Chapter 29

Mid-afternoon, Thom and Rin were standing on the top deck as the ship pulled into Birkemi. Looking around the harbor, Thom saw people rushing about loading and unloading goods from ships moored there. Their belongings were nearby and ready to be offloaded first per the captain's request. He and Rin had packed their things after supper, and one of the crew had brought them topside.

"I see that our ride has arrived," Rin commented, pointing to a man standing near their dock with a cart and a horse.

"Are we staying in Birkemi?" Thom asked.

"Yes," Rin replied. "Until I find a place for my shop, we'll stay at the inn Captain Musa suggested. While I'm searching, I want you to continue learning Glakkadian. I'd also suggest you walk around and listen to conversations to get a sense of the cadence of their speech. Khali was good, but she grew up in Dridley. You might pick up other nuances from those born here."

Before departing the ship, Rin and Thom thanked Captain Musa for the voyage. Thom had earlier thanked Cooke, Budergi, and Momodou.

Within a week of their arrival, Rin found the perfect location for his shop. It was in the southwest corner of the town. The previous owner had moved to another island a month before. The front of the shop included built-in shelves, a counter, and an area to see patients. An added benefit was a miniature stove big enough for a pot to brew teas and prepare other treatments. The back rooms included a combined kitchen and dining area, two bedrooms, and a water closet. Behind the shop was a stable that could house two horses. It also had a garden with herbs still growing in it.

Settling into his room, Thom unpacked his belongings. Because the walls of their new residence were thick, the window in his room had a deep ledge that he could use as a shelf. Carefully pulling his treasure jar out of his saddlebags, Thom placed it on the ledge next to his mended angel statue. Opening the jar, he removed his special object, tracing his finger around its triangular shape. "It's the start of another adventure," Thom murmured, gazing at his mysterious item. He was now living in a land with people who held diverse beliefs and didn't look like him or speak his language.

As soon as they moved in, Rin dedicated his time to setting up the shop, visiting the older healer, Gethen, and getting the word out about his arrival. He also bought a horse, large enough to pull a cart, should they need one. Noting a curved marking on his forehead resembling the moon, Rin suggested calling him Crescent.

Much to his dismay, Thom's first task was weeding the garden. Then, he sowed the seeds Rin had brought from Dochalan and added vegetable plants they'd purchased at a nearby nursery. He came across a narrow creek while foraging for firewood among the trees behind the shop. Along its banks laid a deposit of decent-quality clay suitable for making storage jars. He'd have to shape them by hand since he didn't have a pottery wheel. And without a kiln, he wouldn't be able to fire them. He'd have to rely on the occasional sunny day to harden them.

Exploring the neighborhood, Thom came upon a clothier, trading post, and bookshop. Exploring the bookshop, he joyfully shouted when he discovered that the shop carried the complete Demba's Chronicles series. The owner wasn't pleased, and he still felt embarrassed.

His wanderings further led him past a Chapel of the One a few doors down from Rin's shop. After his chat with Cooke, he was curious about the Aaliswan faith. He wanted to visit it in the next couple of weeks.

When he had an afternoon free, Thom intended to explore the bi-weekly market fair near the town center. He understood that the fair boasted of an array of new and used goods. And most vendors were willing to bargain. Thom wanted to see if he could find a good hat. When it wasn't raining, the sun was quite intense.

During those initial weeks in Glakkadeth, one of the first things Thom noticed was the presence of a few others who had his same beige skin color. But he could tell that he was still an unusual sight for many. Once in a while, he'd walk by a mother and child, and the child would point toward him. It was an odd feeling to stand out. When Davi moved away, he'd tried to stay as invisible as possible to hide from Kevar and the other kids. He couldn't do that here.

Chapter 30

Rin heard a loud thunk and a groan from the front room. "Having some trouble, Thom?"

"I dropped the scuttle. Now there's coal all over the floor after sweeping it clean. By the time I scoop up the pieces, I'll have to clean the floor again, and probably me too."

Returning to labeling the salve jars for a time, Rin heard another groan. "Problem?" he asked, getting up from the table in the back area and walking through the curtains separating it from the front room.

"Oh, I don't know," Thom responded, crouched below the counter where Rin couldn't see him.

"Talk to me," Rin encouraged.

"I've been clumsy lately, which makes all my chores take extra time," Thom said, standing up.

Rin tried to keep a grin off his face when he saw Thom had coal smudges on his nose and cheek. He had heard Thom complain before about the drudgery of some of his chores. It wasn't unusual for someone his age. He knew that as Thom got older, he'd understand. Speaking aloud, he said, "I know, Thom. I was clumsy when I was a kid, too. Your body's growing rapidly. I'm not surprised, given the work we've done on your healing gift, not to mention your self-defense training and how much you eat."

Thom stilled with an odd expression on his face.

"What are you feeling?" Rin asked him.

"I didn't realize I had grown," he said happily. "I know my trousers are a little short. The kids at home always made fun of how short and skinny I was. Was it because my gifts were blocked?"

"I wouldn't say they were blocked, so much as mostly dormant. My suspicion is that there was a symbiotic relationship between them and your size. They started emerging when you worked with your mother. Samiltun also triggered the release of your gifts when he tried to manipulate you. Your healing of Rindo had the biggest effect."

"I guess that makes sense," Thom said. "Since you mentioned Samiltun, I worry about my family. Will he hurt them because I'm not there? Or even try to force them to tell him where I am?"

"First, because of my shield, Samiltun believes your gifts are minimal, making you useless to him. Second, even if he wanted to test you again, he doesn't know where you are just like your family. What else?"

"Well, I really miss my family. Reta must be helping Da in the pottery. Kavan's weeding the garden. Bedum's married by now. And my Mam's about to have the baby."

"I understand. Being away from your family can be hard for one as young as you, and you haven't yet made friends here. I am glad Khali was your friend in Dridley, even if it was limited to a few weeks."

"Me too. I miss her."

"I'm sure you do. Unfortunately, as for your family, we won't return to Docha-leigh soon. You have more learning to do with your gifts, in particular your major gift, which I still can't identify."

Thom grimaced. "I know. And I can't get the texturing of my shields to stay put. Sorry."

"No need to apologize. You've come a long way. And I am impressed with how well you picked up Glakkadian. You almost speak like a native. You're better than me."

"Thanks," Thom said.

"You still look troubled."

"It's sorta... overwhelming. At home, even though I was busy, I had time to write and think about things on most nights. I also feel like I'm not meditating enough."

"OK. Let's make sure that's part of your day," Rin told him. "What about having your training in the morning rather than after dinner. Then, you'd have the evening to yourself."

"Oh, thank you, Rin," Thom said, sighing.

"Anything else contributing to your feelings?"

"Some of their beliefs and customs, I don't know... They're... strange."

"Like what?"

"The other day, I went into the Chapel of the One. Since you said the One is Deu, I thought I'd see if anything felt familiar to the Iosan chapel at home."

"And, did it?"

"I don't know. Maybe," Thom said. "They had an altar and candles on it, like our chapel. But they didn't have any statues. "While looking around, I overheard two people talking about being born multiple times."

"I see. The Aaliswan faith is somewhat different from what you know," Rin explained. "The two were talking about reincarnation, one of their beliefs."

"I don't understand how that works," Thom admitted.

"Ah," Rin responded. "I could try to explain, but it's better if someone who practices Aaliswan tells you."

"OK, I guess," Thom said, shaking his head.

"Remember when I told you about wanting to find someone at the monastery here to teach you about your gift."

"Yeah."

"I also hope to find someone to teach you about their faith. I'm sensing it's connected to your major gift."

"Really," Thom replied.

"Sometime soon, we'll visit there," Rin said. "I know we've been here over a month, and it might seem like a long time to wait, given how much I pushed us to get here fast. But the message from my guides was to give your gift more time to heal. You're still a bit raw after healing Rindo."

"OK."

"Anything else?"

"Same-gender couples. In Docha-leigh, we don't have them. All couples are a man and a woman."

"That's not quite true. There are same-gender couples. But they mostly live west and north of where you grew up."

"They do?" Thom said.

"Yes."

"I haven't seen any."

"My understanding is they intentionally don't venture far from their villages," Rin explained. "Some in Docha-leigh have a limited view of relationships. What do you think about same-gender couples? Didn't you say you saw a few holding hands in the market fair the other day?"

"Yes," Thom replied. "A male couple was sitting on a bench. They seemed tender with each other, like Da and Mam. And I saw a young girl who seemed to be their daughter run up to them. How does that work?"

"While we're here, you'll likely meet same-gender couples. Maybe you can ask them."

"I guess. It feels like I have a lot to learn, including about their beliefs. I think it's important. I wish someone would show up to help me with it."

"What about praying?" Rin asked.

"I suppose," Thom replied, frowning.

"I'll help you clean up," Rin offered.

Chapter 31

One morning in Mercha, Thom was helping Rin create herb packets for people to take home. His Mam and Rin believed that providing them encouraged people to look after their health. He was shelving packets behind the counter when the door chime rang and a girl entered the shop. She looked around Thom's age. She was also taller, with golden brown skin and black braided hair to her shoulders.

Rin turned to her and, speaking in Glakkadian, asked, "Can I help you, lass?"

"Yes, please, sir," she answered. "My mother helps care for residents at the Holders of Lumen-anima monastery, and some older monks need herbs for their internal problems. I first went to Healer Gethen's, but she said to come here because she's retiring soon."

"Certainly, I also understand the monastery lost its healer rather suddenly."

"Yes, sir," she responded. "Brother Binder had a heart seizure."

"I'm sorry to hear that," Rin replied. "Such a loss. Might I ask what happened?"

"I heard he was teaching his apprentice Rafi in the infimarium when he clutched his heart and collapsed. My mother, a beginning healer, wasn't there. Brother Binder also mentored her. By the time she arrived, there was nothing she could do."

"How did Rafi handle it, lass?" Rin continued. "I'd imagine he felt some guilt."

"Oh yes, sir," she replied. "He kept blaming himself, thinking he should've been able to do something."

"I feel for him. That's hard for anyone, much less an apprentice," Rin said.

"Thank you," she replied. "Brother Binder was a nice man."

"I'm sure he was. What kind of internal problems are the older monks having? Can you be specific?"

"They aren't able to, um..." she paused, shifting her feet. "They have problems going to..."

Rin jumped in, "Do you mean they're constipated and unable to relieve themselves?"

"Oh, yes, that's the word. Mamie was running out of the medicine for it."

"How much do you need?"

"Um," the girl thought. "I'm pretty sure seven monks are having these problems. They're all male if that matters."

"It doesn't, but thanks," Rin replied. "I think I can cover that. Are you aware of any other medicines your mother might need?"

"No," she answered. "But Mamie doesn't usually mention those things to me."

Turning to Thom, Rin said, "Why don't you chat with the lass while I get the packages together in the back?"

"Hello, I'm Thom, Rin's companion," he said in Glakkadian. "What's your name?"

"I'm Mekial. But I don't think you're the healer's life partner," she replied with a little smile.

"What? Oh, Digi!" Thom said, turning red. "I used the wrong word. I'm still learning your language. That word never came up when I was studying Glakkadian with my friend, Khali, in Dridley. I help Rin by growing and drying his herbs, and um... care for patients when I can."

"Oh, do you mean apprentice?" Mekial replied.

"Yeah. Sorry."

"You speak our language pretty good," Mekial replied. "And you even know a curse word. Didn't you get here two weeks ago?"

"No. It's been over a month. But I started learning Glakkadian three weeks before we sailed. I've been studying it for almost four months."

"Wow, that's not much time, given how good you are," she answered. "Glakkadian's hard. I'm impressed!"

"I do struggle with vocabulary, like you heard. I also get stuck on the future tense sometimes."

By this time, Rin had returned. "You're Mekial. I overheard."

"Yes, sir," she replied.

"I'm Healer Rinbalden," he introduced himself. "Thom apparently has a knack for learning your language. It took me a few years to get to his level."

"Oh, you've lived here before," Mekial commented.

"Yes, but on the capital island. Here are the medicines for your mother."

Mekial pulled a few coins out of a pocket in her trousers and offered them to Rin. "Is this enough?"

Rin took a few and left the rest. "Perfect," he said. "Thom and I would like to visit the monastery at some point to introduce ourselves, especially to your mother and Rafi."

"Oh. I think Mamie would like that. She hoped to visit you, but she's been too busy."

"I understand," Rin replied. "By the way, how many people are at the monastery, and what's their age range?"

"Nearly a hundred. Seventy are professed monks; forty are brothers, and the rest are sestras. Then, I think there are four postulants and five novices. The support staff numbers to about ten. There are also some children. As far as their ages, they range from a few months old to the late 80s."

"Clearly explained, lass," Rin replied with approval. "You have a good mind."

"Thank you," she answered. "My younger brother would disagree with you. He calls me a smarty-pants."

"As you heard, Thom could use further assistance learning your language," Rin said. "Would you be interested in making a little money to help him improve his skills?"

"Oh, I would, but I'll have to ask my mother," Mekial answered. "If Mamie approves, maybe you can teach me your language, Thom?"

"Sure," Thom replied.

"Would you also ask your mother when we might visit her and Rafi?" Rin asked.

"Yes," Mekial replied. "I'd best get back. Nice meeting you, Healer Rinbalden and Thom."

"Nice meeting you too, Mekial," they replied.

After Mekial left, Thom looked at Rin, "You didn't mention anything about finding me a teacher at the monastery."

"No," he replied. "I'll ask Mekial's mother when we meet her."

Thom was restocking the salves when Mekial returned.

"Hi, Mekial," Thom called out in Glakkadian. "I've had another chance to use the word apprentice since I last saw you."

"I'm glad," she replied. "My mother was OK with me helping you learn our language. Are you still willing to teach me yours?"

"Sure. I've got a book that could help you out. It's a basic reader with lessons. Rin found it, but I don't need it. It's got phrases in Glakkadian that match the same in Dochalan."

"Thanks," Mekial answered.

"I'll get Rin from the back room and fetch the book." When he returned, Rin was behind him.

"Good morning, Mekial," Rin greeted.

"Good morning, sir," Mekial replied.

"I heard that your mother approved of you teaching Thom," he said. "I also see Thom has the primer for you."

Thom handed Mekial the book, which she put in her carrying bag.

"Ma made some breakfast muffins for me to give you," Mekial said. "My favorites are the ones with chocolate pieces. But Ma also made some with cinnamon and apples and others with figs and a little spice."

"That's very generous," Rin replied. "We could use a break. Would you like to join us for some tea as we try the muffins?"

"Yes, please," Mekial replied. "But I can't stay long."

"Um," Thom interrupted, "what's chocolate?"

Rin smiled. "Mekial, would you tell him?"

"Chocolate comes from the cacao tree, which grows where it's warm and humid."

"Humid, I don't know that Glakkadian word," Thom replied.

"It's when there is a lot of water in the air, but it's not raining," she answered. "The moisture, along with the heat, is needed for the tree to grow."

"I see," Thom replied. "We have some humidity back home, but not as much here."

"Thom, would you put the larger kettle on our stove in the back?" Rin asked. "I'll get a tray with cups and a few napkins to put on the table."

Coming back into the room, Thom said, "Please sit."

When Rin came back, he placed the tray on the table.

Mekial took some muffins from her basket and placed them on the tray. "I have a few more for you too."

Thom could smell the cinnamon and apple muffins. His mouth was already watering.

Noticing his reaction, Rin said, "Thom, please wait until the water is ready for the tea."

Thom nodded with a sigh.

"Mekial, did you have a chance to ask your mother about us visiting her?"

"Yes," she replied. "Mamie asked if late morning next Tas-dae would work for you."

"That should be fine," Rin replied. "I'll post a sign on my shop door that morning, letting customers know we'll be gone most of the day."

Thom scratched his head, looking puzzled. Mekial had referred to her mother as Mamie but also as Ma. He wondered if they were nicknames for the same person or had other meanings.

"Thom, is something concerning you?" Rin prompted.

"May I ask you a question, Mekial?"

"Sure, anything," she replied. "After all, I'm your teacher now," she said, grinning.

"You said your Ma made the muffins. But earlier, you also used the word, Mamie. Are you using a different word for the same person?" he asked.

"They're both variations of mother. But in my case, Mamie is Lauret Gambi. She's the healer who works with Rafi in the infimarium. Ma is Bea Gambi. She's my other mother. She's the one who baked the muffins. She's also a blacksmith, by the way."

Thom nodded tentatively.

"Thom," Rin interrupted. "I think you have another question, and I suspect Mekial knows what it is."

Mekial smiled and nodded. "My mothers are married. They raised me and my younger brother, Budaj."

"You don't have a father, then?" Thom remarked.

"Well, there's a man who's our father, but we don't call him that because he didn't raise us. He's one of the monks."

"Thom, do you recall our conversation about relationships in Glakkadeth?"

"Yes. You explained there are couples of the same gender. Am I using the correct term, Mekial?" Thom asked.

"Yes," she replied.

"Thom, I think the water's boiling," Rin interrupted. "Would you go make up the pot?"

"Of course," he replied.

Shortly after, Thom returned with the tea and poured them a cup.

"Thom, why don't you try one of the muffins with the chocolate pieces," Mekial suggested. "They're the ones with the dark bits. I wonder what you'll think."

Thom grabbed one and took a bite. His eyes rolled in bliss. "Wow, this is amazing," he exclaimed. "It tastes incredible. Rin, do you love them, too?"

"I do like chocolate," Rin admitted, "but I prefer the cinnamon-apple muffins. They're quite wonderful."

"I'm glad you like them," Mekial replied. "I have more in the basket. There's more of the others, too, Healer Rinbalden. Ma likes to bake. She makes biscuits and buns. Buns have a filling."

"You can call me Healer Rin, Mekial," Rin offered.

They were silent for the next few minutes as they enjoyed the muffins.

"May I have another?" Thom asked. "They really are fantastic!"

"Thanks," Mekial replied, "I'll tell Ma. But did you know you have chocolate on your chin?"

"Oh," he cringed and wiped it with his napkin.

"I should go," Mekial announced. "I'll tell Mamie you'll be coming next Tas-dae."

Mekial stood, as did Rin and Thom. Before she left, she took the remaining muffins from her basket and placed them on the tray. It was an impressive pile.

"Your mother is most generous," Rin said. "If she's at the monastery when we visit next week, we'll thank her personally."

"She will be," Mekial replied. "She offers her black-smithing skills there three times a week."

"Yes, thanks again for the muffins," Thom interjected before stuffing the last bit of his second chocolate muffin in his mouth.

Mekial smiled, replying, "You're welcome. Bye."

Chapter 32

Thom rose early on the day they'd travel to the monastery. The night before, he and Rin had gathered herb packets for Mekial's mother and Rafi. They were also bringing burn salves and other ointments. As a gesture of thanks for the muffins, they added some thyme and rosemary that Mekial's other mother could use for baking.

Rin opened the shop at their usual time, 7 am. They waited on customers for two hours before Rin said, "Let's close up and get ready to leave. Would you saddle up Crescent? The bag with the salves, ointments, and herbs is on the table."

"Alright," Thom replied. He also retrieved a bag containing the Glakkadian dictionary and his novel. Thom didn't think he'd have time to read but wanted to bring it anyway. Entering the stable, he called out, "Hi, Crescent. We're going on an adventure."

Crescent whinnied in response.

Thom picked up a brush and started grooming him. Crescent leaned into him, his indicator that he wanted more. "I know you love this, you greedy beast. I gave you a thorough grooming yesterday. This will be a short one." He also inspected Crescent's hooves to make sure nothing was lodged there. Finally, he ran his hand over Crescent's body, where the saddle would sit, to confirm it was still smooth.

Thom arranged the saddle blanket and the saddle on him before cinching the front and back straps. While he had liked Brule, he felt more connected to Crescent. Perhaps Thom's sensitivity was related to his work on his gifts. After strapping on the saddlebags, he led Crescent down the alley, alongside their shop, to the front door.

"Is everything ready?" Rin asked, locking the door behind him and confirming the closed notice was prominently displayed.

"Yep," Thom replied.

The monastery was located outside the town's northwest gate. Rin would ride Crescent, and Thom would walk alongside. After about an hour, they reached the gate. It didn't look very wide or tall to Thom.

"Good morning, sirs," the guard there greeted them. "Would you mind waiting? A cart's about to come through."

"Not at all," Rin assured him. "Let's stand over by the guardhouse, Thom."

"Duck your head," the guard called to the cart driver. "Duck your head!" he yelled. Turning to Rin and Thom, he said, "We've told the steward who oversees this gate that it needs to be widened and made taller, but nothing's happened. Sorry about the wait."

They watched as the driver carefully led two horses and his cart through. The cart was laden with enormous barrels. As it went by, Thom heard what sounded like liquid sloshing inside them. He wondered what they contained.

"Thank you for waiting," the guard said, beckoning them forward. "You might've been fine passing through at the same time. But a month back, a similar cart, also carrying barrels, rode through, and one of its wheels came loose. Two of the barrels fell off and busted open, nearly injuring a monk walking in the opposite direction. She did get drenched from the ale that spilled. She wasn't pleased."

"Thank you for your precaution, sir," Rin called out, nodding.

"You're welcome. Have a good day."

Passing through the gate, Rin and Thom made their way to the crossroads and the signpost. One of the signs displayed the monastery's name and pointed toward the northwestern road. Heading in that direction, they passed by an apple orchard and a meadow, where some residents were grazing sheep and goats.

Soon after, they approached an adobe wall about six feet high on the right. Traveling further, they came to a wooden archway. Above the archway, carved in the wood, was a spiral symbol with wavy lines passing through it. Above it were the words, Holders of Lumen-anima Monastery.

Since the gate was open and had no attendants, they rode through into a large courtyard. Off to the side, Thom saw a small garden with stone benches upon which two people sat. A young man was tending some plants. Ahead of them, running more than half the length of the courtyard, was a building with mud walls and a tiled roof. Hearing whimpering, Thom looked to the left and saw a sheltered area with benches. Sitting on one was a woman, wearing an apron and cradling a child of about six, who was the source of the sound.

Mekial came out of the leftmost door of the building and went to the woman and child. Noticing Rin and Thom, she smiled and waved. Then she directed the woman to follow her into the door she had exited.

While they waited for her to return, Rin dismounted, and they made their way closer to the building.

Soon after, Mekial returned and walked over.

"Welcome, Healer Rin and Thom!" she greeted them. "I'm excited you're here. Mamie's inside with Rafi caring for the little girl."

"What happened to her?" Rin asked.

"She was helping her mother prepare noon supper and burned herself on a pot."

"Oh, do you know if your mother and Rafi have burn salve?" Rin asked. "We brought some with us."

"They do. But I'm sure more would be welcome," Mekial replied. "Mamie asked me to take you to the stable."

"Thank you," Rin replied.

Thom took the Crescent's reins, and they followed Mekial along the road that curved behind the building.

They found themselves in a sizeable compound, with buildings connected by covered walkways. One building, off to the left, had six floors with windows running along its first floor.

"That's where most of the monks live. The lowest level is where everyone eats," Mekial explained, noticing where Thom was looking. In front of us is the chapel."

Glancing at it, Thom noticed the same symbol above the doorway as the entry gate.

"The stables are a little further along against the monastery wall. You can see it from here," Mekial said, pointing."

"That's a large stable. How many horses do the monks have?" Thom asked.

"About thirty. I know some of the mares are pregnant. So, they'll have more soon."

A middle-aged woman with a solid build was walking their way when they entered the stable.

"Hi, Maden," Mekial greeted her. "These are the people Mamie mentioned. This is Healer Rinbalden and his apprentice Thom." Turning to Rin and Thom, she said. "This is Maden, the stable manager."

"Nice to meet you, Maden," Rin greeted her. "And you can call me Rin."

"Nice to meet you too," Maden replied. "There are empty stalls ahead."

Thom led Crescent into one of them.

"Brushes and curry combs are hanging on the wall," Maden instructed. "Hay's in the corner, and there's an oats bin next to them. I'll leave you to it."

"Thank you," Thom and Rin replied.

Maden nodded and headed further into the stable.

"Thom," Rin said, "Why don't you get Crescent cleaned up and settled? Mekial, would you take me to your mother and Rafi? I'll take one of the saddle bags, Thom. When you're done, meet us there with the other."

"OK," he replied. Thom unloaded both saddle bags and handed one to Rin. When they left, he got to work making Crescent comfortable.

He had added hay to the feed bin when Mekial returned.

"I brought a treat for your horse if that's OK," she said.

"Oh, Crescent would love that," Thom replied. "Let me get him some oats and water, and then I'll introduce you."

When Thom finished, he led Mekial to the front of the stall. "Crescent," he said, "this is Mekial. Mekial, this is Crescent. Crescent's a strong and proud horse. And mostly well-behaved," giving him a wink.

Crescent snorted.

"He's beautiful. And I like the marking on his face. It looks like the moon."

"Oh, I was wondering what the word for that was in your language," Thom remarked. "That's how Rin came up with the name. Crescent, Mekial brought you a treat."

Mekial pulled the apple out of a pocket in her tunic and placed it in front of Crescent's mouth.

Crescent literally pounced on it.

"Crescent!" Thom exclaimed in annoyance. "That's rude."

"It's OK," Mekial said.

Quickly swallowing the treat, Crescent flapped his lips before nuzzling Mekial.

"I also have a sugar cube for you," she stated before feeding it to him.

"Oh, you're his new best friend," Thom admitted. "Crescent, I don't know how long we'll be, but if it turns out we'll be here a while, I'll come by and check on you."

Crescent whinnied.

"Let's go back to the infimarium," Mekial suggested.

"OK," Thom replied. When they crossed the yard but didn't retrace their steps, he frowned.

"This is the backside of the same building that the infimarium is located," Mekial explained.

"Oh, I'd wondered," Thom said. "It doesn't look like the same building."

"That's because the front of the building has the public entrances to the infimarium, trading post, and storage for garden supplies. This door gets us into the hallway behind them. It's the staff's private entrance."

When they entered the staff door of the infimarium, Thom saw a room twice the size as his Mam's healing room, with two examination tables and cabinets lining the walls on both sides. Rin was standing near a woman and a young man near his oldest brother's age. He assumed they were Mekial's mother and Rafi.

"Thom," Rin said, "I'm glad you're here. This is Mekial's mother, Healer Gambi, and Apprentice Healer, Brother Raphael."

"Nice to meet you, Thom," Healer Gambi said. "You can call me Lauret. I'm sure it'd be fine for you to call Brother Raphael, Rafi."

"Of course," Rafi replied.

"Nice to meet you both," Thom replied.

"Set the other saddlebag on the table," Rin indicated. "Lauret and Rafi, this bag contains the other herbs I mentioned. I'm glad we brought the salves and ointments, Thom. They were running low. We gave the mother and her child, whom we saw earlier, one of the little pottery jars you made with the salve. Lauret thinks there would be a great market for the jars."

"Yes," Lauret chimed in. "We haven't been able to get jars that size, and they'd be perfect for sending medicines home with our patients. The mother who visited is the main cook here, but it still made sense for her to have a jar of salve in the kitchen should other accidents occur."

"I'm glad that helped," Thom said. "Do you know where I might get good clay to work with and a kiln where I can fire them?"

"You should talk with Brother Reyner," Lauret replied. "Mekial can introduce you."

"Yep," she agreed.

"Thom," Rin said, "Rafi, Lauret, and I are going over treatments and herbs for the next hour. You won't learn anything new by staying here." Turning to Lauret, he asked, "Is Mekial needed here?"

"No. Mekial's gift doesn't lie in the direction of herbs or healing."

Mekial nodded.

"Mekial, in addition to introducing Thom to Brother Reyner, would you introduce him to any other brothers and sestras you encounter?" Rin asked.

"Sure," Mekial replied.

"Also, we're hoping to find a spiritual teacher for Thom. He has an unusual and powerful gift I haven't yet identified. I'm hoping one of the monks can. Besides that, I want Thom to learn the beliefs of your Aaliswan faith. Do you know of someone who might be interested in providing instruction?"

"I think I know someone," Mekial replied. "She has powerful gifts, too." Looking at her mother and Rafi, they all chuckled and together exclaimed, "Sestra Berbera."

"Mekial," Lauret said, "I think Sestra Berbera's in the chapel. We'll meet you in the refectory in an hour and a half after the noon supper bell rings."

"OK, Mamie," she replied.

Chapter 33

Making their way to the chapel, Thom commented, "Your mother said you aren't a healer."

"No, I'm not," she said. "I've helped her sometimes, but I really like defense and protection work, as Brother Medelin calls it. I'm getting weapons training from him. I hope I'm good enough to be part of the Prezdan's Guard when I grow up."

"Oh. In Docha-leigh, we have a few women soldiers, but not many. How long have you been training?"

"Six months, but Medelin thinks I have a knack for it. He even mentioned I might get into the Guard Academy a year sooner than most when I'm thirteen. I know that's almost three years away.

"Three years. That makes you ten years old," Thom commented.

"How old are you?" Mekial asked.

"Almost nine and a half."

"We're almost the same age," Mekial replied. "Since your Healer Rin's apprentice, you'll be the same kind of a healer as him, right?"

"Well, I'm kinda unsure," he replied. "I have a strong physical healing gift, and Rin's helping me get better. But I've got another gift that even Rin can't figure out, and it's much stronger."

"Do you know anything about it?" Mekial asked.

"Rin thinks it's related to healing. But it also has something to do with people's spirits and maybe their auras."

"I've never heard of that," Mekial commented. "Have you known about it all your life?"

"Nope," Thom replied. "It first showed up when Rin and I were on the road. You see, we were supposed to go to Eiren originally. But when I healed a boy using that gift, Rin thought we should come here instead."

"What happened?"

"Um," Thom paused. "I'm not sure I should say anything."

"I promise I won't tell anyone," Mekial said.

Thom sensed into Mekial, seeing her blue aura, which indicated honesty and trustworthiness. "OK. A little boy was sick, and nobody could help him," he explained. "The thing is, his mother was pregnant with him and his twin sister. But when she was giving birth, the girl died. Somehow, her spirit got confused and twisted itself around her brother's. I still don't completely understand what I did, but I got her spirit to let go."

"Wow," Mekial replied. "I haven't heard of anyone being able to see someone's spirit."

"From what Rin told me, no one has. Maybe Sestra Berbera can."

"I don't know," she replied. "But now I'm pretty sure she's the best person for you to talk to. She can also teach you about Aaliswan beliefs."

"Good," Thom replied. "The Iosan faith I grew up with doesn't quite fit. I did believe some of it, but the elders kept saying Deu demanded we be perfect. And that doesn't feel right anymore."

"Wait. Your elders expected you to be perfect?" Mekial asked. "I could never be. Oh, there's Brother Reyner," she said, pointing to a man exiting the chapel. "Brother Reyner!" she shouted.

Ahead of them, Thom saw a man with jet-black hair and wearing a light brown robe.

"Mekial," he responded, coming toward them. "Does your mother need something?"

"Oh, no, Brother Reyner," Mekial replied quickly. "This is Thom. He made some small jars Mamie thinks would be good for her salves. He's willing to make more, but needs good clay and a kiln."

"Mekial, take a breath and slow down," Reyner advised. "Nice to meet you, Thom. You're young to be a potter."

"I'm not, sir," he replied. "I'm an apprentice healer. My father's a potter. I worked with him for two years before I left home. He taught me how to make pots, jars, and other things."

"Are you Healer Rinbalden's apprentice?"

"Yes, sir."

"I had heard a healer and his apprentice would be visiting today. Please call me Reyner. Do I understand you're from Docha-leigh?"

"Yes, I am, Reyner."

"And your father's a potter. I wonder if I know his work."

"My Da's name is Uric Macirdan."

"Oh yes," he replied. "I've heard of him. A potter friend on the capital island told me she saw some of your father's work."

"Da would be happy to hear that," Thom replied.

"Yes, she told me your father produces high-quality pottery and creates interesting designs with emboss-ments and etchings. I think she mentioned your father even fires stones into them sometimes."

"He does," he grinned. "I wonder how your friend saw some of it."

"Oh," Reyner replied. "She travels to Docha-leigh occa-sionally but didn't mention meeting your father. I'd love to see his work or yours."

"I can show you some things I made, including little jars we brought from home. I created some jars here, but they're hand-molded."

"I'd still be very interested in seeing them," he replied. "Regarding your request for clay, I can take you to the streambed, where we get ours. And you can use our kiln. Would that work?"

"Yes, sir!" Thom exclaimed, his voice rising in excite-ment.

"Of course. How about meeting me at the pottery after supper? It's behind the chapel. You can see smoke coming out of the kiln chimney."

"I think that's OK, but I should tell Rin."

"Certainly," Reyner concurred. "Mekial, you're very quiet."

"Well, after I introduced Thom, I thought I'd just breathe, like you said," she smirked.

"Oh. May the One bless your mothers for raising such a cheeky daughter. Anything else?"

"Is Sestra Berbera still in the chapel?" Mekial asked.

"No. She left. But I believe Lebrim, her postulant, is still there. He'll know where she is."

"Thank you," Mekial and Thom replied.

When they stepped through the chapel doors, they were greeted by the smell of incense.

Thom sneezed. "Oh no, incense," he whispered, not wanting to disturb the people meditating there. "The elders at home love using incense, especially at the Solstice services."

"Are you allergic?" Mekial asked.

"Not really. But my nose is super sensitive. The few times I smelled it, I sneezed."

"They burn one around the December Solstice that smells like evergreens," Mekial commented.

"Oh, I think I'd like that as long as they didn't use a lot." Gazing around, he said, "This is nice. It's so simple compared to the chapel at home." Straight wooden benches with burgundy pads were arranged in concentric circles. In the center was a stone altar covered with a cloth, hosting an array of candles in various sizes. On the adobe walls, he saw mosaics of figures surrounded by colors resembling auras, including a few with wings.

"What's your chapel like?" Mekial asked.

"It's got fancy benches with carvings that match the marble altar. But let me tell you, those benches didn't have padding. Sitting there made my butt ache. The walls were covered with religious figures that looked like past elders and plaques listing the names of folks who donated them. There are also a few statues. It feels crowded, even without people. This chapel's beautiful, and it feels sort of freeing."

"Yes, it is," Mekial said.

"I wish my Da and my sister Meli could see the mosaics," Thom said. "Meli's an artist. Before I left home, she'd quit working in the pottery to focus on her art."

"Reyner and some of his apprentice potters created them. You can ask him about it. Oh, there's Lebrim," Mekial said, waving to a short, thin man with black hair. "Hi, Lebrim," she said as he drew close.

"Hi, Mekial," he answered.

"I'd like to meet Thom," she continued. "He's an apprentice to Healer Rinbalden."

"Nice to meet you, Thom," he said, extending his hand to shake.

As Thom shook Lebrim's hand, he was immediately struck by Lebrim's energy. It felt strong and calming. He sensed his aura was vivid purple, shaded with blue and turquoise.

"You're a holy one," Lebrim stated suddenly.

"What?" Mekial said.

"I'm sorry," Thom replied. "I don't know that word."

"You have a strong healing spirit," he explained.

"I do? I am learning healing from Rin," Thom explained.

"No. You misunderstand," Lebrim replied. "You have a physical healing gift, but you also have an extremely powerful spirit healing gift. Were you not aware?"

"Spirit healing. That's what it's called?" Thom uttered, looking stunned. "I know my second gift is stronger than my physical healing gift, but Rin couldn't name it. Can you tell me more?"

"Please wait here," Lebrim said.

As Thom watched Lebrim leave, he noticed something strange. Lebrim almost glided away. "What's that about?" he asked Mekial.

"I don't know," Mekial answered, her brow furrowed. "Lebrim joined the monastery a year ago. Sestra Berbera took him under her wing. He seems pretty spiritual, but I haven't spent much time with him."

When Lebrim returned, he was with Sestra Berbera. After introducing her to Thom, he left.

Without saying anything, Sestra Berbera gestured towards one of the benches and sat down.

Sitting beside her, Thom and Mekial noticed her eyes were closed. Uncertain what to do, they sat quietly.

Thom looked at the mosaics again and saw one he hadn't noticed. It reminded him of the dragons in his novels. It also triggered a vague sense that he had met one. Don't be silly.

A few moments later, Sestra Berbera opened her eyes. Turning to them, she said, "Hello, Mekial and Thom. I suspect you had a strange encounter with Lebrim."

"Yes, how'd you know?" Thom asked.

"Lebrim never hurries anywhere. When he rushed up to me, he was very excited. He explained you have a very unusual and powerful gift."

"He called my gift spirit healing. What is that?" Thom asked, puzzled. "Even Rin didn't know. At first, he thought it was part of my physical healing gift. But after I healed a young boy, he realized my second gift was something special."

"I'm not surprised," Sestra replied. "Your two gifts are similar because your spirit healing gift does result in some physical healing. But a spirit healer is more about healing a person's spirit or, more accurately, helping them remember their true nature as a divine spirit and all that comes with it."

"I'm confused," Thom admitted.

"I'll tell you more at another time," Sestra replied. "May I hold your hands?"

"Sure," he answered.

Sestra grasped his hands. After a few seconds, she spoke. "You have shields. Would you mind lowering them? If you're hesitant, sense into me first. I believe you can do that, can't you?"

"Yes," Thom answered. When he tuned into her aura, he saw vibrant purple, blue, and turquoise, like Lebrim, but also lavender, for grace, in addition to green and brown. The colors swirled in a kind of rhythmic dance. It was mesmerizing. He knew he could trust her and immediately dropped five shields. It would have been six had Rin not removed his fake shield a month before.

"Thank you," she replied. Sestra sat quietly, holding his hands and gazing into Thom's eyes.

Wanting to help, Thom imagined his heart opening to her.

She blinked and took a deep breath. "Lebrim was quite correct, Thom. You have a very powerful spirit-healing gift. Your spirit blazes quite intensely. Have you not been aware of it?"

"Somewhat," he replied. "Rin explained that my gift for spirit healing is powerful, as you and Lebrim call it. I know I can detect life energies from quite a distance. Rin also told me I see auras with greater detail than he."

"Good. My sense is your spirit-healing gift recently emerged. In fact, it looks like it was abrupt."

"Yes, it was," Thom replied. He went on to explain his encounter with Samiltun and Rindo's healing.

"That makes sense. I still see some raw edges. But it appears you've worked with your teacher to smooth them out."

"Oh. I'm glad," Thom replied. "Are you a spirit healer?"

"No, I'm not," she said.

"Oh," he said, his face falling. "I guess you can't help me."

"I didn't say that. I have worked with people with unusual gifts," she replied, considering before nodding. "I usually work with one student at a time, but I'd be honored to work with you too, Thom."

"You would? Thank you. But what do you mean, honored?" he replied. "Maybe I don't understand the word. I'm still learning Glakkadian."

"You speak it quite well. But let me try other words. Respected, Worthy, Esteemed. But even they don't convey what I mean."

"I have a dictionary in my bag but left it with Rin. I'll look it up tonight."

"Good," Sestra replied. "Young man... how old are you, eight or nine? You look young, but you sound much older."

"Almost nine and a half," he replied.

"Ah. It all makes sense," Sestra said.

"What?" Thom asked.

"As Lebrim said, your gift is extraordinary, and with it comes some innate wisdom. It is rooted in and comes out of your holiness."

"Lebrim used a similar word," Thom said. "But I don't know the corresponding Dochalan word."

"It means you're very connected to the divine through your spirit," she explained. "In other words, you are blessed."

"What?" he replied. "I never felt like that. For a long time, I felt cursed because I was different."

"That makes sense too. Your uniqueness made you stand out, and I suspect you didn't fit in well with other children."

Thom's eyes welled up with tears.

"Thom, you're a beautiful being, not perfect, but truly beautiful," she said, patting his hands.

Wiping his eyes with his tunic, he mumbled, "Sorry."

"You have nothing to be sorry about," Sestra assured him. "Tears are your body's way of releasing pain and trauma."

"Thanks," Thom mumbled, his head lowered.

"Furthermore, Thom, she stated, "My angels confirm your spirit-healing gift holds immense potential power."

Thom's head popped up as his mouth dropped open. "Your angels? You have angels?"

"I don't have angels," she corrected. "Rather, there are a few angels with whom I have a strong relationship. You have at least one with whom you're connected, yes? Like your guardian angel?"

"I do," Thom agreed. "Rin told me I could connect to other angels and guides too. Since I haven't heard about many angels, I connect with Deu and my guardian angel. Mostly by writing in my journal and sometimes talking in my head."

Deu. His closest connection is with God. How unusual, she thought. Speaking out loud, Sestra Berbera said,

"Back to your spirit healing gift. I will work with you. As mentioned, I don't have your gift. However, I have worked with people with strong divine connections. Before I forget, my angels want me to impart something fundamental. Although your gift is special, it doesn't make you better than anyone else. Always use it with humility and be grateful for having it."

"I will, Sestra," Thom assured her.

"Are you going to teach Thom our beliefs, too?" Mekial interrupted.

"Mekial," Sestra cautioned, "I think Thom can speak for himself. But yes."

"Sorry," Mekial said.

"Mekial's right," Thom confirmed. "Rin wanted me to learn about your beliefs."

"Understood," Sestra replied. "Before I let you go, I want to ask you something."

"OK," he replied.

"When I first arrived, I sensed your interest in the mosaics."

"I am," he replied. "They're very beautiful. A few figures seem familiar, but I don't know why."

"Does your faith have religious images in your churches?"

"I only know my chapel at home. But it has paintings and statues, like I told Mekial," Thom answered. "None of them look like these."

"I see," she said. "Well, I can think of three reasons why some might be familiar: from previous lifetimes, through your higher self dwelling in the divine realm, or through visitations."

"By previous lifetimes, are you talking about reincarnation?"

"Yes," she replied. "That's one of the beliefs of my faith."

"Rin told me," Thom said. "I want to learn more about it."

"What about visitations?" Sestra asked.

"Well, the elders told us about those in the holy book but nothing about people having them today. Would you count a visitation from my guardian angel, Sereh?"

"Yes," she answered. "I'd imagine your elders didn't talk about your higher self either?"

"No," Thom replied.

"Depending on how long you're here, I'll teach you about reincarnation and higher selves, among other things. Do you know how long that will be?"

"No. I'll check with Rin at supper. He's doing some training with Mekial's mother and Rafi."

"Is he?" Sestra mused. "I have an idea. But I must talk with your teacher and a few other monks."

"OK, Sestra Berbera," Thom replied, curious about what she wanted to talk to them about.

"Off with you, Mekial and Thom."

"Thank you, Sestra Berbera," Thom and Mekial replied.

Chapter 34

When they left the chapel, Thom turned to Mekial, "I like Sestra Berbera. She's very wise."

"Even though I haven't known you long, I thought she'd be perfect for you."

"She is. Thanks," Thom said as his stomach growled. "Um...how soon before supper?"

Mekial laughed. "The bell should ring soon. What if I show you more of the monastery before then and end up near the refectory?"

"Sounds good. But what's a refectory?"

"It's what the monks call their dining room."

"Huh," Thom replied. "Hey, can we first check on Crescent?"

"Of course."

After confirming his equine friend was fine, Mekial led Thom to a garden.

"What a big garden," Thom remarked, looking upon the rows and rows of plants.

"It is," Mekial confirmed. "The monastery has many mouths to feed, not to mention patients to treat. The monks have a full plate, don't you think? Get it?" she asked, chuckling.

"You're strange. I am, too," he admitted, smiling. "My Mam has a good-sized garden," he replied. "Not as large as this."

"Do you have a big family?" Mekial asked.

"Yes, I have two older brothers, two older sisters, a younger sister, and a younger brother. And when I left home, Mam was pregnant. So, there'd be eight children by now."

"You have a big family," Mekial replied.

"Yes. Mam came from a big one, and both my Da and Mam wanted the same."

"Do you have a big home?" Mekial asked.

"Not big enough. Da and my oldest brother Bedum added a room for Mam a few years ago. But it was still cramped. Do you have a big family?"

"I have one older brother and one younger besides Mamie and Ma," Mekial replied.

"Do you live here?" Thom asked.

"Oh, no. We do have a room the monks let us use if we stay late," she answered. "It's a big place, as you can see."

"Uh-huh. Last week, you mentioned kids live here. Are their parents on staff?"

"A few," Mekial said. "But the parents of the rest are monks."

"Oh. Somehow, I thought monks had to be... um... celibate," saying the word in Dochalan. "That's what my Mam called it."

"I don't know that word," Mekial said.

"It means they aren't married and aren't, um....intimate," he said, reddening.

"I get it," she replied, smiling. "Some are, but most aren't. Is that how it is with your religion?" Mekial asked.

"Yeah," Thom replied.

"In our faith, monks can marry," she explained. "And that can be someone of the same or the opposite gender. If same-gender couples want kids, often another monk helps, like with my mothers."

"Do the kids become monks?" Thom asked.

"If they feel called to join," she explained. "Neither my older brother nor I were called. I'm not sure about my younger brother, but I have doubts. Kids raised here can choose to leave the monastery when they are 16 if they don't feel called. Some leave earlier if they apprentice to a trader outside the monastery."

"I never heard of that, not that I would. It makes sense. Going back to what I asked earlier, where do you live when you don't stay here?"

"We have a home with three bedrooms and a loft near the northwestern gate," she replied. "But, it's still a little crowded. Mamie uses my room to store some of her healing supplies."

"Sometimes I wish I grew up in a smaller family," Thom confessed. "I've always felt a bit different from my brothers and sisters. They're all noisy and chatty. I like spending time by myself writing and reading. Do you like to read?"

"Not much. My training keeps me pretty busy. I don't have much time for it."

"What does your older brother do?" Thom asked.

"He's in his last year at the Guard Academy. When he graduates, he'll move out. Mamie plans to make his room into her healing room. It'll be nice to have more space."

"Does he want to become a Prezdan Guard like you?" Thom asked.

"Yes," Mekial replied. "But he wants to get specialized training on the capital island and get assigned a post there. I'm fine with getting posted anywhere."

"What does a guard do?" Thom asked.

"They protect the Prezdan and his family and watch over government meetings, including when foreign officials visit. Sometimes, they travel with him when he goes to other countries. I'd love to do that."

"Sounds cool," Thom replied as a bell rang.

"That's the supper bell," Mekial announced. "Why don't we head into the refectory through the kitchen?"

"Sounds good," Thom replied as his stomach growled again. "Sorry."

When they reached the kitchen door, Thom heard the clanking of pots, pans, and dishes.

Mekial peeked in and said, "OK. The coast is clear."

"Are we going to get in trouble for coming in this way?" he asked.

"No. Lots of the servers are novices and postulants. Some are kind of clumsy. I don't want to run into them when they're carrying the food."

"Good," Thom replied with relief. The last thing he wanted to do was anger anyone the first day he was here.

Thom and Mekial entered a bustling scene. Dominating the space was a single hearth where beef roasted, filling the air with its aroma. Thom's mouth watered. The room also boasted of two sizable stoves and three sinks. A young man and woman were scrubbing pots at two sinks. Glancing around, Thom's eyes fell upon a girl peeling vegetables at a corner table. She had a bandage on her arm and winced occasionally.

Noticing where Thom was looking, she said, "Oh. That's Meri. She's the girl Mamie treated earlier. Meri got scalded with boiling water while helping her mother, Awa, the main cook here. It looks like Awa's free. Come, I'll introduce you."

"OK," Thom replied.

They walked over to the woman, adding a dirty pot to the pile by a sink.

"Awa," Mekial called out.

"Yes," she replied, turning towards them.

"I know you're busy, but I wanted you to meet Thom. Thom, this is Sestra Awa. But everyone calls her Awa. Awa, Thom's the apprentice healer who made the pot of salve Mamie gave you."

"Oh. It's nice to meet you, Thom," she replied. "Having the salve here will be a big help, at least for minor burns. Meri's burn this morning was a bit more serious," she said, glancing at her daughter with sympathy.

Thom noticed Awa carefully looking him over.

"You're too skinny," she declared. "There's plenty of food in the refectory. After supper, come back, and I'll give you more rolls and sweet buns to plump you up."

"Thank you, Awa," Thom replied as his stomach growled again. He wondered if any buns would have lemon filling.

"Best you get him some food, Mekial before he passes out," she ordered, laughing.

"Yes, ma'am," Mekial curtsied.

"Oh, you," she replied.

Thom and Mekial pushed through the kitchen's swinging doors into the refectory. In front of him, Thom saw a series of long tables that stretched back three rows. On either side of the doors, Thom saw other tables laden with baskets, dishes, and tureens of food. People were lined up and serving themselves. Scanning the room, he saw Rin, Lauret, and Rafi and pointed them out to Mekial.

"Let's get in line," Mekial suggested. "It looks like the cooks made stew today. They always serve a salad. Plus, there's also warm bread. Grab a bowl and a plate, and take as much as you want. As Awa mentioned, the cooks make a lot of food."

Thom didn't need to be told a second time. Following Mekial's example, he served himself some of everything. At

Mekial's encouragement, he slathered extra butter on his slices of bread.

With full plates of food, they made their way to the table where Rin, Lauret, and Rafi sat. Thom saw another lady and a boy, probably younger than him, talking with Lauret.

"Thom and Mekial," Rin said. "I'm glad you made it. We saved places for you."

After sitting down, Mekial poured them water from the pitcher on the table.

"Thom," Lauret spoke, "I'd like you to meet my wife, Bea."

"Nice to meet you... "um... Mrs. uh."

"Mrs. Gambi. But please call me Bea," she replied.

"This is my younger brother, Budaj, who I mentioned," Mekial said.

"I may be younger," Budaj declared, "but I'm twice as strong as you, Mekial!"

"Are not!" she countered.

"Am too," he insisted.

"Children! Enough," Lauret warned.

"Budaj sometimes works with me in the smithy," Bea explained. "And I must admit, he is getting stronger every day."

"I mostly put more coals on the forge and make sure it stays hot with the bellows," Budaj admitted. "But last week, Ma let me help fix a broken sword. She said I was really good at it," turning to Mekial and sticking out his tongue.

"Thom. Ma baked the sweet muffins I gave you the other day," Mekial reminded him.

"Oh. They were really good," he said. "Thank you. I loved the ones with the... I think it was called chocolin."

"Chocolate," Bea corrected. "Yes, they're Mekial's favorite too. You're very welcome."

Thom and Mekial turned their attention to their food. Thom found the stew hearty and wonderful. The salad was a nice complement to the heavy stew.

"Thom," Rin said. "I spoke with Sestra Berbera and Abbotess Linna."

Thom looked up with his mouth full of stew and grunted an acknowledgment.

"Sestra Berbera was amazed at the strength of your spirit healing gift," Rin continued. "Yes, she told me what it was called. You'll be meeting with her three times a week initially. Also, Brother Medelin agreed to train you in self-defense and weapons. I'll be coming twice a week to train Rafi and Lauret. They're also lending us a horse."

"Wow," Thom replied. "She already spoke with you? That's great." Pausing, he asked. "Um...should I be doing some work for them too?" He hoped he wouldn't be asked to weed.

"Yes," Rin answered. "I understand you talked with Brother Reyner earlier. He stopped by the infimarium and saw the salve jars you made. He was impressed. He'd like you to teach some of his apprentices."

"I can do that," he said with relief.

"Did I detect an unspoken fear that you might be asked to do something else, like weeding?" Rin replied with a grin.

Thom blushed and nodded.

"I know it's not one of your favorite chores," Rin said. "Besides, as I understand it, the novices and postulants handle that. Oh, and Reyner said he'd set you up on a pottery wheel, too."

"Great," Thom said. "I'm supposed to meet him after supper. I'll let him know we talked."

"Thom," Bea interjected. "I noticed the cooks put out the chocolate biscuits I made this morning."

"They did?" Thom said with excitement.

As he started getting up, Mekial said, "I'll get us all some. I'll also bring some berry biscuits for those who don't want the chocolate ones."

"Thanks," Thom said, sitting back down. Turning to Bea, he asked, "Do you own a bakeshop and a smithy?"

"No," Bea answered. "I only have a smithy. I bake at home because it relaxes me, and sometimes I make a large batch. When I do, I donate the extra to the monastery to cover some of Mekial's training expenses. But I think you have an underlying question. Were you hoping I ran a bakery where you could buy some chocolate treats?"

Thom blushed again.

"There are bakeshops in town that sell them," Bea explained.

"But they're not as good as yours, Ma," Mekial chimed in, returning with a plate of biscuits.

"I'll be happy to bake a regular supply of chocolate biscuits as payment for you teaching Mekial your language," Bea offered. "Mekial mentioned you were willing."

"Yes, yes, I did," Thom answered. "She's helping me with Glakkadian. You'll be sitting in when Sestra Berbera teaches me, won't you, Mekial? At least initially?"

"Yes, for as long as you need me," Mekial assured him. "By the way, I've already gone through a third of the primer you and Rin gave me."

"For someone who never reads, that's impressive," Thom replied.

"I didn't say I never read," she protested. "I said I didn't like it much. But for some reason, I think learning your language will be important. I study for an hour every night."

Chapter 35

A few days after his first visit, Thom left the shop for the monastery very early. It was a lovely, dry day in the mid-60s. Since he was training the potter apprentices, Reyner had assigned him a good-sized area to work in.

After two hours of teaching, Thom walked to the chapel to meet Sestra Berbera. When he arrived, he found Mekial already there talking with her.

"Good morning, Thom," Mekial called out.

"Good morning, Mekial and Sestra Berbera," Thom replied.

"How did your pottery session go with the apprentices?" Sestra Berbera asked.

"Good," he answered. "They're very talented. More than me. But I showed them some interesting tricks to mixing the clay and creating salve jars."

"Are you ready for your first official lesson?" Sestra Berbera asked, winking. "I realized I told you much more than I intended the first time we met."

"That's OK, Sestra Berbera," Thom replied. "And yes, I'm ready."

"You're welcome to call me Sestra B. That's what everyone calls me. I'm glad Mekial's with us today," she continued. "I want to talk with you more about our beliefs, and there'll likely be words you might not understand. I'm hoping you'll be able to translate, Mekial."

"I'll try," she replied. "I'm not sure how much help I'll be since I'm new to learning Dochalan. I do have a Glakkadian to Dochalan dictionary to help."

"Let's head back to one of the study rooms," Sestra B directed. "By the way, some sessions might include Lebrim and a novice."

Thom and Mekial followed Sestra B to a door at the back of the chapel, where they entered a hallway with rooms on both sides. She led them to one.

Stepping inside, Thom saw twelve padded chairs arranged in a circle, with bookshelves on two of the walls.

"Let's move three chairs closer together," Sestra B requested.

Sitting there, Thom felt his insides churning a little. Was he nervous or excited? Maybe a little of both.

Turning to Thom, Sestra B said, "First, let me tell you a little about our community's mission. You probably noted that our monastery is called Holders of Lumen-anima."

"Yes, above your entrance gate," he replied.

"That translates to holders of the light soul. The mission of my religious community, the Liberventians, is to help people remember their divine light or self in each incarnation and, as a result, discover their life purpose. Are you with me?"

"Yes," Thom replied.

"The Aaliswan faith," she continued, "teaches that each of us is a divine being who incarnates numerous times to learn, grow, and have new experiences. An essential part of a human's journey is to be attentive to the spirit and ultimately remember her or his divine nature and calling. Hence, the community symbol."

"That's the symbol above the chapel door and the entrance gate of the monastery, isn't it?" Thom asked.

"It is," Sestra confirmed. "The spiral represents journey and growth, and the lines are the spirit flowing through."

"It's neat," Thom said. "It kinda reflects my life over the last couple of years.

"I didn't know that," Mekial interrupted.

"Our founders were called to create a community to support the journey," Sestra B explained. "What's unusual is that our founders were two same-gender couples, Isoc and Augi Kante, and Meggie and Meri Jagne. A fundamental principle is that our members do not proselytize or try to convert people. We simply encourage everyone to live their best selves and from within their profession, whether teaching, pottery making, cooking, or even caring for horses."

"I like that," Thom replied. "People can follow their intuition."

"It's curious that you know that word," Sestra B said.

"Rin told me about it," Thom admitted. "You mentioned people need to remember their calling. Can you explain that? I've heard it used by the elders and Mekial, too."

"Certainly," Sestra B replied. "A calling is a person's life purpose that he or she first decides before birth. The term is more common in religious circles. But it applies to everyone."

"Do you know what my calling is?" Thom asked.

"That's part of your journey to remember it. Also, the same calling might differ depending on the person," Sestra B explained.

"How do you mean?" Mekial asked.

"For example, a calling might be to serve the poor. One man might feel passionate about doing so as a cook and open a soup kitchen. Another might have healing gifts, like you, Thom. She might dedicate her life to healing the poor. And not to leave you out, Mekial, someone like you might work as a constable making sure that the poor get equal treatment as the rich."

"Huh," Thom mumbled. "Are there callings based on specific gifts and sort of result in someone being unusual, like Lebrim?"

"There can be," Sestra B replied.

"And don't forget yourself, Sestra B," Mekial added.

"True," Sestra B admitted, lowering her eyes, "but I don't usually toot my own horn."

"I'm happy to toot," Mekial declared.

"To continue," Sestra B said, "While our monks live their purpose in many occupations, they are dedicated to helping others discover their own. Are you still following me, Thom?"

"Mostly," he said. "But I don't know the word toot."

Both Mekial and Sestra B chuckled.

Mekial looked up toot in the dictionary and explained, "It's the sound a goose makes or a musical instrument, like a horn."

"Oh," Thom replied, also chuckling.

"Anything else?" Sestra B asked.

"You talked about the One. Rin told me the One is the supreme being that my Iosan faith calls Deu. Can you tell me why you call Deu the One?"

"Ah. OK," she replied. "The name comes out of who or what the One is. The One is the creator, as in the Iosan faith. My understanding is that Deu is often pictured as a male. But in Aaliswan, the One is genderless. Out of the One, all things come to be: worlds, nature, humans, and all living creatures. We are expressions of the One. In other words, we are one and reflect the One."

Thom pursed his lips, his eyebrows furrowed.

"Is this too much for you?" Sestra B asked.

"Um," Thom replied.

"Let me put this another way," she said. "All of us are creations of the divine, the One. The One speaks us into existence, as it were. Some utterances result in angels, archangels, and other divine beings. We talked a little about angels when we first met."

"Yep," Thom agreed.

"Humans are uncommon expressions," Sestra explained. "Our soul or spirit, which is divine, attaches to our body when we incarnate. The rest of our divine being, our higher self, is still in the divine realm. Our higher self repeatedly incarnates to live out a particular calling."

"So, according to your faith, we've lived multiple times," Thom said.

"Yes," Sestra B replied. "Some remember bits of their previous lives, but most don't. The primary reason behind reincarnation is for the spirit to have a new experience, limiting the influence of the previous life."

"But why would they want to live more than once?" Thom asked. "The elders only teach about one life. And when you die, if you're good, you go to heaven. If you're not, you go to hell."

"Ah," she replied. "I didn't mean to get to that level of detail in our first meeting. But briefly, since we're part of the One, having our individual experiences broadens the One's being. In a way, they create new possibilities. I'm sure this isn't very clear. Why don't we talk more about this at another time and return to something more familiar to you."

Thom nodded.

"A few thousand years ago," Sestra B continued, "the One, upon seeing that people had forgotten their divine essence, uttered an unparalleled being into the world, Jeshua. From a young age, he fully remembered who he was and his calling. He traveled around teaching and healing. But many in the religious leadership were threatened when people started believing what he taught."

"That sounds like Iosa," Thom admitted. "I was taught he was Deu's only son and was killed by the religious leaders you mentioned."

"The same is true of the Aaliswan faith," Sestra B replied. "But unlike your faith, Jeshua is not the One's only child. Granted, he had an important calling. But, like him, we are all expressions of the One."

"That's not what I was taught," Thom remarked. "The elders said humans are sinful, and it was their responsibility to tell us what Deu wanted. They also taught the Iosan faith was the true faith, and all others were wrong."

"I see," Sestra B commented.

"Mam and Da don't believe that," Thom continued. "It's one of the reasons why my family doesn't always attend services. Another was because my parents saw elders acting cruelly and dishonestly. My brothers and sisters and I still had religious education. My parents thought it was important for us to know about Deu and other religious stuff."

"Thom, have you seen an elephant in your time here?" Sestra B asked.

"Yes, Rin pointed one out on the way to the monastery the other day. I forgot to tell you, Mekial. Why?" he asked, startled at the sudden change in topic.

"I want to use an elephant as an analogy. I know it sounds odd, but bear with me."

"OK," Thom replied. "But what does analogy mean?"

"Mekial?" she said.

Looking it up, she provided the corresponding Dochalan word.

"Thanks," Thom said.

"As you know, an elephant is a huge animal," Sestra B stated. "Both of you visualize people of various faiths standing around one. Imagine they're so close that all they see is one part, like a foot, the trunk, or an ear."

"OK," Thom replied curiously.

Mekial grunted in agreement.

"How would one group of people interpret their part?" Sestra B asked.

Pondering the question, Thom finally answered, "That the one part was all there is."

"Exactly. Would these people be aware of the other parts of the elephant?"

"No," Thom replied. "They'd describe the One and define their faith based on the part they see."

"Oh," Mekial replied in understanding. "I've never heard this before either. That would mean that when someone insists their faith is the correct one, it's because they only see that part."

"Yes," Sestra B confirmed. "What would happen if they stepped back and saw more?"

"They'd figure out there was more to the One than they thought," Thom stated. "And maybe they'd realize everyone was looking at the same thing."

"They'd also have to stop claiming other faiths were wrong," Mekial chimed in.

"Very good," Sestra B replied. "Hopefully, it would even lead them to walk around the elephant to get to know other parts and what they provide, like her trunk, tail, or ears. The same applies to faiths. If people ignore or discount another faith's perspective, their view of the One becomes skewed."

"Skewed?" Thom said.

"Oh, I know that one," Mekial replied, sharing the Dochalan word.

"Thanks, Mekial," Thom said. "Since no part of the elephant is better than another, the same is true for faiths, right?"

"It is. Now, my next point is critical," Sestra B continued. "Because each person possesses their own individuality, each may be drawn to or resonate with one part, as it were. And it's important to honor their choice."

"In that case," Mekial offered, "people shouldn't try to convince others to adopt their beliefs."

"And neither should they judge someone for following a faith that makes sense to them," Thom added. "Is that what you mean?"

"Yes, you're both getting it," Sestra B said. "Even members of our faith and my community don't always remember these basic tenets. One other thing. You must also respect those who don't believe in a supreme being—in other words, those who don't resonate with any faith."

Thom and Mekial sat quietly, thinking about all they had learned.

"Any questions?" Sestra B asked.

Both shook their heads.

"One final thought that's a bit less overwhelming," Sestra B said. "I know the Iosan faith teaches that formalized prayer is the primary way to communicate with Deu. You mentioned, Thom, that sometimes you talk to Deu and your guardian angel in your head. That's what I call chatting, and it's prayer, too. How's that going?"

"Oh, not great," Thom said. "Rin said the same thing about chatting. I've been trying. I'm not sure I'm doing it right. Since I live here, and your faith calls Deu the One, I thought using that name might help. But it didn't seem to. Saying good morning 'the One' felt awkward, though."

"First, there's no right way," she said. "Second, the One doesn't care what name you use. The One has many names. I'd suggest you keep trying but relax and let go of your expectations. As to the awkwardness, I agree. In fact, I refer to the One as God for that very reason."

"Oh, I think I somehow knew that," Thom replied, thinking of how he started his journal entries.

"Enough for today," she said. "Let's meet in two days at the same time. For that session, I'd like to focus on meditation and using it to connect consciously with your spirit-healing gift. Mekial, I don't think we'll need you. But do bring the dictionary, Thom."

"OK, Sestra B," they both replied.

As Mekial and Thom exited the room, Thom remarked. "That elephant analogy makes sense. I can't put it into words exactly, but it feels like there's more room around me. I need to write about all of this."

Mekial nodded. "I'm off to study Dochalan. Thanks for teaching me yesterday. Some of your conjugations are tricky."

"I understand," Thom said. "Good luck. I'm going to meet Brother Medelin. Should I be worried?"

"No," she assured him. "Medelin's tough, but he's a good teacher. He's all about finding your hidden skills and revealing weaknesses."

"Hidden skills, huh? It sounds like I'll get some not-so-hidden aches and pains."

Smiling in agreement, Mekial nodded and walked away.

By the end of the day, Thom knew he had guessed correctly. Medelin was pleased with his balancing and movement abilities but not his strength and endurance. Until the supper bell, he had Thom running at various speeds, between slow and sprinting, and lifting light to heavy grain bags. After the meal, he focused on staff work, first by hitting the pells and ending with sparring. Riding Crescent home, Thom was glad Rin had plenty of the salve for him to spread on his aching muscles.

Chapter 36

"Great job, everyone," Thom said to the potter apprentices. He hadn't been able to train them for the last half week and felt terrible about it. The previous Muns-dae, a runaway horse in the market fair, resulted in injuries that Rin and he had to attend to. Today was his first day back. He'd agreed to spend an extra hour with them to make up for his absence. All of them were making great progress in developing their tactile sensitivity, which was important for ensuring the clays were thoroughly mixed.

Exiting the building, he carefully navigated around the puddles left from last night's rain. Unfortunately, he couldn't avoid the mud. With more than a month left of the rainy season, mud would be a constant companion. Mekial had told him the abbotess had decided to have gravel paths laid down. Apparently, she'd lost her temper when the chapel custodian complained about having to mop up the mud three times before noon supper a few days ago.

Before heading to his session with Sestra B, Thom decided to check on Crescent. Hopping from one grassy section to another to stay as mud-free as possible, he witnessed Rin dash into the infimarium, his tunic splattered in a few places. Rin isn't supposed to be here today, he thought. There must be an emergency.

Entering the stable, he saw Maden tending a mare.

"Good morning, Thom," she greeted him.

"Good morning, Maden," he replied as he went to Crescent's stall. In the next stall was Abu, the horse lent to them by the monastery. Given Rin's hurry, he suspected he couldn't give Abu more than a cursory grooming. Stepping into his stall, Thom greeted him. "Hi, Abu. I'm going to give you a more thorough brush down than Rin could."

Abu whinnied in agreement.

In the next stall, Crescent neighed.

"I'll be there shortly, Cres. I haven't forgotten you." As Thom brushed Abu down, he discovered streaks of mud on the horse's chest and groin. When he finished thoroughly grooming him, including removing a few small sticks from his tail, Abu nuzzled him. "You're welcome." Returning to Crescent's stall, he said, "OK, Cres. Thanks for your patience. How about if I give you a little extra grain?"

Crescent whinnied in agreement.

Thom also checked the hay bin and added more. Running his hand across Crescent's back and flank, he confirmed all was clean. As a bonus, he scratched him on his withers. Sighing with pleasure, Crescent nibbled Thom's head. Lastly, he cleaned up the droppings in both stalls and deposited them in the barrel outside that was used to fertilize the garden.

Giving Crescent a final rub, Thom said, "OK, you greedy one."

"Thom," Maden called out.

"Yes," he answered.

"Thanks for grooming Abu. Rin was in a hurry to assist Lauret and Rafi with a patient. I was going to do that after I was done with Fanta."

"You're welcome," Thom replied. "I saw Rin too."

"When you're done, would you come here?" she asked.

"Certainly. Let me put away the brushes." The bell for supper hadn't rung yet, but Thom would've said yes even if it had. Maden had taken the time to teach him a few more things about caring for horses. He recalled her explaining that horses couldn't really understand human words, but they could detect the tone behind them. As such, addressing them with gentle and caring words was essential. He was intrigued when she told him they could also sense a person's energy.

As he approached Maden and the mare, she said, "Thom, I want you to meet Fanta, who's pregnant. But before you greet her, make sure you're grounded. Fanta's very sensitive to people's energies."

"Of course," Thom replied. After doing that, he moved to Fanta's head and softly said, "Hi, Fanta, I'm Thom." Fanta was-dun colored with deep brown eyes. "My, you are beautiful."

She whinnied in response.

"Fanta's about nine months along," Maden explained. "She doesn't look like it, though, and I have to admit I'm a little concerned about the size of her foal. Most mares this far along are much bigger."

Thinking that this was another teaching opportunity with Maden, Thom listened attentively.

"I had a feeling I should introduce you to her," Maden continued.

That's funny, Thom thought. During his morning meditation yesterday, he sensed that he'd meet someone new today. His intuition was correct again. However, the someone was a horse, not a human.

"I overheard you talking with Sestra B and Rin," Maden said. "I understand you can sense the spirit of humans. I wonder if you can do the same with animals, like Fanta and her foal."

"I think I can," he confirmed. "I'll start with Fanta." First, lowering his fifth shield, associated with spirit healing, he placed a hand on her neck and the other over her heart. Sensing into her, he whispered, "Wow."

"What are you picking up?" Maden asked.

"Fanta's spirit is really alive, and her energy is very strong."

"Horses have twice the energetic field humans have," she explained.

"I didn't know that," Thom replied. "I saw that Fanta's field doesn't have strong colors like a human aura. But it does....um, sparkle, I guess. I don't know the Glakkadian word."

"I think you mean iridescent," Maden offered.

"Yes, that's it," Thom replied. "Fanta also has a determined and loving spirit. She's amazing," whispering that to the mare.

In response, Fanta turned her head and nipped at his hair.

"What about the foal?" Maden asked. "Fanta's uterus is further down her flank if you want to move your hands closer."

Attending to it, Thom did indeed feel something. The fetus, a male, he realized, exhibited the beginnings of an intense energy. Thom saw the same iridescence that he saw in Fanta. Moving his face closer to Fanta's flank, he whispered, "Hi, little one. You're going to be a handsome boy, aren't you?" He felt a flash of energy connecting to his spirit. "Thank you." He turned to Maden with a look of awe.

"A male, you said," Maden commented. "You sensed his gender from his spirit?"

"Yes," Thom replied.

"What happened at the end?" she asked.

"He reached out to me with his energy," Thom answered. "He's going to be a special one."

Maden smiled. Last night, she had seen Thom's face flash before her when thinking about Fanta. She was glad she had followed her instincts. "Thom," she said. "I know your schedule's fairly full, but could you spend some time with

Fanta and the little one, as you called him, through the last months of Fanta's pregnancy?"

"Could I?" Thom asked, excitedly. "Oh yes, please. I'll fit it in somehow. But I'll check with Rin first."

"I would think he'd agree. He's probably still in the infimarium," Maden offered.

"Thanks." Before he left, Thom whispered expressions of love to Fanta and the little one.

Chapter 37

Months passed, and while riding to the monastery, Thom decided to chat with God, as he now referred to Deu. Mind-speaking, he said, *I can't believe we've been here seven months. A lot has happened. Fanta will give birth to her colt soon. Am I crazy that I feel like I already know him? I even feel connected to his spirit.* As he approached the monastery gate, he asked, *Is this part of my spirit-healing gift or my physical-healing gift?*

Soon after, the word, *both,* came to him.

I guess that makes sense, he thought. *Wow. That's the first time I received a direct response from you. Until now, when I've asked you or Sereh a question, the answer has always come from another person, like Rin.* Thinking about the answer raised another question. Mind-speaking once more, he asked, *But how do I know it's from you and not me?*

You don't, and you do, God answered.

Well, that's helpful, he replied sarcastically. Oh, dear, he thought, frowning. He shouldn't have spoken to God like that. But he wasn't dead, though. Maybe it was OK.

No worries, God replied, able to sense Thom's fears. *Think about what I said.*

Passing through the gate, he considered God's words.

I guess I can't be 100% sure because I'm human. But if my spirit is divine, and my intuition comes from that, I should trust it.

Keep going.

When I tap into my intuition and spend time with it, everything lines up between my brain-mind, body-mind, and spirit-mind.

Exactly.

"Thom," a voice called out.

He didn't respond.

"Thom!" the voice repeated.

Looking up, he discovered he was outside the stable. Maden was looking at him with concern.

"Oh, sorry, Maden," he replied.

"Are you OK?" she asked.

"Yes. I was chatting with God."

"Ah. I wanted to tell you Fanta's gone into labor."

"What?" Thom answered excitedly. "Is she about to give birth?"

"Not immediately," she answered. "She's in the first stage, which could take a few hours. I'll send someone to find you when her water breaks."

Thom made his way to the pottery for another lesson with the apprentices. He was going to show them how to create Rin's salve jars. He hoped he could stay focused. When the lesson was over, since no one had brought him a message from Maden, Thom went to his session with Sestra

B. He told her that Fanta was in labor, in case he had to leave.

Knowing Thom would be a little distracted, Sestra B spent the hour introducing him to various archangels and each one's specialty. When she told him about Archangel Metatron and that he mentored lightworkers, he felt he already knew him.

Thom went to the training yard to work with Medelin when the session ended. Since it was Jauli, a month past the end of the rainy season, he no longer had to train in the salle, for which he was grateful. While he liked the salle because the floor-to-ceiling mirrors allowed him to view his positioning as he ran through staff exercises, it often got very stuffy. And if you were unlucky enough to train after Medelin had trained a group, it also stunk from the students' sweat.

Thom was deeply engrossed in his staff maneuvering routine when Jeren suddenly burst in. Jeren was six years old and one of the assistant cook's children. "Um, sorry to bother you, but Maden told me to come and get Thom."

"Is it time?" he asked.

"Yeah, I was deliverin' some apples to her when Fanta's water went, whoosh," he explained. "I just missed gettin' wet."

"Go, Thom," Medelin said.

Thom handed Medelin his staff and dashed after Jeren. Fanta was lying on her side in the corral where she'd been moved earlier that day. Kneeling, Thom briefly touched her flank to encourage her and her foal before standing next to Maden.

"Be aware that Fanta may stand up and lay down a few times to help stimulate contractions before the birthing starts," she explained. "If all goes smoothly, the foal's front feet should appear first, followed by his nose and head, which could still be encased in the amniotic sac. The sac should break on its own, but if it doesn't, I'll want you to help me remove it."

"OK," Thom said.

"Be ready. It'll be any time now," Maden told him.

Thom's eyes were glued on Fanta, his heart racing in anticipation.

"Here come his legs," Maden alerted him. "And there's his nose. Good job, Fanta and…" pausing.

"Apollo," Thom offered. "When I checked on the foal earlier, that name popped into my head."

"Good job, Fanta and Apollo," Maden praised them.

"Good job," Thom repeated.

"Here come Apollo's shoulders," Maden said. "That's the hardest part."

Thom continued sending love and healing energy to Fanta and Apollo.

With Fanta's final push, Apollo's shoulders passed through her pelvis, followed by the rest of him.

"Let's get the sac off him," Maden advised.

Together, they pulled off the remains of a whitish membrane.

"Now, let's help improve Apollo's breathing," she said. "Grab a hay straw and tickle his nose to see if you can get him to sneeze."

Doing as she said, Apollo gave a big sneeze and shook his head.

"God bless you," Thom said.

"It looks like the umbilical cord separated," Maden commented. "And, like I suspected, Apollo's smaller than most foals."

"Will that be a problem?" Thom asked with concern.

"Probably not, since you said he had a strong spirit," Maden assured him. "But I must say that the similarity between you and Apollo is interesting."

"What do you mean?" Thom asked her.

"When you came here, you were small but had a strong spirit. That's the same with Apollo. Your connection almost seems providential."

"I hadn't thought about that," Thom said. "I'll see what Sestra B thinks."

"Good idea," Maden agreed. "She's always attentive to signs and their meanings. Let's step off to the side to give Fanta time with him."

Thom watched as Fanta cleaned Apollo with her tongue. He was amazed. Thom had never seen a foal being born. He was a beauty with hazel eyes, chestnut hair, and what looked like a star on his forehead.

"Stay as long as you wish, Thom," Maden offered. "In about an hour, Apollo should stand and soon after begin nursing. At some point, Fanta should start pushing again to expel the placenta. Let me know when that happens."

"OK," Thom replied, still a bit stunned.

"Before I step away," Maden said, "You said Apollo's name appeared in your mind. Do you think you can speak to animals that way? Remember when I told you animals understand the intent and emotion behind spoken words, not usually their meaning? I wonder if your ability to connect with Apollo's spirit provides you another way to communicate with him."

"No. I wish I could," Thom told her, "I tried to mind-speak with Crescent and Abu, but nothing came through."

"Oh, well," Maden replied. "I didn't hurt to ask."

After Maden had left, Thom sat on the side of the corral. He was so focused on Apollo that he was barely conscious when Mekial placed a stuffed meat roll in his hand. Thom applauded when Apollo finally stood and was fascinated when he had no trouble finding his dam's udder to nurse. When Apollo made his way over to Thom to nuzzle him, his heart almost burst. He remained there throughout the rest of the afternoon. When Rin came by at the end of the day to travel home, he said goodbye reluctantly.

"I expect you to spend as much time as you can helping me care for Apollo," Maden said, with a smirk, as they headed towards Crescent and Abu's stalls.

Lying in bed that night, Thom replayed Apollo's birth. He thanked God and the angels for this new life, grateful for the chance to witness it. Apollo had become very precious to him during the last months of Fanta's pregnancy. Now, he'd get to show his love for him directly.

Chapter 38

I t was too early for his session with Sestra B. After spending time with Apollo, Thom walked around the monastery grounds. He couldn't believe Apollo was almost four months old. With Thom's constant attention and Fanta's mothering, Apollo had grown to the size of other foals his age. This morning, Maden commented that he might start weaning from Fanta soon.

As he wandered about, Thom appreciated the fresh air. With the approach of Uctiba, the minor rainy season would soon begin, but today was beautiful. "Good morning, divine team," he spoke out loud since no one was around. Sestra B taught him about divine teams the previous month, explaining that a team provides support and guidance. She also told him that he had to invite divine beings, with whom he felt attuned, to create one. He remembered feeling weird about it, seeing himself waving his hands in the sky to get a being's attention and saying, "Hey, do you want to be on my team?" What still brought tears to his eyes was how many volunteered. Besides his guardian angel, God, Jeshua, and Archangel Metatron, Archangel Raphael, the divine healer, stepped up. There were also a couple of surprises, like Archangel Orion, who helps people manifest what they need to live their life's purpose.

Since then, Thom chatted most often with Jeshua. Sometimes, he'd hang out with him during breaks in his schedule, sharing how he felt or playing together with one of the monastery dogs. Very quickly, Jeshua felt like a friend. The Iosan elders would have considered such a thing a sacrilege.

Thom decided to sit under one of his favorite trees, the Baobab. Through his earth sense and his spirit-healing gift, he felt a kinship with it, as it was called the Tree of Life. Gazing through its bare branches into the sky, Thom sighed. He enjoyed this time alone as it gave him space to think. He recalled a conversation with Sestra B the other day about his team. She'd encouraged him to be silly with them. The elders would undoubtedly have a fit if he told them that.

He decided to give it a try this morning.

For some reason, Thom imagined that he was a ball of energy. He pictured himself zooming around the divine realm and unexpectedly popping in on his team members. Rather than being annoyed, they were delighted and chased after him, forming a long line. Angels waved at him, encouraging him to go faster. He laughed until his stomach had stitches, and he could hardly breathe, which was strange because neither applied to his imagined shape.

Lying there, Thom's heart warmed from the love of his team. He wondered if they would be his friends like Jeshua had become. "Friendships with God and angels," he said out loud. It should've felt weird, but it didn't. A wave of sadness abruptly engulfed him. In his mind, he saw the kids from home flash before his eyes, with Kevar calling him a weirdo and laughing at him. The other kids laughed, too.

Suddenly, a pile of leaves blew over him, and, in his mind, he heard, *Shake it off, Thom.*

"Jeshua, did you do that?" he called.

With the help of Mother Earth, came the reply. *I'm your friend, and so are the rest of your team. Don't let anyone make you doubt that. Now, let's get back to some fun. Weren't you wondering about giving your divine team nicknames?*

Yeah, Thom mind-spoke, with the beginnings of a grin. *For me, what about Jesh?*

I like it, Thom replied.

Checking in with the rest of his team, they were also willing. He quickly came up with a few. Archangel Orion would be Ori. God would be G, of course. For Archangel Raphael, he couldn't call him Rafi since that's what everyone called the apprentice healer. Thom decided to go with Rafe. But he couldn't come up with a good one for Metatron. Jeshua had suggested Tronnie, but that didn't feel right.

Noting the sun's position, Thom realized he'd better make his way to the study room. Sestra B told him yesterday that Lebrim and Nuala would join him today. When he arrived, he saw that Nuala was already there. "Good morning, Nuala," he said, settling on one of the cushions placed in a circle on the floor. Nuala was a novice in the monastery community.

"Good morning, Thom," she replied.

Thom was adjusting the cushion when Sestra B entered. Because he was still thin, the hardness of the ground sometimes made sitting uncomfortable, even with the padding.

"Good morning, Nuala and Thom," Sestra B greeted them as she entered the room. "Lebrim will be joining us shortly. Today, I'll take you through a guided meditation, starting with visualizing your Sanctuary."

Thom thought back to when Sestra B first introduced him to the idea. She explained that each person's Sanctuary reflected what their mind imagined would be a safe place. She also added that in their Sanctuary, they would feel their most substantial connection to their divine nature. Thom's Sanctuary formed immediately in his mind, with mountains, an open field, and a river. His favorite spot was under a big oak tree, whose roots were shaped into a natural seat. He was still amazed when he accidentally discovered that his Sanctuary played an important role when a new spirit-healing ability emerged.

He had been walking through town when he passed a printing shop where two teenagers were yelling. In front of them, on the floor, was a pile of scattered handbills. Stopping to watch, Thom was blasted with a feeling of wrongness from the older teen, nearly knocking him over. Looking directly at him, he noticed his aura was dark gray, which could mean unhappiness. When he glanced at the younger teen, a girl, he felt a rightness in her, and her aura showed blue.

When Thom shared this experience with Sestra B the next day, she explained what he felt were resonant or dissonant energies. She added that they reflected whether a person's life choices aligned with their spirit. At first, Thom was simply curious. But then Sestra told him two more things that shook him. Apparently, his ability was rare and would be considered holy. Mention of that word still made him uncomfortable. He got scared when she warned him not to tell anyone what he sensed unless they asked. Sestra assured him she'd be there with him and suggested he visit his Sanctuary to find peace.

"Thom," Nuala whispered to him.

"Huh," Thom replied.

"You do go off a lot," she said. "What do you think about?"

"Do I? Oh, sorry," he whispered back.

"It does give you an other-worldly look," she commented. "Anyway, Lebrim's here. We're about to start."

"Thanks, Nuala."

"Let's begin," Sestra said, addressing the group.

"Well done, everyone! Sestra B said at the end of their session. "I sensed that you all became aware of your connection with each other. Since all of you have previously connected to your angels or guides, the next stage was to experience the oneness you share with humans and all creation. What you felt today was the beginning of that. It will grow as you open yourselves up to more of it. Can anyone help reset the furniture for the afternoon class?"

"I can," Nuala volunteered.

"I can help, too," Thom added.

"Thank you both," Sestra B said as she walked toward the door. "It's a little stuffy in here. I'm leaving the door open."

While tidying things, Thom noticed Nuala seemed unsettled and distracted. Focusing on her energies, he detected some dissonance that appeared as dark gray sparks erupting through her aura, similar to the older teen. Her other colors were dim, too. He would've thought they'd be brighter and include purple since she was in religious life. "Nuala, are you OK?" he asked.

"Huh, what? Did you say something?" Nuala answered.

"Now who's in another world?" Thom said, smiling. "And yes, I asked if you're OK. Did something happen in the meditation you didn't share?"

"No," she replied. "Maybe it's nervousness about my first profession to the community."

"When's that?" Thom asked.

"In about four weeks."

"If you ever want to talk, I'm available," Thom offered.

"Thanks," Nuala replied.

They were just finishing restoring the room when they heard a cough.

Looking toward the door, Thom saw Jeren.

"Hi, Jeren. Can we do something for you?" Nuala asked.

"Thom," he replied. "Someone's asking for you and Healer Rin."

"Healer Rin didn't come to the monastery this morning. Did the person give a name?"

"Captain Musa Bittaye."

Oh, my goodness. Thom thought. He hadn't seen the captain since they got off his ship. "Jeren, where is he?" he asked.

"In the reception room," he answered. "I can take you."

"Thanks," Thom said.

"Thom, would you mind if I tagged along?" Nuala asked.

"No, not at all," he replied.

Jeren led them to a room in the same building as the infimarium.

Stepping into the room, Thom came face to face with the captain of the Bittaye Biashara, seated in one of the armchairs. "Captain Musa," he said enthusiastically. "How are you? I wondered if I'd see you again. How's Khali? Why are you here? I mean at the monastery."

Captain Musa laughed, looking him over. "That's quite a greeting. It's good to see you, Thom. I see you've grown, and you look stronger."

Thom's face reddened. "Yes. I have defense and weapons training here. And I'm eating more, too."

"That's natural, lad," Captain Musa replied. "Who is this with you?"

"Oh. Sorry," Thom replied. "This is Nuala. She's a novice here."

"Good to meet you, sir," she answered.

Thom immediately noticed a shift in Nuala's energy.

After they had all seated, Thom said, "Rin isn't here now. But he did say he was coming for noon supper."

"I'm glad. I'd like to see Rin. But I came to see you," he admitted.

"Me? Why?"

"Khali," he answered. "Every time I port at Dridley, she asks me how you are. I promised her I'd look you up the next time I came."

"How is she?" Thom asked.

"Fine," he replied, clearing his throat. "Khali's still selling her twisters. Before I left Dridely, she started selling hot tea in the morning. Some prefer it over coffee."

"Oh, how thoughtless of me!" Thom said. "Would you like something to drink, captain?"

"Water would be nice," he answered.

"I'll get it," Nuala replied, jumping up. "Do you want me to find Mekial, Thom?"

"Oh, yes, please," he replied. "Thanks, Nuala." Turning back to the captain, he said, "I wanted you to meet her. She's been helping me improve my Glakkadian."

"I must admit you almost sound like a native," the captain confirmed.

A few minutes later, Mekial dashed through the door.

"Mekial, this is Captain Musa Bittaye," Thom said. "I think I told you he captained the ship that brought Rin and me here."

"Yes, you did," Mekial replied, offering her hand to shake. "Nice to meet you, sir."

"It's good to meet you, Mekial," he replied. "I understand you tutored Thom in our language. Well done!"

"Thanks. He's teaching me Dochalan. And sorry for being sweaty. I was on my way to get washed up after training. Medelin pushed me hard today, Thom. Brace yourself for a good workout."

"Ugh," Thom groaned. "Thanks for the warning."

"Good idea to learn Dochalan," the captain admitted. "Our land does a lot of business with Docha-leigh. It'll be to your advantage."

"Thank you, sir," Mekial replied.

"She's picking it up fast," Thom admitted.

Just then, Nuala rushed in the door, out of breath and panting. "Here's.... your.... water, sir."

"Thank you, Nuala. I see you added a slice of lemon. Very considerate."

"You're very welcome, sir," she replied, blushing.

Looking towards Nuala, Thom detected another surge of energy in her. Tuning into her aura, he noticed the gray sparks had become less frequent. He also saw more purple in her auric field, but it was light, indicating an almost hopeful feeling. Shaking his head, he wondered how he even knew that.

Thom, Nuala, and Mekial chatted with the captain for some time. The captain talked about Khali's doings and told them about his travels. In turn, Thom shared what he'd been doing and learning.

"You've been a busy lad for being here, for what, seven months?" Captain Musa noted.

"Yes, but it's been great," Thom answered.

"Have you gotten used to the spiciness of our food?" he asked.

"Mostly," he replied. "Once in a while, I've had trouble." Glancing at Mekial, he asked, "Should we give him a taste of our new drink?"

"Good idea," Mekial agreed.

"Your new drink?" he asked, bemused, as the bell rang announcing the noon meal.

"We'll explain it to you at supper," Thom replied.

During their meal, Nuala and Budaj bombarded Captain Musa with questions. Budaj was interested in whether his ship had ever faced pirates, and Thom had to admit he was interested, too.

Rin arrived when they were halfway through the meal. "Oh. Captain Musa, what a surprise to see you!"

"Khali demanded I visit Thom on this trip home," he explained. "I wouldn't hear the end of it if I didn't. I saw the note on your shop door and came here."

"It's good to see you," Rin said.

"What happened to the ship about to run into you?" Budaj demanded from the captain.

"Ah," he said. "We were able to change direction, thankfully, and the wind from the storm helped us avoid a collision."

"That's cool," Budaj said.

"It was stressful, but my crew is well-trained," he replied.

Thom noticed Rin was also interested in the captain's travels. He was puzzled when Rin asked if the populace, where the captain visited, expressed any discontent. He wondered why a healer would want to know about that.

Mekial was returning to their table when she whispered to him. "Awa agreed to make a batch of Timbu, even though it's not very cold out."

"Oh, great," Thom whispered back. "Why don't you get a pitcher, and I'll get a plate of sweet biscuits. Captain, we have something we want you to try."

"Is this what you and Mekial were talking about earlier?" he asked.

"Yes. Mekial and I will be back shortly."

When Thom returned, he carried a plate of cinnamon biscuits. Mekial followed behind with a pitcher and some mugs.

"Who wants Timbu?" Mekial asked.

"I do," Budaj said.

"I'll pass this time," Lauret responded.

"I'll try it," Nuala added.

The captain spoke up. "What's Timbu?"

"We'll tell you after you've tasted it," Thom replied.

The captain paused, looking skeptically at the dark liquid in his mug. Shrugging a little, he took a sip.

Thom, Mekial, and Budaj watched his face closely.

A smile erupted before Captain Musa declared, "This is wonderful. It tastes like chocolate. On a cold day, it would warm you to the bone. What is it?"

"We invented it!" Mekial, Thom, and Budaj announced.

"Mekial, why don't you tell the story?" Thom suggested.

"Why not me?" Budaj demanded. "I threw the chocolate."

"Yes, you did," Lauret remarked. "And you remember the extra chores you got for doing that, don't you? Enough. Go ahead, Mekial."

"Some months ago, Thom hadn't gotten used to our food's spiciness," she explained. "Mam and Rin advised him to drink hot milk to help his stomach. The next day, he had more because he still had troubles. Budaj was acting particularly bratty that day."

"Mekial," Bea warned.

"Sorry, Ma," Mekial apologized. "But he wasn't sharing the bowl of chocolate bits the cooks had put out by the biscuits."

"I brought them back to the table, didn't I? Shouldn't I get to eat them all?" Budaj justified.

"We share at this table, young man," Bea warned.

"Yes, Ma."

"Anyway, Budaj started throwing them at me," Mekial continued. "Rin wasn't there. And Ma and Mamie didn't see because they were talking to Abbotess Linna who stopped by our table. Budaj didn't aim well. Many fell into Thom's hot milk. Thom, do you want to continue?"

"Sure. The chocolate bits had started melting. I stirred them in because I didn't know what else to do. My milk darkened. I'm not sure why I did the next thing since I hadn't even tasted the milk. But I grabbed the bowl of chocolate bits and poured them all into my mug. Budaj and Mekial looked at me with their jaws hanging open. When I took a sip, I had the same reaction you did captain. I was in heaven."

"His eyes were all bugged out," Budaj added.

"I told Mekial she had to try it," Thom said.

"I had the same reaction," she admitted.

"I tried it too," Budaj interjected.

"We decided to share it with others, including Awa and the rest of the cooks," Mekial continued. "Most of them loved it. Awa decided to make it regularly, especially on cold days."

"Good decision," Captain Musa agreed. "Where does its name come from?"

"Our combined names, Thom, Mekial, Budaj, TMB," Thom explained. "That naturally became Timbu."

Reaching for one of the cinnamon biscuits, Thom had an inspiration. "Do you think Khali would want to sell it with her Twisters?" he asked.

"Great idea," the captain replied. "I'll add a sack of the chocolate bits to my cargo. Mekial and Thom, would you take me to Awa so I can learn how many chocolate bits to add?"

"Of course," they answered.

As Thom sat there, a strange thought arose in his mind. Timbu's going to save your life one day. Shaking his head, he asked himself, where did that come from?

Thom was leaving his individual session with Sestra B when he ran into Nuala. Her energy seemed lower and more dissonant than the last time he saw her. While checking her aura, Thom noticed that purple was nonexistent. He also detected more flashing gray sparks. "Nuala," he spoke up.

"What? Oh, I'm sorry, Thom. I didn't see you," she answered.

"Are you OK?" he asked.

"Um. No. I didn't sleep well last night." she explained.

"Only last night?"

"No. How did you know?" Nuala asked.

"You probably heard one of my gifts is spirit healing, haven't you?"

"Yeah. That's one of the reasons you study with Sestra B."

"Uh-huh," he confirmed. "Well, through my gifts, I can feel people's energy levels. With my spirit-healing gift, I can also sense when someone's life choices match their spirit. Over the last few days, your resonance has been all over the place, as Sestra B calls it. I haven't been probing you. It's... the thing is, I can naturally sense things, and it feels like you're out of alignment."

"What do you mean? I've been dedicated to my lessons and chores," she replied defensively. "I meditate twice a day. Even my advisor praises me for my dedication."

"I'm sure you are dedicated," Thom replied. "Have you talked with your spirit guides?"

Nuala stood there but said nothing.

"Do you have time to talk? I'm willing to listen," he offered.

"OK. But can we go someplace where no one can hear?"

"Sure," Thom said.

Nuala led them to a bench near one of the gardens.

After they sat, Thom asked, "What's going on?"

"Well, I told you first promises are coming up at the beginning of Nuvima," she said.

"You did."

"You see, the other novices are all excited about making their year-long commitment to the community."

"Aren't you?" Thom asked.

She looked down but didn't say anything.

"Nuala, I promise I won't share this with anyone unless you say it's OK."

She was silent for a time before saying, "It's just.... how old are you, nine? I'm almost sixteen."

"I'll be ten next month," Thom said. "But, if you don't want to tell me, that's OK. I'm worried about what could happen if you don't talk about what you're going through. Keeping it inside might make it worse." He felt Archangel Metatron's presence and confirmation of his words. At the same time, he saw an energy take shape behind Nuala, which took the form of an angel. He heard a name. "Nuala, is your guardian angel, Darielle?"

"Did someone tell you?" she asked.

"She did. She's standing behind you with her hands on your shoulders."

Nuala looked down again. "I haven't been speaking to her lately. I was afraid of what she might say."

"Did you think she'd get mad?" he asked.

"I don't know," she shrugged.

"I really think you should talk to someone. And, to let you know, one of my divine team members is Archangel Metatron. He's with us now and agrees with me."

"Truly?" Nuala asked.

"Yeah," he replied. This is about your first promises, isn't it?"

"I don't want to take them," she blurted out.

"What's going on?"

"You know I grew up here. My father's a brother in the community, and my mother works in the stables."

Thom smiled, inviting her to continue.

"They were happy when I decided to become a novice last Siptema. It felt like the natural thing to do. Because everyone knew me, they readily agreed and accepted me into this year's class."

"It made sense to you."

"Yeah," Nuala confirmed. "It all was fine for the first six months. But then, I heard my novice mates talking, and they were all passionate about being of service through the community. I didn't feel that. When I checked with Darielle and my guides, they told me to wait because it would be revealed in time. But it hasn't come. Or maybe it has, and I'm missing the messages. I don't know what to do. I don't want to let my parents or the community down."

"Can I ask you something?"

"Sure," Nuala said, looking forlorn.

"Isn't the point of the novice year for the community to look at you and you at it to see if you're a good fit?"

"Uh, huh."

"And haven't two other novices left?"

"Yeah. But they didn't grow up here. For them, it was a mutual decision. Everyone here knows me and knows I'm committed to helping people."

"Hmm," Thom responded, considering what to say next. He recalled how Nuala's energy changed when she met

Captain Musa. That seemed important. But how should he bring this up?

She needs to make the connection herself, Metatron mind-spoke to him. Darielle nodded in agreement.

Thom had an idea and asked, "Have you ever felt really excited or passionate about something yourself?" Glancing to his left, Metatron gave a nod.

"Yes," she replied. "When we have festivals and people from all over come."

"Like who?" Thom said, encouraging her to continue.

"Oh, people from other islands with food and gifts to trade," she said. "Sometimes, even a few sailors come and talk about their travels. It's interesting to hear about who they've met and the lands they've seen."

Thom noticed a jump in Nuala's energy. "Is that why you wanted to sit with us during Captain Musa's visit?"

"Yeah. I never met a captain before. It was exciting to hear about how he became one."

"It was. I noticed you asked him questions about sailing life," he commented.

Nuala smiled and nodded. "He was a nice man."

"Nuala," Thom said, interrupting her recollections. "What do you feel when you think about a sailor's life? If you could name a few, what would they be?"

"Happy. and my heart races," Nuala answered quickly.

"Anything else?" Thom prompted.

"Um... Maybe yearning," she said, pausing.

Thom remained silent.

"I want to be a sailor!" she finally blurted out. "It's ridiculous. I know. The whole community expects me to profess."

"Nuala, isn't your community's mission to help people remember who they are and their life purpose, no matter what it looks like?"

"True, but..." Nuala replied.

"Nuala, let me ask," he said. "What do you want to do?"

"Go to sea, and one day be a captain," she blurted. "I can't believe I told you."

"That's your passion, as Sestra B calls it," Thom added. "And it's great you did."

Thom looked at Darielle and Metatron and saw both smiling and nodding. "Darielle and Metatron agree," he told her.

"They do?"

"Yes. Maybe it's time you chatted with Darielle and your guides? And maybe your parents and your novice director?"

"Good idea."

"I've got to get to weapons training. I'd better run."

"Thank you, Thom."

"You're welcome." Making his way to the salle for training, Thom smiled. Talking with Nuala felt good, he said to himself. It makes sense that people must remember their purpose rather than someone telling them. This could be his calling.

After dinner that night, Thom shared his thoughts with Rin. The following morning, he also talked with Sestra B. One thing really struck him from their conversation. She explained that honoring a person's free will is important, even when their choices take them in unhealthy directions and away from their purpose. She said the hope is for those bad choices to become a learning experience that leads them back.

Chapter 39

Thom had the rest of the day to himself. Mekial was busy with her family. The Liberventians also had their three-day retreat every year in early Uctiba. Since Thom had spent time with Apollo yesterday, he decided to go to the market fair to find a crystal. Sestra B had told him they could help someone connect more strongly to their highest self. Rin suggested he pick one out as a gift for his upcoming birthday.

When Thom left the shop, the streets were still damp from last night's rain. Breathing in the clean air, there was a lightness to his step. Walking through the town, he was careful to avoid the puddles. Making his way through streets crowded with people rushing about on business, Thom was especially conscious of the young messengers running by. Most were probably legitimate, but a few could be thieves. He made sure his money pouch was secure and hidden before heading out. In case the crystal was expensive, he'd brought some of the money he'd earned as Rin's apprentice in addition to what Rin had given him for his gift.

The fair was in the center of town and divided into four sections: food and herbs, trinkets and jewelry, clothing and housewares, and entertainment. Thom first visited the food and herb section and his favorite food vendor.

"Good afternoon, Maru," Thom greeted a middle-aged man with a touch of gray in his hair. Thom could hear meat sizzling on the grill behind the vendor. Maru specialized in meat skewers. Drawing closer, the savory aroma of the cooking meat made his mouth water.

"Good afternoon, Thom. No stand today?"

"No," he replied. "We sold most of our packets the other day, and Rin said he didn't need my help with patients."

"That's great that you have the afternoon off," Maru commented.

Thom grinned. "You wouldn't happen to have any over-cooked skewers, would you?"

Maru returned the grin. "As a matter of fact, I do. I was wondering if anyone might want them. I have two chicken and three beef."

"I'll take one chicken and one beef. A penny each?"

"Yes."

When Thom was turning to leave, Maru added, "Tell Rin that my mother came up with another spice blend from the herbs she bought from him. We'll invite you both to dinner one night to sample the result."

"I will. See ya."

Thom strolled away, savoring the beef skewer. It was good and, as expected, very spicy. Swiftly finishing it, he moved on to the chicken. Cutting through the clothing and housewares section, he walked by a knife vendor.

"Young sir," the knife vendor called out, "I'll give you a good deal on a knife."

Thom shook his head. Throwing knives still gave him the willies, even though Medelin had introduced him to them a few months before. Finally arriving at the trinkets and jewelry section, he headed towards the vendors who sold crystals and colored stones. He spotted a stand with colored stones and approached.

"Get away," the rotund man behind the stand yelled. "My stones are for well-bred people, not vagabonds like you."

"That's weird," Thom muttered. His clothing might not be the fanciest, but they were clean. Why would that man shout at him like that? Walking away, he remembered Kevar's mother and how she reacted to him back home.

Thom stopped at another stand that sold stones and crystals. He was dazzled by their beauty. A deep purple crystal caught his eye. It had an interesting shape, resembling a pie wedge with triangular pieces pointing upward. "May I pick it up to look more closely?" he inquired politely of the vendor, who looked to be Rin's age.

"Yes. Aren't you Healer Rin's apprentice?" I saw you both at your stand a month ago," the man commented, adding a few more crystals from a nearby box to his display.

"Yeah."

"Are you familiar with that crystal?"

"No, sir."

"It's amethyst. A monk told me it supports healing and helps people connect to their intuition and their higher self."

"Thanks for letting me know. I wondered why I felt drawn to it," Thom replied. Besides its shape and color, he liked how it sparkled in the sun. While examining the crystal, Thom overheard the vendor in the jewelry stand to his left explaining to his customer that the blue stone in the bracelet was a precious stone imported from Docha-leigh. When he heard his home mentioned, he looked over and recognized the stone. It was not the most common, but it wasn't precious. Peering at the customer, he saw a well-dressed man wearing a tunic and trousers with detailed embroidery.

Looking back at the vendor, a tall, thin man, Thom felt drawn to lower his fifth shield to view his aura. He saw it was primarily blue, but one area was faded and overshadowed by something he couldn't see clearly. Focusing on it, something shifted inside him. He could now see threads with a muddy yellow tinge pulsing in a grid pattern. The threads pulsed more rapidly as the vendor espoused the stone's rarity.

Did that mean he could tell when someone was lying? Thom was shocked by the idea. Rin had said he'd develop new abilities. He didn't think it would happen so soon, though.

Turning back toward the customer, Thom also studied his aura. He saw purple, blue, and a touch of green, but no muddy colors. The customer's honest, Thom concluded. He had to speak up. "Excuse me, sir." When he didn't respond, Thom repeated, "Sir."

"Yes," the man said, looking over at Thom.

"I'm sorry to intrude, but that stone isn't rare. It's not the most common, but it's not the rarest. I'm from Docha-leigh, and my Da uses stones like that on some of his pottery."

"Hmm?" the man replied, frowning. "Are you Healer Rin's apprentice?"

"Yes, sir. Do you know him?"

"I haven't met him, but my servants have picked up medicines and herbs from his shop." Turning his attention back to the vendor, he growled, "Trying to overcharge me, are you?"

Shaking a little, the vendor's face fell. "Sir. Money's been tight, and my wife is expecting again," he said desperately. "Since I've seen others selling jewelry for more than they're worth, I thought I would too. I'm sorry. I'll sell the bracelet at a discount if you still want it. Please don't turn me into the constable."

As the vendor spoke, Thom observed the muddy yellow threads fading and the blue growing brighter. That meant the brightness was the vendor's spirit coming through, a sign of greater alignment. It seems like a person's honesty affects their alignment, he concluded. And it also changes their auric colors. He'd have to ask Rin and Sestra B about it.

"Why should I believe you?" the customer asked the vendor.

"Sir, I believe him. He's telling the truth now," Thom interrupted.

"And how do you know that?"

"Um, I don't...I can't explain."

"Hmm," the man mused. "Let's talk when I'm done here." Looking toward the vendor, he asked, "What's your name?"

"Nordin, sir."

"Nordin, I'll still take the bracelet, as my niece favors this shade of blue. I won't be turning you into the constable, but I will keep an eye on you."

Knowing Nordin was telling the truth about his finances, Thom wondered if he could help him. "Mr. Nordin?" he spoke up. "That bracelet would be more valuable if you etched a design into the stone. You'd have to heat it first, though."

Nordin looked at Thom skeptically.

"I know it sounds strange, but that's what my Da does sometimes."

Nordin responded, "I guess it couldn't hurt."

The customer completed his transaction with Nordin and turned to Thom. "Are you hungry?"

Even though Thom had eaten meat skewers not long before, he nodded yes.

"Ahem."

"Oh, sorry," Thom said to the vendor, realizing he was still holding the amethyst crystal.

"Do you want to purchase the crystal?" he asked.

"How much?" Thom replied. After bargaining, they agreed on a price, and he pocketed the crystal.

"Ready to go," the customer asked him.

"Yes, sir."

"Good. Let me first introduce myself. I'm Mikazel Jacobreit. I'm a goods broker. What's your name?"

"Thom."

"Nice to meet you, Thom."

"Nice to meet you, sir."

"Please call me Mik. I know a place nearby that serves a nice afternoon tea."

Two blocks away, they approached a building with a signboard hanging above the door. The name Hinna Tea Salon was carved into it above an image of a painted teapot. Stepping inside, Thom saw round tables draped with pristine white tablecloths. Each was set with dishware that Thom could tell was made by a potter as skilled as his Da. A hearth at the room's far end cast a warm glow with a fire crackling within.

Once seated, Mik ordered and asked Thom, "Have you had high tea before?"

"No, sir, um... Mik," Thom admitted.

"I think you'll enjoy it. It comes with small sandwiches, scones, sweets, and tea, of course."

"It sounds good," Thom said. "Thanks."

"You're welcome. By the way, I understand the proprietress got the salon and high tea idea from your land."

"I never heard of it," Thom responded. "But before coming here, I hadn't traveled a lot."

"Ah. Now, regarding Nordin," he said. "Thanks for your assistance. I was about to purchase the bracelet at the original price when you spoke up. However, your comments seemed to go beyond your knowledge of the stone. How did you know Nordin spoke true after you challenged him?"

"Um," Thom mumbled. He didn't know what to say. Rin had told him to be cautious about telling others about his gifts. Up until then, only the people at the monastery knew. And no one knew about his new ability.

Mik spoke again, interrupting his thoughts, "Are you unsure about what you can say without checking with your teacher?"

"Yes, sir," he replied.

"I think it's time I meet Healer Rin then. Would you check with him about getting together? I'd like to invite you both to my home if that's OK. I'll send a messenger to his shop in the next day or two to propose a few dates."

"OK," Thom responded, sighing with relief.

"I see our tea is arriving," Mik commented. "Let's enjoy it, shall we?"

Thom's eyes grew big and round when he saw a three-tiered stand filled with food placed before them.

"Go ahead. Dig in," Mik encouraged.

Thom picked up a scone and began slathering it with what Mik told him was lemon curd and clotted cream.

When they finished their food, Mik announced, "I must return to my business. But it's been wonderful spending this time with you, young man, and hearing about your home. I look forward to seeing you again and meeting your teacher."

"Thank you for the tea, sir."

"You're welcome. But again, please call me Mik."

Returning to the shop, Thom noticed Rin had yet to return from visiting his patient. Since it was nearing dinner, he took charge of preparing it. Thom retrieved the soup pot from a cold bin in the floor and saw it could use more vegetables. He gathered a few more from the garden, sliced them into pieces, and added them to the pot with more water. After hanging the pot on a hook on the left side of the hearth, he removed the cloth from the bread dough Rin had prepared earlier and placed it in the small brick enclosure set in the hearth.

When everything was in order, Thom picked up the latest book in the Demba's Chronicles series. Last night, he had left off at the point when Abi's dragon had laid three eggs. As he sat down, he recalled a recent discussion with Mekial about the author, Nadia Sanneh, who had claimed to have seen a dragon while visiting another land. In her novels, Sanneh described dragons as wise creatures endowed with gifts similar to Thom's.

Wouldn't it be something if it were true? Thom mused to himself. But everyone knows dragons aren't real. He was sure Sanneh mistook large flying birds for dragons. It was nice to know others had an active imagination.

Thom had read two more chapters when Rin walked in.

"Ah. I smell bread," Rin said. "And I see you put the soup on. Good lad. After my treatments on the merchant's wife, I could use food to replenish my energy."

"How's Mistress Xanderan doing?" Thom asked.

"Much better. I think she's turned the corner and will return to full health."

"Good."

"Let me wash up," Rin said. "Then, we can sit down if everything's ready."

"I'll check the bread, but I think it is."

Neither talked much during the meal. Thom could tell Rin's energy was low like he said.

When they finished, Rin said, "Since you prepared the meal, I'll clean up."

"Thanks," Thom said.

Thom was reading in one of their lounging chairs when Rin placed two cups of tea on the small table between the chairs.

Sitting down in the second chair, Rin let out a contented sigh. "It's good to sit down. How was the fair?"

"Good," Thom replied. "Maru said to tell you that his mother created another spice blend from our herbs. He said he'd invite us for dinner one night to taste the results."

"That'll be a treat," Rin replied.

"I also found a purple crystal, amethyst," he shared, taking it from his pocket.

"It's very nice. Was the birthday money enough to cover it?"

Thom remained silent.

"Thom, you don't have to spend your money for a gift I'm giving you," he assured him. "Didn't you tell me that your family has a "family hold back" motto to make your money stretch?"

"Uh, huh."

"You're still living the motto, which I appreciate. But this time, you don't have to. Go into my room and take whatever you spent of your own money out of the box in my dresser."

"Thanks," Thom replied, reddening a little. "There's something I did want to tell you first." He shared his encounter with the vendor and the merchant and what he believed was his new ability.

"Let's go over your interaction with the vendor again. Nordin, was it?"

"Yeah."

"You said you overheard Docha-leigh mentioned and Nordin's claim that the stone was rare. When you saw the stone and knew it wasn't, you lowered one of your shields to view Nordin's aura."

"Yes. My fifth," Thom answered. "That's the one dedicated to spirit healing. When I did this, I remembered what you taught me about auric colors."

"And that's when you saw the yellow threads?"

"No. Only after I wanted to see more detail."

"Was there anything else you noticed?"

"A lot of Nordin's aura was blue, which meant he was mostly honest. I also sensed that the muddy yellow would take over if he continued to lie. I'm not saying this right."

"That's OK," Rin replied. "I think I'm getting it. I must admit I haven't heard of pulsing colors and patterns. When we worked together on your shields, you told me the detail you could see. And I agree. Another aspect of your gift has made itself known."

"That's what I thought," Thom said, pleased with himself.

"You were. And I think your ability to see greater detail resulted in your desire to see more. In effect, it refocused your gift through your shield."

"It did?"

"That's my suspicion. One question. Why did you want to look at the merchant's aura before speaking out against Nordin's dishonesty?"

"Because if he was dishonest too," Thom explained, "then he deserved to get cheated."

"And Nordin would have continued his behavior with other customers."

"I guess," Thom mumbled, his stomach twisting in shame.

"Thom, please look at me. What happened with Nordin was an opportunity for you to be of service and offer spirit healing. If you hadn't intervened, he might have defrauded the wrong people and ended up harmed or imprisoned. Of course, you aren't responsible for another person's choices, but it was an opportunity for you to use your gift to help people."

"OK," he replied, still feeling bad about his hesitation.

"You did a good thing," Rin explained. "What's interesting is this new aspect of your spirit healing gift: the ability to determine when someone's lying. I wonder what degree of dishonesty you can detect. We might play around with that."

"I don't understand," Thom said.

"For example, suppose someone's exaggerating rather than outright lying. I wonder if that would impact what you saw and sensed."

"I see. Do you want me to go around the fair and read people when they talk?" he asked.

"Not by yourself, no," Rin replied. "If we're out together, I might ask you to casually observe an interaction. I don't want you to intervene. Just notice."

"OK."

"You know, Thom," Rin continued, "this ability is something few others have experience with. You remember our chat about alignment and what Sestra B told you, don't you?"

"Yeah."

"To a certain degree, sensing alignment does tell you the overall nature of the person, but it doesn't provide details about daily interactions. This ability is extraordinary, but it could also be dangerous."

"Dangerous, sir?" Thom said with a tremble in his voice.

"Yes," Rin replied. "If using your gift results in you accidentally saying something out of turn to the wrong person, you could also be considered a threat. Given that, I'm glad you've been training with Medelin."

"Oh," Thom replied uneasily. "I can stop doing it."

Rin smiled with understanding. "It's too late for that lad since your gift continues to expand and evolve."

Thom remained silent.

"Thom, your gift is a good one. We'll ensure you have the tools to stay safe, and the wisdom to determine when to use it and speak out. You've already followed your intuition admirably. That's a good starting point."

"Sir, what about Mikazel Jacobreit, the goods broker? And by the way, what's a goods broker?"

"Someone who trades goods, working as a go-between for suppliers and sellers."

"Oh."

"I commend you on your response to the broker," Rin said. "I wouldn't have wanted you to share details before we had a chance to talk. However, I'll be happy to meet him. You said he would send an invitation in a day or two?"

"Uh huh," Thom said.

"Good. When it arrives, I'll propose some days next week when we might meet."

"Thank you, Rin."

"You're welcome. It's getting late, and we've both had busy days. Let's get some rest."

Thom snuggled under his covers and closed his eyes, but sleep wouldn't come. He was disturbed by his conversation with Rin. He still felt ashamed for considering not helping Mik. He prided himself on being a decent and honest person. However, he did remember wishing Kevar harm because of his bullying. Is it wrong to want bad things to happen to bad people?

The other thing that bothered Thom was the possible danger that could come with his newfound ability. He was glad he was training with Medelin. He knew he had a lot to learn. But he didn't know if we could even control this thing. What if he accidentally checked people's honesty and blurted something out? He'd better talk to Rin again. Realizing he was on edge, he visualized being in his Sanctuary. Soon enough, he felt his body relax sufficiently to sleep.

The following day, at breakfast, Thom shared his thoughts with Rin.

Rin smiled. "I suspected you would think about our chat. I'm glad you're working things out. The older you get, the more you'll discover that while there will always be teachers like me or Sestra B, you'll have to make decisions based on your intuition. No one person has all the answers. Too many rely on others to tell them what to say and do. The worst become zealots, insisting people follow their teacher or their way. Can I presume you wrote about your new ability in your journal?"

"Some," Thom replied. "This morning. I also chatted with my divine team. I got a sense from them that you'd help clear things up."

"I'm glad you checked with them. About accidentally reading someone's honesty, I don't believe that'll happen. In describing the interaction, you mentioned you wanted to view the vendor's aura more closely, which I'll call your intention. I think it's a matter of holding an intention, which focuses your gift."

"An intention, huh," Thom repeated.

"Let me think about it some more. I'll take you through some exercises to explore the extent of your ability."

Chapter 40

Thom and Rin were riding in the covered carriage that Merchant Jacobreit had sent. Through its side windows, Thom watched as they were driven north out of the town. The day was warm, but a gentle breeze made the carriage comfortable. After working with Rin this past week, Thom was confident he could control his lie-detecting gift. As Rin had thought, holding the intention was all he needed to do to see greater detail. Through their exploration, they also discovered Thom could detect exaggerations. For those, he didn't even need the extra focus. It was a matter of paying attention to the person's aura. If someone who was honest exaggerated, only a tiny spot of their primary color faded. The greater the exaggeration, the larger the spot. If the person was consistently dishonest, the muddy yellow color appeared along with pulsing threads. Considering this information, Thom was silent for a time.

When they entered a neighborhood with larger and grander homes, Rin spoke, "We should be getting there soon. When Merchant Jacobreit raises the topic of your gifts, I'll take the lead. I want to evaluate the nature of his interest."

"OK."

"Are you nervous?" he asked.

"Some. I'm glad I know more about this ability, but I'm still a little scared of it."

"I understand. That's why I'm taking the lead."

The driver turned into the open gates of a two-story adobe manor. Thom saw Merchant Jacobreit waiting by the door.

"Welcome to my home, Thom and Healer Rinbalden. I'm glad you were able to join me today."

"Thank you for inviting us, Merchant Jacobreit. And please call me Rin."

"Of course, Rin. And please call me Mik," he replied. "I don't stand for formality, even with my servants. Do come in."

Stepping into the large entrance hall, Thom saw it opened to the second floor, with a curved wooden stairway leading up to it. The floor was composed of mosaic tiles with interlaced diamonds and spirals. As Rin and Mik talked, he looked more closely.

"I see you've noticed my tiles, Thom," Mik said during a lull in the conversation.

"Yes, the design reminds me of symbols I've seen at the monastery," he replied.

"Good eye," Mik noted. "Yes, it's based on one of the angel images in their chapel."

"It's beautiful," Thom admitted. "The spiral's also part of the community symbol."

"Yes, it is. And thank you for the compliment."

"You're welcome."

"Noon supper will be ready shortly and served in the courtyard," Mik told them. "Don't worry about the heat. Our table is set under a pergola. A nearby fountain also keeps it cooler. Would you like something to drink? We have chilled berry juice, ale, and a cool white wine."

"I'll have the white wine," Rin said.

"The berry juice, please," Thom said.

"And I'll join you with the wine, Rin," Mik said, gesturing to the servant waiting nearby. "Please follow me."

They walked along a short hallway to a door at the back, which opened into the courtyard. Soon after they sat at the table, their drinks arrived.

"Again, thank you for coming, Rin and Thom," Mik repeated. "I suspect Thom told you about my encounter with the vendor Nordin."

"Yes, he did," Rin agreed.

"I hope you aren't offended by this question, Rin, but are you the same healer who lived on the capital isle of Umojai some years back?"

"Why do you ask?" he replied cautiously.

"I'm a cousin of Gallen Gessama, the husband of Prezdan Modu Gessama. At a family gathering last year, Modu mentioned, in confidence, that he had worked with a healer who was an advisor to the monarchs of Docha-leigh."

Rin analyzed Mik's comment. His relationship with the Prezdan and his meetings with him were primarily secret.

This meant Mik was one of Prezdan's ghost advisors and would thus be told about him. "Might you be one of Modu's advisors?"

Mik nodded with a knowing smile. "We both have interesting jobs."

"To say the least," Rin replied.

Thom looked confused.

"Thom, you know I lived here previously," Rin reminded him. "I don't want to say much other than we both work for our respective leaders."

Before Thom could respond, the servants brought out the food.

"Please help yourself," Mik said. "It's marinated pork. My cook prepares it with an interesting spice blend, a little hot and sweet. She provided a sauce with the same spices if you want more," pointing to the bowl the servant had placed on the table. "She also prepared an herb salad."

"Thank you," Rin and Thom replied.

After Thom had finished a second helping of pork smothered in the sauce, the servants cleared the plates.

"Now that we've verified our identities, Rin," Mik said, "I'm curious about what Thom did last week. I respect your hesitancy in telling me, Thom, but I hope you'd explain what you observed about Nordin."

Thom looked at Rin, who nodded.

"One of my gifts allows me to read a person's spirit and whether their life choices align with it," he explained. "When I look at people, their auric colors show me that."

"Auric colors?"

"Basically, each person gives off a colored energy that reflects their personality, including their thoughts and actions," Rin explained. "While everyone should be able to see auras, healers are most sensitive to them."

"I...see," Mik winked.

"Good one," Thom replied.

"Do you automatically see their colors, Thom?"

"No. I have to...um... open myself up."

"Can I presume that when Nordin espoused the rarity of the stone, and you knew it wasn't, you wanted to see his colors?"

"Yes."

"What did you see?"

Thom shared what he had discovered.

"Does that mean you can detect when someone's lying?"

"Yes. It first appeared with Nordin, and Rin and I have been exploring it since then."

"Ah. I now understand your hesitancy," Mik remarked. "When you said that Nordin was honest most of the time, does that mean you can see the degree to which people are honest?"

"That's what it seems like," Thom admitted. "Rin explained that it comes from my ability to see how aligned someone is with their spirit."

"Is this a common gift in your land?" Mik asked.

"No," Rin replied. "Healers, in general, have the ability to perceive auric colors, but Thom well surpasses them. As strong as my healing gift is, I can't see the details he can."

"Thom mentioned his gift involved the spirit," Mik commented, "do you think this ability comes from the One? What a silly question. Of course, it does. I'm trying to ask whether it comes through his spirit?"

"I do, to answer both questions. Sestra Berbera, Thom's teacher at the monastery, calls his gift spirit healing. She believes it reflects his growing connection to the divine. And we're both certain it will grow much stronger. Thom is truly a unique lad."

Upon hearing Rin's last comment, Thom's stomach began to churn. He was reminded of the kids back home, calling him a freak. Maybe they're right, as his stomach lurched. He was also beginning to think his second helping was a mistake.

"Thom," Rin called. "Thom."

"Oh, sorry. What did you say?" he replied shakily, sipping his berry juice, hoping it would calm him.

"Mik asked if you ever felt different from others because of your gift," Rin replied.

Why does this keep happening? Thom wondered, feeling further unnerved. "Yeah, I do, especially after Rin told me new abilities might show up as I use my gift more. Sometimes it feels like too much," he gasped.

Rin interrupted, "You didn't say anything to me about it, Thom. Why not?"

"Um... I think I'm gonna throw up."

Gesturing to a servant waiting nearby, Mik asked, "Would you get some seltzer water for the lad?"

After the servant returned and Thom had taken a few sips, he answered, "I didn't have the words until now. I haven't even written about it in my journal. I felt like I needed to let my feelings be."

"Very wise, Thom," Rin complimented him. "In your chats with your angels and Deu, I'd suggest you bring up situations like this."

"OK."

"And please don't keep it inside for long," Rin exhorted. "Sestra, Mekial, and I are willing to listen, even when you don't know what to say."

"Thanks," Thom responded, feeling his stomach settle.

For a short time, no one said anything. Thom could see Mik was pondering something.

"Mik," Rin interjected. "Both of us can tell you're thinking about something, and I suspect it's connected to Thom's new ability."

"Your suspicion is correct, but I hesitate to say anything, given that Thom is new to it."

"Go ahead and tell us, and we can consider it," Rin encouraged.

"Alright. As you know, I'm a goods broker. Twice a year, merchants, brokers, and traders convene on Umojai to assess each trade and discuss surpluses and shortages. Our objective is to maintain fair pricing, ensuring a smoothly functioning economy where everyone has equal access to products. Following the meetings, the Prezdan and his husband host a gala as a gesture of gratitude for everyone's efforts."

"We have a similar gathering in our land," Rin commented. "If I can read between the lines, is there something amiss with trading?"

"You read very well, Rin," Mik confirmed. "For the last few years, some products have become less available, even though we're unaware of shortages. We haven't yet determined what's been happening."

"Are they only for imported products?" Rin asked.

"No," Mik replied. "Two months ago, our investigators heard rumors that our storage warehouses might be involved. After monitoring them, we still haven't come up with anything certain. We do have suspicions. Prezdan Modu, two other advisors, and I have speculated that one or more of our merchant leads are involved."

"Is this where you're hoping Thom might help?" Rin asked.

"Me?" Thom gulped, suddenly worried that his stomach would start revolting again.

"Yes," Mik replied. "But we wouldn't be asking Thom to investigate. I was hoping he might use his ability to identify whether any traders in attendance are being deceptive in their dealings."

"What exactly are you thinking?" Rin asked.

"Since Thom is the age of many of the servants who will be serving at the gala, I was hoping he'd be willing to take on that role."

"A server, which means he won't have to talk with the guests," Rin said.

"Yes, for the most part," Mik answered. "Some traders might ask him questions, given his fluency in our language. While other people of your race live in Glakkadeth, you're still somewhat of a rarity. Interactions should be brief since you'd be acting as a servant. Oh, and to be clear, Thom would serve at the opening cocktail hour, not at the dinner afterward."

"Will Rin be there?" Thom asked, taking deep breaths to keep calm.

"Yes, if you agree," Mik replied, turning to Rin. "You could function as a wealthy Docha-leigh merchant considering doing business with us."

"That would make sense," Rin said. "What do you think, Thom?"

"I've never been a servant before," Thom responded, feeling a sense of relief settle his stomach knowing Rin would be with him. Taking a deep breath, he asked, "Will someone train me? And is there a uniform I'd have to wear?"

"Yes, to both," Mik replied.

Thom sat quietly, taking a few more deep breaths. "Can I think about it?"

"Certainly," Mik answered. "I haven't presented this idea to the Prezdan or the other advisors yet. And, even if you say yes, we may not go through with it."

"When is the gala?" Rin asked.

"Two months."

"And you think you can get Thom sufficiently trained in time?" Rin asked.

"Yes," Mik replied. "Of course, we'd pay for everything, including outfitting both of you."

"Hmm," Rin responded. "We'll consider it and get back to you."

"Thank you, Rin and Thom."

"You're welcome," Thom replied.

Thom walked with Mekial towards the training salle after telling her about his new ability and the merchant's request.

"Wow!" Mekial exclaimed. "You've got a new ability, and you're being asked to use it at the trader gala. I've heard those are important. Sometimes, new business deals start there."

"That's not helping, Mekial," Thom moaned.

"Sorry. I didn't mean to make you nervous. What's going on?"

"My new ability. I'm worried I might make a mistake. What if I read a person wrong? Or worse, what if I read a person correctly, and they're doing something wrong, and they find out about me?"

"Hmm," Mekial replied. "Isn't being able to protect yourself one of the reasons you train with Medelin?"

"Yeah."

"But you mentioned being afraid of making a mistake," she commented. "Since your gift emerged, have you ever done that while reading someone?"

"Not when it comes to reading someone's aura," he replied. "But I haven't used this ability to figure out if they're dishonest, other than Nordin."

"I understand," Mekial said. "But didn't you say you've felt more guided by your angels and the One lately, and they've encouraged you to trust your intuition?"

"Yeah, and I do feel more confident."

"Maybe your worry comes from doing something new. Remember how you told me you automatically get scared in those situations."

"I didn't think about that," Thom replied, considering.

"Tell me something," Mekial said. "During the thing with Nordin, did you get scared when you used your new ability?"

"No. Because I just did it."

"And you also felt confident enough about what you saw to say something."

"Yeah."

"It seems to me," Mekial continued, "that when you naturally use your gifts, you are confident. But when you think about it, like when it's new, you get scared about making a mistake."

"Oh, maybe."

"I'd suggest you talk with Sestra B about it too."

"Good idea. Thanks, Mekial," Thom replied. "I'll see if she can chat with me before I go home this afternoon."

Looking towards the door of the salle, Mekial further commented, "It looks like Medelin's waiting for us. We'd better get a move on."

The following morning, Thom woke up and groaned as he rolled over on his side. After his hard training session yesterday, his body was yelling at him. Maybe he'd lie here a little longer, lying flat once more. He thought about his chat with Sestra B. She assured him he could trust his intuition. She also took him through an exercise he could use if he started worrying about making a mistake.

Speaking aloud, Thom repeated the steps. "First, acknowledge the fear and talk with it, like it's a separate being, and thank it for trying to keep me safe. Second, invite it to look around and see if anything nearby can harm me. Third, ground fully in the present. And fourth, restate my intention to only use my gifts for the highest good, knowing my divine team stands with me."

As he completed the last step, a calm washed over him, and he knew his answer to Mik's request. Climbing out of bed, he grabbed the salve jar from his window ledge and smeared it on his legs and arm, where Mekial had gotten through his defenses. After dressing, he walked to the main room, where he found Rin.

"I heard some grunts," Rin commented. "Feeling some pain from your training?"

Thom grunted in agreement as he sat down.

"While I finish preparing breakfast, why don't you apply the salve."

"I already did," he replied. "I'm waiting for it to work."

Soon after, Rin set a bowl of porridge, bread with jam, and tea before him.

"The ginger tea should help you too," Rin commented, pouring him a mugful.

"Thanks," Thom replied. "Rin, I've thought more about Mik's request. I've decided to say yes."

"Ah. Do you want to tell me anything about how you came to your decision?"

Thom recounted his chat with Mekial and Sestra B.

"I'm glad you talked with them," Rin said. "I presume they'll keep it to themselves."

"Oh, yes," Thom assured him.

"Good. I was pleased when you asked Mik for more time. I'm even more pleased now, given your careful consideration. You're developing good discernment skills. I'm also glad Sestra B gave you the exercise. Fear does have its place in our lives. But if it prevents us from taking well-thought-out risks or trying something new, it limits us."

Thom nodded as he sipped his tea.

"Besides that," Rin continued. "Saying yes strengthens our relationship with the Prezdan and this land. I said nothing to you earlier because you needed to decide without pressure. I'll send a message to Mik."

The next afternoon, they heard back from Mik. He was effusive about Thom's acceptance and told them he'd let them know if the Prezdan and the advisors agreed to the plan.

Over the following week, while awaiting a response, Thom experienced sudden waves of fear and doubt. Each time they arose, he practiced Sestra B's exercise. Staying active also helped occupy his mind, preventing him from dwelling on worst-case scenarios.

Chapter 41

Late Muns-dae afternoon, Rin met Thom in the stable after Thom had returned from the monastery.

"You received a note from Mik," he explained, handing it to him.

"You didn't open it?" Thom asked.

"Of course not. It's addressed to you."

They went inside and sat at the table. Taking a deep breath, Thom opened the note and started reading it. "They agreed to Mik's plan."

"You know, you can change your mind," Rin reminded him.

"Thanks. But my intuition tells me it's important I do this, even though I'm afraid."

"What else does Mik say?" Rin asked.

"There's a local tailor who can make our outfits. The shop's not too far from us."

"Good," Rin replied.

"About the servant training," Thom continued. "I'm to take a class with a local lady. He's going to contact her. It starts on Nuvima 1 and lasts for three weeks."

"Does it meet every day?" Rin asked.

"Um," Thom scanned the message again. "No, four times a week. But it goes all morning."

"Ah. You'll have to talk with Sestra about adjusting your sessions and alert Reyner. But you'd still be able to train with Medelin in the afternoon."

"Yeah," Thom said.

"On the days you have your servant training, I'll handle the chores here," Rin said.

Thom raised his eyebrows, giving Rin a questioning look.

"And yes, I'll even weed the garden. Anything else in the note?"

"Mik says the gala will take place on the capital isle of Umojai, in one of the governmental complex buildings."

"I expected that," Rin replied. "We'll take an interisland ship there two weeks before. I want you to see the capital. I also suspect Mik will want you to act as a servant at trader meetings before the gala."

"I had wondered what the capital was like. What do I tell Medelin and Reyner?"

"Tell them we're taking a vacation."

"OK," Thom replied.

"You know, I'm very proud of you," Rin added.

Inside, Thom felt a warm glow suffuse through him.

"Watch yer step! Watch it, I say," a female voice yelled. Thom was jolted awake and looked toward the window through which the sound came. For the last two weeks, he and Rin had been housed at an inn paid for by Merchant Jacobreit. During their first week, Rin had shown him the sights of the capital, including the famous Pathway of Honor, which boasted statues representing notable Glakkadians who stood up for equality. Thom had been impressed that the figures not only included government leaders, but also teachers, seamstresses, and bakers, to name a few. For the last few days, Thom had functioned as a servant, providing snacks and drinks to the traders at their meetings.

Tonight was the gala, with a dinner preceded by a cocktail hour. Realizing he couldn't get back to sleep, Thom got up. Listening through the adjoining door to Rin's room, he didn't hear any sounds. Rin must sleep deeply. Grabbing his towel, he headed for the washroom. When he returned, he heard sounds from Rin's room. He had finished dressing when he knew someone was outside his door.

"Come in, Rin."

"Did you sense me outside?" Rin asked.

"I think I did," Thom admitted.

"Bravo and good morning, Thom," he added. "I see you already bathed and dressed. Before heading to the dining room, hang your uniform with my outfit on the back of my door. I'll carry both when we head out. I'll meet you downstairs shortly."

By the time Rin arrived, Thom had already consumed two bowls of porridge and was eating a chocolate bun between sips of tea.

"You've got chocolate on your chin," Rin commented.

"Oh. Thanks. I keep doing that," Thom replied, grimacing, before wiping it off.

Rin gestured to one of the servers, who knew their usual breakfast order by then. Turning to Thom, he spoke, "How are you feeling about tonight?"

"I'm a little nervous, but knowing you'll be there helps."

"If you run into any trouble, which I don't expect, or need a break, send me a pulse of energy. I'll be monitoring you. But I know you can do this."

"Thanks. I even visualized it going well. Sestra B also reminded me to check in with myself regularly to ensure I'm grounded and feel connected to my divine team."

"Good idea. You've developed a strong bond with them. That'll help you both at the gala and throughout your life."

"Um... Thanks," Thom mumbled, swallowing the last piece of his muffin.

The cocktail hour was set to start at 4 p.m. and last for two hours. Via a messenger, Mik asked Thom and Rin to arrive at 2 p.m., after Mik's last meeting, to have a quick check-in and see if Thom had any questions. At 3 p.m., Thom would join the other servants for any final set-up needs.

At 1:30 p.m., they made their way to the complex in a public carriage. They were going to dress for their respective roles in Mik's suite. Gallen Gessama would be there to greet them. When they arrived at the main entrance, Rin handed the guard the note Mik had included with his message, identifying them as guests.

Inspecting it, the guard gestured to a page nearby and directed her to escort them to Mik's suite.

Arriving at the door, the page knocked. When Mik answered, the page stammered, "Oh, sir. I was expecting another servant to answer. I'm sorry, sir. I'm babbling. Your guests have arrived."

"Thank you, page," Mik replied, inviting Rin and Thom in as the page scampered away.

They entered a spacious sitting room with large windows that overlooked a courtyard. Off to the left was a fireplace with stuffed chairs and a couch in front of it. Two gentlemen were already seated in chairs.

Mik directed Thom and Rin toward them, who rose. One was of average height and a well-muscled, stout man. The other was taller and slender but also muscular."

"Prezdan Modu," Rin replied in surprise as he greeted the first man. "We weren't expecting to see you before the gala."

"It's good to see you again, Rin. It's been too long," Modu replied, hugging him.

Hi, Gallen," Rin said, embracing the taller man shortly after. "You're looking fit."

"Thanks," Gallen replied. "The guard commander demands we stay current in our training."

"I can tell," Rin said. "Modu and Gallen, this is my apprentice, Thom, that Mik told you about."

"Hel…, hello, sir, Prezdan, sirs," Thom stuttered, starting to bow.

"None of that young man," Prezdan Modu spoke up. "A handshake will suffice. This is my husband, Gallen. And, in these quarters, call us Modu and Gallen. Relax and get comfortable. Mik has water, berry juice, or wine."

"Indeed," Mik agreed. "What would you like? Rin, can I presume wine?"

"Yes, thanks."

"Water, please," Thom added.

Rin settled on the couch while Thom sat on the edge of a chair.

"Please do relax, Thom," Modu said. "To answer your question, Rin. When my meeting was canceled, I decided to drop in and meet Thom."

Gallen spoke up, "Come on, Mod. You must admit you can be intimidating, particularly when you wear your formal garb. Thom, you should see him wearing a torn pair of drawers when he first wakes up."

"They're comfortable," Modu protested.

"Not to mention," Gallen continued, with a lopsided grin, "Mod stumbling around, looking a little like the walking dead."

"Very true. I'm not much of a morning person. Yet my councilors always want meetings early. I suppose it makes sense, given the demands of their own businesses. But I grumble until I'm fully awake and have a chocolate bun with my coffee. I'm addicted to them."

"We both are," Gallen added.

"Oh," Thom smiled. "I'm addicted to them, too. In that case, you might like to try a new hot drink that some friends and I have invented. We call it Timbu."

"Timbu?" Gallen asked.

Thom repeated the story that Mekial and he had shared with Captain Musa.

"We're both very interested in trying Timbu," Modu said. "We'll contact the cook about getting the recipe. Awa, you said?"

"Yes," Thom confirmed. "When we return home, I'm really going to miss chocolate."

"Let's see if we can do something about that when the time comes," Gallen suggested, turning to Rin and Modu, who nodded.

"Thom, I know you've been trained as a servant and have done well assisting at the trader meetings," Modu said.

"Thank you, sir... Modu," Thom replied.

Modu continued, "You've been assigned to serve beverages during the cocktail hour. Some might ask you questions, given that you're quite fluent in our language and are obviously from another land. But your conversations should be brief. If someone does probe, take note of who and excuse yourself, explaining that another guest is beckoning you."

"I must admit I'm a little worried about that. I don't want to be rude."

"You won't be," Modu assured him. "That's standard behavior for a servant. I still must say I don't completely understand your gift. Gallen and Mik have tried to explain it to me, but I'm a little dense with the energy stuff."

"Aura, Modu. It's called an aura," Gallen admonished.

"Um," Thom said, trying to figure out how to explain. "My spirit healing is new, especially my ability to detect lies. With it, I can tell if someone is aligned with their higher self. Auras are energies that sort of lay over a person's spirit. Rin and I can see their colors, which come from someone's personality. I can also see patterns, shapes, and even pulses. They tell me if the person's choices are aligned."

"Does someone have to say something to you before seeing their aura?" Modu asked.

"No. I do need to be near and lower two shields," he explained.

"Let me add something," Rin spoke up. "I'm not sure I mentioned this earlier. Doing this kind of reading uses Thom's energy, which means he'll have to step away occasionally to recharge."

"Understood," Gallen replied. "I'll let the head server know. The other servers will likely need to do that, too."

"Thanks for mentioning that, Rin," Thom said.

"OK," Modu continued. "Finally, I want to assure you we won't be upset with you if you don't identify people whose... auras... reveal deception," looking to Gallen to show he was learning. "While we do have some ideas about how to identify the culprits, this is another avenue we agreed to explore. Finding them tonight would be a great help, though. And I want to thank you both for your willingness to do this."

"You're welcome," Thom and Rin replied.

"Since we have a little time, Rin," Modu added, "let's hear about the trouble you've gotten into since we last heard from you."

"Trouble. Me?" Rin protested. "I'll tell you as long as Gallen shares any stories about overseeing the academics at the Guard Academy. Given the gray hairs on his head, I'm sure he faced some difficulties."

Thom had been serving drinks in the West Room. He'd already replenished his tray four times. The room derived its name from the large west-facing windows. Two doorways, strategically positioned along that wall, led out to a garden plaza. The remaining walls were adorned with intricately woven tapestries depicting various scenes of trades and professions in Glakkadeth.

Eight majestic chandeliers were suspended from the ceiling. Thom and the other servers had lit their candles earlier, a fascinating process. Their handlers, stationed above the ceiling, had carefully lowered the chandeliers on their long metal chains until they were two feet from the marble floor. Once the candles were aglow, they slowly raised them back into position. At the time, Thom had wondered whether any candles blew out, making the work more tedious.

Circulating among the guests, Thom saw a few traders who attended the business meetings, along with their spouses and elder children. They were all dressed in finery. The men wore silk tunics that fell below their knees, with trousers beneath them. Some tunics bore a design. Others were multi-colored, like a stylized patchwork quilt. The women wore similar tunics that seemed more like gowns, which pooled at their feet. Many had scarves around their necks, while others bore head wrappings that matched their tunic. Thom also noted jewelry and medallions prominently displayed on the garments.

Thom hadn't yet encountered any disingenuous people. But it didn't look like all the traders had arrived. Forty more minutes had passed, and he was tired. He'd been intensely scanning everyone they approached. He decided to step into the garden and take a brief rest.

Before Thom slipped outside, he looked at Rin, who was across the room with Mik and sent a pulse of energy to get his attention. When Rin returned his gaze, he nodded towards the garden doors to indicate he was taking a break. Stepping into the garden, he found a bench behind some bushes. His nose twitched, detecting the scent of the nearby white and pink gardenias.

Taking a deep breath, he closed his eyes and re-grounded, connecting to the earth's strength and his divine team. He was getting ready to return to the gathering when he heard two voices on the other side of the bushes.

"Everything's set then?" a woman asked.

"It will be soon," a man replied. "I need to reconfirm with my father which shipments will include the premium dishware and finely woven cloth that's most in demand."

Thom froze where he was, listening carefully.

"Do it soon," the woman replied. "There are investments I intend to make in a few months. I need a good amount of cash for that. People must believe there's a shortage and are willing to pay more."

"I will," the man agreed. "During the meal tonight, I'll make sure my father's wine glass is never empty. At home after the gala, I'll ply him with his favorite brandy to loosen his tongue. He loves it when I stroke his ego and play the admiring son. The fool."

"Good," she replied. "We must be cautious when choosing the warehouses. And you'll have to ensure one of your inventory recorders is placed there."

"Don't I always do that?" the man responded with annoyance.

Thom immediately focused his gift through his fifth shield and sensed into the two.

"Yes, yes," the woman replied, placating him. "Don't get angry. I heard rumors about a few people questioning the shortages and wondering if something criminal was happening. Nothing more has come from them. They've attributed the higher prices to unrest in some countries. Of course, I started those rumors. I'll let our silent partner know that everything's proceeding nicely."

"I still don't understand why you can't tell me who our silent partner is," the man muttered. "Wouldn't it be more efficient if I spoke to this person directly?"

Throughout their conversation, Thom had been examining their auras. The woman's colors were muddy yellow and red, indicating deceit and aggression, with a tight pattern overlaying her spirit. The man's aura had the same muddy yellow. But he also displayed green for jealousy and gray for boredom. His pattern was almost as tight. He returned to the conversation in the hope that the speakers would mention their names.

"We'd best get back to the gathering," the woman warned. "Why don't you go in through the garden doors first? I'll stroll around here for a bit."

Thom needed to get away. He probably shouldn't enter the room through the garden doors if the man was watching. Thom decided to walk around to the main entrance to the building. But how would he explain to the guards wanting to enter there?

Thom cut through the bushes lining the entrance road, where carriages dropped off the guests. Something sparkled on the ground. He saw a silk scarf with a large, dog-shaped brooch attached. Picking it up, he noticed the dog had sapphires for eyes and diamonds adorning much of its body. His sisters would have called it gaudy. This must have come from one of the guests, which gave him an idea.

Stepping towards the front door, a guard raised his hand. "What are you doing out here?" he asked haughtily. "Slacking off?"

"No, sir," Thom bowed to him awkwardly. "One of the guests lost a scarf and brooch and I was asked to search for them."

"I didn't see you leave!" the guard challenged.

"I'm sorry, sir. I'm small, and most people don't notice me. Perhaps someone was coming in while I was leaving."

"Humph," the guard grumbled. "Get back in there."

"Yes, sir," Thom replied, attempting to look humble and at the same time grateful.

"Thanks for your help, divine team," Thom whispered. He shoved the scarf and brooch into his pocket and returned to the gathering. He needed to talk to Rin.

After slipping into the room, Thom weaved his way to the beverage table and grabbed another tray of drinks. Looking about, he saw Rin talking with Gallen and made his way there.

"Thom, are you OK?" Rin asked, frowning. "You've been gone a long time. Were you that depleted?"

"I was tired, but I'm OK now. But something else kept me." Thom explained what he had heard.

"Good idea to return through the main entrance," Gallen approved. "Did either say their name?"

"No," he replied.

"Do you think you'd recognize their voices?" Rin asked.

"Maybe. But I would recognize the man and woman's auras," Thom offered.

"Good," Gallen said. "About the scarf and brooch. Would you show them to me?"

Thom pulled them out of his pocket.

"Ah yes, I know exactly who they belong to," Gallen stated. "I'll return them to their owner, who's quite fond of her poodle. Excuse me."

"Thom, do you need more time to rest?" Rin asked.

"No, I'm fine. Like I said, I think I can find the two easily. For the third, I still need to scan everyone."

"When you identify them, find me, and I'll pass the information on."

"OK."

Thom continued circulating with drinks, searching for the two. More time passed with no luck. By then, the crowd had doubled in size. He decided to focus on the young man. He searched for family groups with an older son. Luck was with him this time. The father was already inebriated and looked like he was holding court. The son, dressed in a gold and black tunic and standing nearby, conversed with two young women.

After circling the room several times, Thom finally encountered the female trader, wearing a vibrant teal tunic with silver beads draped around her neck. She exchanged a word with an older gray-haired male but didn't stop for long. He discreetly followed the older trader to see if he was the third.

When the man stopped to talk with a group of women, Thom decided to approach. "Would you like another beverage, ladies, sir?"

The male trader nodded and took a glass of wine off Thom's tray.

"Oh!" one of the women exclaimed, nearly spilling her wine on her oversized blue tunic, befitting her stature. "My wife told me there was a servant from another land here," she continued, nodding to the slender trader beside her. "Where are you from?"

"Docha-leigh, ma'am," Thom replied.

"I've never been to Docha-leigh. I've been asking her to take me there for ages."

While Thom listened, he again focused his gift through his fifth shield and looked at the male trader. His aura was faded blue, mixed with some muddy yellow in a loose pattern. But he also had some black, indicating unhappiness and even a little remorse. He was sure this was the unnamed partner.

"Would you tell me why you're in our land, young man?" the woman continued.

"Oh," Thom replied. "I'm sorry, but someone's summoning me. My apologies," he said as he bowed and excused himself.

Thom returned to the beverage table, pretending the head server had summoned him. He refilled his tray and made his way back to Rin.

After pointing out the people he'd detected, Thom continued serving. For the rest of the event, while he noted a few people showing colors of exaggeration and a little deceit, no others stood out as disingenuous. When the head server announced the meal was being served, Thom sighed with relief. His feet and back were sore, and he was plain tired.

Exiting a side door, along with the other servers, Thom sat on a bench nearby. When Rin sought him out, he escorted him back to Mik's room.

The gathering was limited to Mik, Rin, and Thom this time. "I can't stay long," Mik replied, "because I'm expected in the dining hall. Did you discover anything, Thom?"

"Yes." He recounted what he learned, and he and Rin provided Mik with a description of the traders.

Nodding his head, Mik said, "I know who they are. My sense is that we've found the key people. We'll take the investigation from here. On behalf of Modu and Gallen, thank you very much."

"You're welcome," Thom replied.

Chapter 42

I t was Mercha. Vern and Finn had been living in Glakkadeth for a couple of months. After they failed to kidnap the kid in Bethemel, they returned to Potai-cruth, demanded their money from Mitch, and resumed their lives as thieves. Last Uctiba, Mitch contacted them again, informing them the healer and the kid had gone to Glakkadeth. When he asked them if they'd be interested in making a great deal of money, they couldn't say no.

"Mind me what Mitch wrote," Finn asked Vern as they ate supper at a small ale and grub tavern in a poorer section of town.

"I don' understand why ya cain't remember," Vern grumble. "For the last time, Mitch tol' us to kidnap the kid, like we planned in Bethemel."

"Yeah, I know'd thet. But da other part with da tradin' still confuses me," Finn persisted.

"He wants us to make it look like Rinbalden is doin' some illegal tradin' and makin' lots a money," Vern explained. "When the constables find out, he gits arrested. That messes things up between our king and queen and the Prezdan here."

"Thets whut I don' unnerstan'," Finn said. "How does thet git im in trouble? And whut does thet hev to do wit' da kid?"

"Mitch said Rinbalden lived in Glakkadeth before. Supposebly, he knows healer stuff they don' here. He thinks he an' the Prezdan become friends."

"Ya didn' mention thet," Finn whined.

"I didn' want to confuse ya," Vern said.

"I'm still confuse," Finn replied.

"Let me finish," Vern said. "We knows healers ain't rich. When we gots here, I opened an account in the healer's name at the countin' house. I've been depositin' money there every week. Ya do remember Mitch sent us the money that I'm usin'."

"Yeah," Finn replied.

"Afta we kidnap the kid, we hol' him for a week. Then one o' the punks'll slip a ransom note under the healer's door. By then, the healer be frettin' big time 'cause he cain't finds the kid."

"I unnerstan," Finn replied. "Didn' ya say sumpin about utter notes?"

"Yeah," Vern replied. "Ya do listen. We planted notes showin' the healer's been gittin' payments from a trader here."

"How's thet gunna work," Finn asked. "Is da trader writin' em?"

"No, I wrote em," Vern explained, gritting his teeth. "The girl punk already planted em in the shop."

"How'd she do thet?" Finn asked.

"I cut her arm and had her go to the healer to git help," Vern explained.

"I hope ya didn' cut her as bad as ya did me," Finn complained. "I still hev a scar."

"Leave it," Vern replied. "After the healer gits the ransom note, he's prolly gonna git the constable. When the constable gits there, both punks'll be near. When the healer is bein' all loud about not havin' the money, the boy punk'll say he seen someone depositin' money for him at the countin' house. The girl punk'll tell em she seen the trader messages when she was bein' treated."

"Oh," Finn replied. "I git it. What will we do after we git da money?"

"We're not gittin' the money," Vern said. "The scandal happens when they fin' out the healer was stealin'. While they's takin' him to jail, I'll kill im. Ya knows I'm very good with a knife, specially knife throwin'."

"What about..." Finn started asking.

"The kid? You kill im."

"I don' like thet, Vern," Finn said. "I niver killed no one. I beat people but niver killed. An I don' think I can kill a kid."

"Then, I'll kill im too," Vern stated. "That'll make the leaders of Glakkadeth and Docha-leigh unhappy with each other."

Finn covered his grimace by taking a gulp of his ale. "Have ya decided when we kidnap da kid?"

"Yeah," Vern answered, "the girl punk learnt the healer will be treatin' someone in town in two days, on Fwi-dae.

The kid'll be spendin' the day at the monastery. On his ride back to the shop, the punks'll grab im and take im to the abandoned shack we found a couple weeks ago. It's supposed to rain hard and should be dark. That'll help cover the kidnappin'."

"And we're meetin' em at da buildin'?" Finn asked.

"Yeah," Vern said. "You do have a brain."

Finn remained silent.

It was dark and pouring rain when Thom left the monastery, his body weary from today's training. Even though the weather was typical for the season, he didn't like it. The wind made it worse as rain blew into his face and ran down his neck. Since his afternoon session with Medelin had run long, he had stayed at the monastery for dinner. A good part of his sword training was with his right arm because Medelin noted it was not as strong as his dominant left. Because Crescent knew the way home, Thom let him take the lead.

"Thanks for doing all the work on the ride, Cres. I know you're wet. Me too. I'll get you a nice hot mash when we get home."

Crescent whinnied in approval.

Thom saw there wasn't anyone else out. He didn't blame them for staying indoors. When he got home, Thom would make himself some hot tea. He wasn't sure if Rin would be there because he'd been spending extra time with a young patient at her parent's home.

Peering forward, Thom saw something lying on the muddy ground. As he drew closer, he heard a moan. Is an animal hurt? He was a few feet away when he saw it was a young man. Quickly dismounting, he approached. "Where are you hurt?" he asked. Crouching down over him, he started to say, "I'm an apprentice heal..." when he felt something hard hit his head.

"Agggggh," Thom moaned, feeling his head throbbing. Opening his eyes, everything appeared blurry. The world spun, and a dizzying sensation swept over him. "Where am I? What happened?" Realizing it hurt too much to think, he surrendered himself to sleep.

Thom stirred. He didn't know how long he'd been out, but his head wasn't pounding as much. Shivering, he sat up, noting that his back was stiff from lying on a wooden floor. While surveying his surroundings, Thom found himself in a small room with worn, cracked walls and a mostly boarded-up window. The faint brightness outside suggested it was early morning.

"Where am I?" he wondered again. "I'm definitely not at the shop or monastery. Something's seriously wrong."

Turning his head, he felt a lump. "Ow," he yelped. "I don't know how I got here or why, but someone's taken me. The last thing I remember is riding Crescent through town. I think there was something on the road in front of me. Where's Crescent?"

Thom shivered again and sneezed. Oh no, he might be getting sick. Wiping the mud off his cloak, Thom wrapped himself again, hoping to get warm, and closed his eyes. He was roused when he heard two male voices in the room. Keeping his eyes closed, he listened, realizing they spoke like people native to Docha-leigh.

"I think they thunked him too hard, Vern. He's still out. He gots a big bump on his head," a man said.

"No matter, Finn," a different man replied. "He's still breathin'."

"I don' like it. What if he dies?"

Thom heard a grunt in reply. So their names are Vern and Finn. And someone hit him on his head.

"Why don' we git sumpthin to eat," Vern said. "The healer prolly hasn't noticed the kid's missin' yet."

Thom heard the door to his room close. Still listening, he heard Vern say, "Yo, punks, wake up. We're goin' to git some eats to bring back. Keep watch."

"They're working with others," Thom whispered. Keeping his ears tuned to the other room, he heard them return. Closing his eyes to concentrate, he strained to hear their conversation.

"This bun good," he heard a female say in accented Dochalan. She sounded younger.

"You coulda' brough' cider," Thom heard another male say, also accented and younger.

"Na," Vern replied. "You can git your own when you go out and scope out the healer's place."

"When you gunna deliver da ransom note, Vern?" Finn asked.

"I told ya before. Not for a week," he replied. "I want the healer sore upset."

Thom heard Finn grunt in reply.

Chapter 43

Rin was startled awake by the sound of a braying donkey outside. He stretched his arms overhead and sat up. He'd come back late the night before, having stayed at the home of the young patient longer than usual. Out of gratitude, her parents had invited him to dinner. Climbing out of bed, he dressed and made his way to the front, hollering, "Thom, you up?"

When he didn't hear a response, he went back to Thom's room and tapped on his door. "Thom," he repeated. "Time to get up." Opening the door, he saw that his bed hadn't been slept in. Maybe he stayed at the monastery last night. He knew Medelin had been training him hard lately. Thinking of the monastery, he realized he'd better get something to eat and head there himself. He was teaching Lauret and Rafi a new stitching method. Before he went to the stable, he grabbed the bag of herbs he'd promised to drop off at another patient's home.

Riding into the stable at the monastery, Rin noted Crescent's stall was empty. "Maden," he called out.

"Yes, Rin," she replied, walking towards him.

"Crescent's not in his stall. I thought Thom stayed here last night. Have you seen him?"

"Not today," Maden replied. "The last time I saw him was after dinner yesterday. He was saddling Crescent, and I presumed he was heading back to your shop."

"He didn't sleep in his bed last night," Rin said.

"Did he stay at the Gambi's?" Maden suggested.

"I'll check with Lauret," Rin replied.

Stepping into the infimarium, he saw Lauret and Rafi. "Good morning, you two. Lauret, did Thom stay at your place last night?"

"Good morning, Rin," she replied. "No. He didn't. Why do you ask?"

"He didn't come home last night. Maden said she saw Thom leave after dinner but hadn't seen him since. Do you know if Mekial knows where he is?"

"I don't," she replied. "She's with Medelin now."

"Thanks. I'll go check with her."

"We'll come with you," Lauret said.

Entering the training salle, they found Mekial sparring with Lebrim while Medelin observed.

"Sorry to interrupt, Medelin," Rin said.

"Did you need something?"

"No. Yes. I need to ask Mekial something."

"Certainly," Mekial replied.

"Do you know where Thom is? Crescent's not in his stall. But I hoped Thom said something to you."

"He didn't, Rin," Mekial answered. "When I left yesterday afternoon, he was sparring with Medelin."

Medelin nodded. "And when we finished, he mentioned he'd get a quick dinner here and head back to the shop. I think he said something about wanting to read his book."

"What's happened?" Mekial asked.

"Thom didn't come home last night, and Crescent isn't in his stall."

"That's not good," Lauret said. "Do you think he had an accident on his ride home? It was raining heavily last night, and the wind was lashing the trees. Perhaps a branch broke off and hit him or his horse."

"I hope not," Rin said, his breath quickening. "Now I'm even more worried. It's not like Thom to take off without telling anyone."

"Where could he be?" Mekial asked, her voice quivering with fear.

"Did you see any signs of an accident on your ride here, Rin?" Maden asked who had stepped into the salle a moment before.

"I didn't, but I rode here along a different route from our usual. I had to deliver herbs to a patient first. Sorry, Lauret and Rafi. I'm afraid I have to cancel your training this morning. I need to search for him. I have a bad feeling."

"I'll do anything to help," Mekial said.

"We'll all help," Lauret stated. "I'll also let Reyner and Sestra B know."

"Mekial, would you ride to the Constable Station and tell Captain Jallow?" Rin asked.

"Yes," Mekial answered before dashing off to the stable.

"Should we meet you at your shop in a few hours?" Lauret asked.

"Since Maden said Thom was returning to the shop, yes."

After being unsuccessful, Rin returned to the shop, hoping to find Thom and Crescent. He didn't. Where could they be? Sitting down, he was considering his next options when Mekial arrived.

"Any sign of him?" Rin asked.

"No," she replied unhappily. "I even rode your route home a few times and checked side streets and alleys. I didn't see any signs of accidents either. But the ground was churned up with the mud."

"True," Rin said. "I hope one of the others found him."

"Me too," Mekial agreed.

When Lauret, Bea, Rafi, and Sestra Berbera arrived, they shook their heads.

"We went by the market fair to see if anyone saw him," Lauret said. "No one did."

"Where else should we look?" Rin said, standing up and beginning to pace.

"Perhaps the retired healer?" Rafi suggested.

"Good idea," Rin said.

"I'll ride over there now."

"Thanks, Rafi," Rin replied.

As he was leaving, Captain Jallow and Mik walked in.

"Mik," Rin said. "How?"

"Jallow came by my place after he learned Thom was missing," Mik explained. "I take it no one has found him yet." Thom and Rin had met Captain Jallow when they had first arrived in Glakkadeth. He had come by to welcome them. He also let Rin know he and his fellow fire brigade members might need his services from time to time.

"No," Rin said. "But we haven't heard from the rest of them."

Sometime later, they walked in. All were shaking their heads.

"I don't know what else to do," Rin said, running his hands repeatedly through his hair. "Maybe Thom wasn't injured, and something worse happened to him. Mik, can I talk to you in the back?"

"Certainly," Mik replied.

Once they were away from the others, Rin asked, "Do you think the traders whom Thom identified found out about him and took him?"

"I don't see how. Besides Modu, Gallen, and two advisors, no one else knew Thom was involved. And when we mentioned his name, we did it in a private room."

"Could someone have been listening at the door?" Rin asked.

"I can't rule that out, unfortunately," Mik admitted. "Since you have plenty of people searching, I'll head to the capital and talk to Modu and Gallen. I wonder if Jallow should know about this."

"I think that's a good idea," Rin said. "Thanks. Let's go back to the others."

"Rin, I'll ride back to my office and ask my deputies to scour the town," Jallow said.

"I'm heading in that direction myself, Jallow," Mik said. "I'll walk with you."

"Anyone have any other ideas?" Rin asked.

"Might someone have come to the shop last night sick, and Thom went to tend them?" Lauret asked.

"That's not impossible," Rin said.

"I'll ask around."

"I'll go with her," Bea added.

"I'll check at the Chapel of the One down the street to see if anyone saw anything," Sestra B said.

"Thanks," Rin said. "Would the rest of you keep looking?"

When they left, Medelin lingered. "Rin, if you're wondering whether someone took Thom, I wanted to let you know that he has come along well in defending himself. Thom's even learned how to use everyday objects as weapons."

"I appreciate you letting me know, Medelin," Rin replied.

"I'll continue searching, too," he said.

Rin nodded.

Chapter 44

The following morning, Thom felt miserable. Coughing and sneezing relentlessly, he felt achy and a rawness in his throat. Putting his hand on his forehead, Thom confirmed his suspicion. He had a fever. The day before, Vern warned him not to scream or make a fuss, or he'd shut him up. To demonstrate the consequences, Vern brandished a sharp-edged dagger and threw it at the same spot on the wall repeatedly, never missing. Unsuccessfully, trying to hide his terror, Vern had laughed, bringing back memories of the female bandit.

Last night, before he went to sleep, he connected with his divine team. Sereh and Jeshua said people were looking for him. That helped a little. They had also suggested that he check Vern and Finn's auras. Vern's had streaks of muddy red and yellow overlaid with swatches of black, which confirmed he was dangerous. In contrast, while Finn's aura did have some muddy red and yellow, he also had spots of pink and green, indicating some caring. Thom wasn't in any shape to do something with the information, but it might be useful.

Another fit of coughing seized him. Once it subsided, Thom curled back into a tight ball on the floor, attempting to find comfort. Laying his head on his arm, he was almost asleep when he heard the door open. Looking up, he saw Finn enter carrying blankets.

"I hear'd ya coffin', and got ya sum blankits," he said. "They's gots some holes in em, but thet's all I could fin'."

"Thanks," Thom replied, sniffling for what seemed like the hundredth time.

"I'm gunna get ya sumpin hot ta drink too," Finn said. "Vern's outside. Don' try nuthin."

After Finn left, Thom piled two blankets on each other, fashioning them into a makeshift sleeping pallet. At least, they'd be softer than the floor. Removing his damp tunic, he tried to brush off the remaining bits of mud. Stumbling to the window, he hung it on a nail he found on the wall next to it, hoping his tunic would dry. Laying down again, he pulled the third blanket over him and fell asleep.

He was awakened when the door opened again. It was Finn.

"Sorry, it took sa long. Vern had me run'd an errand. Here, I brough' ya hot cider and a meat bun, in case ya hungry."

"Thanks, Finn," Thom replied, sitting up and reaching for the bun and the cup of hot cider. "That's very kind." Taking a sip, he felt the hot liquid bathe his throat and warm him.

"Ya welcum," Finn said. "I'll be in da udder room. Vern went out scoutin'."

Thom swiftly finished the cider and bun. He realized he felt a little better and noticed he wasn't coughing as much. But Thom needed to use the privy. Feeling his wet trousers, he grimaced, suspecting that some dampness wasn't from rain. "Um, excuse me," Thom called out, a cough punctuating his words. "Excuse me," he yelled, feeling the rawness of his throat.

Finn came in. "Wutcha need?"

"I need to pee and poop," Thom stated outright.

"Ah, I was wunderin'," he said. "There's a privy out back. I'll take ya."

After returning, Thom asked Finn, "Can you stay a bit?"

"Er, sure," Finn replied. He went to the other room and returned with a chair.

Thom scooted up against the wall behind him, wrapped in his blankets.

"Ya feels any better?" Finn asked.

"Some. The cider helped. Can I ask you something?"

Finn nodded.

"You're from Docha-leigh, aren't you?"

"Yeah," Finn replied. "But before youse ask, I'm not sayin' why we took ya."

"What happened to my horse?" Thom asked instead.

"We gots him tied up," Finn said.

"Are you feeding him?"

"We is, hay," Finn admitted. "He ain't happy. Keeps tryin' ta escape."

"Thanks," Thom replied. "I was worried. And thanks again for the cider and the bun. It helped."

"Welcum."

Based on his aura, there's some good in Finn, Thom thought. He needed to get him to talk. "My name's Thom," he told him. "Your's is Finn."

"Oh, ya hear'd thet, did ya," Finn said, "Vern won' be happy."

"I won't tell him if you don't," he assured him. "Um, I'm still a little hungry. Would it be possible to get another bun and hot drink?"

"Not now," Finn said. "But when one of da punks comes back, I can git ya more."

"Thanks," Thom said. "When you were getting the bun and cider... did the vendor sell something called Timbu?"

"Is thet da brown drink?" Finn asked.

"Yeah," Thom said. "It's delicious and made with something called chocolate. They might even sell muffins with small chocolate bits. They're good, too. When you go, could I ask for that instead? I don't have a right to, but it would help me feel better."

"I don' know," Finn replied. "Brown drink don' sound good. I better go. Vern don' want me getting friendly-like wit' ya."

Once Finn left, Thom wrapped himself back in his blankets.

Thom must have dozed because, before he knew it, he heard the door creak open.

"I got ya thet Timbu drink and the muffin with them dark bits," Finn announced. "The guy convinced me to git it, too."

Before drinking his Timbu, Thom watched as Finn took a sip. A big grin appeared on his face.

"This be good," he said. "Thenks for tellin' me about em. I niver had it afore."

"You're welcome. Try the muffin," Thom encouraged.

Taking a big bite, Finn nodded vigorously. "This be good too," he said. "Ya knows, youse a nice kid. Sorry bout what we doin' ta ya."

Inwardly, Thom smiled and took a drink himself, followed by a bite of the muffin. He knew cider or tea would've been better for his throat, but these were comforting. Thom was glad he'd suggested the Timbu. He wanted to get Finn to like him even more and get him to talk about himself, including whether he ever had any dreams.

Rin trudged back to his shop in the rain. No one had found a trace of Thom. He'd also caught a cold from his long days of searching. When he arrived, he found Mik inside.

"Mik," Rin said, coughing.

"You don't sound good, Rin," Mik said. "You need to take care of yourself. Sit down. I'll make you some tea."

"I know. But it's been six days since Thom disappeared. I've got to keep searching. What am I going to tell his family? He could've been hurt or killed."

"Don't go there, Rin," Mik said. "You don't know what's happened. Modu's guards have been searching for Thom, too. And neither Modu nor Gallen thinks the traders Thom identified are involved in his disappearance. They've had people following them the last few days. The traders are still on the capital island, and no one has visited them recently. I'll be back with your tea."

They were sitting quietly, drinking their tea, when they heard the clomping of an animal outside.

Looking up, Rin saw a horse. "Is that Crescent?" he said, shocked. Jumping up, he ran to the door and yanked it open. Mik followed.

"It is Crescent," Rin said. "I don't see Thom, though."

"Rin, look at the rope tied to his saddle," Mik said. "It's frayed.

"Someone did take Thom," Rin concluded. "But Crescent got away."

"It seems like it," Mik confirmed.

"I wish I could have Crescent tell me where Thom is," Rin said.

Mik nodded. "I'll take Crescent to the stable and get him cleaned up. I'll also let Jallow know about his return. You stay here, Rin. You need to rest and get well. We don't want you catching pneumonia. I know Mekial's scouting out the market fair again. I'll have her come by."

Rin nodded slightly, holding his head in his hands.

"Turg!" Vern yelled. "How did the horse git away? Didn' you tie im up good?"

"Horse tied strong," the boy punk insisted in Dochalan. "See rope. Broke."

Thom heard Vern in the other room. He was happy Crescent escaped and was hopefully back at the shop. Thom was now tied to a chair. Vern started securing him to it days earlier when he caught Finn talking with him. Thom overheard Vern accusing Finn of getting soft.

Shifting in the chair, Thom's back and shoulders ached terribly. Vern had insisted he remain tied through the night, making sleep difficult. His wrists burned from the ropes rubbing against them. Turning his attention back to the front room, he strained to hear snippets of any further conversation.

"Aight," Vern said, his voice barely carrying through the wall. "Finn, you stay here watchin' the kid. I'll go scope out the constable's to see what's happenin'. Youse punks, see what's goin' on at the healer shop. Tonight, one of youse will deliver the ransom note. I knows the healer's crazed. He's prolly not thinkin' straight."

Shortly after, Finn walked in. "Thom," he said. "We hev ta talk."

When Finn left, Thom was shaking. "Finn believes Vern's going to kill me tomorrow," he whispered in horror. "He thinks Vern's going to send him on an errand." His heart pounded rapidly; it felt like it would burst from his chest. His stomach was also tied up in knots.

"Team," Thom whispered desperately, "what do I do?"

In his mind, he immediately heard the words *Breathe* and *Ground.*

He inhaled and exhaled slowly a few times. As his heartbeat began to slow, he tried to relax. It was challenging, but he kept at it. Finally feeling a little calmer, he heard *Good* from them.

OK. Thom knew he needed to figure out how to defend himself. There wasn't much in the room he could use. Looking at the pile of blankets, Thom could kick them toward Vern to trip him. But if Vern came at him with his dagger, he wouldn't have a chance, especially if his hands were tied.

Considering his options, an idea came to him. He'd ask Finn to untie him before he left on his errand. Then, when Vern came in, he'd catch him off guard by leaping from the chair and using it to topple him. Hopefully, he'd be able to escape. *Archangel Michael and divine team, I'm counting on you to help.*

Mostly satisfied with his plan, Thom found himself thinking about Finn. He'd changed these last few days. Or should he say, he's come back to his true self. Finn had a hard life with two thieving parents who forced him to steal. His saving grace was when his parents made him cook for them and his two younger siblings. Even though he was only nine, he loved it. That's always been his dream. When Thom looked at Finn's aura this morning, its muddiness was almost gone. And there was more pink and some blue. His spirit is starting to shine through again. He was pleased.

Chapter 45

T he morning dawned bright after having rained all night. Thom hadn't slept much because he knew what would happen that day. As he'd done for the last few days, Finn brought him a cup of Timbu and a chocolate muffin. When he finished, Vern tied his hands behind the chair again. Using the trick Rin used with the bandits a year and a half ago, he held his hands slightly cupped to ensure the ropes would be a little loose.

Still listening into the next room, Thom heard Vern tell the punks to run to the shop but to stay hidden until after the healer found the note and the constable arrived. After they left, he heard Vern tell Finn, "Leave for the shop in a few minutes. I want ya there when the punks play their parts and the healer gits nabbed. I'll come soon after."

"OK, Vern," he heard Finn reply. "I lef' my cloak in da room with da kid. I'll git it and take off." Finn came in and stepped behind Thom's chair. "I see ya loosed da ropes. Thet makes it easier," he whispered to him. "I know ya learnt some self-dufens. Vern be strong, but sometimes he's slow. I'm goin' ta constables' ta let em know. I don' know if I'll iver see ya agin, Thom. But thenks."

"Thank you, Finn," Thom whispered, as Finn grabbed his cloak from a hook and walked toward the door. "May the One be with you."

Before Finn left the shack, he heard Vern yell, "Stay hidden and keep yer cloak over yer face."

Then there was silence.

OK, *guys, this is it*, Thom mind-spoke to his divine team. He grounded himself and took a few deep breaths.

The door opened, and Vern stepped in, clutching his dagger.

"Sorry kid, but I gots no choice," he said, moving towards him.

Thom stood up, grabbed the back of his chair, and pulled it in front of him as a shield.

"Finn untied ya," Vern said. "I knew'd he was goin' soft. I'll deal with im."

Thom remained silent but watchful.

Vern grabbed a leg of the chair with his free hand to rip it out of Thom's hands, but Thom held firm.

"Youse a stronger bugger than I thought," Vern commented. "Ya gonna lose. I can make this quick if you don' fight me."

Thom stood defiantly.

"Nah? OK."

Vern yanked the chair from Thom's hands and dropped it.

Seeing the dagger coming at him, Thom grabbed one of his blankets and whipped it toward Vern's leg, making him stumble a little. He barely avoided getting stabbed in his heart.

"Think yer clever, don't ya," Vern muttered.

Grabbing the chair again, Thom whipped it around with all his might before slamming it against Vern. A resounding crack echoed through the room as the chair shattered into pieces.

Vern dropped to his knees and groaned, rubbing the side of his head. "Ya gonna pay for that, kid." Rising to his feet, he advanced on Thom.

Realizing he was backed against the wall, Thom's instinct kicked in. Bending his knees, he twisted, narrowly avoiding the dagger that grazed his head before becoming lodged in the wall.

As Vern pulled the dagger loose, Thom scooted out of the way, ignoring the blood running down his face. Stay grounded, he reminded himself. He needed to get the dagger. Grabbing one of the chair legs off the floor, he took the sword stance Medelin had taught him.

"That's not gonna do ya much good against this," Vern laughed, waving the blade in front of him.

Determined to stay strong, Thom used the chair leg to strike Vern's hand and sent the dagger flying.

"You busturd!" Vern yelled, grabbing the chair leg and pulling Thom close.

Thom dropped the leg, but not before Vern had used his momentum to throw him across the room. When he crashed to the floor, he felt a shooting pain in his left arm. "Aagh," he yelled, briefly stunned.

"Now ta end this," Vern snarled.

Turning his head, Thom saw Vern retrieve the dagger. Remembering the tale Rin had shared about the woman tossing a heavier man over her shoulder, he decided to try it himself. When Vern approached him from behind, Thom reached back, seized Vern's arm, and successfully hurled him over his shoulder. Vern's head collided with the remains of the chair, accompanied by the ominous sound of something snapping.

All was silent except for Thom's heavy breathing.

Vern's eyes stared sightlessly.

"What? No!" Thom yelled in horror. "He can't be dead. I don't want him to be dead. He's not supposed to be dead! Killing's wrong! Healers aren't supposed to kill, especially spirit healers. Digi, Digi, Digi!" he repeated.

As Thom attempted to rise, his face contorted in pain, forcing him to abruptly sit down again. Touching his left ankle, he winced. Carefully cradling his broken arm in his hand, he was overcome with sobs of despair.

Rin was an absolute wreck. He hadn't slept much since Thom went missing and was exhausted. At least his cough was better because Lauret had insisted on treating him yesterday. Forcing himself out of bed, he heard the clanking of dishes. Mik had been staying with him the last few days as Rin increasingly unraveled.

"Tea and porridge are ready, Rin," Mik called out. "Bea dropped by with some sweet cinnamon muffins for you. They're warming by the fire and smell great."

Rin stumbled in and said, "Thanks, Mik."

While Mik set the table, Rin tottered to the front door to check the weather. Despite others advising him to rest, he couldn't bring himself to remain idle. Approaching the door, he noticed folded paper protruding from underneath. Retrieving it, he began reading its contents.

"Rin," Mik called out, "Breakfast's ready."

Rin didn't respond.

"Rin," Mik repeated as he came up next to him. "Did you hear me?"

Rin turned and handed Mik the note.

"Someone did kidnap Thom, then," Mik concluded. "That's quite a lot of money."

Rin looked at Mik before collapsing on the floor, sobbing.

"Rin, Rin!" Mik exclaimed. "Let me help you to the chair."

After settling him, Mik said, "This means Thom's alive."

"Maybe. Give me a minute, Mik," Rin replied, wiping his face with a handkerchief.

"OK," Mik replied. "After I get you tea, I'll head to the Constable Station to inform Captain Jallow."

While Mik was fetching the tea, Mekial walked in, "Rin, I searched near the docks and didn't..." Her words trailed off as she observed Rin's expression. "What happened? Is Thom... dead?" she gulped, tears appearing in her eyes.

Rin shook his head, pointing to the ransom note on the table.

She picked it up and read its contents.

"Ransom," Mekial said. "Thom's alive?"

"I hope," Rin murmured uncertainly.

Mik returned to the front room with a cup in his hands. "Ah. Mekial. I'm glad you're here. Will you stay with Rin while I get Captain Jallow?"

"Sure," she replied.

Upon Jallow's arrival with Mik, they discovered Rin pacing back and forth with his shouts filling the air. A crowd had gathered outside.

"I'm glad you're back," Mekial said with relief, "Rin suddenly went from hopeless to raging. He's been detailing how a healer could make Thom's kidnappers pay."

"Rin, where's the note?" Jallow asked.

Mekial handed it to him.

By then, Rin had quieted.

"That's a substantial amount," Jallow admitted.

"I don't have that kind of money," Rin said, his voice tinged with sorrow.

"Don't worry," Mik said. "I can help pay it, and I'm sure Modu and Gallen will too."

Standing by the shop door, a tall young man interrupted, "What about da money you have in your countin' house account? I was dumpin' trash there last week when I hears someone depositin' money for you."

Jallow turned around. "What did you say?" he asked.

Stepping into the shop, he repeated it.

"I don't know what you're talking about," Rin insisted. "I don't have an account there."

"The guy depositin' it seemed all secret like, but I was next to him, and I hears the healer's name, sir," the man said to the constable.

"Ask the healer where he got da money, constable," a young woman, who had also stepped into the shop, said. She was shorter than the young man, with braided hair cascading down her back. "I was here last week when I gots cut. When the healer was in da back room, I saw messages in a drawer. They said sumpin about payments for help with tradin' business."

"What are you talking about?" Rin demanded.

"They's over there," the young woman insisted, pushing her way through and pulling several sheets out of a drawer.

Taking the messages from her, Captain Jallow looked through them, occasionally glancing at Rin. "Mekial, would you check if my deputies have arrived yet?"

"Sure," she replied. Something about the young man and woman didn't sit right with her. When she returned with the deputies, she stood across from them watching.

"You asked for us, sir," one of the female deputies asked.

"Yes," he replied. "Did you bring the restraining chains with you?"

"Yes, sir," the other one answered. "They're in my saddle-bags."

"Please bring them to me."

Mekial noted the subtle grins on the young man and woman. "Constable," she interrupted, "I think..."

"Not now, Mekial."

When the deputy returned with the chains, the constable looked first at Rin and said, "Deputies, arrest these two on suspicion of kidnapping."

"No! No!" the young man protested as he and the woman tried to escape out the door.

Still sitting on the floor holding his arm, Thom heard footsteps approaching. Looking towards the door, he saw part of a face appear.

"Apprentice Thom?" a female called out.

Thom nodded.

Two deputies in uniform entered, a man and a woman.

"Where's Vern?" the man asked.

With his right hand, Thom pointed to where Vern had fallen.

The male deputy rushed over to Vern's body to check him. "He's dead."

The female deputy frowned before crouching next to him.

"Arrest me," Thom pleaded, staring at her with bleak eyes still filled with tears. "I killed him. I'm a murderer. I broke the One's rules."

"I doubt that," she replied. "You're hurt. I'm not a healer, but let me see what I can do." Looking at her partner, she said, "Would you cover the body with one of the blankets and tell the others that Thom's safe?"

"Sure," he answered.

"Also, if you can find a few clean cloths, bring them to me, and wet one if you can. I want to clean Thom's face."

Thom was sitting in the front room with a makeshift sling on his arm. His head had been wrapped to staunch the bleeding. He was sipping a cup of Timbu when he heard Rin's voice.

"Thom! Thom!" Rin yelled.

"I'm here, Rin," he replied weakly.

Charging through the door, Rin stopped suddenly when he saw Thom's arm and head. "You're hurt. What did they do to you?"

The female deputy stepped over to Rin and said, "Besides a broken arm, he has a cut and a bump on his head and a twisted ankle. I don't think it's broken. But it is starting to swell."

Rin looked at her questioningly.

"My Ma's a mid-wife. I learned a few things from her," she explained.

"Thanks for taking care of him, deputy," Rin said.

"You're welcome, sir."

Thom heard more footsteps, and soon after, Captain Jallow, Mik, and Mekial rushed in. Thom watched as Captain Jallow conferred with his deputies. When Jallow disappeared into the other room, Thom lowered his head in shame.

Completing his assessment of Thom's condition, Rin said, "It's not as bad as I thought. It will take some time, but you'll heal. You may have a small scar on your head. I'm sorry we couldn't find you sooner. I'm sure it was awful."

"I killed him," he whispered.

"What?" Rin asked.

"I'm a murderer," he said, starting to cry again.

"Nothing I said convinced him he's not a murderer, sir," the female deputy said.

"Thom, we'll talk more when we get home. But you are most definitely not a murderer."

"You're not, Thom," Captain Jallow confirmed, stepping back into the room. "From the looks of things, the man called Vern broke his neck when he hit the remains of the chair. At some point, when you're back at the shop and rested, I'd like to find out what happened."

"Um, OK," Thom said reluctantly. "What happened to Finn?"

"He's in custody, back at the Constable Station," Jallow answered.

"Is he OK?" Thom asked. "He helped me, Rin. He even remembered his purpose. He's changed."

"We'll talk more about that too, Thom," he assured him.

"Hey, Mekial. Hey, Mik," Thom said to them.

"Hey, Thom," Mik replied.

"Are you OK?" Mekial asked, her face wet with tears.

"I guess," he answered.

"Mik," Rin said. "Can you fetch a cart and horse so I can get Thom back to my shop?"

"One's outside, healer," the male deputy said.

The next month was all about recuperation for Thom. Rin had temporarily changed rooms with him because it better suited the endless number of visitors. Mekial was the most regular. She'd wait on him most days, bringing him a constant supply of Timbu and chocolate muffins.

Sestra B visited him, too. She helped him understand he did not break the One's rule against killing. While he believed her, he still couldn't reconcile himself with the fact that he, a spirit healer, had caused someone's death, however accidentally.

Maden even came by with Apollo. He laughed with delight when she walked him through the shop to his bedside, after which Apollo nuzzled him. It was wonderful seeing him again.

When Thom's ankle had healed, he could finally relocate to a chair by the hearth. One afternoon, he was sitting there reading when Rin came in.

"How do you feel?"

"Good," he said. "My arm's no longer itching. When can I return to the monastery? I know I won't be able to work in the pottery until the cast's off, but I could meet with Sestra B and even do some training with Medelin."

"How about in a few more days?" Rin replied. "You went through a terrible thing. I want you to feel better physically and emotionally. Are you still having nightmares?"

"Once in a while," he admitted. "But I don't wake up all sweaty anymore."

"Good," Rin said. "I wanted to tell you what's happening with Finn."

"Yes, please," Thom said, leaning forward in the chair. He was aware that Rin and the constable had already questioned Finn. Both had been disappointed when Finn couldn't offer more than a vague description of the noble who hired them and couldn't tell them the man's real name.

"Finn's going to be sent to a rehabilitation camp on another island," Rin explained. "While I trust his sincerity about being a changed man, he does have to accept responsibility for the harm he's done. He'll be there for a few years at least."

"Oh, OK," Thom replied, a little saddened.

"But," Rin continued, "you'll be pleased to know the warden will assign him to assist the cooks in their kitchen. In a way, he'll get to follow his dream."

"I'm glad," Thom said. "And what about the two punks, as Vern called them, and the money? Was there really an account in your name?"

"The two punks are in jail," Rin replied. "I don't know anything more about them. As to the account, there was one, and it held the money to cover the ransom. We suspect it came from the noble. At Modu and Gallen's request, the money was donated to Glakkadeth charities."

Chapter 46

Five months had passed since Thom was kidnapped. He had recovered from that terrible experience, at least physically. His body was in the best condition it ever had been. When he returned to the monastery, with his left arm still in a cast, Medlin had him sparring with his right again. He wondered if he had been stronger on that side, whether he could have disarmed Vern and gotten away rather than killing him. He still felt guilty.

Today, the weather was nice and in the high 70s. Thom spent it at the pottery. Brother Reyner had a big commission and needed help finishing the pieces. Thom and Rin had returned to the healing shop and were preparing a late dinner when they heard the chime ring at the front of the shop.

"I'll see who it is," Thom offered. Returning soon after, he stepped into the back room and said, "It was a messenger with a note from Mik. I wonder if it's something about Finn?" They hadn't heard from Mik since his kidnapping.

"What does it say?" Rin asked.

"It's about the traders I identified," Thom said. "I completely forgot about that with my kidnapping and all." Reading it, he handed it to Rin.

The message detailed that the investigation had taken almost nine months, requiring Mik to travel to Dridley. The traders Thom had identified were arrested and subsequently convicted. The principal culprits were stripped of their trader medallions and received a five-year sentence. The silent partner, driven by desperation, faced a shorter imprisonment. Mik once again conveyed gratitude on behalf of Modu and Gallen. The message concluded with him expressing their intention to offer a reward as a token of appreciation.

"What do you think?" Rin asked.

"That's something they were caught," he replied. "I didn't think it would take so long. I'm glad I could help."

"And what about the reward?" Rin asked.

"Oh, I don't know," Thom replied. "I don't think I need more crystals. I could check if Nadia Sanneh wrote another book in the Demba's Chronicles series. What about you?"

"Oh, maybe another floppy hat," Rin replied, smiling. "Maybe you could use one too? Your hat only shades your face. Mine shades my entire head."

Thom gave him a look. "I wonder what ship Mik took to Dridley. Maybe it was Captain Musa's."

"You're thinking about Nuala, huh?" Rin commented.

Six months after Nuala left the monastery, Thom had learned she had signed on as an apprentice seafarer on

Captain Musa's ship. "Yes," he admitted. "I was happy when I heard she'd gotten an apprenticeship. I guess Captain Musa was impressed with her. I hope she's happy."

Chapter 47

Thom rode to the monastery for a training session. He was glad the rainy season was over, and they were training outside again. As usual, the salle smelled. After Thom's kidnapping, Medelin also insisted that he learn offense work. He was a bit better with knives than swords. But he much preferred using the staff. It seemed more natural. He supposed the good news was that Medelin still had him working with dull swords.

Life mainly had returned to normal. It was a month past Solstice Day, and school was back in session. It wasn't wholly normal because Rin had asked him to enroll in the monastery school. Up until then, Rin had tutored him. But he expressed concern Thom would get behind, especially in mathematics. He also asked him to take a new offering called science, which taught about biology, nature, and astronomy. This afternoon, Thom would have his first class in both. He had mixed feelings about going back to school. He liked learning but hoped the teachers would be more interesting than those back home.

Arriving at the monastery stable, Thom unsaddled and groomed Crescent. Because he was a little early, he snuck into the kitchen to see if he could get a cup of Timbu. Thom could smell beef slow roasting in the hearth. He was looking forward to supper. But Timbu always made him happy. Awa was happy to oblige.

When Thom walked into the training yard, Medelin commented, "Begged Awa for some Timbu, did you?"

He grinned.

While Thom sipped his drink, Medelin reviewed sword attack angles. He reminded Thom of the importance of watching his opponent's eyes because less skilled swordfolk often betrayed their next move by looking toward their next strike location.

After finishing his Timbu, Medelin, and Thom began to spar. After a good workout, Thom wiped the sweat from his brow, grimacing and embarrassed that he had a few more nicks and bruises.

"You're doing better," Medelin commented. "But you're still not protecting your right side enough."

"I don't know why I keep forgetting. Sorry," Thom apologized.

"You'll get it," Medelin assured him. "Now, off with you. I know you want to spend a little time with Apollo before you meet with Sestra B."

Thom found Apollo peacefully grazing in the paddock, accompanied by Fanta and other horses. The warm air carried a subtle scent of grass, mingled with the barest hints of manure, a testament to the daily upkeep by the stablehands. Gazing fondly at Apollo, he recalled Maden's words about Apollo's rapid maturation, possibly ready for limited riding in a few months, around the age of two. Thom eagerly awaited that milestone. As he approached the fence, Apollo made his way over and greeted him with a friendly whicker.

While petting him, Thom reflected on the healing he'd helped Rin and Lauret with a month ago. One of the hired hands of the local cattle breeder had been trampled when a lightning strike scared the cattle. When the injured man was brought in, he was near death. At Rin's request, Mekial had sought Thom out. As it happened, Sestra B had recently taught him how to tap into the healing energy of his divine team in addition to using his own. By channeling their energy, including that of Archangel Raphael, they saved the hired hand's life, even though he did lose his arm.

Apollo nudged him. "Sorry, I was distracted," Thom admitted. "Now that I'm fluent in Glakkadian and Mekial's doing well with Dochalan, I'd thought I'd have more time to spend with you. But Rin wants me to take classes. I have some time now. And I'll make sure I spend time with you, too, even if I have to get up earlier."

Apollo whinnied.

Thom headed to Sestra B's office for his session.

"Today, I'm going to help you deepen your connection to your divine team," she explained after Thom had settled into a chair. "Your ability to tap into your team's healing energy last month opened another channel between them and you. I want you to build on that, enabling you to channel more of your divine team's gifts. This will strengthen your spirit healing gift and enable you to connect with their wisdom more easily."

"OK," Thom replied.

"Bring to mind an image of your team sitting around a table, let's say," Sestra B instructed him.

Thom envisioned a circular table, its surface luminescent but opaque, made from a material he couldn't identify. Around it were placed tall green padded chairs of a simple design constructed with the same material. His divine team filed in and took their seats. "OK. They're here or there or something," he told her, smiling.

"Good," Sestra B replied. "Now, look around the table, greet each of them separately, and ask about their special ability. Then, one by one, invite them to merge with you and feel their ability so strongly that it becomes part of you."

"Merge with me? Are they supposed to come through the table somehow?"

"Remember, the table isn't real; it's merely a metaphor symbolizing your team gathered around you," she clarified. "But by merging, yes, they join their spirit with yours. If seeing their hands and arms overlay yours helps you visualize it, imagine it."

"OK," Thom replied. "I'll try."

"Who do you want to start with?"

"Archangel Raphael, the healer," Thom replied.

"OK. Proceed, and don't rush," Sestra B advised.

"That's the last, Thom said after finishing with Jeshua.

"Good job, Thom," she praised him. "Now, thank them and let the image fade."

"Done," he replied, opening his eyes.

"How do you feel?" Sestra B asked.

"Amazing," Thom replied. "I feel tingling along my body."

"That's because you raised your vibration to match your team's," Sestra B explained.

"I understand now," Thom commented.

"Say more," Sestra B encouraged.

"The first time I felt tingling was after I left home while building my connection to God. Later, I felt it when I was healing Rindo. So, all this time, it meant I had increased my vibration to make me more connected to the divine. That would also help me channel healing, wouldn't it?"

"Yes. As you get older, you'll gain greater understanding about other past experiences, including painful ones, that didn't make sense."

Thom remained silent, considering her words.

"Anything else?" Sestra B asked.

"Yeah. At the end of each chat, each team member said they were in awe of my growing abilities and the good I could accomplish," he replied. "That's hard to accept. How could anyone be in awe of me?"

"You're a special young man, Thom," Sestra B replied. "Since you can't see that at this point, let us be the keepers of that truth for you."

After leaving the session, Thom headed towards the refectory and ran into Mekial coming out of the training yard.

"How did training go?" Thom asked.

"Good," Mekial replied. "Medelin had everyone break into groups of three to spar. Sometimes, I was the defender, and the other two were the attackers. Other times, I was an attacker."

"Wow," Thom replied. "Sounds difficult. I'm still only sparring with one person. How did you think you did?"

"It went OK," she replied. "We've done three-person sparring before. But today, Medelin had us switch up the group a few times, and we had to adjust immediately. I didn't adapt as fast as Medelin wanted."

"Oh, sorry."

"Thanks. I'll get it," Mekial said confidently.

"Are you ready for supper?"

"Yes," Mekial replied. "I want you to meet two novices. They're twins."

"OK," he replied.

Mekial and Thom sat down with their food at a table that was still half empty. This time, they were having beef, which was served inside warm bread rolls with slices of tomato, lettuce, and onions. Thom was quite hungry and decided to take two.

"I don't see them," Mekial said, scanning the room.

"Should we wait before eating," Thom asked.

"No," she advised.

Halfway into their meal, Mekial shouted and waved, "Sanna and Sona!"

Thom looked towards the refectory doors and saw a boy and girl entering.

"Hi, Mekial," Sanna and Sona greeted her in unison as they approached their table.

"Sanna and Sona, this is Thom," Mekial introduced them. "Thom, this is Sanna and Sona."

They both looked to be teenagers. Sanna had high cheekbones, and curly hair cropped closely to his head. Sona had a rounder face and straight hair down to her shoulders.

"It's nice to meet you both," Thom replied, shaking their hands.

"Sanna and Sona started as novices three months ago," Mekial told him. "Can you join us for supper? There are plenty of seats."

"Thanks for the invitation, Mekial," Sona replied. "Unfortunately, we're taking our supper to go. We have a philosophy test in about an hour and need to study more. Another time, though."

"OK," Mekial replied. "Good luck with your test!"

As they walked away, Mekial said, "Aren't they attractive? Sanna's cheekbones make him look rugged. And Sona, I want to touch her soft, round face."

"What?" Thom asked.

"I wonder if either of them is dating?" Mekial said, not noting Thom's reaction.

Thom saw that Mekial's eyes had a faraway look. "Mekial," he interrupted, "why do you want to know if they're dating?"

"I wouldn't mind if either of them asked me out?" she admitted. "Of course, that's not encouraged for novices or postulants, but a girl can dream."

"You're attracted to boys and girls?" Thom asked, astonished.

"Yes," Mekial replied. "Haven't you heard of people attracted to both genders?"

"No," he said. "In Docha-leigh, I only knew of people attracted to the opposite gender. Of course, after I arrived here, I learned about same-gender couples. But I've never heard of someone attracted to both."

"Oh," Mekial replied. "Sorry, I should have told you before I went on and on about Sanna and Sona. I know you're a little younger than me, but haven't you noticed who you're attracted to?"

"I don't know. Maybe. I had heard girls go through puberty before boys."

"True," Mekial replied.

After they finished supper, Mekial walked towards the infimarium to check in with her mother. Thom had a little time before his mathematics class. Walking back to the paddock again to be near Apollo, he found him playing with a filly. Sitting on a hay bale nearby, he thought about what Mekial had asked him. Who was he attracted to? Was he even attracted to anyone?

Mekial was pretty, but she felt like a sister like Khali. Thinking about Nuala or the other women at the monastery, he couldn't say he felt attracted to any of them. They were nice, but that was it. Thinking of boys, he remembered how he liked spending time with my best friend, Davi. But that was a few years ago. Lebrim's kind, but he seemed otherworldly. Considering the other male monks, he thought of Brother Reyner. He was handsome. Then, thinking of the twins, if he was truthful, he felt more drawn to Sanna. Did that mean he was attracted to boys? Suddenly, a word popped into his head that sounded like "sense." That's odd.

Chapter 48

Coming out of his session with Sestra B, Thom took a deep breath, appreciating the mid-70-degree temperature typical for Jauna. He decided to head to the training yard and practice the footwork Medelin had recently taught him. Classes had ended and wouldn't resume until the end of Aegisa, which gave him more free time.

After working out for an hour, Thom was taking a sip of water when Jeren came running in, out of breath. "Jeren, what's going on?"

"One sec…," Jeren whispered, his breath coming in quick pants.

"Here," Thom said, handing him a ladle full of water.

After a pause, Jeren gasped, "Looking…you… everywhere. Lebrim…bad."

"In the infimarium?" Thom asked.

Jeren nodded.

Thom dashed there, where he found Lauret and Rafi on one side of the treatment table, working on Lebrim.

Moving to the opposite side, he asked, "What happened?"

"Something to do with his heart," Lauret answered. "He was in the chapel meditating when he collapsed. Sestra B was there. She and two other monks carried him here."

Thom saw Sestra B standing out of the way, looking on worriedly. Lebrim's skin was ashen, and his lips were light blue. "Oh no," he uttered.

"Rafi and I have been trying to heal him," Lauret explained. "Since Rin's not here, we've done everything he taught us, but it's not working."

"Let me put my hands over yours, Lauret," Thom said. Together, they directed healing into Lebrim's heart. From his science class, he'd learned about blood flow and imagined any clots that might have formed breaking up and enabling good flow. They seemed to make some progress.

Pausing briefly, Thom sensed the clots reforming. Looking at Lebrim's aura, he saw its colors fading, except for purple.

"We're losing him," Rafi warned.

"No, no, no," Thom insisted. "Lebrim has his whole life ahead of him as a spiritual teacher. He's always been fully aligned with his highest self. He has to live out his purpose. I'll ask for help from Archangel Raphael and the healing angels."

Closing his eyes, Thom remembered Sestra B's teachings about an angel's purpose: to help. Rather than asking, he knew how to phrase his request. "Angels, thank you for helping us heal Lebrim in keeping with the highest good."

Thom and Lauret felt a surge of golden energy pass through them and into Lebrim.

"He's improving," Rafi stated, "Look, his lips are losing their blue tinge."

Thom noticed Lebrim's aura colors were brightening. "Lebrim, Lebrim, we're here," he assured him. "Sestra B is too."

Lebrim mumbled something.

"Did you get that?" Thom asked.

"No," Lauret and Rafi replied.

"Come," Lebrim whispered, "close..."

Thom still couldn't make it out.

"He said to come closer," Rafi told them.

Thom gestured for Sestra B to stand next to him.

"OK," Lebrim whispered a little louder. "Time."

"What?" Thom replied. "What's OK? You're not saying it's your time!"

Lebrim nodded slightly.

"No, no, no," Thom insisted. "It's not your time. You have much to do. Archangel Raphael, we need more healing! Divine team, you gotta help!"

"Is... OK," Lebrim whispered again before losing consciousness.

"We need to give him more healing energy!" Thom demanded.

Lauret and Rafi stepped away. "No, Thom," Lauret stated, "Even if Rafi and I could offer more, we wouldn't. You heard Lebrim."

"No. Lebrim can't die," Thom insisted. "My gift. I should be able to heal him. There's got to be something else I can do." Turning his attention back to Lebrim, Thom sent all his healing energy into him. He also realized he wasn't feeling energy coming from his divine team.

"Thom," Sestra B whispered, taking hold of his hands. "Thom," she repeated.

With tears streaming down his face, he turned to her, "What am I doing wrong? Please, God, help!"

"Thom," Sestra B repeated. "Lebrim told you himself. It was his time. You must let go. Look at his face. His spirit has returned to the divine realm and is at peace."

Wrenching his hands from Sestra B, Thom ran from the infimarium. He had to find Rin! He could bring Lebrim back. He's a better healer. "I'm a failure," he muttered in despair.

Running into the stable, Thom came upon Maden.

"I've got to find Rin," Thom explained. "Can you help me saddle Crescent?"

"This is about Lebrim, isn't it?" Maden replied. "Jeren told me he collapsed."

"Yes, Rin needs to bring him back. I need to get Rin!" he insisted.

Sestra B had followed Thom and overheard his request. Maden looked at her, who shook her head.

Walking over to Thom and touching him on his shoulder, Maden replied, "No, I'm sorry, Thom. No. Lebrim's in spirit. Rin won't be able to help."

"You don't know. You weren't there," Thom shouted. "Are you a healer? You're nothing more than a stable keeper. Take your hands off me! I'll do it myself."

"Thom!" Mekial cried out, rushing in. "Sestra B confirmed it. Lebrim's gone." Mekial moved over to Maden, as did a few other stable hands preventing Thom from saddling Crescent.

"I hate all of you! I wish I never came to Glakkadeth!" he yelled, running out the stable doors.

"Thom, stay!" Mekial cried out. "Talk to me. I'm your friend."

"Leave me alone," Thom replied. "Why couldn't I save him?" he moaned as he raced out of the monastery entrance and toward the town. Where was Archangel Raphael? And why didn't his divine team help when he asked for more healing energy?

Stopping, Thom shouted up to the sky, "Why didn't you help me? Did I do something wrong? It's because I killed Vern, isn't it? I killed Vern, and now I've killed Lebrim. I'm a failure as a spirit healer."

Running further, he continued berating himself. Rin and Sestra B are fooling themselves, thinking he was gifted. What a joke! Looking ahead, Thom realized he had run to the town gates. Stopping, he tried to catch his breath. Bending over, he threw up.

"Young man," the guard at the gate said. "Are you OK? Do you need a healer?"

"Huh. A healer. That's a laugh. I couldn't heal him. I'm a failure," he repeated.

"What?" the guard asked, sounding confused.

"Leave me alone," Thom yelled.

"Excuse me!" the guard yelled. "With that attitude, if you think I'm going to let you into town, you've.... wait. Wait. Aren't you the healer's apprentice? You should know better!"

"Leave me alone," he yelled again, running back towards the monastery. Coming upon the apple orchard, he knew that on the other side was a grazing area with a brook running through it. Stumbling through the orchard, he dropped down next to the brook. Cupping his hands, he scooped up some cool water and drank before sprawling, exhausted, on its bank. By then, his mind was numb, and he soon found his eyes closing.

When Thom opened his eyes, he saw that it was almost dark, and stars were beginning to appear. His mind immediately returned to Lebrim and his failure. Calling out to his divine team, he cried, "Where were you? Why didn't you heal Lebrim? You should've taken me instead of him. He was better than me. I'm nothing. Kevar was right. I'm a freak and misborn, and I don't deserve to live."

Thom tried to visualize his team gathered around the table but couldn't. And he felt no tingles. Looking up toward the stars, he murmured, "Ori? Archangel Orion, are you there? You're supposed to help with my purpose. Sereh? God? But he heard no response. "Jeshua, I thought you were my friend." The silence was deafening. Even the brook seemed silent, as were the usual night sounds from crickets and owls.

"You've abandoned me. I guess I would've, too. I'm not the great healer that everyone thought. I'm a murderer! I don't deserve to live." Thinking of Lebrim again, he moaned in despair, "I'm sorry. Please forgive me," breaking down into sobs again. "Take me, I want to die! Please take me!" he whispered, finally falling into a troubled sleep.

When Thom awoke again, it was fully dark, except for the light cast by the stars and the moon. He was still alive. What should he do? Thom didn't want to fail anyone else. He needed to get away. That's what he should do. He should just leave.

Aching inside, he considered his options. He needed to go somewhere to hide. Should he go to another island? Or would his skin color make him stick out too much? Part of him yearned to go home, but he knew he couldn't. He didn't want to bring shame to his family, he thought, as his stomach rumbled. How can his stomach hurt and be hungry at the same time?

Returning to the orchard, Thom picked two apples and sat down against a tree. After polishing them off, he felt a little more settled and came to a decision. Thom would leave Glakkadeth and catch a ship to any destination but Docha-leigh. Come morning, he'd offer his services to the captain as an assistant to the cook in exchange for passage. By now, his cooking skills had improved sufficiently. Estimating it to be a few hours after midnight, he realized there was one thing he had to do before he left, say goodbye to Apollo. It would hurt to leave him, but Apollo would be better off without him.

Stumbling back to the monastery, Thom found the main gates locked, but the side gate near the stable was open. Navigating to the large stall, Apollo still shared with his mother, he stepped inside. Apollo nickered upon seeing him. He felt Apollo's distress and knew he was the cause.

"At least you haven't abandoned me," he whispered. When Apollo nuzzled him, Thom was overcome with emotion once more. He wrapped his arms around Apollo's neck, and as his legs gave way, Apollo gently lowered both of them to the ground, where sleep claimed him.

"He's here," Mekial called out.

Thom opened his bleary eyes and looked up at her.

"You idiot!" she yelled at him. "How could you run away like that?"

"I'm sorry. I know I failed," Thom said, turning his face away in shame. "I should've been gone by now. I'll leave and won't bother you anymore."

"What are you talking about?" Mekial asked.

Rin and Sestra B ran in.

"Thom, Thom, are you OK?" Rin said with concern.

Thom buried his face in Apollo's flank and said nothing.

"Thom said he knows he failed and will leave, so he won't bother us anymore," Mekial shared.

Rin crouched next to Thom and spoke softly, "Thom. I know you feel you failed Lebrim. You didn't fail him or us. And you didn't fail with your gifts either. You did all you could, but it was Lebrim's time to return to spirit and the divine realm."

Thom looked up at Rin and Sestra B, who nodded.

"Everyone was worried about you after you ran out," Rin explained. "After Rafi found me at the shop, the entire monastery went looking for you for the rest of the day and even after dark. When we couldn't find you, we feared you'd been hurt or done something foolish."

"And we searched and searched," Mekial added. "Rin, me, and my family all stayed overnight here."

"Why?" Thom asked. "I'm nothing. I'm fooling myself, thinking I'm a healer. I'm not special. Even my divine team abandoned me because I killed Vern, and I couldn't help Lebrim."

"Vern?" Rin said. "You're still feeling guilt about accidentally killing him. Oh, Thom, dear lad. I didn't realize you hadn't let that go. It's time you did."

"But if I was stronger or more skilled," Thom said, "he would only have been knocked out. It's my fault."

"You did your best with what you knew, Thom," Rin said. "No one can fault you for that. Why don't you chat with Archangel Jeremiel? He's all about forgiveness and Deu's mercy."

"That won't work," Thom insisted. "They aren't listening to me anymore."

"Thom," Sestra B interrupted. "Listen to us then. You didn't fail, and your team hasn't abandoned you. Your shields are too thick and stiff for anything to get through, even help from your team."

"What?" Thom asked, finally sitting up, his hand still resting on Apollo. "I blocked them out?"

By then, Bea, Budaj, Maden, and a few others stood outside the stall, looking at Thom with concern.

"I don't understand," Thom said. "You don't hate me?"

"No, Thom," Sestra B said, "we love you."

"Thom, can we talk somewhere more privately?" Rin asked. "That is, you, me, and Sestra B."

"And me too," Mekial insisted.

"Yes, Mekial, and you too," Rin replied. "Is that OK?"

"Sure," Thom replied in resignation.

"Let's go somewhere we can sit," Rin suggested.

"How about the study room behind the chapel?" Mekial suggested.

"Good idea," Sestra B agreed.

"Are you hungry?" Rin asked Thom.

"A little. I still have a knot in my stomach. But I could eat."

"I'll bring you some Timbu and one of my muffins with the chocolate bits. I added raspberries. I think you'll like it," a female offered.

Thom looked around and saw Awa standing there. "Yes, please, Awa," he replied.

Rin helped Thom to his feet. With Rin holding one of Thom's hands and Sestra B the other, they made their way to the study room. Mekial ran ahead to open the doors.

They were settling into chairs when Awa came in with a pitcher of Timbu, four mugs, and a large plate of muffins.

"I brought extra in case the rest of you wanted some, too," she said.

"Thank you, Awa," Thom said.

"You're welcome, Thom. You worried us. Don't do that again," she said, both sternly and lovingly, before leaving.

"Go ahead, Thom," Rin instructed him.

Thom poured himself some Timbu. Looking at the others, Mekial nodded, but no one else. After handing a mug to her, he picked out a muffin and took a large bite. "Wow," he said, "raspberries and chocolate go well together."

Mekial grabbed one, took a bite, and smiled. "Mmm."

"Like Sestra B said, we don't hate you," Rin replied. "We love you. But we're a little angry with you. Not because you couldn't save Lebrim but because you ran away. You scared us, and me especially. All the desperate feelings I felt when you were kidnapped came flooding back."

"I did?" Thom mumbled with a full mouth. "You were desperate... about me?"

"Yes. I was worried you might take your own life. I know your history and remember what you told me about how the other kids treated you."

Thom turned away.

"What?" Mekial said. "You were going to kill yourself!"

"I wasn't going to kill myself," Thom defended, "but I did ask God to take me. But God didn't..."

"What kind of stupid..." Mekial yelled, bits of muffin flying from her mouth. "I could punch you!"

"Mekial!" Sestra B warned. "You're not helping. If you can't be silent, you'll have to leave."

"Sorry, Sestra."

"Like I was saying," Rin continued. "I know your self-esteem isn't always strong. And I knew you were going to take full responsibility for Lebrim's death. I was also certain your head talk would reinforce your feelings of worthlessness. I know you don't believe it, but you are worthy."

"How did you...?" Thom replied with surprise.

"Because I know you, Thom," Rin answered, "at your deepest level. You are a gifted young man who is hurting and imperfect but gifted nonetheless."

"May I speak?" Sestra B interrupted.

"Go ahead," Rin said.

"Thom, I want to echo what Rin said. You are a gifted spirit healer and a gifted physical healer, too. But no one, not even you, can save everyone, especially those who know it's their time to return to spirit. It might sound harsh, but it's the height of arrogance to think you can save everyone."

Thom looked down again.

"We all know you're not arrogant," Sestra B continued. Rin and Mekial both nodded. "But focusing on where you failed keeps the attention on yourself rather than on the person you tried to heal. As a healer, service must always be foremost in your mind. We talked about that in your lessons."

"Service," Thom repeated.

"And with that must come the awareness that you don't control all outcomes. That means you must recognize when you've done all you can or should do. As you know, each spirit chooses to be born into its current incarnation and is aware of possible challenges it might face. My sense is that when you were working on Lebrim, he was straddling our world and the divine realm. He likely recalled his pre-incarnation meeting, where he discussed the possibility of dying young. When you called upon your divine team, I suspect they offered enough healing to enable him to tell you that possibility was coming true."

Thom remained silent for a while before saying, "Sestra B, you talked to me about the pre-birth meetings before. I believe and trust you, and it makes sense to my brain-mind. But I don't feel its truth in my heart and stomach."

"That's OK. Some in our community still wrestle with it," Sestra B admitted. "Let's go back to what Lebrim said. I want you to recall them because remembering the experience will help you heal."

"Thom," Rin interjected, "Bring his words to mind like I had you do after you healed Rindo. But, at the same time, hold yourself as an objective observer to ensure you don't get swept up in your emotions."

Thom visualized himself back in the infimarium, tending Lebrim. At first, seeing himself standing over him, he felt his emotions threatening to overwhelm him. *Archangel Haniel, thank you for helping me contain my feelings,* Thom called out silently. He immediately felt her assistance as his feelings became more distant.

"What is Lebrim saying?" Sestra B prompted him.

"He's saying, OK. *Time,*" he admitted.

"Exactly," Sestra B said.

"Maybe I haven't failed, like you said," Thom admitted. And Rin's right about Vern, too." He felt like a deflated ball. As he glanced at Sestra B, Rin, and Mekial, he saw tenderness, concern, and love reflected in their eyes.

"You understand," Rin said.

"Mostly," Thom replied.

"That's OK. Give it time," Rin replied.

Thom sighed in response.

"Now, as much as sleeping next to Apollo must have been comforting," Rin continued. "I'm thinking you could use a good rest."

"Yeah," Thom said, taking his last sip of Timbo.

"Mekial, would you lead Thom to one of the guest rooms here?"

"Of course," Mekial replied, rising from her seat and walking over to him. "Give me your arm," she told him. "In your condition, you won't make it alone, even if you know where the guest rooms are."

Mekial escorted Thom from the study room into the monastery proper and to one of the guest rooms. "I'll get you a glass of water if you get thirsty. But first, let me help you get out of your clothes."

"What? No," Thom said, turning red. "I can undress myself."

"OK," Mekial replied. "I don't want to find you on the floor because you couldn't."

"I can manage," Thom insisted.

"I'll be back with your water," Mekial said.

When she returned with the water, Thom had removed his filthy clothes and slipped under the covers.

As she was leaving, Thom said, "Thank you for everything."

"You're welcome, you idiot," she answered. "For a gifted person, sometimes you are thick-headed. But I think I understand."

"Thanks," Thom replied.

"Get some sleep," Mekial said, closing the door.

Lying on his back, he sought out his divine team. "You didn't abandon me, after all."

Feeling their tingling assurances, he fell sleep.

Chapter 49

Even though Lebrim had died three months before, the strain of it still weighed on Thom. As he had the afternoon free because classes were canceled, he decided to head to his usual Baobab tree to think. Sitting there, he opened himself up to his divine team's wisdom.

Everything Rin and Sestra B had told him about Lebrim made sense. Why was he still disturbed? When no answers came, he quieted his mind and visualized his Sanctuary. It was usually Spring there.

Surveying his surroundings, Thom noticed the blooming meadow nearby. He inhaled the fragrance of roses, lavender, sage, and the smell of soil. Thom cherished his time here, surrounded by the grandeur of his mountains as he thought of them and the soothing burbling of a river flowing nearby. Not too long after, he felt himself more at peace.

Relishing his tranquility, Thom was startled when a male voice shouted, *Ho, the Sanctuary.*

Looking towards the forest path along the meadow's edge, he saw two figures approaching. No one had ever visited him in his Sanctuary. Rising to his feet, he was astonished when they drew near and saw who one of them was. *Jesh?* he exclaimed in disbelief. Although Thom had chatted with Jeshua recently, the last time he'd seen him was eight months before, when Sestra B taught him how to channel his divine team's abilities.

Yes, Jeshua replied with a smile. *Hi, Thom.*

Hi? Thom answered, still getting over the shock of seeing him. *I'm always happy to see you, but you've never visited me in my Sanctuary before.*

I hope you don't mind, Jeshua continued. *By the way, it's breathtaking and peaceful here.*

Thanks. And no, I don't mind. What are you doing here?

Before we get into that, how about a hug? he asked.

Yes, he replied. As they hugged, Thom vaguely remembered a greeting routine. How odd. And who was this other being?

Stepping apart, Jeshua introduced the other. *This is Lightworker-Reliant, but we call him Rel.* Rel was a muscular male, taller than Jeshua, with light brown hair.

Oh, you're on my divine team! Thom exclaimed. *You were one of the first to volunteer. Can you tell me why?*

Because you're on a remarkable journey as a spirit healer, Rel replied.

Thanks. Nice to meet you, Rel, Thom said, offering his hand to shake. When their hands met, an immediate connection occurred. Why did he seem familiar?

Nice to meet you, Thom, Rel replied.

Shall we sit? Jeshua suggested.

Sure.

How are you doing with Lebrim's death? Jeshua asked.

I'm a little disturbed, he admitted. *I liked Lebrim even though I didn't know him well. But it's hard to wrap my head around it. Despite what Rin and Sestra B said, there are times when I still feel I let him down.*

Yeah, your divine team has been getting that from you, Jeshua said. Reliant also nodded.

Thom glanced at Rel again but didn't say anything.

It seems you've let go of Vern's death, though, Jeshua commented. *Chatting with Jeremiel helped?*

Yeah, Thom admitted.

Good. But we know that took a while, Jeshua said. *Sometimes that happens. It did for me in one of my incarnations when a childhood friend died. It's important that you honor your feelings. You're also still learning about your spirit-healing gift. Your sensitivity, along with your approaching adolescence, naturally elevates them.*

It does, Thom admitted. *Even though I don't feel guilty about Vern anymore, I still do about Lebrim, and I'm even a little angry. At the same time, I feel peace and acceptance that it was his time. How can I feel both at the same time?*

It must all seem a bit wonky to you, Thom, Jeshua remarked.

Yeah, it does.

Wonky, Jesh? Rel interrupted.

Rel calls Jeshua, Jesh, too, Thom observed.

I like the word, and I think it conveys Thom's mixed feelings, Jeshua defended himself. *It's part of being human, Thom. Be gentle with yourself. You're doing great. You've faced many challenges for one so young. We know it's been difficult. But your team and others in the divine realm are keeping a close eye on you. We love you very much.*

Thanks, Thom replied. *That means a lot. But, can I ask…?*

About Lebrim? Jeshua interrupted. *Yes. He's fine. He's still processing his short life with his team.*

I'm glad, Thom replied, feeling a part of him relax and then sat quietly.

Change of subject. Would you agree that we have gotten close over the last two years? Jeshua asked, breaking the silence.

Yes. You're like an older brother. I like chatting with you, like I have with God and others. I'm glad I finally let go of my belief that you were unapproachable.

Me, too. If truth be told, we've been close for much, much longer. We've even shared lifetimes.

Lifetimes? Thom said. *You're talking about reincarnation.*

Yes, Jeshua confirmed. *You've talked about this with Rin and Sestra Berbera, haven't you?*

Yeah, he replied. *I had wondered if we knew each other longer,* noticing that Rel was smiling.

Did Sestra Berbera talk to you about higher selves, too? Jeshua asked.

She did, Thom replied. *I still don't really understand how a part of a higher self incarnates.*

Why don't you answer that, Rel, Jeshua suggested.

OK, Rel replied. To be direct, Thom. I'm your higher self.

Thom's mouth dropped open, and he sat there stunned.

Are you OK? Rel asked him.

I guess, he replied, a little uncertain. It's one thing to hear about higher-selves. It's another to meet your own higher self, face to face. I thought you looked familiar, like a relative.

That's intentional, Rel admitted. All beings in the divine realm are energy spheres, like your sun. But we can take human form as needed. I thought you might feel more comfortable if I had similar features.

That means your natural form is a sphere, too, Jeshua? Thom asked.

Yes, Jeshua replied.

Thom sighed. *Sometimes, I think I'm getting a handle on everything when a new idea comes along.*

Is this too much? Rel asked. I don't have to say anything further.

No. Go ahead, Thom said. *Wait, sometime after we first met, didn't I imagine myself and all of you as energy balls zooming around the divine realm?*

You did, Jeshua replied, smiling.

We all had a great time, Rel added, chuckling. I still laugh when I see Archangel Michael running through a guardian angel and profusely apologizing.

You remind him of it enough, Jeshua commented.

True, Rel replied. Thom, do you still want to understand how a part of me incarnates as you?

Please, Thom answered, grinning at the image of an embarrassed archangel.

Let me keep this brief, Rel replied. Since you know our natural state is an energy sphere, a part of my energy attaches to a human form when I incarnate as I did with you. Some call that your soul or spirit.

OK, I learned about that from Sestra B.

Your soul is still part of me, Rel further explained. I'm indeed with you every moment.

If you're me, does that mean you can control my body and make choices for me? Thom said, squinting at him in concentration. I'm not saying this right.

I know it's hard for a human mind to comprehend, Rel acknowledged. But no to both questions. You're independent. But I send messages and signs, along with the rest of your divine team, to help guide you. It's up to you to follow them, of course. I'd also encourage you to chat with me.

I guess. But... how would that work? Would I say, "Hey me, it's me? Thom said with a crooked smile.

It's nice to hear your humor again, Jeshua admitted. It hasn't shown itself much since Lebrim died.

No, it hasn't, Thom replied.

To answer your question, Rel commented, you could say, Hey, Rel, or higher self. There are no rules.

OK, I'll give it a try.

Good. I look forward to it. There's another reason why Jeshua and I wanted to visit with you today. Your time in Glakkadeth is coming to an end soon. Since your spirit heal-

ing gift is fully activated and you've completed the basic training, you're ready for the next stage.

We'll be leaving Glakkadeth. Where will we go? Thom asked.

Back to Docha-leigh, Rel replied.

We're going home. Rin hasn't said anything.

Do you remember why Rin brought you here in the first place? Rel asked.

Yes, Thom replied. He said Lord Samiltun wanted to manipulate me into using my gifts for his plans. And it wouldn't be safe for me or my family if I stayed at home.

Did he say anything else? Rel asked.

He told me he put a shield over me to make Samiltun think I wasn't gifted. He removed it after I learned to shield myself.

Good, Rel replied. I'm glad Rin explained what Ruefell Samiltun could have done to you. And that you can shield yourself. We're both impressed with your shielding. Good job.

Thanks. You know about Samiltun, too, Thom said.

Of course, Jeshua responded. Samiltun has been misusing his gifts for a long time. His father was a Dochalan lord who was having an affair with Samiltun's mother. When Ruefell was thirteen, the lord's wife learned of it and had her poisoned. When Ruefell learned of it, he used his emerging gifts to manipulate a thief to infiltrate the manor and kill everyone but the lord. Having no other heir, the lord adopted him. A few years passed, and the lord died in a supposed hunting accident, elevating Ruefell to Lord Samiltun.

Samiltun's higher self hasn't been able to get through to him, Rel added. In fact, Samiltun has essentially blocked his connection to the divine realm.

Wouldn't that impact access to his gifts? Thom asked.

Good question, Jeshua remarked. Unfortunately, no. Gifts are innate and, therefore, remain.

His higher self is at their wits' end and is a bit angry, Rel commented.

Not to mention his guardian angel, Jeshua added. For the last twenty-five years, poor Turil has been perpetually close to a nervous breakdown, if that was possible for angels.

I assume you're telling me this because I'll be going home soon, Thom commented. But I don't understand why. Doesn't Samiltun still believe my gifts aren't strong?

Likely, Rel answered. But if you encounter him, we want you to be on your guard if he recognizes you.

Would he really be able to? I wasn't even nine when he last saw me. And since then, I've changed. I'm taller, and my body has filled out from my training.

True, Jeshua said. And very well done, I might add.

He may not recognize you, Rel agreed. But if he learns your name, he could remember you.

Knowing his type, Jeshua added, Samiltun's probably hired criminals to watch for anyone with gifts. Since you wouldn't recognize them if they were nearby when you used your gifts, they would alert Samiltun.

I see, Thom replied.

This lifetime is very important for you, Rel said. Do you know you're a powerful spirit healer?

Yeah, Thom answered. *Rin and Sestra B told me that.*

The strength of your gift has never been seen before on your planet, Rel explained. Not to mention the new abilities you've demonstrated, like healing Rindo and truth-telling. More spirit-healing abilities are certain to arise as you continue training.

But that won't be by Rin, will it? Thom said. Since he didn't know what this gift was in the first place.

True again, Jeshua replied. You'll find out who soon enough.

Can't you tell me now? Thom asked.

No, Jeshua said. *Circumstances can change and may require someone other than the one we've identified. Consider that in the original plan; you were destined for Eiren instead of Glakkadeth.*

Oh, yeah, Thom replied.

I want to mention a few other things, Rel continued. Because you're part of me, you share my traits and gifts, including your healing gifts. They're the primary gifts associated with my purpose as a lightworker, as we call it in this realm. That's what you are.

A lightworker, Thom repeated. Why does that sound familiar?

Metatron mentioned it when he visited you a few years ago, Jeshua informed him.

Huh, Thom grunted.

Talk to Rin, Rel suggested, before continuing. You also have an earth-sensing gift, which comes out of your physical healing ability.

Rin did tell me that, Thom said.

What you don't know is that you have a few other abilities, Rel explained. You're clairsentient because you easily tap into other people's feelings like you did with Rindo. You're also clairvoyant, which is apparent from the vividness of your Sanctuary. And finally, you're clairaudient, because you can hear our messages. Our chats, for example.

Um, I'm getting a bit overwhelmed, Thom interjected.

Sorry, Rel replied. My point is that you are a very gifted person. As you continue developing your spirit healing gift, each of the abilities I mentioned will grow stronger.

Thom remained silent.

I'd suggest you talk with Rin about that, too, Jeshua added.

You mean I'll remember this visit, then, Thom said. I know that's not usual.

Forgetting the details was intentional, Rel replied. We know you can get caught in your head trying to figure every-thing out. Because of that, we only wanted you to recall each experience in a general way. But this time, it's important that you remember what we talked about.

OK, Thom responded.

We know you can handle this, Thom, Jeshua assured him. Listen to Rin, your teachers, and us as we continue to support you. Please know that while you may face challenges, you will have positive experiences too.

What challenges?

Sorry, I can't tell you, Jeshua replied. That'll take some of the fun away, not to mention impacting free will.

Fun, yeah, Thom replied, frowning.

That's all we wanted to tell you, Rel remarked. You're doing a great job and are truly magnificent and precious to us.

Thom shook his head in wonder as Jeshua and Rel dissipated like fog. He remained in his Sanctuary for a little longer. Finally, he opened his eyes and determined it was late afternoon from the sun's position. It was time to ride home. Walking toward the stable, he said, "Thanks, Jeshua and Rel. Nice to meet you in person, Rel, sort of."

Entering the stable, Thom went to Apollo's stall to say goodbye before saddling Chestnut. Apollo greeted him with a gentle nudge and a whinny. Thom had much to talk about with Rin. He was going home! He was going to miss this place. Halting suddenly, he was struck by a realization. "What about Apollo? Will the monastery let me take him home?

Chapter 50

Since it was Siptema, the weather was perfect for Rin and Thom to sit outside after dinner. The sun was close to setting, casting warm hues of red and orange across the sky. It was a few days since Jeshua and Rel's visitation. He hadn't yet told Rin anything about it because he wanted time to reflect on what they had told him. Bending his head over his journal on his lap, he wrote, *G, it meant a lot that Jeshua and Rel visited me. And Jeshua's hug was great. It really helped me let go of the rest of my guilt about Lebrim. I'm glad he's safe and pray that his life review goes well. I still think he could have done a lot of good if he'd lived. But I accept it was his time. If he gets reincarnated, I hope he can live a longer life to share his gifts.*

Lifting his head, Thom noticed that Rin was deeply immersed in his book, a mystery. Returning to his journal, he continued, *I can't believe I'm going home soon, G. I wish I'd asked Jeshua and Rel when that would happen. Maybe I'll be back in time for the Solstice Day celebration. It'll be great to see everyone. I guess I should ask Rin.* Closing his journal, he spoke, "Rin." When there was no response, he repeated his name.

"Huh. Oh, sorry, Thom. Did you want something?"

"Yeah, I want to tell you about a visitation I had."

"A visitation," Rin replied. "Do you mean someone came to the monastery?"

"No," Thom replied. "To my Sanctuary. You see, I was still a bit disturbed by Lebrim's death and how I handled it."

"Do you want to talk more about it?"

"No. I'm OK."

"Well, who visited you?" Rin asked.

"There were two. One was Jeshua."

"Jeshua's on your divine team, isn't he?" Rin asked. "You said he feels like a brother, didn't you?"

"Yes," Thom said.

"How was it seeing him?"

"It was great. Jeshua gave me a big hug. Sometimes, I imagine him beside me when I walk around the monastery. Do you think that's weird?"

"No," Rin assured him. "I'm sure he's with you."

"Good," Thom replied. "Sometimes, I still worry what other people think about me."

"I know, Thom," Rin said sadly. "We'll keep telling you that you're a good person."

"Thanks."

"Who was the other person that visited you?" Rin asked.

"It was my higher self, Lightworker-Reliant. He goes by Rel."

"Oh, my!" Rin exclaimed. "That's something. What was that like?"

"Very strange. When I shook Rel's hand, it felt like we shared the same energy. That was before Jeshua told me who he was."

"That makes sense because you are an incarnation of Rel."

"That's what Rel explained. Jeshua also told me that we shared previous lifetimes together."

"You and Jeshua, huh? And how was that to hear?" Rin asked.

"Strange, too," Thom replied. "It sort of felt true, but I don't remember my other lifetimes."

"Sestra B has spoken to you about reincarnations, and why you forget, hasn't she?"

"Yeah," Thom answered. "And Rel told me more about it."

"Did it make sense?"

"Mostly. It still feels strange. I keep using that word."

"Understandable," Rin replied. "Please let it be. My experience is you'll encounter someone or something that will bring it to mind and help you understand it more. And, assuredly, your divine team will send messages about it too."

"You think?" Thom asked.

"Yes. What did Jeshua and Rel say?"

"They said my two gifts for physical and spirit healing mark me as a lightworker. Rel suggested I talk with you about it."

"Ah. I should have guessed that's where your calling came from. Do you know what that is?"

"Someone who brings light and hope," Thom said.

"Exactly," Rin replied. "It's a unique role for beings in spirit. Put succinctly, they're committed to helping humans see who they truly are. You did that with Nuala when you asked her about her passion, which enabled her to name her shadows and ultimately identify her path."

"I see," Thom replied. "Around the time Apollo was born, Sestra B told me Archangel Metatron oversees lightworkers."

"That's correct," Rin replied. "I'd imagine he plays an important role for your higher self."

"Rel's on my divine team, too," Thom admitted. "I didn't understand why he asked to be on my team because I'd never heard of him. Now I know."

"Did Jeshua or Rel say anything else?" Rin asked.

"Yes. They said we'd be returning home soon. They didn't tell me when, though. Can you tell me?"

"Yes, but I want to explain something first," Rin replied. "You see, I didn't know when that would be. My guides told me I would know. I guess your visit was what I was waiting for. Before I tell you when we're leaving, would you tell me what else they said?

"Alright," Thom said. "They told me you wouldn't be teaching me when we got home. I figured that, but I did wonder who."

"Very true. What else did they say?"

"They warned me that I could run into Samiltun, who might still be looking for people with gifts to use."

"Indeed," Rin acknowledged. "You've advanced to a point in your training where a new perspective is necessary. Sestra B confided in me that you're approaching a stage where she'll have nothing more to teach you. And they were correct that I won't be teaching you. Next fall, you'll attend the Acadium in Docha-leigh, where others with special skills like you will teach you."

"The Acadium!" Thom shouted. "I've heard it's a top school for students with special gifts. But I know it's expensive. My family could never afford it."

"It is a prestigious school, and it can be expensive," Rin admitted. "But no student was ever turned away because they couldn't pay. Scholarships are available."

"Are you saying I'll be given a scholarship?" Thom asked excitedly.

"Yes. As a matter of fact, you will."

"You said next fall," Thom commented. "That's a year away. Why are you, Jeshua, and Rel telling me now?"

"Because we need to get on our way in early Aprali to allow us time to travel. The Acadium is in the capital. I want to be there six weeks before the start of the term, which occurs in mid-Siptema. That should also give me enough time to get a sponsor for you."

"What's a sponsor?"

"Someone who keeps an eye on the academ during the school year. That's what students are called at the Acadium. The sponsor gives him or her a place to stay during the holidays if the academ's family doesn't live nearby," Rin explained. "Some may provide monetary support."

"Wouldn't that be you?" Thom asked, a little confused.

"No. I'll have other responsibilities to attend to, Thom."

"Do you mean as a healer?" he asked.

"Not exactly," Rin replied. "Listen, I'll tell you something you must keep in the strictest confidence. I trust you after coming to know you these few years and seeing how you remained quiet about the help you provided the Prezdan. I'm a member of COMDC, which stands for Covert Observers and Messengers for the Docha-leigh Commonwealth, or COM for short. We keep our eyes and ears open on behalf of the monarchs for anything that might impact the commonwealth."

"Do you mean you're a spy?" Thom asked.

"I don't know if I'd call us that. But we do keep watch," Rin admitted.

"But why," Thom asked. "Who or what do you watch?"

"Ah," Rin considered. "That comes with a story. Queen Niamh and I met during our first year at the Acadium. At the time, she was the daughter of the reigning queen. She, her cousin Gabi, also a student, and I spent a great deal of time together."

"You're a friend with the queen," Thom remarked.

"Close friends," Rin corrected him. "By the way, Gabi's now the queen of Eiren, where we were originally headed when we left your home. She's married to the king, of course."

"What about King Pethuric?" Thom asked.

"Pethuric came to the Acadium a year after we started," Rin explained. "When he joined us, we became an unstoppable foursome, much to the chagrin of some of our teachers, not to mention Niamh's mother."

"Do you mean you were troublemakers?" Thom asked, shocked that someone like Rin would misbehave.

"Perhaps a little bit, but not in a bad way," Rin said, chuckling. "I remember once when Peth suggested we drop bags of shredded multicolor paper on sixth-year students during their graduation ceremony. It didn't quite go as planned, and the paper went all over the hall. For punishment, we had to pick up every shred and work in the kitchen for six months the next school year."

"Even Queen Niamh," Thom asked, "I guess she was a princess then."

"Oh, yes," Rin replied, still chuckling.

"But where does COM come in then," Thom asked, bewildered.

"It was created after Niamh's mother unexpectedly died. She and Peth had been married little more than a year, and suddenly, Niamh was thrust into the limelight as queen. Niamh felt overwhelmed because she was still learning to govern."

"It must have been hard to lose her, Mam," Thom said sympathetically. "What happened to her, Da?"

"He had died ten years before," Rin explained. "A bit desperate, she turned to her friends for guidance and support.

COM became particularly important in the first year because many tried to flatter her to gain influence, including emissaries from neighboring lands. Niamh realized she needed advisors with her and the commonwealth's best interests at heart."

"COM," Thom commented.

"Exactly," Rin said. "We, the four of us, determined this group of advisors should be covert and that its members had to possess special skills to provide the kind of help Niamh needed. Their duties would require them to act as secret couriers to the leaders of other countries and conduct undercover investigations related to commerce, governance, and human rights violations. I became its first member and used my healing profession to camouflage my covert activities. Gabi didn't join because she was moving to Eiren soon after.

Recalling Rin's question of Captain Musa when he visited the monastery, Thom asked, "Was that why you asked the captain whether there was any unrest in the places he traveled?"

"Ah, I thought I detected curiosity from you when I asked," Rin replied. "And yes, since I'd been away on my COM duties for a few years, I've been out of touch with where things stood in Docha-leigh and other lands."

Thom was silent, thinking about their trip home. "If we leave in early Aprali, we'd be home by late Jauli."

"Your mathematics class seems to be a benefit," smiled. "Your figuring would be correct except for a couple of things. The voyage shouldn't take us as long due to ocean currents. We also won't have the delays we had coming here. But I want to make a few stops before going to the capital."

"Where?" Thom asked.

"I'd imagine you'd like to spend a few days in Dridley to see Khali again."

"Oh, yes. I have a lot to tell her," Thom replied.

"I thought we also should stop by the Barrelsons to see how Rindo is doing. What do you think?"

"Yes. I've been thinking about Rindo, too. I've wanted to ask if we could visit him, but I didn't know when we'd return to Docha-leigh."

"I also thought you'd want to spend at least a month with your family before heading to the Acadium," Rin said. "I'm thinking we'll get there at the end of Jauna if everything goes according to plan."

"Oh, wow. I have a lot to tell them. And I want to see everyone, including my newest sibling. I don't even know if it's a he or a she."

"On this end," Rin continued, "I'll need to start making arrangements, including finding a ship and letting people know we're leaving. I'll tell Lauret, Rafi, and Reyner, as well as Mik. Will you let Mekial, Sestra B, and Medelin know?"

"Yes. Oh goodness. I'll let Mekial know tomorrow. What about Maden?" Thom asked.

"Will you let her know?" Rin asked.

"Yes," Then Thom's face fell.

"What's wrong?" Rin asked.

"Apollo. I don't suppose we could take him with us?"

"Probably not," Rin replied. "Oh, Thom. I'm sorry."

"I've been helping Maden train him. She said I might be able to start riding him a little in a couple of months after he's used to a saddle."

"I don't see why you couldn't still do that since we'll be here for another seven months," Rin replied with sympathy.

Thom nodded but looked forlorn.

"Let's head in, Thom," Rin said. By then, the sun had set, and it was getting too dark to read, not to mention cooler. Walking through the back door, he realized he also needed to let the monarchs know and ask for their help finding a sponsor.

Chapter 51

Thom oversaw the healer shop in the late afternoon as Rin left just after supper to tend to a patient in her home. Now that it was Disime, the minor rainy season had ended. Even though it didn't rain as hard as the major rainy season, he was still grateful it was over. Too many times, he was out without his waxed cloak and had gotten drenched. But even that wasn't always effective. Someone needed to invent something better that could keep him completely dry. He had finished helping a customer when he heard someone yelling 'fire.' Stepping out into the street, he stopped a woman running by and asked, "What's going on?"

"Fire at the Chapel of the One," she answered before hurrying away.

Thom followed her and was taken aback when he discovered Rin and two other men slamming their bodies against the chapel door to break in. He smelled acrid smoke but saw that the front of the building remained undamaged, including its ornate painted windows.

Spying Thom, Rin called out, coughing, "Thom! Get the constable. We're having trouble breaking in. Something's blocking the door. The fire's spreading rapidly."

Sprinting toward the Constable Station a few blocks away, Thom was relieved, knowing none of the monks would be at the chapel. Since today was the fourteenth, the monks were at the monastery honoring the anniversary of the community's founding with their Day of Thanksgiving. Arriving at the Constable station, he spotted Captain Jallow. Gasping for breath, he cried, "Fire...chapel."

"Thanks," he said, turning into the station door to inform the deputies within and then darting next door to alert the fire crew at fire brigade headquarters.

When Thom returned to the chapel, Rin and the rest had successfully breached the door. The remains of a bench lay outside, which Thom presumed was previously blocking it. A line of people diligently passed water buckets into the building. Rin was outside directing them.

"Rin!" Thom called out. "The fire brigade is on its way."

"Good," he replied tiredly, still coughing. "We're slowing its spread, but we need help."

"What can I do?" he asked.

"Find another water barrel. The ones we're using are almost empty. See if you can get more people to join the bucket line."

"OK," Thom replied. Shortly afterward, he located another barrel around the corner from the chapel and rounded up more volunteers. His bucket line had finally gotten into a rhythm of passing buckets when a young man with un-kempt black hair clad in a vest rushed past him and crashed into a woman behind him, causing her and a few other volunteers to tumble. Hearing a loud crack, he inspected a few of the buckets the volunteers had dropped and found two were useless.

Thom frantically searched for new buckets when he heard the bell of the steam-powered fire wagon ring out. Turning toward the sound, he saw two horses pulling a cart with a huge metal barrel come to a stop by the chapel. A muscular man wearing a leather coat and a brimmed hat shoveled coal into the fire bin below the barrel. Another was attaching a cloth hose to a pipe protruding from its side. Two others, similarly outfitted, began pumping water through the chapel door. He and the others who had passed buckets stepped back.

The smoke billowing out of the chapel was lessening. It looked like the brigade was getting the fire under control. Glancing around, Thom saw all but one man looking re-lieved. The man's eyes seemed ablaze, and his lips were pursed tightly. Thom thought he looked like the man who had bumped into their bucket line earlier and decided to investigate.

Navigating behind him, Thom recognized his clothes. Upon closer inspection, he saw that the edge of his vest was singed. Lowering his fifth shield, he perceived a black mesh enveloping the man, and his aura displayed shades of muddy red and yellow. The mesh erratically pulsed, reflecting the man's anger. There was no doubt that this was the guy. Thom knew he had to inform Captain Jallow.

Surveying the scene, he spotted him overseeing brigade members replenishing the water barrel on the wagon. Moving stealthily to ensure the man didn't notice, Thom reached Jallow and whispered, "Captain Jallow."

Frowning at being interrupted, Jallow turned towards him. Recognizing Thom, he said, "I know you wouldn't distract me without good reason. What is it?"

"I think I know who started the fire," he said, explaining why he suspected the man.

"Can you describe him?" Captain Jallow asked.

"Sure, but I can point him out to you," Thom explained.

Assigning another brigade member to take over his task, Jallow moved discreetly behind the man Thom had pointed to but remained still.

The crowd erupted in cheers when the brigade announced the fire was out. The young man, however, did not. Thom witnessed Jallow grab the man, who attempted to escape. Two nearby deputies ran to Jallow's aid. After they escorted the man away, Captain Jallow returned to Thom by the wagon.

"Thanks, Thom. You have a good eye," Captain Jallow commended him. "That fellow did start the fire. We found a flint and a piece of iron in his pocket. It also helped that he couldn't keep his mouth shut about wanting to burn out the evil believers. He's one of the fanatics associated with a fringe sect of the old religion."

"People believe the monks are evil," Thom said, incredulous.

"Some, but it's not only the monks they believe are evil. They also believe the same of anyone who practices the One faith," he replied unhappily. "I've got to get back to the station and deal with the young man. Thanks again for alerting us about the fire and helping us quickly catch the culprit."

"You're welcome."

Thom and Rin were relaxing by the hearth reading that night after dinner.

Cough—Cough—Cough—Cough.

"That sounds bad," Thom commented.

"It sounds worse than it is," Rin confessed, taking another sip of chamomile tea. "Once we'd broken into the chapel, we inhaled a lot of smoke before the brigade arrived. I made sure the two men with me had a supply of tea to take home with them."

"I'm sorry," Thom said. "You said you were near the chapel soon after the guy started the fire."

"Yes," Rin admitted. "It was a bit of a fluke. I was returning home. I stopped briefly to admire the chapel windows when I saw a shadow inside. Knowing no one should've been there, given the monastery celebration. So I looked closer."

"How bad was the damage?" Thom asked.

"They lost their altar, wall hangings, and a few benches. But not much more. Jallow told me the culprit had piled paper and cloth on the altar to get the fire going. Miraculously, the structure wasn't damaged, but they will have to do some cleaning and repainting before they can use the chapel again."

"That's good news," Thom sighed. "I'm glad you were there."

"And you used your spirit-healing abilities to confirm the young man was the culprit," Rin commented.

"Yes," Thom said. "Captain Jallow called him a fanatic."

"Fanatics are an unusual breed," Rin explained. "They come in many forms, not only religious. They can be obsessed with a particular viewpoint, belief, or person."

"The guy also had some kind of meshed shield around him, but not like mine. Do you think he was like Samiltun and had gifts he was misusing?"

"Ah. I know what you're talking about," Rin replied. "His shield is not like ours. It's more of a filter someone unconsciously creates due to their rigid beliefs and prejudice. It means the person dismisses opinions different from their own. They also disregard facts that challenge their viewpoint, referring to those facts as false news. Those folks are dangerous. They're willing to deceive and harm people in their mission to convert everyone to their beliefs."

"That's terrible," Thom replied.

"It is. It's getting late. We should get to bed. You have a lesson tomorrow with Sestra B, don't you?"

"Yeah," Thom replied. "And my classes in math and science."

"How are those going?"

"Pretty well. We're learning geometry and trigonometry, about angles and stuff. I'm mostly getting it. Science is interesting. We're covering anatomy now, specifically the cardiovascular system. I wished I had learned it before Lebrim... I know it wouldn't have saved him, but...," Thom admitted sadly. "Oh, and I also learned that inanimate objects give off energy, too, like rocks, clay, and metals. I thought only living things did that."

"That should be helpful to you, given your earth sense," Rin commented.

"I agree," Thom answered. "It's giving me words to describe what I sense."

"Good," Rin said. "Well, goodnight, Thom."

"Goodnight, Rin."

Chapter 52

A few days after Solstice Day, Thom sought out Sestra B.

"Good morning, Thom," she greeted him as he entered the chapel. "We don't have a session this morning, do we?"

"No," Thom answered, suddenly sneezing.

"Bless you," Sestra B responded. "The incense?"

"Yeah," Thom replied, wiping his nose on a handkerchief in his pocket. Rin had forced him to carry it after having observed Thom wiping his nose on his tunic sleeve one too many times.

"One of the novices was overly enthusiastic with the incense at our Solstice Day service. Even after opening the doors. I can't believe that the scent still lingers."

"I thought he was using quite a lot," Thom admitted. "I held my nose through part of the service. I didn't want to disturb it with my sneezing. Um, I wonder if you're available to talk?"

"Certainly. Let's go to my office," she suggested. "The air's clean there, I can assure you. My window's also open, and the breeze is coming in. It's the perfect temperature, don't you think?"

"Yeah," Thom replied, remembering his ride here, especially past the orchard and grazing field. The view resembled a painting with the light blue sky as the backdrop. It made him think of Meli, whom he would be seeing soon. He wondered if she ever painted landscapes.

Easing into his usual chair in Sestra B's office, Thom glanced around. He knew he'd miss this place after he left. He always enjoyed his private meetings here. Her office featured two plush chairs, a well-stocked bookshelf, and a neatly arranged desk with a matching chair. The energy here felt peaceful and evoked trust.

"What do you want to talk about?"

"I really liked the Solstice service the other day and Sestra Ndey's homily," Thom stated.

"What did you like?"

"A few things. First, when Ndey stressed that we don't look to one spiritual teacher for all the answers. I also liked it when she warned us to be wary of those who claim their way is the true way. And I appreciated when she told us to trust our intuition."

"Does that make sense?" Sestra B asked. "If you recall, we discussed this when we first met."

"Yes," Thom replied. "At first, I thought it would create all kinds of problems. But I realized it encourages people to be real. Rin called it authenticity. The elders demanded blind obedience at home."

"What's your question?"

"I'm finding myself drawn to the Aaliswan faith. So many of your beliefs make sense, like reincarnation. Of course, it also helped that I met my higher self, Rel," he said, smiling. "My question is whether my calling as a spirit healer also includes telling others about my new beliefs."

"You're using the word, calling, like my community uses," she commented.

"Yes," Thom agreed. "I feel like it describes my divine connection more accurately than the word, purpose."

"I understand," she replied. "About sharing your beliefs, what would that look like? Do you mean standing on a corner, like street preachers, or bringing them up while treating a patient?"

"Oh, no," Thom said. "For the first, that's not me. And for the second, it doesn't seem appropriate."

"Good," Sestra B approved. "Healing should never be tied to beliefs."

"Rin told me the same thing back when we ran into the bandits," he commented. "He said healing must never be offered with conditions."

"Did you agree?" Sestra B asked.

"Mostly," Thom replied. "I keep coming up with scenarios where a bad person who has hurt someone needs healing. Given the suffering he inflicted, shouldn't he suffer?"

"I see your point," Sestra B replied. "On the other hand, what if offering healing prompts him to rethink their behavior, to use your pronoun?"

"Huh," Thom answered. "I hadn't considered that."

"Back to your question about whether sharing your new faith is part of your calling," Sestra B said. "I have an answer, but I'd like to check with my angel guides."

"Sure," Thom replied.

While he was waiting, Thom looked around her office again. He noticed a book on the table next to her chair. It was titled "Understanding the Akashic Records." He imagined it could be about some sort of bookkeeping.

Sestra B cleared her throat to indicate she was ready to speak. "My angels conferred with your divine team and agree your focus should remain on spirit healing and the abilities you develop. Their concern, if you included faith sharing, is that it might inadvertently take precedence. They agree you can share your beliefs with others if they ask."

"OK. I guess that makes sense," Thom replied. "One more question. Are there Chapels of the One in Docha-leigh?"

"I believe there are," she answered. "I don't recall if there's one in your capital, though."

"I hope there is. Thank you, Sestra B."

"You're welcome. What are you up to next?"

"Oh, Maden and I are going to do some training with Apollo."

Chapter 53

It was midway through the first month of the new year. Since Rin and Thom would leave Glakkadeth in a couple of months, Rin had told Thom not to enroll in academic classes this term. He'd still meet with Sestra B and train with Medelin, though. With the extra time, Thom was freed to help with Apollo's training. He had recently begun riding him. The rides were brief, considering that Apollo was six months shy of three when trainers typically waited before introducing a rider. However, as Thom was still considerably lighter than an adult, even with his muscle growth and increased height, Maden had determined Apollo's spine and skeletal structure could support him.

Today, as part of the training, they introduced Apollo to obstacles. It was a perfect day, with clear skies and temperatures in the high 70s. The air smelled fresh, even with the scent of cut grass and the musk of horses from the nearby stable. In the middle of the corral, Maden had placed a log, eight feet long and six inches in diameter. Thom was trying to get Apollo to step over it. Up until then, Thom had communicated his instructions verbally using emotional cues and through his connection with Apollo's spirit. He had always responded well. This time, Apollo wasn't. Maybe if he showed him, Apollo would understand.

"Apollo, watch me," Thom said, stepping over the log. Turning around, he then prompted, "Now it's your turn. Come on. Step over the log."

He still wasn't getting it.

"Thom," Maden called out. "I have an idea. You've done visualizations with Sestra B, haven't you?"

"Yes," he replied.

"Why don't you try visualizing the instruction? Given how connected you two are, he may receive the image."

"OK," Thom replied. Closing his eyes, he visualized Apollo picking up each hoof and stepping over the log. Going through the exercise again, Apollo successfully completed it.

"Fantastic, Apollo!" Thom exclaimed, giving him a friendly pat on the neck. Retrieving a carrot from his pocket, he presented it to Apollo, who eagerly devoured it.

"Now repeat that, but this time riding him," Maden suggested.

Apollo once again responded perfectly.

"Great, Thom. Why don't you ride him back to the healer shop this afternoon?"

"Can I?" he said, hoping. "Wouldn't that be too much for him?"

"I'm certain he'll be fine. But pay attention to his energy and spirit. If you sense any discomfort, dismount and walk him the rest of the way. When you come back tomorrow, let me know how he did."

Three days passed, and it was late afternoon. Thom and Rin were making salves to treat cuts and scrapes in the healer shop. The neighborhood was quiet, free of children dashing about, as school resumed the previous week. Now, they had the opportunity to replenish their dwindling supply of the salve. Over the preceding three weeks, a continuous flow of parents had sought it out, responding to the inevitable accidents caused by their overactive children during winter break. Thom was grinding herbs in the pestle on the back counter when the chime above the door rang. Turning around, he saw Mikazel Jacobreit's smiling face.

"Hello, Thom, and a belated Happy New Year!" Mik greeted him.

"Mik. It's good to see you. Belated Happy New Year to you, too," he replied.

"Thanks," he said. "Another beautiful day."

"Yeah, it is," Thom agreed. "I know I've been in Glakkadeth a long time, but it still amazes me that it's warm. At home, it could be snowing."

"I'd imagine you're looking forward to going home," Mik commented.

"Yeah," Thom said. "I can't believe I'll be there soon. Let me get Rin." Stepping to the curtain between the shop and the back area, he called, "Rin. Mik's here."

"Hi, Mik," Rin said, entering the front room. "How have you been?"

"Very good. Apologies for not visiting sooner. I've been doing a fair amount of traveling."

"No worries," Rin said. "What can we do for you? Do you need any herbs or salves? Or is someone ill?"

"None of those things," he replied. "I'm here as a courier of a sort: to give you and Thom an invitation."

"An invitation?" Thom asked, his eyes wide.

Mik pulled an envelope from his satchel and handed it to Rin, who opened it.

The invitation was a folded ivory card bearing the embossed blue Glakkadian coat of arms on its front. Extending it to Thom, Rin suggested, "Why don't you read it aloud?"

Looking down at the gold characters, Thom cleared his throat and began:

With sincerest thanks for the service provided to the people of Glakkadeth, Modu Gessama, Prezdan of Glakkadeth, and Gallen Gessama, First Husband, cordially invite Healer Rinbalden and Apprentice Healer Thom Macirdan to a farewell dinner at 6 pm at our official residence in the capital city, Benjil, on the island of Umojai, Glakkadeth Archipelago, the 32nd of Fibre, in the year 1063

"It's signed simply Modu and Gallen," Thom concluded, "We're being invited to a farewell party."

"Yes," Mik said. "And it's in your honor."

"That's very kind of them," Rin said. "I had wanted to visit them before we left, but this is very special."

Thom looked at Mik dumbfounded.

"You were a big help to them a year and a half ago," Mik reminded him. "Now that everything's settled, they wanted to thank you officially. They also told me it was a way of making amends for not being able to find you when you were kidnapped."

"It wasn't their fault," Thom protested. "After all, the kidnappers were from Docha-leigh."

"Nonetheless," Mik said, "they were embarrassed."

"You were very important for Glakkadeth, Thom," Rin reiterated.

"This is in your honor, too, Rin, as the invitation indicates," Mik stated. "Do not discount the work you've done here either."

"Oh, well," Rin replied, waving his hand in dismissal.

"He's right, Rin," Thom said, nodding.

"Mik," Rin interjected, wanting to change the subject. "Modu and Gallen normally dress casually. But I wonder if there's a formal dress requirement?"

"Yes, as a matter of fact, there is," Mik replied.

"What are we supposed to wear?" Thom asked. "I don't think I have anything."

"Modu and Gallen will pay for your formal wear," Mik answered, "as a gift from Glakkadeth."

"That's very nice of them," Rin replied. "We'll thank them at the party."

"Yes, it's very generous," Thom echoed.

The next day, Rin and Thom went to the same tailor shop where Thom had gotten his servant outfit for the trader gala. After reviewing tunics of various colors and designs, Thom chose a silver linen tunic with purple embroidery. Rin chose a white one with deep green embroidery. They each chose trousers that matched the embroidery color.

When Thom returned to the monastery the following day, he shared news of the invitation with Mekial. While she expressed her excitement for him, he couldn't help but wish she could be there. However, she assured him that they'd have another farewell celebration. The ensuing six weeks passed swiftly. Medelin intensified Thom's weapons training, wanting him to reach peak strength before their departure. In between training sessions, Thom devoted his time to Sestra B and Apollo.

Thom and Rin took an interisland ship to the capital island three days before their farewell dinner. This time, at the Prezdan's request, they would stay on the government grounds in the building where visiting dignitaries stayed.

The suite to which they were assigned had four rooms: two bedrooms, a sitting room, and a bathing room, with a built-in tub with pipes that pumped hot and cold water. Thom had taken a long, hot bath the first night there, a welcome contrast to manually filling up the tin bath at the shop.

Seeing the capital again was fun. Thom especially liked exploring its market, which was twice the size of the one on Rohan where they lived. On one visit, he picked up another journal. What was nice about it was that each page had inspirational quotes reflecting the beliefs of the Aaliswan faith. Each afternoon, when they returned to their suite, he couldn't help feeling self-conscious. He kept expecting someone to tell them they didn't belong and kick them out—well, at least kick him out.

They were invited to Modu and Gallen's residence the morning of the party. Upon arrival, the porter immediately led them to the sitting room.

"Healer Rinbalden and Apprentice Thom Macirdan have arrived, sirs," the porter announced.

"Send them in," Thom heard a male voice respond.

Upon entering the room, Thom was struck by its inviting, well-worn charm. Blue-upholstered couches and chairs were arranged in two groupings about the room, with the cushions bearing indentations, a testament to their frequent use. Along one wall stood bookshelves displaying an array of books and bric-a-brac. Across from them, a large table hosted a jigsaw puzzle that someone was assembling.

Beneath it, a large maroon rug added a touch of warmth, slightly worn where the two chairs sat, revealing that two people spent considerable time there.

For a leader, he would've expected a room filled with expensive furniture that was uncomfortable to sit in. Not that he had visited the homes of any leaders before. The room also gave off an earthy aroma, with a touch of sweetness, likely from the array of plants and gardenias situated about the room. Thom was quite thankful the scent didn't make him sneeze. Patting his tunic pocket, he confirmed he had a handkerchief to wipe his nose if he did. He definitely didn't want to wipe his nose on his tunic in front of Modu and Gallen.

"Thom, Rin, please come in," Gallen called out. "Help yourself to some beverages and pastries," he said, gesturing to a side table. "Modu will be in shortly."

"Thank you, Gallen," they both responded.

Thom walked to a side table and found an array of options. He helped himself to a scone, splitting it and spreading jam and clotted cream on each side. Thom remembered how much he enjoyed them when he had high tea with Mik a while ago. He also took one of the muffins with chocolate bits. Moving to the beverages, Thom stopped suddenly. "Wha...?" he exclaimed.

"Might you have found the pitcher of Timbu, Thom?" Gallen asked, holding up a mug and smiling. "I'm having some myself."

"When? Did you..."

"Soon after you told us about it, we contacted Awa, and she provided us with the recipe," he explained.

As Gallen was speaking, Modu walked in and interrupted. "I like it too, but I usually add cinnamon to mine. There's cinnamon by the pitcher if you want to try it. But for now, I need some coffee."

"Thanks," Thom replied. "Maybe I'll try a little." After pouring himself some, he sat on the couch across from Gallen and placed his plate and mug on the table between them.

Rin sat next to Thom with his own plate and mug of tea. Modu sat in a chair next to Gallen.

"You arrived three days ago, didn't you?" Modu asked.

"Yes," Rin answered since Thom had a mouthful of scone.

Swallowing quickly, Thom replied, "Yes. And thank you for the tunic and trousers."

"You're welcome," Modu answered. "We wanted to give you something of our culture to take with you."

"Thank you again."

"Will you have a few more days to explore the city?" Modu asked.

"Yes, that's the plan," Rin replied. "We need to find another place to stay for those days."

"Don't be silly, Rin," Gallen spoke up. "You can stay where you are for as long as you want. By the way, there's a new theater troupe in residence. I'd suggest you go to a show. We could arrange for tickets if you'd like."

"That would be wonderful," Rin replied. Seeing Thom focused on taking a bite of his muffin, Rin gave Gallen a wink.

"Mmph," Thom grunted in agreement, looking up.

"When do you sail?" Modu asked.

"Early Aprali," Rin replied. Turning to Thom, he said, "I booked passage home on Captain Musa's ship."

"Truly?" Thom said with excitement. "It'll be great to see the captain and Nuala again."

"Nuala?" Gallen asked.

"Nuala's a former novice from the monastery," Rin explained. "She's now a junior seafarer on Captain Musa's ship."

"I'm sensing there's a story," Gallen said.

"Thom?" Rin said.

"Oh. When Nuala was a novice a couple of years ago, I sensed she was unhappy. I was with her when Captain Musa visited me at the monastery. When she met him, her energy and aura perked up."

"Can I presume you used the same spirit-healing gift that helped us root out our trading culprits?" Gallen asked.

"Yes," Thom replied. "Another day, during a chat with her, Nuala realized her calling was not to religious life but to the sea."

"Once again, you're serving our people," Modu said. "You are a remarkable young man."

"Oh, it's nothing," Thom countered, reddening. "Anyone would've done that."

"Perhaps," Modu replied. "But you did it. And for that, we are once again grateful. As you know, tonight's party recognizes your help with the traders, which impacted many people. What you offered to Nuala is equally important and valued."

Thom blushed even more.

They chatted for a bit longer before it was time to leave.

As Thom and Rin left, Modu called out, "See you tonight. It's bound to be a memorable evening."

Walking back to their room, Thom turned to Rin and asked, "A memorable evening. I'm sensing something more is behind that than just having a goodbye party."

"Do you?" Rin said mysteriously.

Dressed in his formal wear, Thom looked at himself in the full-length mirror in his room. He liked the outfit. The geometric embroidery was beautiful. Behind him, he heard his door open.

"Admiring yourself, I see," Rin smiled.

"Oh. Um," Thom stammered.

"It's OK," Rin replied. "You look nice."

"Thanks," he replied. "You look nice too."

"Thank you. Are you ready?"

"Yes."

"Let's walk to the residence," Rin suggested.

Like before, the porter greeted them at the entrance. He led them to the reception room's doors and knocked. The porter stepped aside as the doors opened.

Stepping inside, Thom's jaw dropped when he saw who was there. Smiling behind Modu and Gallen were Mekial, her mothers, and her younger brother. Next to them stood Sestra B, Awa, Rafi, Medelin, Maden, and Reyner. On the other side, he saw Mik, Captain Musa, and Nuala. At the back, he was shocked to see Captain Jallow.

"I think Thom is a tad surprised," Gallen announced, who was wearing a white tunic with navy blue embroidery.

Everyone laughed.

"You're all here," Thom remarked. "I expected Mik and a few others. But I didn't expect all of you."

"Thom, in the few years you've been here, you've touched many people, both knowingly and unknowingly," Modu explained, wearing the opposite of Gallen: a navy tunic with the Glakkadian coat of arms on his chest. We had to bring together those closest to you and Rin to give you a proper farewell."

"But, why all the formality?" Thom asked.

"Because we also wanted to make our thanks official," Modu answered. "More on that at another time. Please come in and join our little gathering."

Turning to Rin, Thom commented, "You were in on this, weren't you?"

"Yes. Modu and Gallen contacted me and explained they wanted to include our friends in the gathering. But they wanted it to be a surprise for you."

Thom dabbed at his teary eyes and surveyed the room, three times the size of the healing shop. Towering walls reached at least fifteen feet high, and paintings of men and women dressed formally were hung on them, similar to Modu and Gallen's clothing. Crown molding graced the top of the walls, showcasing intricate floral designs that added a touch of elegance. Two walls boasted large windows with luxurious emerald drapes framing them.

"Hey, you," Mekial said, pushing her way through to him.

"Hi, Mekial," Thom said. "You look pretty."

"Thanks," Mekail replied. "I don't often wear burnt orange, but Ma found the cloth on sale at a store in town. Did you like how I played it cool when we discussed this gathering? I could be an actor."

"Yes, I didn't know."

"And speaking of acting," Rin interrupted, "Modu and Gallen purchased tickets for us to see the theater troupe's show tomorrow night."

"Oh, wow," Thom replied. "That's sounds great."

"And... Mekial," Rin prompted.

"I'll be sticking around for a few days and will join you."

"I can't believe it. It'll be fun having you with us," Thom replied.

"Let's mingle," Rin suggested.

Mekial and he wandered about together, accepting a glass of sparkling cider from a server bearing a silver tray. She was dressed in the same servant garment Thom had worn when he acted as a server.

"Did you hear her call me, sir?" he asked Mekial.

"Well, you are one of the guests of honor," she admitted. "But another server called me, sir, before you arrived. Should we get some appetizers from the servers before Budaj eats them all? They have stuffed mushrooms, oysters, figs with goat cheese, and spicy breaded meatballs. I can smell the meatballs from here."

"Good idea," Thom agreed. "I'd like at least one of each, especially the meatballs. I'm glad I finally got used to your spiciness."

They had made the rounds a few times, and Thom was swallowing another meatball before he said. "Given how good the appetizers are, I could eat more. But I guess I should save room for dinner."

"Me too," Mekial said, biting into another mushroom. "This is my last."

"All of this must have cost them a lot," Thom commented, looking around the room again. "I get it if they have this for Rin, but not me."

"Why do you keep dismissing what you did, Thom? As the invitation said, you did a great service for the Prezdan."

"I don't know about that. Speaking of the Prezdan, I want to introduce you to him and Gallen."

"But I'm no one in particular," she protested.

"Now, who's underestimating herself? Come on," Thom encouraged, dragging her over to them. "Modu and Gallen, I'd like you to meet my friend, Mekial. She helped me learn Glakkadian."

"Good to meet you, Mekial," Gallen responded.

"Yes, good to meet you, Mekial," Modu echoed. "And, given your tutoring, we are indebted to you too. Thom's fluency in our language was essential in helping us deal with our past trading anomaly." By then, everyone knew of the traders' illegal actions from an article published in the land's main newsprint. Few knew of Thom's involvement.

"Oh. Well, Thom knew a lot of the language by the time I started helping him," Mekial protested.

"Yeah, but you helped me with my accent and to learn trading terms," Thom said. "Mekial's also a wicked sparring partner. She beat me six times out of ten in our training runs."

"Correction. Seven," Mekial said with a smirk. "I beat you the other time even though you still deny it."

"Maybe," Thom said.

"Do you like training, Mekial?" Gallen asked.

"Yes. Medelin works us pretty hard, and I do get bruises. But I enjoy learning about fighting and defensive styles and how to use weapons effectively."

"Do you know what you want to do with your life?" Modu asked.

"Um...," she stammered, embarrassed.

"She wants to be part of your guard, Modu," Thom answered.

"If you keep working hard, that may happen," Modu said.

Taking a deep breath, Mekial said, "I will, Prezdan Gessama."

"See you later, Modu and Gallen," Thom replied before they went to get another glass of cider.

"Let's mingle," Mekial suggested.

Seeking out Nuala, Thom approached her. "I can't believe you and the captain are here. I thought you'd be on the ship somewhere."

"We'll be heading out tomorrow for a brief voyage," she explained. "But we couldn't miss your party."

"Thanks," he replied. "How are you? Is being a sailor all you hoped it would be?"

"Yes," Nuala answered. "I did have a little seasickness at first, but that's passed. I love traveling at sea and seeing the large expanse of the ocean without any land in sight. It's kind of a spiritual experience."

"Sounds great," Thom said. "You're happy then."

Just then, the head server announced dinner was ready in the adjoining room.

"I am," Nuala said, "thanks for asking. "We'd better go in and take our seats.

Walking through the sliding doors, Thom was captivated by the room's beauty. Crystal chandeliers hung from the ceiling, and the tables were covered with emerald cloths, matching the drapes over the windows. On the tables were settings of exquisitely etched dishware. Accompanying it were gleaming silver utensils and crystal goblets. Thom couldn't believe this was all in honor of him and Rin.

At the conclusion of the meal, Modu stood, tapped his wine goblet, and asked, "Would you all return to the reception room?"

Stepping back in, Thom saw it had undergone a change. There was now a podium with chairs arranged in front of it. He and Rin were directed to sit in the first row. Modu stood behind the podium, with Gallen to his left.

"What's going on?" he asked Rin.

"I'm not sure," Rin admitted.

Modu cleared his throat and spoke, "Welcome again, everyone, to this gathering to thank Rin and Thom for their service to the people of Glakkadeth. Service is a key principle of the Aaliswan faith. With this comes the requirement to recognize those who provided outstanding service. Tonight, it is my pleasure to give that."

"Healer Rinbalden, would you please step forward?" Gallen called out. He directed Rin to stand to Modu's right, facing those gathered.

"For the last few years, Rin," Modu continued, "you shared your great gifts as a healer. When you learned the monastery had lost its primary healer, you stepped in to help and trained both Healer Lauret and Healer Raphael."

Thom turned in his seat to look for Rafi. Seeing him, he mouthed, "Congratulations!"

Rafi mouthed back, "Thanks."

"We also thank you for organizing the bucket brigade during the recent chapel fire. Had you not acted, the neighborhood might have been consumed and possibly resulted in the loss of lives."

Thom saw Rin shifting his feet uncomfortably. He was grateful to Rin for training him. He thought it appropriate that Rin was honored for all he had done. Before they even came to Glakkadeth, Rin had saved him from Samiltun and the bandits.

"For all of your service," Modu announced, "and for having offered great friendship and advice over the years, we award you, Healer Rinbalden, with the Silver Order of Merit for Service."

Gallen turned to the table behind him and picked up a navy blue, cloth-covered box emblazoned with the Glakkadian coat of arms. Turning back towards Modu, he opened the box, revealing a silver medallion with a blue ribbon at the top.

Inviting Rin to turn towards him, Modu pinned it to Rin's chest. Then, Modu and Gallen each embraced Rin and kissed him on both cheeks, followed by resounding applause.

Looking through tears of joy, Thom noted Rin had turned red and smiled. Even adults turn red sometimes.

Directing Rin back to his place, Modu invited everyone to sit again.

"OK," Modu continued, "This next recognition has been too long in coming. We have someone in this room who showed great bravery on behalf of the people of Glakkadeth, especially for someone of such a young age."

Thom gulped, getting a little uncomfortable himself. "Uh, oh," he muttered.

"Thom Macirdan, please come forward."

Thom stood and stepped next to Modu.

"Without knowing us very well," Modu continued, "this young man willingly agreed to use a special gift that was still new to him to help us route out some very clever and inscrutable traders. Had these traders gone unchecked for much longer, they would have seriously damaged our economy and threatened our trading partnerships with other lands."

Thom gulped again, feeling his face grow warm.

"His action," Modu added, "restored our trading system to its proper balance, which impacts every citizen of Glakkadeth in small and large ways. For that alone, we are indebted to him. But his service didn't stop there. During the same chapel fire, he used his alert eye and unique gift again to identify the arsonist. As a result, Captain Jallow and his deputies were able to apprehend him."

Thom saw Captain Jallow smiling and nodding at him. He felt his face getting even redder.

"Thom used his gifts unselfishly to help all of us," Modu explained. "But his assistance wasn't limited to these more visible situations. He also offered help on a personal level. He provided a listening ear and keen observation to a young novice struggling to find her purpose. That helped her realize that rather than being called to a religious life, she was called to a life at sea. All of us have searched for our purpose at one time or another. How precious a gift it is to help someone identify their purpose. And we mustn't forget the healing he offered humans and animals."

Looking towards Nuala, Thom saw her nodding at him and mouthing, "Thank you again!"

"On behalf of the people of Glakkadeth," Modu announced, "we award Thom Macirdan with the Silver Order of Bravery for his courage, quick-wittedness, and overall support of our ideals."

By this time, Thom was nervously shaking.

"Take a deep breath, Thom," Modu whispered to him.

Taking the medallion from Gallen, Modu pinned it on Thom's chest.

As Modu was about to hug Thom, Gallen interrupted, "I have one more thing to add. I also want to thank Thom, Mekial, and Budaj for inventing Timbu. It's becoming a common drink and a lucrative export from our land."

Thom laughed, looking at Mekial and Budaj, who wore big smiles on their faces.

"Now, can I give him a hug?" Modu said to Gallen with a smirk.

"Of course," Gallen replied.

No sooner had Modu and Gallen given Thom a hug and a kiss on both cheeks when everyone applauded.

To Thom, it seemed to last forever. He was preparing to sit down when Modu said, "We're not done yet."

"A certain stable manager mentioned you aided in the birth of a foal two and a half years ago. A colt named Apollo, I believe," Modu stated.

Thom nodded.

"I understand you've been training him under Maden's watchful eye."

Thom noticed Maden nodding.

"Maden explained you have a special bond with him. She and Abbotess Linna have agreed that he can continue being your companion and return with you to Docha-leigh."

"What?" he replied, stunned. "I don't want to take him from Fanta if he doesn't want to go."

Maden spoke out. "Thom, I don't have the gifts you have, but I and the other horse trainers agree that Apollo and his dam Fanta want this. While it will be sad to lose him, it would be wrong to separate you."

"But how will we get him to Docha-leigh?"

"We offered to pay the extra cost to Captain Musa to cover Apollo traveling with you," Gallen explained, "but he's waiving the cost. Apparently, Timbu is extremely popular in Dridley and has resulted in extra income to the entire Bittaye family."

"Indeed," Captain Musa added.

"But," Gallen continued, "we're covering the cost to ensure your riverboat from Dridley can transport Apollo."

"Oh. Thank you... so much," Thom choked out, tears streaming down his face.

Gallen pulled a handkerchief from his pocket and gave it to Thom.

"Thanks," Thom said, wiping his face, embarrassed by how much he was crying.

"Keep it," Gallen insisted when Thom attempted to return it.

Looking down at the handkerchief, Thom noticed the embroidered Glakkadian coat of arms.

"But I have my own," Thom protested.

"Consider it another Glakkadian keepsake," Gallen replied.

Once again, the room burst into applause.

When the room grew quieter, Modu spoke. "Please continue to enjoy our hospitality. There are some desserts, coffee, tea, and Timbu, of course."

The servers quickly rearranged the chairs to accommodate small groups.

Mekial rushed up to Thom and gave him a big hug. Budaj did the same soon after.

"Can we see your medallion, Thom?" Budaj asked.

Standing together, Thom lifted it from his chest. On the front, around the edge, was a green laurel wreath. In the center was a silver imprint of a majestic lion with a flowing mane and alert eyes. The Glakkadian coat of arms and Thom's full name were on the back. Below it were the words, "Member of the Silver Order of Bravery, 32 of Fibre, 1063."

At the end of the evening, Thom and Rin said their goodbyes and returned to their suite. Before they went to bed, Rin turned to Thom and said, "Congratulations. Your medallion and Apollo were well deserved."

"Thank you," Thom replied. "You deserve yours too. I can never thank you enough for saving me, not to mention teaching me."

"You're welcome," Rin replied.

"You knew about Apollo, too?" Thom asked.

"Yes," Rin replied. "But it was Maden and the monks who suggested it."

"Wow."

"You've had a big impact on Glakkadeth in your few short years here, Thom. I'm certain you will also have a big impact at the Acadium."

"Thanks, Rin. Good night."

"Good night, Thom."

Chapter 54

Thom's final month in Glakkadeth was focused on training Apollo, as he needed to be accustomed to a rider for extended periods. However, the onset of the major rainy season challenged their routine. Whenever Rin sensed a lull in the rain, Thom adjusted his schedule. Unfortunately, his forecasts weren't always accurate. On more than one occasion, Thom would be out riding when the rain started. As a result, he soon learned to bring his waxed rain cloak. Of course, it helped him more than Apollo, even if it didn't protect his legs. Sometimes, he'd beg the kindness of strangers to use their barn and wait out the downpour. Other times, they simply endured it.

Two days before they departed for Docha-leigh, Rin had given Thom the day off to spend with Mekial. Rin was meeting with the new healer, Lule, and her apprentice, and he wasn't needed. The two had moved from Benjil to Birkemi at the Prezdan's request to take over Rin's practice. Thom was sweeping the shop floor when the door chimed, and Mekial stepped in.

"Good morning, Mekial," Thom said.

"Good morning, Thom," Mekial replied. "Oh, I had a flash-back to the first time I visited, when you said you were Healer Rin's life partner."

"You had to remind me," Thom grimaced.

"Of course," she replied, chuckling. "What are friends for?"

"Yeah, thank you...sooo... much," he replied with a wry grin. "I really am going to miss you."

"Me too," Mekial echoed. "But I don't want to think about that now. Today's all about fun."

"OK."

"Are you ready to go?" she asked.

"Yeah," he answered. "Let me get my bag, and I'll meet you out front."

"OK," Mekial replied.

When Thom stepped outside, he was carrying his bag, which contained a pair of old trousers he cut off for the occasion. The sun shone with a few wisps of clouds in the sky. He had worried it would be raining since it hadn't rained for a week. Since it was mid-morning, it was a little cool, but he knew it would get warmer. He was glad because he was finally visiting a beach. He'd never been to a beach, even at home, since it was inland. Thom's schedule had been packed, not to mention Mekial's, with whom he wanted to go. He hadn't found an opportunity.

"Do you want to go to the beach now?" she asked.

"No. Let's wait a little until it gets warmer," Thom suggested. "What if we go to the market fair first? I want to say goodbye to Maru. Maybe we could buy some meat skewers from him for our supper."

"Good idea," Mekial agreed. "Ma also gave us some chocolate biscuits she made yesterday."

An hour later, they left the fair and headed to the island's east side and the beach Mekial had suggested.

"I'm glad we stopped at Maru's cart," Mekail said. "I know I had breakfast an hour ago, but I could've eaten one of the chicken skewers there. They looked juicy."

"Yeah. And the smell of the sizzling beef made my mouth water," Thom added. "I can't believe Maru gave us twelve skewers. We have enough for three people."

"I think it was his way of giving you a farewell gift," Mekail said. "I'm glad it's just the two of us. Earlier this morning, Budaj was pestering Ma to make me invite him."

"I'm glad, too," Thom agreed. "Thanks for suggesting we buy a few apples. I could've brought a couple from the shop. By the way, how far is it to the beach?"

"About twenty minutes since we both walk fast," Mekial informed him. "It's north of where you'll catch your ship. There's an inlet there that protects the beach, which helps the water stay warm."

"I can't wait," Thom replied.

Arriving at the coast, Mekial led them down a path between tall palm trees laden with coconuts. Reaching the crest of a low hill, Thom saw before him a pristine white beach and a gorgeous ocean in shades of blue, turquoise, and azure. The view and the hypnotic sound of the waves crashing against the shore mesmerized him. Why hadn't he come here sooner? This would've been an excellent place for him to meditate.

"Thom!" Mekial yelled.

Looking left, Thom saw that she was fifteen feet ahead. "Oh, sorry," he replied, running up to her. "This place is beautiful."

"Yeah," Mekail agreed. "I thought we'd sit near the palm trees. That way, we'd get shade in the afternoon. I don't want you to return to the shop as red as a lobster. Did you bring your hat? The sun's especially bright."

"I did," Thom answered. "I'm glad Rin forced me to get one. I feel a little guilty about making fun of his floppy hat. It's come in handy."

"Only a little?" she laughed. "Since my skin burns, I also need to be careful."

After enjoying their skewers, biscuits, and apples, Thom settled onto the blanket, his gaze wandering across the expanse of sand. He appreciated the scene: seagulls gliding gracefully overhead and the sun casting brilliant sparkles upon the ocean waves. Glancing at Mekial, Thom saw her head buried in the pages of her book. Thom couldn't help but smile, realizing he'd passed on his love for reading to her. As he closed his own book, he glanced toward the water. His grin widened as he thought about their most recent swim. They had joyfully chased after rainbow-colored fish darting around them, bursting into laughter whenever the fish changed direction or swam within the coral reef. The water had been crystal clear, allowing them to follow easily. Its temperature was perfect, neither uncomfortably warm nor too cool.

Thom couldn't wrap his head around the fact that he'd be setting sail for home tomorrow. The mere thought of seeing Khali and his family again filled him with anticipation. He wondered how much they changed while he was away. It wasn't lost on him that he had undergone significant changes. The most apparent was his physical growth, but he also recognized his deepening sensitivity, a direct result of his expanding gifts. Perhaps the most profound change was mentally. He felt more confident. Though he still had doubts, they no longer held the same grip over him—at least, he hoped. As he sat up, an irresistible pull drew him toward the water's edge.

Walking there, Thom observed the waves rhythmically flowing towards the beach and back again to the sea. The movement reminded him of Sestra B's urging to go with the flow for whatever new abilities might emerge with his gifts. She had challenged him to be curious about them rather than afraid. At the time, despite her suggestion, Thom immediately feared it would be overwhelming. When he confided in her, she reminded him to stay grounded and trust his connection to Mother Earth and his divine team.

Standing there with the waves gently lapping over his feet, Thom noticed how his feet were sinking into the wet sand, even as the water flowed around them.

Use this image as a metaphor, Thom, a voice spoke in his head.

Jeshua? Thom replied in his mind.

No, it's Archangel Metatron.

Oh, sorry, he replied. *Sometimes, you all sound the same. What do you mean it's a metaphor?*

Consider your current stage in life and what lies ahead. It's quite apt, I'd say.

Thom stood still, with the waves lapping over his feet, reflecting on it.

"Thom," Mekial said, interrupting him.

"Huh? What?" he answered, shaking himself to return to the present. "Mekial?"

"Yeah," she replied. "Your face was all scrunched up in concentration. What are you thinking?"

"Archangel Metatron asked me to think about standing on the beach looking at the ocean as a metaphor for my life now."

"He's one of the beings on your divine team, isn't he?"

"Yeah, and he mentors those on life paths as lightworkers," he explained.

"I think Sestra B used that word for Lebrim," Mekial commented.

"That makes sense," Thom replied, then frowned.

"Do you still feel guilty about not saving him?" she asked.

"No," he answered. "I do wish he could've lived. But I know it was his time. He could've helped many people see their goodness and realize they're supported by God and the angels."

"That fits with you as a spirit healer, you know."

"Uh, huh," Thom said, still thinking about Lebrim.

"What do you think the metaphor means?"

"Oh," Thom answered. "Well, this place and everyone have come to mean a great deal to me. And I've learned a lot about myself, who I am, and who I'm not. I feel more grounded because of that and my bond to my divine team."

"OK. Makes sense."

"I guess the beach sort of represents my grounding. But in two days I'll be traveling home and soon after to the Acadium, where I don't know anyone. You know how I get when I face something new. All collywobbles."

"Mm-hmm," Mekial agreed.

"In front of me, the water keeps moving, washing over my feet. These waves are tiny, but they'd be huge if there were a storm. So, they're always changing, kind of like life."

"OK," Mekial said, listening intently.

"If a wave's big, it could sweep me off my feet. And even if it wasn't, when the wave went back out, it would remove sand from around my feet and could make me unsteady."

"Are you saying you're scared?" Mekial asked.

"I'm not sure," Thom replied. "But who knows what might happen. Maybe there'll be a huge wave, like if everyone hates me. They might even make fun of me like Kevar. And

Lord Samiltun could find me," he said, his voice speeding up with anxiety. "He might try to kidnap me like Vern and Finn and make me do awful things. I'd never see my family or anyone again. Plus, if I develop new abilities, Rin and Sestra B won't be with me or even you. It could all go wrong."

"Thom, breathe," Mekial suggested. "Doesn't Medelin tell us to do that when we face a bigger or more skilled opponent?"

"Oh, yeah," Thom uttered, taking a few deep breaths.

Mekial looked out at the crashing waves. "First, I think you are scared. That's OK because you don't know what's going to happen. With the Samiltun guy, you're more prepared and stronger, don't you think?"

"Yeah."

"Now, I can't predict the future," Mekial said. "But it seems like you're all focused on bad stuff. What about the good stuff that might happen? Look out at the ocean. Didn't we have a great time chasing those fish? We didn't plan to do it. And it was fun, wasn't it?"

"Uh, huh."

"Couldn't amazing adventures be waiting for you at the Acadium? Maybe the waves are an invitation to go with the flow and be open to whatever comes."

"You sound like Sestra B," Thom commented, smiling.

"You're not the only one who's been called an old soul."

"I wish you were coming with me."

"I know," Mekial said. "But I'm headed to the Guard Academy in the fall."

"Yeah. And you'll be great there unless someone takes you off guard," Thom smirked, shoving her a little.

"See, you couldn't knock me down," she declared confidently.

Dissatisfied with his failed attempt, Thom pushed her again, leading to a wrestling match. It ended with them tumbling into the water, getting their hair matted with sand, and laughing hysterically.

"Thanks, Mekial," Thom said as they returned to their blanket.

You're welcome."

"That reminds me of something Sereh told me," Thom added.

"What?"

"She said the spiritual path isn't all about seriousness. It must include play and fun."

"I hadn't thought about that," Mekial admitted. "I need a guardian angel."

"You already have one," Thom assured her. "Ask the angel to send you a sign. I got a white feather."

"Oh, yeah. You showed me yours a while back, along with your weird triangular thing," Mekial responded.

"I did," Thom replied. "How about if we enjoy the rest of the afternoon, not trying to figure anything out?"

"Good idea."

Thom rose at dawn the following morning and had a quick breakfast to get to the monastery early. Last night, there'd been a downpour. The patter of rain on the roof had lulled Thom to sleep. Riding through the streets now, they glistened with the fresh wash. The air smelled of wet earth as he navigated Crescent around puddles of water in the road. This would be the last time he rode him. Patting Crescent's neck, Thom said, "You've been a good companion. Thanks for breaking free when I was kidnapped. You were brilliant. You helped Rin and everyone find me."

Crescent whinnied.

"I'm sorry you can't come with us when we leave. Rin told me you'd get a new home. But he wouldn't tell me with whom. Maybe Mik or the new healer. I'm sure you'll be treated well." Since they were sailing to Docha-leigh tomorrow, Thom would be riding Apollo back to the shop at the end of the day. He'd been a little worried that Apollo wouldn't be able to handle the long days of riding that was soon to come. But Maden had assured him Apollo could handle it. Rin would return Abu to the monastery today and ride Crescent back instead of him this afternoon.

Arriving at the monastery, Thom curried Crescent, settling him in his stall. He then walked over to Apollo. "Hello, dear one," he said, hugging him around the neck. "We'll be traveling on a ship tomorrow back to my home. I hope you adjust to the ship's movement. My stomach wasn't too happy at the start of our voyage here."

Maden walked up to him. "Reminding Apollo about his upcoming trip, I hear."

"Yes. Will Fanta really be OK without Apollo?" he asked again.

"Oh, yes," she replied. "She's had other colts and fillies who no longer live nearby. And once again, Apollo will be fine, given the bond you have."

"Good," Thom replied, sighing with relief.

After spending time with Apollo, Thom walked to Sestra B's office.

"Good morning, Thom," she called out as he knocked on her door.

"Good morning, Sestra B," he answered when he entered. "Did you sense me, like I can sometimes do?"

"No. Given the time, I expected you. "We're going to meet here in my office, just the two of us, for our last session."

"OK," he replied, settling into his usual chair across from her.

"Let's start with a meditation. Then, we'll check your shields and gifts."

"Great job," Sestra B complimented him a while later. "Your shielding is impressive. You're quickly able to change the texture and thickness without much thought. Your fake shield is strong enough to deceive anyone except those with the strongest gifts. I'm certain Samiltun would be fooled if you ran into him."

"Rin, Jeshua, and Rel said the same thing."

"I wouldn't worry too much," she assured him. "You can still work on your shields at the Acadium."

"I will," Thom assured her. He also hoped that his looks had changed enough from four years ago that Samiltun wouldn't recognize him.

"As to your physical healing gift, it's on par with strong practitioners. The Acadium healers should be able to teach you skills that will improve your use of it."

"Thanks," Thom replied.

"Regarding your spirit-healing gift, we've already explored all the abilities that have emerged thus far. I suspect that others will arise as you continue working with it. That's why it was important for you to continue recognizing the relationship between your intuition and your intention. As you inevitably face a new situation and your intuition identifies a need, that becomes an intention from which a new ability could arise."

Thom furrowed his brow. "Rin said the Acadium might not have someone like you on staff who can work with me. How do I keep working on it?"

"Perhaps there will be a teacher who can work with unusual gifts," Sestra B suggested. "I did check with the abbotess, and she confirmed there's a chapel staffed by our community in the capital. Still, I recommend you turn the question over to your divine team."

"Good idea," he agreed. "Sometimes, I still get afraid things won't work out. My divine team keeps reminding me to trust them and not get caught up in the details."

"You have many examples of times that it did," Sestra B reminded him. "Think of what happened with Apollo and your worry about leaving him behind."

"Yeah," Thom said. "I still can't believe you all gifted him to me."

"You underestimate your impact on our community, Thom," Sestra B said.

"I don't know," he mumbled.

"We do," Sestra said. "Our time is almost up. It's truly been an honor working with you these last few years. You've been an adept student. You usually didn't resist when I asked you to try something that struck you as odd."

"Usually," Thom said, grinning.

"Like Lebrim said, you are a holy one and are certain to be a blessing to all you meet," she told him.

Thom lowered his head, turning a little red.

"I'm glad you still blush," Sestra B remarked. "At its root is your humility. With gifts like yours, some people can become arrogant. But you're yourself. One other thing. Always remember to be grateful for all you have, even for the challenges you face. They're opportunities to learn, expand, and remember that no one is perfect."

"Yes, Sestra B. Thank you for how much you helped me. I'm gonna miss you," he said, his voice breaking. "Can I hug you?"

"Of course. And I'll miss you too, but I'm sure we'll meet again. Now, off with you, young man," Sestra B stated gruffly. "I have other students to attend to."

Turning back after opening Sestra B's door, Thom saw her wiping tears from her cheeks, matching those falling from his eyes. Next up, he had his last session with Medelin. Goodbyes were hard.

Walking into the training yard, he found Mekial standing in the grassy area holding two staves. It was the rainy season, so Medelin would soon move training into the salle. He was glad his last one was outside.

Mekial called out, "Medelin suggested we spar. He said I was getting sloppy. As if."

When they finished an extended match, both were sweating.

"You're very good, Thom," Mekial commented. "I don't like to admit it, but you're even better than me."

"Thanks," he replied.

"I'm going to wash up and head over to the refectory to help set up for your final supper," Mekial said. "I hate saying that. Who will I complain to when Budaj is being a pest?"

Thom shook his head before saying, "I didn't think I would ever have a close friend after my friend Davi moved away. Thank you. And it's been fun annoying your brother."

"Yeah, it has. Anyway, I'd better go. I'll see you soon," Mekial replied. "I think Medelin wants to talk with you."

Turning around, Thom saw Medelin standing by the storage bins for the training equipment. "Can I wash up first?" he asked.

"Please," Medelin answered.

Like Sestra B, Medelin shared with him how much Thom had improved since they started working together. He did point out areas where he needed more training, like defending his right side. Medelin was correct since Thom was naturally left-handed. Walking from the yard, he saw Rin coming out of the infimarium.

"Everything good in there?" Thom asked.

"Yes," Rin replied. "Thankfully, there were no patients. Shall we enter the refectory together?"

"Let's," Thom replied, stepping into the room to a loud chorus of "jolly good fellows."

In the late afternoon, Thom headed to the stables. Rin was going to spend another hour with Lauret and Rafi. He'd ride back to the shop by himself. Saying goodbye to everyone had been emotional. They all wished Thom well and hugged him. They had become part of his family. Mekial hugged him, too, even though she would ride with them to the ship tomorrow. With all the gifts he'd received, including an aquamarine crystal Sestra B gave him, which was supposed to help calm someone and bring clarity, he was glad he'd brought extra bags.

"Do you have room in your bags to fit everything, Thom?" Maden said, walking up to him.

"I hope," Thom replied. "I need to find a way not to crush the chocolate biscuits and muffins Bea made for us."

"I can imagine," Maden said. "That was a large bag of chocolate bits that Awa gave you."

"Yeah," Thom said with a big grin. "I'm going to be careful with them, too. Thank you again for letting me take Apollo with me."

"You're very welcome," she replied. "Given your strong connection, Apollo would have a hard time without you."

"Thanks again, Maden," he said, giving her a final hug before mounting Apollo. After passing through the monastery gates, he stopped. Looking back, he said, "I'm sure going to miss this place. I know you will, too, Apollo, especially your dam. I missed my Mam when I left home."

Chapter 55

The rising sun peeked through the window of his room. Thom hadn't slept well last night. His thoughts about leaving and his emotions had swirled inside of him. Lying in his bed, he realized it was the last time he'd sleep in it. He was excited to be returning home, but it was still hard to leave people he had come to love: Mekial, Sestra B, and Medelin, most significantly. But Reyner, Maden, Lauret, Bea, and Lebrim, and even Budaj held a special place in his heart. Hearing Rin in the other room, he knew he'd better get up. Quickly getting dressed, he went into the front room.

"The porridge is still warm in the pot. I already ate," Rin told him. "After you finish, would you wash the pot and your dishes? We're leaving them for Healer Lule."

"Sure," he answered, smelling the comforting scent of cinnamon in the porridge.

"Are you all packed, including your treasure jar and the angel statue?"

"Yes, they were the last things I slipped into my bags."

"Good."

The driver and cart for their belongings arrived, and soon after, Mekial. Thankfully, Rin's prediction that it wouldn't rain held true. Carrying his stuff to the cart in the rain wouldn't have been fun.

"Good morning, Mekial," Thom greeted her as he loaded his first bag.

"Good morning, Thom," she replied. "Do you need help with the rest of your stuff?"

"Please," Thom said. "Rin's inside. He can tell you what to get. By the way, did you come from the monastery?"

"No, from home," Mekial replied. "I'll go this afternoon."

Thom returned to the shop and emerged with his second bag. Dropping it into the cart, he heard a loud clunk. He knew it was his Demba's Chronicles series. He had persuaded Rin to let him take all seven books. They were very special to him. He and Mekial had even run into the author, Nadia Sanneh when they visited a bookstore in the capital two months before. They were scanning the shelves in the fantasy section to see if another book in the series had been released when Nadia entered. He and Mekial gushed when they introduced themselves and told her how much they loved her series. Curious about Thom's fluency in Glakkadian and his presence in Glakkadeth, Thom shared some of his story, as did Mekial. Intrigued, she hinted that her next book, which she was close to finishing, might include characters based on them.

When they finished loading the cart, Rin asked Mekial, "Would you get Crescent from the stable?"

"Sure," Mekial replied. When she returned with him, she said, "I couldn't find his saddle or the other gear."

"That's because they were loaded into the cart already," Rin replied. "Mekial, for being a great friend to Thom and me, I'm giving you Crescent."

"What? No!" she protested. "I thought you were going to leave him for the healer."

"Oh, no," Rin replied. "She doesn't need one. Crescent is for you."

"Crescent always liked you," Thom assured her, "especially after all the treats you gave him."

"Thank you. But how are you getting to the quay?"

"I'll be riding in the cart with the driver, of course," he replied.

Before they knew it, they reached the quay, teeming with activity. The scent of salt and fish permeated the air, mingling with the sounds of bustling dock workers carrying goods from the nearby warehouse. Two ships were moored nearby. The second was the Bittaye Biashara. Thom saw Captain Musa and Nuala on the top deck and waved to them.

"I'll help you load your stuff, Thom," Nuala yelled. "I'll get a few others to help, too."

"Thanks," Thom shouted back.

After their belongings were transferred, she and Thom led Apollo onboard and into the structure on the top deck designed for housing animals. Along one wall were barrels of grain and stacks of hay, sufficient for the voyage and a trough for water. After brushing Apollo down and ensuring he was comfortably secured, Thom returned to the quay where Mekial stood with Rin and Captain Musa.

"Is Apollo all set?" Rin asked.

"Yes."

"Good. Let's depart," Captain Musa stated.

"I'll see you on board, Thom," Rin said, walking up the gangway with the captain.

Thom and Mekial looked at each other, knowing they had already said everything they needed to. After a long hug between them and kisses on each other's cheeks, wet with tears, Thom made his way up the gangway.

As the ship pulled out, Thom and Rin stood on deck waving goodbye to Mekial. Thom remained there until he could no longer see her. Heading to their cabin to unpack his belongings, he hoped their voyage would be easy.

Chapter 56

The return journey to Dridley went by swiftly. With favorable winds, Captain Musa reached the port in under five weeks. To Thom's delight, Khali awaited them at the dock and waved madly when they pulled in. During their few days there, he enjoyed spending time with her and her family. He discovered she now worked as an associate buyer at the trading store. Annan had taken over her cart business and started selling Timbu, too. Apparently, it had been an immediate hit. He learned that children even liked to dip their Twister into it.

The day before their departure, Rin secured space for themselves and Apollo on a flatboat headed northeast. The additional funds provided by Modu and Gallen were enough to cover the cost of the journey and convince the skipper to construct a temporary shelter for Apollo. The trip passed without incident. Thom devoted much of his time on deck grooming Apollo and sharing stories with him about Docha-leigh and his family. In between, he revisited the first book in the Demba's Chronicles series, which remained his favorite thus far. Ten days later, around mid-morning, they disembarked at a wharf about an hour from the Barrelsons' homestead. Rin purchased a second horse from a local trader.

When they arrived at the Barrelsons' place, Thom noted significant changes. A substantial clearing had been made in the surrounding woodland, expanding its footprint. The cottage was now twice its size and could no longer be characterized as a cottage. It still had green shutters but featured a shingled roof instead of thatching. The homestead boasted of a second barn, also with a shingled roof, and another smaller brown building, the purpose of which Thom couldn't determine.

"Let's dismount and see if we can find someone," Rin suggested.

Thom saw a boy exit the home as they led their horses closer. "Is that Rindo?" "He's taller, and his hair's a little darker. He'd be about seven, wouldn't he?"

"Yes," Rin agreed.

"Rindo," Thom called out. "Rindo!"

The boy glanced toward them with a puzzled look before coming closer. "I think I know you, but I don't know how."

Thom noticed Rindo held a piece of wood and a metal tool.

"We were here a few years ago when you were sick," Rin explained. "Thom helped you."

"Oh, yeah. You sorta feel familiar, too. Weird, huh."

"Not at all," Thom assured him.

"You saved me, didn't you?" he asked, giving Thom a hug.

By then, a woman had also come outside, calling, "Who is it, Rindo?" Walking closer, she exclaimed, "Oh my goodness, Healer Rin!" Turning towards one of the barns, she yelled, "Storen! Come here. We have guests! Storen!"

"I heard you the first time, Lida," Storen replied, stepping out from the newer barn, his head down and wiping his hands. "What do you mean we have guests? I already know your brother's here." Finally, he looked up. "Healer Rin. Is that you?"

"Yes," Rin replied.

Both he and Lida came closer and stared at Thom.

"But this can't be Thom!" Lida said.

"It's me," Thom answered.

"You've changed."

"You're over a foot taller, and you've put on weight and some muscle, I see," Storen commented.

"I was small when you first saw me," Thom admitted. "Plenty of food and physical training made the difference."

"Indeed," Storen answered.

"Come into the house," Lida said.

"I'll be there shortly. I need to put my tools back in the workshop," Storen said, walking toward the second building Thom couldn't identify.

Thom trailed behind Lida and Rindo as they entered the home. Rin was a step behind. Inside the spacious room, a sturdy gray-stone hearth was the focal point. Nearby, three padded brown chairs were arranged. In one of them sat a middle-aged man with a slightly receding brown hairline reading to a red-headed young boy nestled in his lap. Thom couldn't help but be drawn to the glint of gold rings on two of the man's fingers and a long silver chain around his neck, which the boy idly played with. Their quality reminded him of the jewelry Mik sometimes wore back in Glakkadeth.

"Thom and Rin, I'd like you to meet my brother, Padraic Byrne. He's a …"

Rin interrupted her, "Paddi?"

"Rin, what are you doing here?" Paddi asked. "Wait, Lida, is Rin the healer who came with the young lad a few years ago and saved Rindo?"

"Yes," she replied. "As you can see, the young lad is almost a teenager. Aren't you, Thom?

"Nice to meet you, sir," he said, shaking his hand.

"Paddi's a textile merchant who lives in the capital," Rin explained. "He's also a member of the trading council and a friend of the king and queen."

"Correct," Paddi said. "And Thom, please call me Paddi."

"Thank you, Paddi," Thom replied.

"Would you like some cider to warm you up on this cool morning?" Lida asked.

"That would be lovely," Rin replied.

"Yes, please," Thom said.

"Go ahead and make yourselves comfortable at the table," she said, pointing to the large table across the room from the hearth.

"Me, cider," the young boy on Paddi's lap demanded.

"Yes, Benno," Lida said. "Rindo, would you settle Benno on his chair and pull it up to the table."

"Yes, Mama," Rindo replied.

Thom observed Rindo carefully setting down the tool and piece of wood he had held on a small table before turning his attention to Benno.

"I think we still have warm blueberry muffins that Benno didn't gobble up," Lida added.

They were sitting at the table when Storen joined them.

"I poured a mug of cider for you, too, Storen," Lida said.

"Thanks," Storen said, sitting at the head of the table.

"What brought you here?" Lida asked.

"Is Rindo healthy?" Thom asked, his brow furrowed.

"Oh, yes," Storen assured him.

Thom sighed with relief, his tense shoulders easing as he reached for a muffin. Biting into it, he appreciated its sweet taste.

"However," Storen continued, "he's developed some unusual abilities."

"To answer your question, Lida," Rin replied, "We're here because Thom insisted we see Rindo."

"You did?" Rindo asked, sitting across from Thom.

"Yeah," Thom admitted. "I wanted to make sure you were OK after I healed you. It turns out that what I did wasn't something healers can usually do."

"What you described back then did seem unusual," Storen admitted. "When we told our local healer, she said she hadn't heard anything like it."

"I'm not surprised. I learned that my ability to see Rindo and his twin's spirit is part of my spirit-healing gift. But I did use my physical healing gift, too."

"Spirit healing?" Paddi said. "I've never heard of that."

"Neither had I," Rin admitted. "We learned its name in Glakkadeth."

"Glakkadeth? That's a good distance to travel," Storen commented.

"It was," Rin agreed. "But Sestra Berbera at the local monastery was able to train him."

"Storen," Thom said, "what abilities?"

"Rindo," Storen prompted his son.

"I like to carve," Rindo said.

"Nice. Was that a carving I saw you with earlier?

"Yeah."

"Maybe you can show me some pieces you've finished."

"Sure, I'll go get them," Rindo answered.

While Rindo was gone, Storen explained, "We know that carving isn't unusual in and of itself, but Rindo started carving within a month of you saving him."

"But he wasn't quite three years old," Thom said, his eyes wide.

"Exactly," Storen replied. "Rindo had found my whittling knife and carved a cow with it. I was shocked at how lifelike it was. I took the knife away, of course. But, after a week of insisting he knew what he was doing, I told him to show me. And he did."

"He's a natural," Lida added. "It's almost like he's carved before. He even talks like he's been working with wood for many years. It's like he thinks he lived another life."

"I think maybe I have," Rindo responded, coming back into the room with a wooden box. "But I don't know how."

Thom looked at Rin, who shook his head.

"Not to interrupt," Rin stated. "Might I ask about your beliefs?"

"Sure," Storen replied. "It seems like a strange question, though. Our family follows the Iosan faith for the most part."

"What Storen means is that we believe the basic tenets about Iosa and God," Lida added. "After you healed Rindo, we talked to an elder, who denied that such a thing was possible. He insisted Rindo got better on his own. We knew that wasn't what happened, and we started questioning some of the elders' teachings."

"My parents raised me in the same faith, Storen and Lida," Thom confessed. Glancing at Rin again, who nodded this time, he continued, "Like you, my parents said they became disenchanted with our local elders, as they would say, for similar reasons. The thing is, some people believe humans have lived more than one lifetime, like the Aaliswan faith in Glakkadeth."

"I've never heard of that," Lida commented. "Is that even possible?"

"Some believe it is," Thom responded. "Rindo could be right."

All were silent until Rindo asked, "Do you want to see my carvings?"

"Please," Thom replied.

Reaching into the box, he pulled out a carving of a cow. "This was my first. It has a few bite marks because Benno chewed on it when he was a baby."

"Beautiful," Rin commented.

As Rindo retrieved more, he explained, "Ten of these are for you, Uncle Paddi, to take to the capital." Besides other cows, there were sheep, horses, and a small two-wheeled cart.

"Can I look at the cart?" Thom asked.

"Sure," Rindo replied, handing it to him.

The cart was very impressive. Its smooth wheels were attached to the cart with a wooden dowel. Two long pieces of wood stuck out from the front with holes at their ends. Taking the cart back, Rindo placed it on the table and put a horse in front of it. Then, taking a piece of twine from the box, he threaded it through the holes and around the horse.

"I need to add something around the horse's neck for the twine," Rindo explained. "But look, the horse can pull the cart now," he said, demonstrating.

"Wow," Thom exclaimed. "The cart's amazing."

"That's the second cart I created," Rindo informed. I gave the first to Benno, but our cow stomped on it."

"Ax-dent," Benno said softly, fidgeting.

"I'll make you another," Rindo assured him.

"When Rindo first started carving," Storen interjected, "he gave a few to neighbor children whose parents couldn't afford toys."

"I wanted them to have nice things to play with," Rindo said.

"That's very generous of you," Rin told him.

Thom decided to check Rindo's auric colors and saw white for innocence, green for generosity, and bright purple for spiritual sensitivity. He also sensed that Rindo was fully aligned with his divine being. That's incredible. Maybe he'd accidentally opened a channel between Rindo and his higher self.

Since the others were still examining Rindo's carvings, Thom checked in with his divine team, mind-speaking to them. *Did I do that?*

Yes.

Is that you, Archangel Metatron? Thom asked.

Yes, again.

I'm not supposed to, am I? I mean, it should have opened naturally.

Correct, Thom, Metatron replied in his mind. *But before you start getting hard on yourself, remember that you didn't do it on purpose. You weren't trained, and neither you nor Rin knew what your gift was. It's had some interesting results with Rindo.*

Thanks, Metatron, Thom replied, returning his attention to those in the room.

"Rindo, would you wrap up your carvings and put them in my room?" Paddi asked. "I have space for them in my saddle bags." Looking at Rin and Thom, he said, "I brought a few back to the capital from my last visit here six months ago. A toymaker jumped at the chance to sell them."

"Oomgh," Lida suddenly groaned.

"Are you OK, luv?" Storen asked.

"I'm fine," Lida replied. "It's the little one. We're expecting our third child. It's been very active since Rin and Thom came in. It kicked again, almost as if it wanted our attention."

"Congratulations, Lida and Storen," Thom replied. Thom hadn't noticed Lida was pregnant under her loose clothing.

"Twin," Rindo said, pointing to his mother.

"Are you expecting twins, sis?" Paddi asked.

"Not that I'm aware of," she answered.

"My twin," Rindo stated more firmly.

"Rindo's said that before," Storen admitted. "He's become quite sensitive to people, knowing when someone is near, for example, and even when something's going to happen. That's another of his abilities."

"Interesting," Rin replied. "Perhaps he has some emerging gifts. If Rindo shows this more, send a letter to Paddi, and he'll pass it on to me."

"Of course," Paddi confirmed.

Rin seems to know Paddi well, Thom thought. He wondered if it was through COM?

"What are you thinking, Rin?" Storen asked.

"Thom might have inadvertently opened a channel to a gift in Rindo," Rin explained.

"I wondered the same thing," Thom said, "given Rindo's comment about Lida's pregnancy." Turning to Lida and Storen, he said, "You know that when I helped Rindo, I sensed into his spirit and his sister's."

"You mentioned that, yes," Storen agreed.

"Would it be OK if I sensed into the little one you're pregnant with, Lida?" Thom asked.

Thom felt Lida's mixed emotions of uncertainty, fear, and hope.

Lida looked at Storen, who nodded.

"Go ahead," Lida said.

Closing his eyes and grounding himself, Thom lowered his fifth shield. He immediately knew the little one was Rindo's female twin. Opening his eyes, he announced, "Rindo's correct. Your little one's spirit is that of his twin, and she's female too."

"Truly?" Lida replied, her head tilted upward.

"How can this be?" Storen asked.

"I don't know," Thom said. "But it seems that Rindo's twin was determined to be born into your family."

Lida and Storen started crying.

"Were you using your spirit-healing gift?" Paddi asked.

"I was, along with my physical healing gift," he answered. "My physical-healing gift allows me to sense a person's spirit and auric energy. My spirit-healing gift enabled me to determine if her spirit was Rindo's twin."

Paddi sat there stunned, uttering, "That's some gift."

"Would you please excuse us?" Storen asked everyone.

"Certainly," Rin said.

Lida and Storen went upstairs, and they heard a door close.

"Thom," Rin said. "Would you mind if Paddi and I talked privately?"

"No," Thom replied. "Rindo, would you and Benno show me around? This place is much larger than when we last visited."

"OK," Rindo said.

At Lida's invitation, Rin and Thom decided to stay with the Barrelsons for two days. This allowed Lida and Storen to ask more questions and allowed Thom to spend time with Rindo and Benno.

The following day, Thom told them he hadn't detected anything unusual in Benno's spirit, much to the Barrelsons' relief. But he also explained that gifts didn't typically emerge until children were around twelve.

In the afternoon, Rin and Paddi sought out Thom.

"Thom," Rin said, "Paddi's agreed to be your Acadium sponsor."

"Oh, really. Thanks, Paddi," Thom said.

"You're welcome," he replied. "I have a large home. When you get to the capital, you can come by and meet two of my children and choose a room."

"Thanks again," Thom said.

"No problem," Paddi said. "And, if truth be told, I'm looking forward to seeing what other adventures life might bring you, given those I've heard about."

"Rin told you some of them, huh?" Thom said, wondering even more whether Paddi was part of COM.

The next morning was overcast and cool. Thom retrieved his light jacket from his saddlebags, already attached to Apollo's saddle, and was greeted by chittering.

"Good morning to you, Mr. Squirrel," he addressed the furry creature facing him in the home's backyard. "I didn't mean to interrupt your nut gathering."

The squirrel chittered once more before swiftly grabbing a nut in his mouth and scampering into the woods.

"Are you ready for our ride, Apollo? We'll be leaving soon." He was confirming that everything was secure when he received another greeting.

"Hi, Thom," Rindo called out, standing nearby.

"Oh, Rindo. I didn't see you there," he replied.

"I made you something," he answered, handing him a carving of a horse.

"Is this Apollo?"

"Yeah."

"Rindo. It's beautiful." Showing it to Apollo, Thom said, "Rindo carved this of you, sweet one."

Apollo whinnied.

"He likes it, too. How did you carve it so quickly?" he asked.

"I can carve fast. But I stayed up late last night," Rindo answered.

"You have a gift."

"Um... thank you," he mumbled, staring at his shoes and shuffling his feet. "And thank you for coming to see us again. Mama was kinda scared about Benno 'cause of me. Oh, and thank you for saying she's gonna have my twin."

"You do know, Rindo, she won't be your twin," Thom warned, "since she'll be much younger than you."

"I know, but I still feel like she is," he responded.

"I understand," Thom replied. "I need to finish rearranging my saddlebags to make room for your gift. I'll come back inside in a minute."

After exchanging goodbye hugs with the family, Rin and Thom mounted their horses.

"Thanks for the pasties," Thom said to the gathered family. "I'm still full from the great breakfast, but..."

"Yes, I know, Thom," Lida remarked. "Growing boys are always hungry."

Thom nodded and smiled.

"See you in Aegisa!" Paddi called out.

Chapter 57

A few weeks passed, and it was early afternoon when they neared Thom's home. It was a beautiful summer's day, warm but not too humid. Thankfully, on this return trip across Docha-leigh, they hadn't run into bandits.

"Rin, will you live in town while I stay with my family?" Thom asked.

"No," he replied. "I'm going to the capital. I have a few things to handle. Since our journey back here from Glakkadeth was quicker than I thought, I'll ride back here in five weeks. That should give you a good amount of time with your family. Then, we'll head to the capital and Paddi's home as discussed."

"You said Paddi would take me to the Acadium rather than you, didn't you?"

"Yes," Rin replied. "As your sponsor, he'll handle your introduction to the provost."

"OK," Thom replied. "Before we get to my home, I wanted to tell you that I don't want to say anything about my kidnapping. It would terrify Mam, given how much she hated me leaving."

"That's for you to decide, Thom," Rin replied. "But don't rule out sharing it in the future."

Riding up to his home, Thom noticed an extension and a new roof had been added. Two modest-sized flower gardens of freesia, roses, and jasmine were located on both sides of the path to the pottery, their colors vibrant against the mostly blue sky. He could smell their floral scent.

Rin and Thom dismounted and approached.

"Hello, Macirdans!" Thom called out. When there was no response, he called out again, his voice cracking. Thom's voice had started changing before they left Glakkadeth, much to his dismay and the amusement of the ship's crew.

"If you're looking for the potter, he's next door," a female voice yelled from inside the house.

Is that Meli? Thom wondered. Her voice sounds deeper.

"Meli! You know you don't greet people that way," he heard his mother reprimand in a clipped tone. "Go out and escort the customer, now."

When Meli opened the front door, she was wiping her hands on a green apron. "I'll show you to the pot..." she started to say. "Thom?" Meli said in shock. "Oh my Deu, Thom!" she shouted, running up to him and giving him a hug.

Hearing Meli's shout, Thom's mother dashed out the door, her tunic speckled with bits of flour. "Thom!" she exclaimed. "Uric! Uric! Come. Thom's home." Running up to him, she shoved Meli out of the way to envelop him in kisses and a hug.

"Ouch, Mam!" Meli said, picking herself off the ground.

"We didn't know when we'd see you again," his mother stated, her eyes filling with tears. "Let me look at you," she continued. She placed her hands on both sides of his face and said, "You've grown. You're taller than me." Noticing his scar, she asked, "What's this?"

"Oh, it's nothing," he replied.

"Look at his muscles," Meli interrupted, reaching out and squeezing his biceps.

"Yeah, I had some training," he admitted.

"It's good to see you, too, Healer Rin," his mother added.

Soon after, Thom's father arrived, along with Redik and Kavan. Redik wore a vest over his tunic, which was not something that he'd wear in the pottery. Kavan's trousers were covered in dirt, a testament that he had been doing some gardening.

"We've missed you, son," his father said as he hugged him, looking the same as he always did, with streaks of clay smearing his protective apron.

"I missed you all too," he said, looking at them and noticing Reta, who had grown a few inches since he last saw her, coming toward them holding the hand of a blond-haired toddler.

Seeing Thom staring, his mother looked around. Leaning down and picking up the toddler, she said, "This is your sister, Alli. Alli, this is your brother, Thom. Give him a hug."

Alli squirmed in her mother's arms to get away and started crying.

"It's OK, Mam," Thom replied. "Alli doesn't know me. Hopefully, she'll get to know me while I'm here."

"Are you back for good?"

"Um. No," Thom replied. "I'll be here for five weeks. Then I'm going to the Acadium."

"The Acadium," Redik replied with awe. "How did you arrange that? Isn't it expensive?"

"Thom was granted a scholarship," Rin finally said. "He'll also have a sponsor, a merchant living in the capital who will keep an eye on him while he's there."

"But he won't be here," his mother remarked with sadness. "You can't go away again. You've been gone four years. And Lord Samiltun hasn't been around since we finished his commission."

"Mam," Thom interrupted. "I need to continue my studies. And I will be able to come home occasionally."

"Rin, I thought you were going to teach Thom healing," his mother complained.

"I did," Rin replied. "Thom's developing into an excellent healer. But it turns out I couldn't help him with his other gift. He was taught by a sestra in a monastery in Glakkadeth."

"Glakkadeth!" his father yelled. "You mean the archipelago that's south and west of Docha-leigh?"

"Yes," Rin replied. "I wonder if we can continue this conversation inside."

"Oh, certainly," Uric replied. "Redik and Meli, please take their horses to the stable."

"I'd like to take Apollo there myself," Thom interrupted. "But Meli could take Rin's horse."

"She can also show you our new stables," Uric responded.

"New stables," Thom commented as Meli led the way around the back of the house. "I noticed you guys built an extension."

"Yeah," she replied. "Two years ago, we had a horrendous storm, and a tree crashed through the roof of our old stable. It was a blessing our horses weren't injured. When we built the new one, we made it bigger to hold a few more horses since Da's business had picked up. Da even hired another potter since Redik isn't here much."

"Why? Did he take up another trade?" Thom asked.

"No, he still works for Da. But he's more of a salesman now," Meli replied.

"That's why Redik was wearing a vest."

"Yes. He wants to look professional, he says. I don't know why he's wearing it now since he's home. Anyway, Redik takes pieces of Da's work to other shop owners in towns who sell them. He also leaves pamphlets in case people are interested in commissioning pieces. So, Redik's often on the road."

"And he doesn't mind traveling?" Thom asked.

"No. Redik loves it. He's even been to the capital. Da's had a few commissions from there, too."

"If Redik plans to come to the capital again, I'll tell him to visit me at the Acadium. And maybe you can come with him sometime."

"I'd like that."

"By the way, do you still add designs to some of Da's pieces?" Thom asked.

"Once in a while," she replied. "A few months after you left, I started painting. And I love it. I play with geometric shapes and repetitive patterns. They kind of mesmerize and transform the viewer."

"Mesmerize and transform. You still like using big words," Thom said, smiling. He recalled that Sestra B had told him that Archangel Metatron, a member of his divine team, was known for a sacred cube composed of the same shapes representing creation. Given Meli's description, Thom wondered if Metatron somehow inspired her.

"Indubitably," she responded with a large grin.

Laughing, Thom added, "You sound passionate about your art."

"Oh, I guess I am. When I paint, it feels like I'm transported to a place full of light and possibilities," Meli agreed, her face exhibiting an unearthly glow. "I even sold a few paintings in town. I can show you some pieces I'm working on."

"I look forward to it," Thom replied. Painting sounded like her calling.

"You know, Thom," Meli continue, "I wasn't kidding about your muscles. You're bigger than when you left. If Kevar was still around, he wouldn't have the nerve to bully you."

"What?" he replied. "You knew?"

"Me, Mam, and Da," she answered. "We were sorry that happened. But we didn't say anything because you always tried to hide it."

"Thanks for telling me. You mentioned Kevar isn't around."

"Yeah," she replied. "They moved away about a year after you left. I say good riddance. The whole family was too big for their britches."

Meli led them into a stable with eight stalls. Four were occupied. He recognized two of the horses. He assumed the others belonged to Redik and the potter his Da hired. Meli pointed Thom to one stall while she led Rin's horse to another.

After settling the horses, Thom asked, "Do you want to meet Apollo?"

"Yes."

Moving to Apollo's head and making room for Meli, he introduced, "Apollo, meet my sister Meli. Meli, this is Apollo."

Apollo whinnied and blew into her hair.

"Amazing," she said. "He doesn't even know me."

"But he knows me very well. I helped with his birth and trained him. He understands he can trust anyone who I trust."

"It sounds like you were busy when you were away."

"I was," Thom replied. "Let's go in. I'm sure everyone will want to hear about it."

"Thom and Meli slipped into the house through the newly added wing. Inhaling deeply, he couldn't help but sigh; the air carried a comforting blend of freshly baked bread, the lingering fragrance of soap, and unmistakable hints of rosemary and eucalyptus—likely traces of his Mam's healing work. Thom was home. He wondered if she still made the disgusting burdock root tea she forced him to drink when he was younger.

Pointing to the first door on the right, Meli said, "That's Mam's healing room. It's much bigger than her old one." Walking further down the hallway, she said, "My room has the open door. Reaching it, she quickly closed it and said, "Um... I'll show you tomorrow."

As they entered the front room, Thom noticed everyone gathered around the familiar long, dark wooden table. He couldn't help but wonder if his initials were still etched on its underside—a secret remnant of his early writing venture. Among those seated, he spotted a slender young woman with reddish-brown hair pulled back into a ponytail. She must be the new potter.

"Thom," his father said, "this is Brigid. We hired her last year. She lives down the road with her parents."

"Nice to meet you, Brigid," Thom replied.

"Nice to meet you, Thom," she said in return.

"Hurry up and sit down," Kavan demanded. "Healer Rin wouldn't tell us much until you got here."

Thom's father sat at one end of the table, and his mother, holding Alli, sat at the other. Reta, Kavan, Meli, and Rin sat along one side. Brigid sat next to Redik along the other, close together.

"Where are Deena, Rian, and Dana?" Thom asked. "Rin, Dana is Deena and Rian's daughter."

"They have a second daughter now, Liviana. We call her Liv," his mother explained. "She's almost three."

"I'm sorry I missed her birth, too," Thom said. "What about them and Bedum and his wife?"

"Deena and Rian still live one town over. Bedum and his wife, Saoirse, also live there. Redik will ride there tomorrow. I'm sure they'll come by in a day or two."

"Good. I look forward to seeing them," Thom said. "How was Bedum's wedding?"

"It was nice," she replied. "I'm sorry you missed it."

"Me too," Thom agreed. He sat down next to Redik, nudging him and giving him a wink.

Redik smiled.

"OK," Thom said. "I'm seated. You can continue, Rin."

"Why don't you take over?" he suggested.

"What do you want to know?" Thom asked.

"Everything," Kavan demanded.

Thom shared about his last four years, starting with the day they first rode out.

"You were really captured by bandits," Kavan said. "Weren't you scared?"

"I was," he admitted. "But we were fine, Mam. Rin helped us escape, and after that, he began teaching me self-defense."

"I taught Thom the basics," Rin explained.

"It felt like more at the time," Thom smirked, thinking of some of the aches and bruises he'd gotten after sparring with Rin. "When we were on the ship to Glakkadeth, some sailors taught me, too. And when we got there, Brother Medelin, a monk at the monastery, trained me."

"A monk trained you," his father interjected, raising his eyebrows. "That's not like any religious elder I know."

"Yeah," Thom replied. "He was tough. Some days after training, Mekial and I were ready to collapse."

"Wait," Meli said. "Mekial? Who was he?"

"Mekial's a girl," Thom corrected. "She helped me learn Glakkadian. And I taught her Dochalan."

"Ooh. Was she your girlfriend?" Kavan remarked, making kissing noises.

"No. We're only friends," Thom said.

"They train girls too?" his father asked.

"Yes, and she's really good. Better than me by a lot. She wants to be a guard for the Prezdan of Glakkadeth."

"That's different from here," Brigid said. Some people still say it's shameful when girls do the same work as boys. Mam's a blacksmith, but she's even better than Pa."

"Oh, that's awful," Thom replied. "Mekial's Ma is a blacksmith in Glakkadeth. She's highly respected for her craft."

"I hope it will change for my Mam's sake and mine," Brigid admitted.

"Rin," Winni interjected. "You mentioned you couldn't help Thom with his other gift. What is it?"

"Spirit healing," he replied. "Sestra Berbera at the monastery was able to identify it. It's even much stronger than Thom's physical-healing gift."

"Lebrim, a postulant there, first identified it," Thom said, still feeling sad about his death.

"What's spirit healing?" Winni asked. "I've never heard of it."

"Nor had I," Rin admitted. "Briefly, Thom can see deeply into another person's spirit, including their auric colors. He can tell if the person's life choices align with their higher purpose. Because Thom is fully aligned, his spirit emits energy that acts as a catalyst to encourage people to make good choices."

"What's a catalyst?" Reta asked.

"It's sort of like a spark to get a fire going?" Redik explained.

"I understand about a person's spirit and auric colors," his mother said. "I've begun to see colors too."

"Good," Rin replied. "I'm glad your gift is growing."

"But for the other," she continued, "do you mean Thom can control another person, like Samiltun tried?" she uttered in horror.

"Wait," Meli interrupted. "Samiltun? Wasn't he the lord who demanded you finish creating his pieces early."

"Yes," his father replied. "Samiltun tried to manipulate Thom and me to allow him to apprentice Thom. Rin told us that his intentions were criminal."

"Was that really why Thom had to leave suddenly?" Meli asked.

"It was," her father answered. "We didn't want to worry you."

Meli let out a frustrated 'Humph,' her tone dripping with displeasure.

"Back to your question, Winni," Rin resumed. "Thom theoretically could do that. But if he did, it would sever his alignment to his highest self, which I know Thom would never do."

Thom shook his head. "Rin's correct. Sestra B and my divine team taught me, and I believe that each person must find her or his own path. Since I'm fully committed to my purpose, I can't force anyone to behave in a certain way. All I can do is live my best self and be available to offer healing energy. I'm still trying to understand it. I do know my gifts are stronger when I remain aligned."

"Thom helped a former novice in the monastery in this very way," Rin added. "With his help, she realized her purpose was to be a sailor."

"Wait, your divine team?" his father asked. "What faith do these monks practice?"

"It's called Aaliswan," Thom said. "They believe in the One, who we call Deu. Iosa is called Jeshua. They also believe we've all lived many lifetimes. And, before we're born, people decide on their purpose."

"I think I've heard about that in the capital," Redik commented.

"And to answer your question, Da," Thom continued, "my divine team are divine beings who advise and guide me."

"Wow. This is too much," Kavan uttered.

"About this spirit-healing gift, Rin," his mother interrupted, "you said it was stronger than his physical-healing gift."

"Yes, Winni," Rin said. "I've never experienced a gift as strong as that one."

"Have you seen Thom use it other times?" she asked. "I'm trying to understand how it might be related to physical healing."

"The first time I experienced it was when Thom saved a young boy's life," Rin explained. "While he did use a bit of his physical-healing gift, it was mostly his spirit healing." Turning to Thom, Rin asked, "May I share the story?"

"Yes," Thom replied.

Rin told them about Rindo and his twin. He even shared their most recent visit with the Barrelsons.

"I don't know what to say," Winni replied, dumbfounded.

"I don't either," Uric agreed.

"What's important," Rin continued, "is that Thom's spirit-healing gift is still evolving. I'm newly formulating this, but when Thom intuits a need, his intention triggers a new ability to arise."

"Intuition and intention," Thom echoed. "Sestra B mentioned something like it in my last meeting with her. I didn't quite grasp it then, but it's starting to make sense now, especially considering how I healed Rindo and what happened with Nordin."

"Don't forget the dishonest traders and the fanatic arsonist you identified," Rin added. "It applies to that, too."

"Oh, yeah," Thom agreed.

"The spirit-healing ability also enables Thom to detect whether someone is lying or exaggerating," Rin explained.

"I'd better be careful what I say when Thom's here," Kavan mumbled.

"What did you say, Kavan?" his father asked.

"Um, nothing, Da," Kavan replied.

Thom remained silent, hiding a grin.

"Hold on," Meli said, "You're saying Thom dealt with dishonest traders and an arsonist?"

"Yeah," Thom confirmed. "Again, don't worry, Mam. I wasn't hurt or anything."

"I'm not sure that makes me feel any better," his mother replied.

"He did get a medal from Prezdan Modu of Glakkadeth and his husband, Gallen, for his service," Rin added.

"You got a medal," Kavan said. "Can I see it?"

"Sure, but not right now," he assured him.

"Um," Redik interrupted, "you said Prezdan Modu and his husband."

"Yes," Thom replied.

"Are same-gender couples common in Glakkadeth?" his father asked. "I know of places west of here, but I didn't think there were many."

"Yes, it's common. Here in Docha-leigh, there are a few places in the north, too," Rin replied. "But you're correct. There aren't many."

"Rin, you said Thom might exhibit other abilities depending on the situation," Winni asked.

"I did."

Turning to Thom, she said. "It sounds like that could be unsettling."

"It can be," he admitted, appreciating her question. "When it happens, I talk with Rin, Sestra B, and my divine team. I also write in my journal and meditate to help me get my head around it."

"It sounds like you're more religious than us," Redik commented, "except for Deena."

"Deena? What do you mean?" Thom asked.

"You know Mam and Da have had issues with some of the elders' teachings," Redik replied.

"Yeah," Thom replied. "That's why we didn't attend many services, even before I left."

"About a year and a half ago, Deena went in the other direction when an elder claimed she saved Dana's life."

"What?" Thom said with shock, "Dana almost died?"

"Yes," his mother replied. "She got very sick with a fever and became pale and weak. I tried various treatments, but nothing worked. When Dana became unresponsive, Deena went to the local chapel and asked the elders to help. One came, Elder Ouna."

Meli groaned. "She's awful. I had her in one of my religion classes a few years ago."

"Meli, please don't interrupt," her mother warned. "When the elder got to their house, she claimed evil spirits had attached themselves to Dana. She performed a ritual with water and a lot of hand waving and smeared mud mixed with ash all over her body."

"Rin, have you heard of anything like this?" Thom asked.

"No," he replied. "This doesn't sound like healing."

"There's more," his mother stated. "When she finished, the elder proclaimed Dana would get better soon and demanded that Deena and Rian donate most of Rian's carpenter commissions to her for the next four months. I pulled them aside and told them Ouna was a fraud. But they were desperate and wouldn't listen."

"What did they do?" Thom asked.

"Rian gave his word he'd pay," his mother explained. "That didn't stop the elder from warning them if they ever missed a payment, Dana would die. She also said they couldn't mention the money to the other elders. Rian worked himself into the ground, taking on extra non-carpenter jobs to get by."

"They didn't even have enough money for food," Meli added. "Most of the time, they ate here during those months. It was heart-rending. Dana did get better. But nothing we said to Deena could convince them Elder Ouna didn't perform a miracle. Da even tried to tell the head elder what she did, but he wouldn't listen, insisting Elder Ouna was faithful and honest."

"Did you find out if there was anything special in the mud, Winni?" Rin asked.

"There wasn't," she said. "I had wondered, too. I asked the elder what to do if we ran out. She said to dig it from the ground and get ashes from our hearth. I stayed with Deena and Rian a few days a week and did what I could. I also applied the mixture to Dana to placate Deena. I figured it wouldn't do Dana any harm."

"Deena and Rian were really upset!" Kavan added, his mouth turned down in a frown.

"They were," his mother confirmed. "It tore my heart out to see Dana struggling and what Deena and Rian endured. Now, Deena strictly follows what the elders teach. And she believes Elder Ouna is divinely touched. We avoid talking about it or her faith these days."

"I'm so mad," Thom said. "The elder used Dana's condition and Deena's desperation to steal from them."

"I agree," Rin stated, anger also evident in his voice. "Her behavior was counter to Iosan principles. I'm sure that's why she wanted to keep the so-called donation secret."

They all nodded grimly.

Breaking the silence, his mother said, "We've always been committed to encouraging you to develop your gifts. I must admit I still don't understand your spirit-healing gift, Thom. Do you think you could say something to Deena?"

"I don't know," Thom admitted. "She has to realize on her own that something's off about her beliefs and adoration of Ouna. I could ask her questions about her attitude, though."

"Thanks, "his mother said. "I do fear for you and your gifts. You might face people who dislike or distrust you because of it. But I know you must follow what's best for you."

"Thanks, Mam," Thom replied.

"I'd best tend to the dinner preparations," his mother told everyone. "It's nothing special: vegetable beef soup and bread. But it will be filling. Reta, please go to the garden and get more carrots and peppers?"

"Yes, Mam," Reta replied.

"Rin, of course, you'll be joining us for dinner," Uric stated.

"Yes, thank you," Rin answered. "Would you mind if I slept by your hearth tonight?"

"Oh," Winni replied. "You don't have a place in town? I thought you might set up your practice again."

"No," Rin answered. "I have some other work to attend to. I'll be leaving tomorrow morning. But I'll return in five weeks to take Thom to the capital."

"OK," Winni responded, shaking her head unhappily. "In that case, there's a bed in my healing room if you want to stay there."

"Thank you," Rin replied.

Thom watched his father get up and walk towards his parents' room. He decided to follow him. "Excuse me," he said to the others at the table.

"Da," Thom called out. "Can I ask you something?"

"Of course."

"When I left with Rin, I was worried Samiltun would come back and punish you when I wasn't here."

"Ah," his father replied. "Your Mam and I discussed it after you left. While we believed Rin when he said he was no longer interested in you, we thought we should be prepared. Just in case, we coached Redik to complain about you not being there to help when he returned. We decided I would respond by reminding Redik that you were delivering medicines. When Samiltun returned, I think our little act helped."

"I'm glad," Thom replied, relieved. "Thanks." Returning to the front room, he played with Alli for the next hour, intent on getting to know his baby sister.

Early the next morning, Rin said goodbye to everyone. "I'll see you in five weeks, Thom," he called out.

"Bye, Rin," he replied. It would be strange not seeing him every day.

Late morning the following day, Deena, Rian, and their two girls came by.

"Thom," Deena cried out. "Look how you've grown!"

"It's good to see you, Deena and Rian."

"Dana and Liv, this is your Uncle Thommy," Deena said, introducing him. "Dana, you might not remember him because you were two when he left."

"Nice to meet you," Dana replied.

Liv, who hadn't been born when Thom left, smiled bashfully.

"Girls, why don't you go see what Kavan and Alli are doing," Deena suggested. "Oh, by the way, Bedum and Saoirse should arrive before supper."

Thom summarized the last four years for Deena and Rian, telling them about his physical healing, weapons training, and work at the pottery. He didn't say anything about his spirit healing. But since Thom had promised his mother, he needed to think about what to say. Wanting to end the conversation, Thom told them a small lie, explaining he had promised to help Reta in the gardens.

Once outside, Thom found Reta trimming plants. "Do you need any help?" he asked.

"Sure," Reta replied. "I know you don't like it, but would you mind taking over weeding the vegetable garden? I started yesterday before you arrived. But I first wanted to plant flowers under the oak tree."

"Not at all," Thom replied. "And you're right, I still don't like weeding, but I know it's necessary."

"At least that part of you hasn't changed?" Reta replied with a smile.

"Yeah. I know. Many things happened to me while I was away." Thom agreed. "But look at you. You've grown. And the gardens are beautiful."

"Thanks. I love doing it," Reta replied. "I feel like I'm a part of nature. I do help Mam with her patients and work some in Da's pottery. But my heart's out here."

"It shows," Thom said. "You have a real gift. And by gift, I'm talking about the earth-sensing gift. I have a bit myself. But yours must be very strong. Maybe one day you'd go to the Acadium."

"I don't know," Reta replied.

For the next twenty minutes, Thom concentrated on his task. As he did, he thought about what he might ask Deena. He mind-spoke to Archangel Uriel: *I know you guide those looking for answers and bring light to those lost in their darkness. Thank you for giving me the words, and always for the highest good.* He had started working on the last row when Reta whispered.

"Don't look now, but I think Deena's looking for you."

Thom saw her coming around the side of the house.

"I think I know what she's going to ask you," Reta said.

"Me too," Thom replied.

"Thom, can we talk?" Deena asked.

"Sure," he answered, standing and wiping his hands on his trousers.

"Let's go further towards the back of the house," Deena suggested. "I don't know if you remember, but when you were a toddler, you wandered away from Mam one morning and came back this way. There's a wooden bench that Mam and Da put here a couple of years ago. Let's sit there."

Once seated, Thom said, "It's a nice view of the valley. What's up?"

"You mentioned you spent some time at the monastery."

"Yes, I did."

"Was their faith, Iosan?" she asked.

Thom knew this was coming. He didn't want to upset her, but he had to be honest. "No. They practice the Aaliswan faith."

"I don't know it. Did you tell them about the true faith?" Deena asked.

"What do you mean by the true faith?" he asked cautiously.

"The Iosan faith. That's what Elder Ouna calls it."

Thom sat there quietly, sensing her aura. He saw small areas of muddy pink, which Rin said could mean insecurity, confusion, or obsession. Thom hadn't checked the arsonist's aura in Glakkadeth, but Deena gave off some of the same energy. He doubted she'd be open to considering his questions. But Thom had to try. Best if he answered carefully. "I didn't. A few already knew about the Iosan faith."

"Did you try to convert the non-believers to the true faith?" she asked.

"No, Deena. People have a right to believe what they choose."

"Wait, you didn't say true faith. Don't you believe Iosan is the true faith?" she asked.

"No, I don't," Thom stated bluntly.

"I was going to ask you to go with me to the service tomorrow," Deena said. "No one else in our family goes. You're still Iosan, aren't you?"

"I don't know what my faith is," he responded. "I can tell you I feel closer to Deu and Iosa than ever. They're very special to me."

"Hmm, I don't know," Deena commented. "I will tell you that you must return to the Iosan faith. Your soul is in jeopardy if you don't."

"I'm sorry, Deena," Thom replied. "I don't believe that."

"You have to, Thom!" she insisted. "You don't know what you're saying. You're not even thirteen. I'm almost twice your age."

"I know I'm young, Deena. But I know in my heart and in my soul what's right for me."

"Are you saying people should believe what they want? That's crazy talk. No. You must listen to me."

"Actually, I don't," Thom replied. "I have to follow my calling and live out my purpose." *Guys, what do I do,* he asked his divine advisors.

"Your calling, how can you have a calling? You're not studying to be an elder."

"Deena, I love you as a sister," he said with sadness, "but I don't agree with you."

Ask how she's feeling.

How she's feeling? I'm not sure how that will help, but OK. "Deena, how are you feeling?"

"What does that matter?" she frowned.

"Please, Deena," he pleaded, still wondering why he was asking the question.

"I'm a little tired," she answered. "We got up early to get the girls ready to come here."

Ah, he thought. Now he knew what his team meant. "I'm sorry you're tired, but I'm not asking about your health. What are you feeling now, after all you've said?"

"I'm worried for you and what Deu will do to you," she replied.

Silent again, Thom reflected on Deena's concerns. She believed Deu was vengeful and waiting to catch him doing something wrong to condemn him. He used to believe that, too.

"Do something for me, Thom," she said. She pulled a well-worn prayer card from her pocket and handed it to him. "Elder Ouna gave it to me. Would you pray these words every day? Perhaps you'll realize the mistake you're making."

Thom read the prayers. It described Deu like he thought it would and called on humans to abase themselves due to their sinfulness. Looking at Deena, he said, "No, I won't pray those words. I will and do pray every day. But I don't believe in a Deu who is judgmental and condemning. And I don't believe humans have to throw themselves at Deu's feet to ask for mercy. Do you honestly think humans are such awful beings, and you're a sinful person?"

"Well, I try to be good," Deena replied, pausing. "You have to admit there are some terrible people who think only of themselves and don't care about hurting people."

"Yes, I know there are bad people," Thom admitted. He knew from personal experience. "Although, I also believe deep down they are good, and do those things because they've forgotten who they are, their blessed selves. And, by the way, Deu isn't out to get us either."

"You're wrong," Deena insisted. "Did those Aswan people tell you that?"

"The faith is called Aaliswan, Deena," he replied. "And no, if you look in the holy book, you will read that Iosa talks about Deu's love and understanding."

"Maybe, but Elder Ouna says we have to fear Deu," Deena stated.

"I know it's your choice to believe Elder Ouna and the Iosan faith because it makes sense to you. But it sounds like your faith in Deu centers on fear. Is that really how you want to live?"

"How else?" Deena responded. "The elder knows better than me."

Thom knew he couldn't say anything against the elder. "My teacher at the monastery, Sestra Berbera, told me their holy book had a similar phrase but realized it was a mistranslation from the original language in which the book was written. They eventually determined the correct word is respect or esteem."

"Well, she's not Iosan, and I don't know her," Deena replied dismissively.

Realizing there was nothing more he could say, he added, "I understand. As I said, it's your right to follow a faith that makes sense. That's your decision. And it's my decision to live a faith that makes sense to me. I'm sorry, Deena."

"You will be sorry," she said, standing up and walking away, her shoulders slumped.

Thom got up and went back to the garden. *I'm sorry, guys. I did the best I could.*

You did well. You planted seeds. Sometimes, that's all you can do.

Thanks, Thom replied, returning to weeding.

"How did it go?" Reta asked.

"As expected," Thom replied.

Reta nodded.

The weeks flew by. Thom rode Apollo almost daily, except when the weather was too hot and humid or rained. He longed for the drier air of Glakkadeth. Occasionally, he allowed Reta and Kavan to ride him in case long rides were in their future. Memories of the aches and pains from his early rides with Rin came flooding back all too easily. He did like being home. It felt comforting to slip back into a familiar routine. He spent half the morning working in the pottery and a few afternoon hours assisting his Mam with her patients. Nevertheless, he made sure to carve out time with Alli and his other siblings.

One evening, Thom chatted with his divine team from the bench overlooking the tranquil valley. *I'm heading to the Acadium soon,* he shared, with a mix of nerves and excitement evident in his belly. *I wonder if they'll like me? I hope they don't think I'm strange like the neighborhood kids think. The other day, I walked by some of them. One pointed at me and said something to the others, and they all laughed. I guess it wasn't only my size they didn't like. I know you'll be with me. I'll try to stay positive.* Sitting there, a memory tugged at his mind. He had the feeling something remarkable had happened here. He thought it might have occurred when Deena said she found him nearby as a toddler. But he wasn't sure.

The night before Rin was expected to return, Thom was writing about his upcoming trip when his mother approached him, sitting at the dining table.

"Do you want some tea?" she asked. "I have the kettle on."

"Yes, please," Thom said, continuing to write.

Setting a steaming cup before him, she said, "It's chamomile to help you get a good night's rest."

"Thanks, Mam," he replied.

"I also made you something else," she said, placing a basket in front of him covered with a cloth.

Removing the cloth, he whispered, "Are these..."

"Yes, ginger buns with lemon curd filling," his mother said, smiling. "I know it's not your birthday, but I missed four while you were away."

"Thanks, Mam. Oh, I forgot to thank you for giving Rin the recipe. At the inn where we stayed when I turned nine, he asked the cook to bake them. I didn't even think he knew it was my birthday."

"I made sure he did. I wanted you to know we were thinking of you. We had ginger buns on your birthday, too, and we all toasted you and hoped you were well."

"Oh, Mam," he replied, his voice breaking. "That means a lot."

"Rin gave you our gift, too, didn't he?"

"Yes. Thanks. It was funny that it was a book about a teenager on a ship."

"I hope you enjoyed it."

"I did," Thom assured her.

"Well, have a bun before it gets cold. I pulled them out of the oven before you came down."

Picking one up, Thom brought it to his nose and drank in its slightly spicy and sweet aroma." Taking a bite, he smiled and said, with his mouth full, "Mmff s'ill as ood as ev'r."

She smiled. Glancing at Thom's journal, she remarked, "I see you still use that."

"Yeah," he replied. "I don't write every day. Just when I have a new idea or something's on my mind, especially now that I chat with God, Jeshua, and my team daily."

"You said God and Jeshua are what they call Deu and Iosa in Glakkadeth?"

"Yes," Thom replied.

"And you hear back and get comfort from them?" his mother asked.

"Most times. They don't always answer immediately and often not directly." He decided not to mention that he didn't feel them soon after Lebrim died.

"That's nice," she said. "The elders never talk about chatting with Deu or Iosa. Can anyone do it?"

"Of course," Thom said. "When I started, it was mostly telling them about my struggles and feeling their support. The back and forth came later."

"Hmm. Maybe I'll try sometime."

They sat silent for a time, enjoying this private time together.

"Something else is different about you besides your height and muscles," his mother commented.

"What do you mean?"

"You were always more advanced than others your age by your intelligence," she said, "but hearing you talk about your experiences, I'd guess I'd say you're more settled."

She's right, he thought. He wondered if part of that was because he grounded himself first thing in the morning. He hadn't considered that.

"Healer Rin returns tomorrow, then," his mother said.

"Yes," Thom replied. "He'll probably want to get on the road sometime after breakfast."

"Are you sure you want to do this, Thom?" she asked, her voice breaking a little.

"Yes, Mam. I do. I have learned a lot these last few years but have more to learn."

"You've grown very wise."

"Thanks."

"I'm going to miss you," his mother said. "I've loved having you back, even if it wasn't long. You've been a great help to my patients. I'm sure you'll be a blessing to them in the Acadium."

"Jeshua tells me the same, but sometimes I still have doubts," he admitted.

"I know. That's part of being human. Doubts are the flip side of humility. They remind you that you can always learn more and to be grateful for what you have."

"Sestra B said something similar."

"Wise woman."

Rin arrived the next day, precisely as Thom had anticipated. The weather was clear and, thankfully, not humid. Thom was in his old alcove, packing the final items, when he caught Rin's call through his window. Quickly climbing from the loft and running outside, he greeted him, "Hi, Rin. It's good to see you."

"It's good to see you too."

Looking around to ensure no one else was nearby, Thom asked, "Did you get your...errands done?"

Rin cocked his head and said with a grin, "Yes. All but one. I'll finish that when we get back to the capital."

"Do you want to go inside and say hello to everyone while I get Apollo ready?" Thom asked.

"Sure. And thanks for presuming I'd want us to leave early today. You know me well."

"You're welcome."

When Rin and Thom were on their way, Rin asked, "How was your visit?"

"Oh. It was nice. Redik's probably going to get engaged next year. He even talked about possibly moving to the capital to open a shop to sell Da's pottery."

"Interesting," Rin replied. "Any difficulties?"

"Mostly no," Thom replied.

"Say more," Rin insisted.

"My sister, Deena."

"Ah. I expected that, given what your family said," Rin replied. "What happened?"

"Basically, she said I was going to hell if I didn't return to the Iosan faith," he answered. "I knew it wasn't my place to convince her otherwise. My divine advisors suggested I ask her some questions, but she didn't understand. All I could do was tell her I had to follow my path like she followed hers."

"I'd imagine she wasn't pleased with your response."

"No, which was probably why she only visited one other time while I was there."

"I'm sorry," Rin replied.

"I'm sad for her, Rian, and the girls. Her energy was a milder version of the arsonist's."

"That makes sense," Rin replied. "Some people hold onto their beliefs so tightly that anything that doesn't match theirs is viewed as a threat. Their worldview would collapse if they dared to question even the smallest thing and are too scared to let anything new in."

"It seems to me that a collapse might be a good thing," Thom remarked. "Of course, they'd have to deal with all of the emotions they've shoved down inside like my sister did when my niece nearly died."

"You are growing in wisdom, Thom," Rin replied with approval.

"I can't take all the credit," he said. "Sestra B started me thinking about the arsonist's behavior, and I began wondering what would release people like him from the imaginary cage they created around themselves."

"Well said, Thom. Well said."

Chapter 58

Thom and Rin's ride to the capital was uneventful. Early afternoon on the first day of Aegisa, they came to a sign at a crossroads. The arrow pointing to the right indicated Freas-a-chos was twenty miles away.

"Freas-a-chos. We're almost there, huh?" Thom commented, wiping sweat from his brow. Glancing at his handkerchief, he noted it bore streaks of dirt from the dusty road.

"Yes," Rin replied. "We'll stop at an inn about five miles from here. We should get to the capital in time for a late supper tomorrow. I want both of us rested when we get there."

"OK," Thom replied. "I wish the breeze would return."

"Me too, or rain to cut the humidity," Rin agreed. "By the way, people who live in the capital call the city Freasa."

"Freasa," Thom repeated. "Thanks."

The following day, they both awoke much earlier than planned. With much gratitude to Mother Earth, the rain had cooled things down. Opting to forgo breakfast, they grabbed some pasties for the road. As they approached what Thom hoped would be the final hill after more than a handful, Rin called out.

"At the summit, you'll behold Freasa. It's truly a sight to see."

Gazing across the valley, Thom saw the city sprawling beneath Monarch's Keep. Nestled against the side of a mountain, the Keep had a regal quality, with its imposing conical towers linked by sloping roofs. Flanking them, to the left and right and slightly lower, stood narrower towers. A fortified wall, punctuated with turrets, encircled the Keep.

"Impressive, isn't it?" Rin remarked. "You may not realize, but the spires atop the towers of the tallest stone structure are fashioned to resemble the nearby mountain peaks, with a subtle hint of a crown. Doesn't quite capture it, does it?"

"No," Thom agreed.

"The series of monarchs who built the Keep had particular ideas," Rin explained. "It didn't turn out the way they hoped. When we get closer, you'll notice that the monarchs were fascinated with geometrical shapes, to put it nicely."

Just like Meli, Thom thought. *Metatron, did you have something to do with this, too?*

"Equally important was their desire to leave a personal mark," Rin continued. "Starting at the back, the building shapes progress from rectangles to hexagons and octagons and finally end with circles. Even the turrets follow the same pattern."

"No triangles," Thom asked with a grin.

"No. We can be grateful for that. I think it would be odd living in a triangular-shaped building."

Thom found his left hand reaching into his tunic pocket and rubbing his mysterious triangular object. "How old is the Keep?" he asked.

"It varies," Rin replied. "The rectangular building was constructed around 400 and is the oldest. The rest were built every five generations. The most recent was the Acadium. It's located outside the Keep's walls and was erected around 900. It's to the right of the Keep, down the hill on the lower plateau. Thankfully, those monarchs were more practical and returned to a square shape for the building."

"That's where I'll study for the next six years?" Thom asked.

"Yes," Rin replied.

"What's the building with the towers called?" Thom asked.

"Cleirigh Hall," Rin replied. "It's the building where most business is conducted. It includes two large halls, offices, and quarters for servants, staff, and visitors. I have a room there myself."

"Do the monarchs live there too?"

"No," Rin replied, "They live in the Royal Residence behind it. Let's continue, shall we?"

When they reached the city's outskirts, Thom noticed that the homes were closer together but still had a yard. Many were filled with squawking chickens, braying goats, and a cow. Their residents barely gave them a glance as they passed by.

As they continued their journey, the activity along the road increased, culminating in their approach to a sizable bridge. The river it spanned was twice the width of the one they had traveled from Dridley. Boats bustled with activity along its banks as crews hurriedly loaded and unloaded cargo. Pedestrians called out to neighbors. Children chased each other, dodging carts and workers. Crossing the bridge, the air was saturated with the mingled scent of freshly cut timber, fish, and tar. Meanwhile, kingfishers darted overhead, swooping down in attempts to snatch fish offal from boat decks.

"A lot of activity," Thom remarked.

"Yes, Freasa's a busy port," Rin agreed.

Once across the bridge, Thom noticed many buildings now held shops, with second or third stories, that looked like family dwellings. Unlike the homes they had passed, which were made solely from wood, only the upper levels were wood. The first was made of stone. The road they traveled appeared to be the main thoroughfare. What struck him as odd was that it was no longer stretched straight ahead. Turning to Rin, he asked, "If this is the main road, why does it wind around rather than go directly to the Keep?"

"Think about it," Rin suggested.

At first, Thom thought of reasons for it to be straight. It would be more direct and take less time than a winding road, which could annoy diplomats. A messenger would also be able to deliver messages quicker to the monarchs. Why would the king or queen want to slow someone down? An image of the bandits they encountered when he first left home flashed into his mind. Of course. *Thanks for the reminder, Sereh.* Turning to Rin, he said, "Defense. If enemies wanted to attack the Keep, they couldn't easily get to it."

"Exactly," Rin said. "Now, when we get to Paddi's, you'll stay there for about a week before he escorts you to the Acadium."

"OK," Thom replied.

"We're now coming up to the square where there's a bi-weekly market fair," Rin commented.

Riding through, Thom saw a fountain at its center with a grand marble sculpture depicting a king and queen astride horses. The king's horse, poised with one hoof raised, commanded attention. Nearby, a young man diligently scrubbed away bird droppings from the figures. "Which king and queen are they?"

"King Adan and Queen Cara Cleirigh, who built Cleirigh Hall," Rin replied. "King Adan had a bit of an ego."

Thom also saw booths around the square selling food and goods, like in Glakkadeth. When they rode by a food vendor, Thom's stomach growled.

Smiling, Rin remarked, "Given our early start, we'll arrive at Paddi's well before noon supper. Your stomach will have to endure a bit longer."

"Sorry," Thom replied, feeling a tad embarrassed. "Where is Paddi's?"

"It's in a section on the right side of the Acadium plateau. Some homes are larger because there's more space, as the river doesn't hem them in."

"Do only wealthy people live there?" Thom asked, recalling that there was an exclusive section in Dridley.

"If you're comparing it to Dridley, then no," Rin replied. "King Pethuric and Queen Niamh were adamant that people of all incomes should be able to afford to live there to help ensure the populace didn't become stratified."

"I'm glad," Thom replied.

After some time passed, they found themselves traveling down a wide, graveled street. Rin broke the silence, pointing, "That's Paddi's place on the left."

Paddi's residence stood three stories tall, boasting a central portico spanning two floors, its off-white facade radiating a timeless charm. The bottom story was constructed of a reddish-brown stone and accented with a sizable bay window on one side of the home and two smaller windows on the other. The upper stories were made of wood. Enclosed within a fence supported by matching stone pillars, the home exuded elegance. As they rode through the gate, Thom caught sight of an older man, resembling his father in age, standing beside a younger man near the home's entrance.

"Healer Rinbalden, Apprentice Macirdan," the older man said. "Welcome. I'm Griffin, the head servant. We've been looking out for you."

"Nice to meet you, Griffin," Rin replied as they dismounted.

"Nice to meet you, sir," Thom echoed.

"Oh no, Apprentice Macirdan, I'm not a sir. Please call me Griffin."

"OK. Please call me Thom, then."

"And you can call me Rin, if you like," Rin suggested.

"How about I address you as Healer Rin?" Griffin proposed, offering a bow. "My father always stressed the importance of showing utmost respect to healers, given their dedication."

"Healer Rin is fine."

"This is Benn," Griffin said, introducing the young man with wavy blond hair, who looked slightly older than Thom. "Benn will take your horses to the stable in the back and groom them. He'll also unload your bags and place them in your rooms."

"Thank you very much," Rin replied.

Before handing Apollo's reins to Benn, Thom leaned into Apollo, "This is Benn, who will take care of you. I'll check on you after supper," he said, giving him a hug and kiss.

"You care for your horse as much as Sir Byrne does," Benn commented.

"Thom helped birth Apollo and also trained him," Rin explained. "They have a special bond."

Griffin escorted Thom and Rin through a four-paneled front door adorned with brass fixtures and crowned by a transom at the top. He then directed them to a room off the entrance hall, where Sir Byrne, accompanied by a young woman and another young man, awaited their arrival.

"Rin, Thom!" Paddi called out with delight. "A little earlier than you mentioned in your message and before noon supper. Good to see you both again."

"Good to see you, Paddi," Thom replied.

"Greetings, Paddi," Rin said. "We made good time."

"Rin and Thom, I'd like to introduce you to my daughter, Eran, and my son, Ciarenn. My oldest son, Iosef, is traveling for business."

Eran was tall and slender, with long, dark brown hair tied in a ponytail. She was dressed in a short maroon tunic and white trousers. In contrast, Ciarenn looked a few years older, quite brawny, and a little shorter than his sister. He had light brown hair and was wearing a gray and blue uniform.

"Hello, Eran and Ciarenn," Thom and Rin said simultaneously, laughing.

Paddi, Eran, and Ciarenn joined in.

"Noon supper is not for another hour. We suspect you're both tired. So, we'll get acquainted then," Paddi stated. "Why don't you get settled? Griffin will escort you to your rooms."

When Griffin led them up the stairs, Thom saw rooms on both sides of the hall. Opening the first door on the left, Griffin stated, "This is your room, Healer Rin."

"Thank you, Griffin."

He led Thom to the next room and said, "This is yours, young sir."

"Thanks, Griffin," he said, stepping in and closing the door.

Glancing about, Thom saw a large bed, a sturdy wardrobe, a modest desk and chair, and a washstand complete with a pitcher and basin. The room carried the pleasant scent of freshly laundered sheets, tinged with a delicate hint of lavender. Each piece of furniture gleamed with what he presumed was a recent application of beeswax. Noticing his saddlebags by the desk, Thom approached the wardrobe to unpack and found that someone had already taken care of the task. Absent were his Glakkadeth dress clothes. He made a mental note to ask Rin.

Appreciating the gentle breeze from his open window, he crossed the room and looked out. His room faced the backyard. He saw the stables Benn had mentioned. Ahead, marking the end of the property, he saw a five-foot stone wall crafted from the same stone found elsewhere on the property and a hill beyond. Intrigued by what lay at its peak, Thom leaned out for a closer look. A gray stone wall towered over ten feet tall some distance up the hill. "That must be a wall surrounding the Acadium."

Stepping over to the washstand, Thom filled the basin with water and washed. Feeling weary from the journey, he decided to test the comfort of the bed.

A knock startled Thom awake.

"Thom," Rin called out. "It's time for supper."

He stumbled to the door and opened it.

"Sleeping, huh," Rin grinned.

"How did you know?"

"Your bleary eyes and tousled hair are dead giveaways. Why don't you take more time to awaken and fix your hair? Join us downstairs in the sitting room when you're ready. That's where Paddi greeted us."

"OK," Thom replied.

"By the way, did you notice our windows look toward the Acadium?"

"I had wondered. But all I saw was a wall."

"Oh, the building's set back quite a way," Rin answered. "I'll see you shortly."

Thom went downstairs to the sitting room, which had walls painted in pale green. Before a central fireplace were white-upholstered armchairs and small tables between them. A large bay window overlooked the front of the house, boasting a padded coral pad where someone could watch for arrivals or even read.

"Ah. There you are, Thom," Rin noted.

"Am I late? I'm sorry," he replied.

"No, perfect timing," Paddi assured him. "Let's go into the dining room. Supper is about to be served."

Soon after, the five sat at an oval table covered in a lace cloth. A man and a woman brought dishes out. Thom saw slices of a roast, mashed potatoes, a platter of long beans, and a cucumber salad.

"Rin and Thom," Paddi said, "I want to introduce you to our cooks, Meggie and Pel. They're a married couple who have been working for us for years. Pel's also our jack-of-all-trades. Meggie and Pel meet Healer Rin and his apprentice, Thom."

"Nice to meet you both," Rin replied.

"The food smells wonderful," Thom complimented.

"Nice to meet you, sirs," Meggie and Pel responded in unison. Meggie, stout with her gray hair in a bun, and Pel, thin yet muscular and bald, offered friendly nods in greeting.

"I'll be back with the bread," Pel added.

As they served themselves, Eran said, "Thom, I understand you're starting your first level at the Acadium. I'm going into my third. Ciarenn's going into his last."

Ciarenn grunted, chewing on a bit of roast he'd eaten.

"What are you studying, Eran?" Thom asked.

"Culinary Science," Eran replied.

"What's that?"

"It's the study of many styles of cooking and baking and how to set up a business," she answered. "We're lucky because visiting dignitaries often bring spices and fruits from their lands. King Pethuric asked them to. My classmates and I learn how to integrate them into our dishes. Some spices have become so popular that they're added to our trading list. That benefits them and us."

"What kinds of things have you added?"

"Pomegranates, for one, which are a fruit grown in warmer lands," Eran explained. "We're hoping to grow them here. When the seeds are dried and ground, they produce a powder that adds a tartness to a dish. Meggie added a small amount to the cucumber salad."

"Oh. That's what I was tasting," Thom commented. "I liked it." Thinking about his favorite food from Glakkadeth, he added, "Have you ever heard of chocolate?"

"No," Eran replied. "What is it?"

"It comes from the cacao tree," he answered. "It's both sweet and rich. I have a large bag of chocolate bits, a gift from people I met in Glakkadeth. Would you like to try it?"

"Yes, I would," Eran said. "It sounds intriguing."

Thom looked over to Ciarenn. He's handsome in his uniform, he thought. "Since you're wearing a uniform, Ciarenn, can I assume you are studying soldiering?

"Yep," he answered. I'm hoping to be accepted into the Monarchs' Guard. I train with a sword, staff, javelin, bow, and knife. I also learn hand-to-hand combat."

"Wow," Thom remarked, clearly impressed. "That's a lot of weapons. Back in Glakkadeth, I learned swordplay, knife handling, and staff combat. I'm more skilled in defense than attack. Rin mentioned it's typical for a healer."

"They have excellent healers at the Acadium," Eran commented. "Ciarenn visits them regularly."

"Not recently," he protested. "I did often in my first few years. Some teachers think the best way to learn how to block correctly is to take you down when you don't."

"I've been there," Thom agreed, grimacing. "You're studying soldiering, and Eran is studying Culinary Science. What else do people study at the Acadium?"

"Oh, everything," Ciarenn jumped in. "Architecture, animal husbandry, geology, and storytelling. Storytelling is sometimes tied to music."

"Some major in metalworking, glassblowing, teaching, geology, and history," Eran added. Others study to be scholars, but the best school is on the West Coast in Bethemel."

"And do all of them have special gifts?" Thom asked.

"Gifts or strong talents," Paddi stated.

"I see. With that many programs, is the Acadium large? I couldn't see it from the guest room window."

"Yes, very large. It's ten stories now," Eran informed him. "They added three floors the summer before I started my first year there. I understand academs had to share rooms before they added them."

"I'll get my own room," Thom exclaimed happily. "That's great. I got used to that in Glakkadeth. Growing up, I shared a loft with two of my siblings."

"Speaking of Glakkadeth," Paddi interrupted, "would you tell us what that was like?"

"Sure," Thom replied. He summarized his experience without mentioning the trading scandal, the arsonist incident, or his kidnapping. With great enthusiasm, Thom also told them about Timbu. He promised to bring some chocolate bits down after supper and see if one of the cooks would heat up some milk to try it.

They were finishing slices of lime pie when Rin said, "Eran's kindly offered to take you to a bookshop to get your books. She's even giving you a few she no longer needs. You'll probably also need a satchel."

"Thanks, Eran," Thom said. "How will I pay?"

"No worries there," Rin replied. "Your scholarship covers your supplies too."

"I'll take you to the tailor's tomorrow to get measured for your school clothes," Paddi explained.

"Oh. Not you, Rin?" Thom asked.

"No. I have one errand to finish. I suspect there might be a few more coming my way," he added, giving Paddi a pointed look, which Thom noticed. "You might not see me much for the rest of today or tomorrow, even for meals. I will be here in two days for supper, though. Afterward, I'll be leaving Freasa. And I'll be gone for a while."

Thom remained silent. While he knew Rin had other work, he still felt a pang of loss in his gut after spending four years with him.

"I'm sorry, Thom," Rin said, interrupting his thoughts. "I'm confident you'll meet new friends at the Acadium. You already know the Byrnes here."

"I can introduce you to my friends," Eran offered, "even if they are older."

"Thanks," Thom mumbled half-heartedly.

Paddi looked at Eran and mouthed 'chocolate' to her.

"Thom," Eran spoke again. "Shall we see if the cooks can heat up some milk?"

Thom's spirit lifted slightly at the suggestion, saying, "Yes, let's."

"May we be excused, Da?" Eran asked.

"Of course," he answered.

A short while later, Eran, Meggie, Paddi, and Ciarenn categorically admitted to being fans of Timbu.

After he'd gone to bed, Thom lay there awake. Once more, he'd be alone, he thought. Despite appreciating Eran's offer to introduce him to her friends, he felt he was starting over. Why did this keep happening? Friends leave, or he left them, like Khali and Mekial. Turning to his divine team, he called out in mind speech, *what will I do? You keep telling*

me you're with me, but you're not here physically. Feeling the tingle indicating their presence, he went on. *That's nice and all, but it's not the same. Even when you visited me in my Sanctuary, Jesh and Rel, you weren't really with me.*

At that moment, as if in response to his distress, Thom heard a faint whinny. "Apollo?" he whispered, relief washing over him. But would he even be allowed to keep Apollo at the Acadium? he wondered, feeling a wave of worry. His changing emotions made him feel as though he was trapped on a runaway cart, careening up and down over hills and valleys of uncertainty.

Thom climbed out of bed and quickly dressed. Grabbing a blanket, he crept downstairs. Soon after, he was tucked up against his friend, appreciating Apollo's warmth, the beat of his heart, and the sound of his breathing.

Thom heard voices. He thought one mentioned his name. Coming awake, he realized it was Eran.

"Benn, have you seen Thom out and about?"

"No, I haven't," he answered. "He's not in the dining room?"

"No. Rin knocked on his door and discovered he wasn't there."

"I wonder. Let me check something," Benn said, walking into the stable. "He's here, Eran. He's with Apollo."

"Thanks, Benn. I'll let everyone know," she replied, dashing through the back door.

Soon after, Thom found himself gazing up into Rin's concerned eyes.

"Thom, you worried us," Rin said with relief. "It feels like déjà vu. We didn't know where you were."

"I'm sorry. I needed someone to hold, and Apollo was here."

"You could have come to me," Rin said.

"I know, but you're leaving. And I felt a little abandoned."

"I see," Rin replied tenderly.

"Do you think I'll be able to keep Apollo at the Acadium?" Thom asked, his voice cracking with hopelessness.

"I don't know," he answered. "We can ask."

"They'll probably say no," Thom said doubtfully.

"Thom," Rin replied. "I know you feel alone. I'm sorry I can't be with you. There have been occasions when I've been asked to come to the Acadium to test certain students. But I can't guarantee it. I wish I could take away your pain and sadness."

"I know you can't," Thom replied. "Somehow, I'll get through it."

"You will. Please know that no one will try to talk you out of your feelings. It's important to attend to them."

"OK,"

"Are you hungry? I think breakfast is about to be served."

In response, Thom's stomach growled.

"Why did I even ask?" he smiled. "Let me give you a hand up."

When Thom stood, Apollo also stood. He hugged him and said, "Thanks for making space for me last night."

Apollo whinnied and whuffed into his hair.

Mid-morning, Paddi took him to a tailor with whom he did business. She agreed to rush Thom's outfits and have them ready in under a week. Thom was getting two sets of formal wear and four of everyday wear.

Chapter 59

A few days had passed and Thom was at breakfast with Paddi when Eran walked in, "Thom, how about if I give you a quick tour of the city and take you to the bookshop?"

"Sounds good," Thom said. "I'll finish up."

"No hurry," she answered. "I'll be in the sitting room."

Eran's first stop with Thom was a small square near the house, with a few vendors selling wares. Like the other square, it also had a fountain in the center but didn't include a sculpture. Then, she guided him to a park a few blocks north, complete with a pond frequented by geese and surrounded by a pebble walkway with benches.

"Let's sit," Eran suggested.

Sitting on one of the benches, Thom appreciated the shade the nearby maple and elm trees provided. He was captivated by a pair of geese leading a parade of goslings from the park edge into the pond. He loved watching the little ones seemingly compete with each other to be first behind their parents. "They're cute," he remarked.

After enjoying the scene for a time, Eran said. "I want to show you something." She led him to the park's northern edge and said, "If you look up to the left, you can see the end of the plateau the Acadium sits on."

"That's some drop-off," Thom commented.

"It is," Eran agreed. "That's why there's the tall wall at the back of the school."

Looking straight ahead, he saw a valley with large grassy areas and a scattering of homesteads. "I thought there would be homes back here, too," he commented.

"It's mostly farms," Eran explained. "With the large population of Freasa, there are a lot of mouths to feed."

"I see," Thom said.

"A good way in the distance," she continued, "I heard there's a special forest the monarchs' oversee."

Thom squinted but couldn't see any sign of it. "What's at the back of the plateau cliff?"

"I don't know," Eran admitted. "I never thought to ask. Let's head to the bookshop."

Stepping inside a spacious shop, Thom inhaled deeply, relishing the familiar scent of books. The shop walls were lined with towering shelves filled with books and brimming with knowledge and adventures waiting to be explored. Around the floor were tables displaying an assortment of merchandise. On one were leather satchels. As a salesperson approached them, Thom took note of their location so he could buy one after he'd gotten his books.

Eran explained to the woman that Thom was starting his first level soon and studying to be a healer. She led them to the applicable shelves and pointed out the books first-level healers used. Before she walked away, Thom asked, "Do you have any fantasy novels?"

"Yes," she answered. "On the other side of the shop."

"Great, thanks."

"Do you like to read?" Eran commented. "With all the reading assigned at school, I'd rather cook than read. It clears my head."

"I understand," Thom admitted. "Reading does that for me. I found a great series in Glakkadeth that included dragons. I'll return here another day when I don't have other books to carry."

When they emerged from the shop, each carried a stack of books tucked under their arms. Thom also had a sturdy satchel slung over his shoulder.

"How are you fixed for quills, ink, and paper?" Eran asked.

"I could use some of each."

"I know the place."

While picking out paper, Thom found a black, unlined notebook with what looked like swirls on the cover. Perfect, he thought. With a handful of pages left in his current journal, he decided it was time to get a new one.

"Ready to head back?" Eran asked after Thom had paid for his purchases.

"Yes."

Chapter 60

After another morning spent riding around the city, Thom was grooming Apollo in the stable when Rin walked in.

"Good morning, Thom," Rin greeted him.

"Oh, you're back," he replied.

"Yes. There will be two guests at noon supper today. I'd suggest you dress up."

"What do I wear?" he asked. "My school clothes aren't ready."

"Put on what you wore to our farewell gathering," Rin suggested.

"The thing is," Thom began, "it's not in the wardrobe. At least it wasn't this morning."

"I suspect one of the servants took it to clean and freshen up a bit. Why don't you look again?"

"OK. Are the people coming important?" Thom asked.

"You could say that," Rin replied. "I'd suggest you head upstairs and get yourself clean. We'll meet in the sitting room in about an hour."

"Alright."

When Thom returned to his room, he confirmed Rin's belief and found his Glakkadian outfit hanging up with his other clothes. After thoroughly washing up, he was still wrestling with his hair when he heard voices downstairs. He'd better hurry. Getting desperate since his hair was still sticking up in the back, Thom dunked the top of his head into the basin. Unfortunately, he tilted the basin, and water poured onto the washstand and the floor. "Oh, Digi!" he cursed.

Thom grabbed a towel and mopped up the washstand and floor as best he could. Since the towel was sopping wet, he couldn't dry his hair. Looking in the mirror, he muttered, "At least my hair's behaving." Dashing from his room and down the stairs, he ran into the sitting room, out of breath, saying, "I'm sorry... I'm late. I had... a problem."

A gentleman seated in a wing chair and dressed in a blue tunic said, "Dare I guess you had issues with your hair, young man?"

"Um. Yes, sir," Thom replied, blushing.

"Peth, don't tease him," the woman beside him admonished. She was dressed in a purple tunic with silver embroidery.

"I'm not truly, luv," the man protested. "I had problems with my hair as a teenager. My only solution was usually dunking my head in a pail of water. I suspect the young man did something similar."

Thom nodded, blushing even more deeply.

"Thom, I'd like to introduce you to Queen Niamh and King Pethuric Cleirigh," Rin said.

Thom's jaw dropped, and his face would have turned an even deeper shade of crimson were that possible.

"I think he's about to explode, Rin," the king remarked, chuckling.

Standing up, Queen Niamh walked over to Thom. "Don't mind Peth. He can be annoying. It's nice to meet you finally, Thom. We've heard a good amount about you. And I see we have a similar taste in clothes," pointing to the silver and purple in their tunics.

"It's nice to meet you, too, Your Majesty," he said, attempting to bow without bumping his head into her.

"None of that," she insisted. "We're here informally. When we see each other on formal occasions, bowing is appropriate, but not here among friends."

"Um, thank you," Thom replied.

Turning to her husband and giving him a look, she said, "Get up, you dolt, and greet Thom properly."

Standing and walking toward Thom, Pethuric extended his hand, saying. "I did mean it. I know what it's like to have hair that won't behave. You'll be happy to know it'll settle down eventually."

"Thanks, Your Majesty."

"Thom," Eran said, "come get chilled cider."

While Thom got a drink, Paddi asked Rin, "Didn't Thom know Niamh and Peth were coming by?"

"No," Rin replied. "I was worried he'd obsess and get himself worked up."

"I see you avoided that," Paddi said sarcastically. "Please, everyone, sit. It'll be thirty minutes before supper's ready."

Thom found a seat on a couch across from the king and queen.

"Niamh, how are you feeling?" Paddi inquired. "Sorry, I didn't ask before."

"That's fine," she answered. "The morning sickness finally ended two days ago. It lasted longer than it did for our son."

"I'm glad to hear it," Paddi replied.

Thom remained silent while the others chatted, trying to work up the nerve to ask a question.

"Queen Niamh," Thom ventured, "you said you heard a lot about me. How? Did Rin tell you?"

"No," Queen Niamh responded, "we learned of you when you were three, even before Rin."

"I don't understand."

"Do you know about foreseers, Thom?" Queen Niamh asked.

"Some," he replied. "There was a foreseer at the monastery in Glakkadeth, but she kept mostly to herself. Someone also told me—I don't remember who—that I have a little ability in that area."

"OK. Good," the queen continued. "Three foreseers had visions."

"About me?"

"Yes. They saw a young boy with extraordinary gifts. Rin determined that the different visions were about the same boy who lived southeast of here."

"Rin, why didn't you ever tell me?"

"I'm sorry, Thom," Rin replied. "I honestly wasn't sure when I should. I wanted to avoid the possibility of you becoming arrogant, knowing the great power of your gifts. I also didn't want to tell you before we knew what to call your spirit-healing gift. After that, I hesitated because your gift kept evolving. I was going to tell you before I left tomorrow."

"Oh, I'm sorry, Rin," Queen Niamh interjected. "I hadn't realized you hadn't told him. Shall I go on?"

"Please," Rin replied.

"Yes, Your Majesty," Thom said.

"Why don't I jump in?" King Pethuric said. "We asked Rin to see if he could find out who the boy they saw was."

"How could you do that?" Thom asked. "It doesn't sound like you knew my name."

"We didn't," Rin answered. "But each vision had specific details which gave us clues. For example, we knew the boy's father was a potter, and his mother was a healer. In one vision, when the boy was about seven, it showed him working in a garden and able to sense a young child's sickness."

"Mirabel," Thom said, nodding.

"Yes," Rin confirmed. "From another vision, we knew that when the boy was about eight, he'd be working in a pottery with a teenager and his father. A dangerous merchant would also be there."

"Samiltun," Thom uttered in horror and amazement.

"Yes," Rin confirmed again. "In the third vision, the foreseer saw a three-year-old talking with a wise female whom the foreseer couldn't see."

"I don't know. I don't remember much from then," Thom admitted. "My sister Deena did remind me I had wandered off on my own one day, but she didn't say anything else. Maybe the vision was of another boy."

"No," Rin said. "Each vision was for a boy living in the same area, and most importantly, he gave off the same, almost blinding, light."

"A blinding light?" Thom said, his eyes wide.

"Yes, Thom, a blinding light," Rin repeated. "I saw it myself when I first met you in my shop in Potai. I mentioned to you how bright your spirit was during your training. The light is your holy spirit, Thom. And before you ask, I didn't tell you this for the same reason I didn't tell you about the foreseers' visions."

"Lebrim called me a holy one when I first met him," Thom remarked.

"I didn't know that," Rin replied.

"Yeah, I guess I haven't told you everything either," Thom said. "What did you do next?"

"For a few years, I went about my usual business. Then, I went looking for you," Rin explained. "When I found you, I set up shop in your nearby town."

Paddi, Eran, and Ciarenn looked stunned.

Rin noticed and said, "Pretty amazing, isn't it?"

"Yeah," Ciarenn admitted. "I've met some very gifted academs over the last five years. None of them said anything about foreseers having a vision about them."

"And Thom won't be saying anything either. Will you, Thom?" Rin asked.

"No, of course not," he replied. "I don't want other academs thinking I'm different or weird. I had enough of that with the kids at home."

"See, Peth and Niamh?" Rin said. "I told you Thom is much wiser than his years."

"Indeed, he is," Queen Niamh answered.

"Can I ask another question?" Thom asked.

"Certainly," she replied.

"How do you remember all the details? The visions happened almost ten years ago."

"Ah. Truthfully, we cheated," King Pethuric admitted. "We record every vision, which enables us to track how close it is to reality. Before this gathering, we reviewed the documents. But honestly, we've often had you in our minds these last four years. Rin usually sent us regular updates on how you were doing. We were concerned when he abruptly took you off to Glakkadeth. He had previously told us you were going to Eiren, where Niamh's cousin Gabi lives with her husband, the king."

"Sorry about that," Rin grimaced. "Our change of destination was quite sudden, and I had forgotten to let you know until we'd been in Glakkadeth a month."

"We appreciate your apology, Rin," Queen Niamh replied. "Gabi was annoyed when you didn't show up."

"Again, sorry," Rin said sheepishly.

Thom smiled inwardly. This was yet another example of Rin being imperfect. Rin also hadn't added an "L" to his words lately. Thom needed to remind himself that he didn't need to be perfect. While he was still considering that, Pel came into the room, announcing that supper was ready.

Peth, Paddi, Eran, and Ciarenn led the way. Before Rin and Thom could follow, Queen Niamh pulled them aside.

"I didn't want to say anything while the others were present, Thom," Queen Niamh said, "But Rin told us about your kidnapping. Peth and I were very upset. How are you doing?"

"I'm OK," he replied. "I don't have nightmares anymore, and Medelin helped me improve my self-defense skills."

"Good," the queen answered. "You'll get more training at the Acadium. I do want to apologize, though, since the kidnappers were from here. We still haven't determined the name of the young noble behind it. Rin's part of the team investigating it."

"Thanks for letting me know," Thom replied.

"You're welcome," she answered. "I wanted to make sure you knew what was going on. Let's join the others now."

Over the meal, they chatted about Paddi's business, trade in general, and family. Thom learned that Paddi Byrne's wife had died three years before.

"How's the breeding program going, King Pethuric?" Ciarenn asked. "Having more horses last fall meant my classmates and I had more time training with them."

"It's going well, and I'm glad you benefitted," King Pethuric said. Turning to Thom and Rin, he explained, "We started this program a few years ago when we purchased some young colts along with mares to increase horse births."

"How's the young filly you mentioned last week?" Paddi asked. "The one whose mare died while giving birth."

"Oh. She's a sad one," the king responded. "Since she couldn't bond with her mother, she's not bonding with any of the other colts or fillies. Head Groom Duncan hasn't had any success trying to train her. She's been too skittish."

"If I may interrupt," Rin said. "Thom might be able to help. With his spirit-healing gift, he connected with his horse, Apollo, before he was born. He also assisted with his birth and trained him."

"Thom's gift isn't limited to humans?" Queen Niamh asked.

"No, it's with all animals, too," Rin explained.

"May I speak?" Thom said.

"Please," King Pethuric said.

"Rin's correct," Thom said. "I can sense the spirit of animals and humans. With some, I can connect deeply, like I did with Apollo. I might be able to connect with the filly. What's her name?"

"Aponi," Queen Niamh answered.

"I'd like to try to connect with Aponi," Thom continued. "But I do have a suggestion."

"Go ahead," King Pethuric encouraged.

"Apollo has a healing and calming spirit," he explained. "If it's not an imposition, I'd suggest he be placed in the stall next to Aponi's when I go to the Acadium. It may help calm her when I'm not there."

"That's a good idea," King Pethuric said approvingly. "I understand you're heading to the Acadium in a few days."

"Yes, after my school clothes come in," Thom said, looking to Paddi, who nodded.

"Good," King Pethuric said. "I'll let Duncan know."

Rin looked over to Thom and smiled.

Meggie and Pel entered the dining room to clear the dishes. Meggie returned with dessert and announced, "We know King Pethuric has a sweet tooth and liked our cinnamon apple crumble the last time he and the queen ate here. Pel made it again."

"That's very kind of you," the king said.

"And," Meggie continued, "after much pestering from Eran, Pel made coffee and some of the Timbu that Thom and his friends invented in Glakkadeth. He's about to bring both out."

"Timbu?" King Pethuric responded. "What is it?"

"It's a hot drink made with chocolate, Your Majesty," Thom explained.

"I've heard of chocolate but never tasted it," he replied. "I thought it came in large chunks."

"No, it comes in bits, too," Thom explained. "And they can be baked into sweet biscuits or muffins or, in this case, melted into hot milk."

"It's quite good, Your Majesties," Eran interjected.

"Bring it on," King Pethuric said enthusiastically.

Everyone was served the crumble. Rin, Niamh, and Paddi had coffee. The rest had Timbu.

King Pethuric lifted his mug to his nose and breathed in its aroma. "It smells good," he commented.

Thom and Eran watched King Pethuric closely when he took his first sip.

"Oh my! This is good," he said, taking another sip. "This would be perfect on a cold winter day. And you said it's good in muffins and biscuits, too?"

"Yes, Your Majesty," Thom replied.

"Did you bring this from Glakkadeth, Thom?" he asked.

"Yes, a large bag, but it's dwindling fast."

"Do you know of a local supplier?"

"I don't, sir," Thom replied. "But Captain Musa includes chocolate bits in his cargo when he travels from Glakkadeth to Dridley."

"Does he now?" King Pethuric commented. "I think I know a trader in Dridley who travels here often. Perhaps the captain might be interested in increasing the size of that cargo?"

"I would think he would, sir," Thom replied with a smile.

After supper ended and the king and queen had left, Thom decided to write about what he had learned. On his way to his room, Rin stopped him.

"Good suggestion about Apollo," he complimented him. "I'm happy Apollo will be close to you."

"Me too. I didn't even think of it as a solution to my situation but rather as a way to help Aponi."

"I know," Rin replied. "That's a clear mark of a healer. I'm proud of you. Now, I'll be leaving tomorrow morning after breakfast. Before I leave, we'll have the chat I mentioned. OK?"

After breakfast the next day, Rin led Thom to Paddi's library, which had two bookshelves, a large mahogany desk and chair, and a seating area with padded dark green chairs and a beige couch. Sitting on the couch, Rin said, "First, I want to find out how you feel about learning of the foreseers' visions yesterday."

"I was surprised and annoyed," Thom admitted. "It might have impacted how I handled Lebrim's death. But I don't know if it would have helped or hurt. After all, I was angry at everyone when he died, including my divine team."

"Again, I'm sorry," Rin replied. "I probably should have checked with my spirit guides about telling you."

"It's OK. I do know you care for me."

"I do, Thom," Rin agreed. "It's been an honor and a pleasure teaching and getting to know you. You're very special to me. And... if I had children, I'd... consider you my... slon," he said, his voice breaking.

"Your slon," Thom smiled tenderly. "I thought you only added an L when you were upset."

"Turg," Rin cursed. "I guess I am since I won't see you daily. Ten years ago, when I first heard the foreseers' visions, I didn't know one of your greatest gifts would be genuineness. No matter the situation, you show up simply as you, even to an old and sometimes cranky healer."

"You're not that old," Thom replied, quirking his mouth a little.

"There you go," Rin replied. Even under your sarcasm, there's an immeasurable amount of love. You're extraordinary and have much to offer apart from your gifts. "Huh," he said, pausing. "An image of your treasure jar popped into my head, probably from my spirit guides. I know that your treasures are important, especially the triangular one."

Thom nodded, wondering where this was going.

"I don't think you realize this, but you are a treasure."

"But...," Thom started to stay.

I know you want to deny it," Rin insisted. "Something is amazing about you that you don't realize. You're a real person."

"What?" Thom asked, confused.

"Let me explain," he continued. No matter who you interact with, whether a street vendor, merchant, sailor, prezdan, or monarch, you show up the same way: honest, straightforward, and uncomplicated. You have great depth, but you are genuine. Before we left Glakkadeth, all our friends described you similarly. Peth, Niamh, and Paddi mentioned it yesterday."

"How else would I show up?" Thom replied. "I'm just Thom."

"Well, just Thom," Rin said with a grin. "It's a rarity. Many people significantly change how they present themselves based on who they're talking to."

"I didn't realize."

Rin continued, "I won't see you for a while."

"Yeah," he said. "I'll miss you."

"And I'll miss you too, Thom," he replied. "Given your history, you'll certainly have some exciting adventures. You'll also face challenges. Try to see them as opportunities to increase your self-understanding and healing abilities. As I've said before, you've only started discovering the extent of your gifts."

"OK," Thom answered. "I'll keep that in mind."

"A few final thoughts. Be wary of others like Samiltun. You do possess the ability to keep them at bay. Also, always remember to be grateful for your gifts and all you have and receive, however big or small. Embrace humility. But, and I mean but, that doesn't include putting yourself down or believing you're not good enough. It means holding an attitude of gratitude."

Thom found himself weeping and unable to speak. "I promise I'll do my best," he said after composing himself. "I want to thank you for all you've done for me: saving me from Samiltun, searching for me when I was kidnapped, and teaching me. I have no words to express how much you mean to me. You said I'll make new friends. Even though it's sometimes difficult for me to believe, I trust you and my divine team, who told me the same thing."

"I'm glad," Rin replied.

"I know you don't know when you'll visit the Acadium," Thom added. "I understand. It's that I want to keep you in my life."

"No worries," Rin said. "You can't get rid of me."

"Can I give you a hug?" he asked.

"I wouldn't leave without it."

Standing up, they shared a long embrace.

"Do you need help with loading your bags onto your horse?" Thom asked.

"No, but thank you," Rin replied. "I brought them down earlier. Benn loaded them up for me. But you can see me out. I already said goodbye to the others."

Thom walked Rin back to the stable, where Benn had Rin's horse saddled and ready to go. Rin mounted and rode out to the front while Thom followed on foot.

"Take care, Thom," Rin called out.

"You too," he replied, watching Rin ride down the street, turn the corner, and disappear from view.

Thom was giving Apollo a prolonged grooming when Paddi entered the stable.

"You take great care of Apollo. It shows that you love him," he commented.

"I do."

"Your school clothes arrived a short while ago," he told him. "I'll take you up to the Acadium tomorrow about mid-morning."

"OK," Thom said. "We'll be stopping at the Keep stables first?"

"Yes, of course," he answered.

"Thanks," Thom replied. "I'll finish grooming Apollo and then pack."

"Sounds good," Paddi said. "We'll take a couple of your saddlebags when we go. Benn will cart up the rest for you."

"OK," Thom repeated, realizing there was nothing more to say.

Chapter 61

The next morning, after breakfast, Thom was finishing packing when he realized he was missing his slippers. The evening before, he curled up in a chair in Paddi's library, reading a book he found on a shelf the other day. The story included divine helpers who incarnated into horses. It made him think of Apollo. Entering the library now, he saw Paddi sitting at the desk. "Oh, Paddi," he said. "Sorry to disturb you. I left my slippers in here."

"You're not," he replied. "I'm handling some correspondence. By the way, I noticed you're reading one of my favorite books. It's the first in a series. You're welcome to borrow it and the others. I'm not sure how much time you'll have for fun reading at the Acadium. I'd imagine you'll have plenty for your classes."

"True," Thom said. "But I always try to get in some fun reading. Thanks for lending me them."

Sometime later, after securing his saddlebags and hanging his satchel over his shoulder, he led Apollo out of the stable to wait for Paddi. Taking a deep breath, he was glad the air was cool, knowing it would get warmer.

Exiting the back door, Paddi greeted him, "It looks like you're ready. I'll be back in a moment."

When Paddi led his horse out of the stable, they mounted and rode toward the front of the house, where Eran stood waiting.

"Good luck, Thom," she said. "Have fun exploring the Acadium. I'll see you in about a month."

"Thanks, Eran," he replied. As they made their way down the road, Thom wondered what he would find in his new home. He hoped he'd make new friends. But for now, at least he had Apollo.

Acknowledgements

Creating this book was a labor of joy, even the tedious editing process. It wouldn't have been possible without the love and support of numerous people, first and foremost my husband, Michael. His constant encouragement as I embarked on a new career as a spirit healer and his example as he lived his calling have become pillars of my strength.

I am also immensely grateful to two groups of individuals who profoundly shaped my journey: my family and the Paulist Fathers. My family provided the bedrock of my beliefs, exemplifying care and selflessness. Their support, alongside that of my husband's family, has been invaluable. Additionally, I owe a debt of gratitude to the Paulist Fathers, whose steadfast commitment to service has helped me unearth my true self and ignited a fiery passion for serving the greater good of all.

Spiritual teachers are also central to my life and this accomplishment. They include Denise Linn, Neale Donald Walsch, Terry Bowen, Dougall Fraser, Radleigh Valentine, and Liz Dawn, along with Gabi, Luke, Dad, and my other advisors from the divine realm. These teachers challenged me to be open to new avenues of learning and experiences, recognize my innate goodness, and take risks to live out my calling.

I'd be remiss if I didn't acknowledge the friends who cheered me on and provided great wisdom as I stepped into this role as an author. They include, but are not limited to, Jeanne, Joan, Karen, Kimberly, Jon, Alison, JoAnn, Mary Anne, Norman, and Alice.

Finally, I want to thank those involved with the publication of this book: my beta readers, Jay, Dave, John, Michael, Sophie, and Lynn; my editor, Kate; my cover artist, John; Katherine, a consultant, the co-owners of As You Wish Publishing, Kyra and Todd; and Liz, who connected me with As You Wish through Misha Productions/Celebrate Your Life.

I am profoundly indebted to each of you. Your support, guidance, and belief in me have been a driving force behind this book. As I embark on the journey of the second book in the series, I carry your encouragement and love with me.

About The Author

Joe McMonagle

Joe McMonagle is a devoted spirit healer, guiding individuals along their life journey in pursuit of healing, connection to their divine essence, and discovery of their purpose. With a diverse educational background, Joe holds a Bachelor of Architectural Engineering, a Master of Divinity, and a Master of Arts in Counseling Psychology. He is also an author, contributing a chapter to the collaborative book *Awaken Your Magic: Real Life Manifestations Journeys*. His professional journey spans 12 years as a religious seminarian/priest and 26 years in the software industry.

Alongside his career, Joe remains steadfast in his commitment to spiritual growth, exploring belief systems and healing practices, and studying under various esteemed teachers.

Contact Joe and discover more about his offerings through his website: www.joemcmonaglehsp.com.